Tropical Depression

Equal and Opposite Reactions Trilogy - 3

Patti Liszkay

Black Rose Writing | Texas

ISBN: 978-1-68513-183-8
PUBLISHED BY BLACK ROSE WRITING
www.blackrosewriting.com

Printed in the United States of America
Suggested Retail Price (SRP) $22.95

Tropical Depression is printed in Book Antiqua

*As a planet-friendly publisher, Black Rose Writing does its best to eliminate unnecessary waste to reduce paper usage and energy costs, while never compromising the reading experience. As a result, the final word count vs. page count may not meet common expectations.

COVER ART: Romaine Rupp
PHOTO OF PATTI LISZKAY: Theresa Liszkay

Praise for
Tropical
Depression

"Liszkay has created a rich world, immersing the reader in the jungles of Nicaragua and into the lives of a family saga with an exciting twist of fate."
–Kirsten Schuder, author of the *Inside Dwellers Series*

"Liszkay's understanding of Nicaraguan culture, combined with her masterful writing, paint a subtle picture of the struggles of her characters and of life in Nicaragua."
–Bill Schweitzer, author of *Doves in a Tempest*

"Liszkay's descriptions are vivid, and her skills as a storyteller are well-honed–so much so that we come to see humanity as a fabric."
–Karen K. Brees, author of *Crosswind*

"Two extended and blended multi-generational and cross-cultural families become intertwined and interwoven with each other to form a tangled web of relationships. Funny and emotionally moving."
–R. Bruce Logan, co-author of the award-winning *Back to Vietnam: Tours of the Heart*

"Patti Liszkay has written a compulsively readable novel about family, love, and sacrifice. Set in Nicaragua, *Tropical Depression* has memorable characters, rich details, and vivid descriptions. It was the best book I've read in a long time, and I was tremendously sorry when it ended."
–Diane Hawley Nagatomo, author of *The Butterfly Café*

To Makaila and Sienna.
I love the music of your voices.

Acknowledgements

Many, many grateful thanks to the following kind, generous, skilled, knowledgeable people who helped me along the way with this book:

Miguel Jimenez Limón for correcting my Spanish and fine-tuning my knowledge of Nicaraguan customs, culture, and food.

Karen K. Brees for editing my English.

My eagle-eyed beta reader and old friend **Janet Wolanin Alexander.**

Artist **Romaine Rupp** for creating the perfect cover.

Maria Reese for her advice on the finishing touches.

Theresa Liszkay for taking my picture.

Tommy Liszkay, Emily Liszkay and **Justin Reese** for their ever-cheerful support.

Tom Liszkay for drawing the family trees; for his tutorial on generators, turbines, and governors; and for being the love of my life.

And thanks to **Claire Liszkay,** who told me about the Momotombo geothermal fields and introduced me to Nicaragua, a beautiful land of beautiful people.

Also by Patti Liszkay

Tropical Depression

Part One

The Nicaraguans

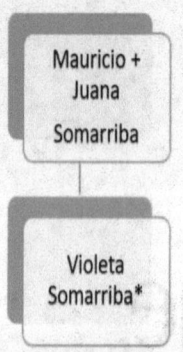

Mauricio + Juana Somarriba

Violeta Somarriba*

*Violeta married Ernesto Guzman

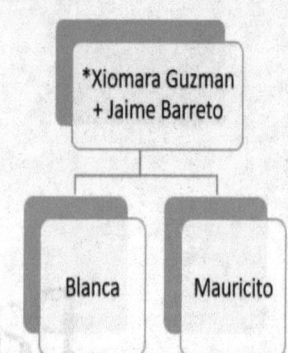

*Xiomara Guzman + Jaime Barreto

Blanca

Mauricito

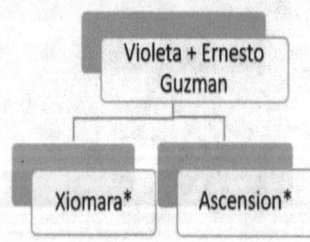

Violeta + Ernesto Guzman

Xiomara*

Ascension*

*Xiomara married Jaime Barreto and Ascension married Lupe Palma

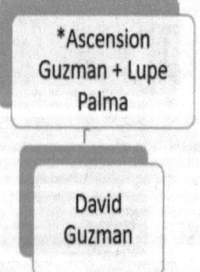

*Ascension Guzman + Lupe Palma

David Guzman

Chapter One

The house belonged to old Mauricio Somarriba, who'd come by it through the family of his deceased wife, Juana. It was one of four houses and twice as many chicken coops, pig pens, outhouses and sheds set here and there around the several acres of jungle clearing shared by Mauricio and his extended family.

The family houses stood several hundred feet apart and, except during the torrential rains of the wet season, were visible to each other through the trees and banana leaf palms that dotted the clearing. The rains fed the streams and aquifers beneath the jungle floor that provided water for the spigots outside each house from which ran the water for drinking, cooking, washing, and bathing. Far off in the distance, between the tree line and the sky, were visible among the ridges of the Cordillera de los Maribios mountain range the smoking peaks of the volcanoes Cerro Negro, El Hoya, Telica, and towering high above them all, the great Momotombo.

The houses were all similar in design but the other houses, each an amalgam of wood, rusted corrugated metal and other found materials, were not as well constructed as Mauricio's, which was sided all around with sturdy, water-proofed cinder block and had a solid concrete floor. His house was also more spacious, consisting of two good-sized bedrooms and a kitchen with a propane-fueled stove, a refrigerator—the refrigerator was used by the members of the other households as well—cupboards, drawers, and a table big enough to seat himself, his daughter and son-in-law Violeta and Ernesto Guzman, their two children and their spouses and his two little great-grandchildren, all of whom lived together in Mauricio's house.

A curtain hung in the doorway between the kitchen and the packed-dirt-floored, three-sided patio that served as a living room and in which there were several wooden chairs, half-a-dozen rusty metal folding chairs, two hammocks, and a table on which sat some books, a pile of magazines, and a forty-two-inch-screen television that the other relatives regularly came over to Mauricio's house to watch. The television plugged into an outlet whose wires ran up the wall then through a small hole in the side of the house beneath the roof overhang where the wires of all the electrical appliances in the house exited then ran bundled together up above the clay tiled roof and attached to the electrical wiring that, thanks to the work of do-gooding foreign volunteer groups—who'd also installed the water spigots—crisscrossed the jungle village of Krukrulitos and ran down to the generating unit outside the city of León, Nicaragua, which bordered the jungle.

On this day Mauricio had just awoken, having slept, as he preferred to, outdoors in one of the hammocks on the patio instead of on the folding bed stored for his use in the bedroom used by his granddaughter Xiomara, her husband Jaime and their two children. He now sat on one of the wooden chairs having his morning cigarette and looking out into the yard where some of the chickens wandered, pecking at the dirt. He liked these cool early winter mornings. The American-style thermometer that Mauricio had bought years ago in the marketplace in León and hung on the patio wall indicated that it was seventy-three Fahrenheit degrees. Later in the day it might reach ninety degrees, but probably not more than ninety-three, it being winter, and winter being the cool, wet season. The tropical rains, which Mauricio also enjoyed watching from beneath the shelter of the covered patio, would sweep in this afternoon and pour down for an hour or so. But there would still be plenty of time this morning for tending the chickens and pigs, as well as his cassavas and the small cornfield behind the housing area. And to say good morning to *señor* and *señora* Frondosa, Mr. and Mrs. Leafy, as the two majestic palm trees that stood in the jungle a dozen yards back from the margin of the clearing had been nicknamed, how far back Mauricio could no longer remember. They were spindly old giants that from many decades of growth now soared over ninety feet above the jungle floor. Mauricio felt a kindship with the two trees, for they were two living things that had been on the earth as long as himself.

"Still alive another day, my old friends?" he might say when he stopped by the palm trees. "Yes, me, too. May we all live a few more days yet."

Mauricio took a long drag on his cigarette. Life was good these days. He congratulated himself, as he occasionally did, for having raised, along with his three sons, an energetic, determined daughter, Violeta, who married well then raised an energetic, determined son, Ascensión. Ascensión was in truth his favorite grandchild, handsome and good-natured and smart. Ascensión and his sister Xiomara grew up not in Krukrulitos with their Somarriba cousins, but in León, where they lived above their father Ernesto Guzman's family's equipment repair shop, *Reparaciónes León.*

Violeta Somarriba had met Ernesto Guzman when she was a girl working at a fruit stand in the marketplace in León, a job for which she would have to wake up at dawn then walk from the village to the road to catch the bus that took the workers from Krukrulitos and the other jungle villages to León. After they were married Ernesto and Violeta worked for Ernesto's father at *Reparaciónes León* until they took over the business. Their children Xiomara and Ascensión grew up working at the family shop. Xiomara married Jaime Barreto, who was fat and cheerful but so lazy that he was practically useless at *Reparaciònes Leòn,* eating more than he earned from the little work that he did.

Ascensión, on the other hand, married a sensitive, pretty girl from a wealthy Managua family who went to the teachers' college in León. Lupe's mother had died when she was young and her father, Daniel Paloma, a cardiologist for well-off Central Americans but certainly not for the likes of the Somarriba's or the Guzman's, disowned Lupe when she married Ascensión. And the rest of the Guzman and Somarriba clans, especially the women, resented that Lupe's rich family neither acknowledged nor shared a bit of their wealth with her in-laws.

But, Mauricio reflected, when the American recession hit Nicaragua like the scourge of God and *Reparaciónes León* went out of business because the customers could no longer pay, it was Lupe's teacher's salary that kept the family from starving until the protests began and in the midst of the chaos that ensued in the cities the government neglected to pay the teachers. Then hungry creditors seized Ernesto Guzman's building and the family fled to Krukrulitos to take shelter with Mauricio, and the meager provisions shared by his extended family then had to be stretched among six more adults, Xiomara and Jaime's infant daughter, and their second child on the way.

It was Ascensión who'd had the spunk to take Lupe and flee to the North, not only lightening the burden on his family but eventually enriching them as well; for the cinder blocks—enough to build the two spacious bedrooms and kitchen—as well as the large kitchen table, the television, the propane stove and the refrigerator, had come to Mauricio's family thanks to the money that Ascensión regularly sent home when he was in the United States working multiple jobs: handyman, night janitor, plumber's assistant, any job he could grab day or night—and how well the jobs in the U.S. paid!—while Lupe stayed in their fine apartment all day and cared for their American-born son.

Mauricio didn't exactly understand why Ascensión and Lupe had returned to Nicaragua. They hadn't exactly been deported, so they said, or not in the usual way; an American judge gave them permission to leave legally and wait for a work visa, so they said. Ascensión, likeable, energetic and hard-working, had apparently made himself an indispensable worker to some American who owned a big plumbing business in a big northern city—New York? Philadelphia? Washington? Well, one of those places (they were all big, crowded abstractions in Mauricio's mind)—and the businessman had promised to get a visa for Ascensión to return someday. Or some such story, which Mauricio wasn't sure he believed.

But what did it matter? Ascensión—good luck that he always brought—and his wife were making plenty of money for the family since they'd returned home, and Mauricio did prefer having his favorite grandson around. But what a shrewd move on the part of Ascensión and Lupe to have a child while in the United States and then to find a rich American woman to raise their child, who would grow up to be a rich American himself and their connection to the United States and their son's future wealth would benefit themselves, their future children and the whole family. Who knew, perhaps the whole family would one day be able to move to the United States!

Truly a bright star of good fortune shone down upon Ascensión and his little wife, both of them well-fed and sheltered and wrapped close and secure in the arms of their family in this sturdy house on this beautiful piece of green land on God's earth.

Mauricio exhaled and watched the curls of smoke dance in the air. Who could be more content?

***

"Get up, *mi amor.*"

Ascensión gently shook his wife's shoulder, but she responded to his touch by curling into herself, her back to her husband. He knew she wasn't asleep; it was possible she hadn't slept all night. And though she'd been lying in bed for the past nine hours she showed no inclination to get up now.

"Lupe," her husband pleaded, "we can't do this today, *querida*, not today, today you have to get up, you know?"

"I can't," Lupe mumbled.

"Yes, you can!"

"No, I can't."

Ascensión's heart lifted. She was talking. That meant she'd get up. Eventually. But it had to be soon. They couldn't be too late for their jobs today. And on this day if Lupe didn't show up for work chances were even Yoolie wouldn't be able to cover for her, even if Yoolie would agree to. But of course Yoolie would always cover for them, Yoolie would always help them, they could always count on Yoolie. Everyone could.

But Yoolie wasn't the problem. The problem was that today a group of American engineers was coming to visit the Momotombo geothermal plant where Ascensión and Lupe worked along with Ascensión's brother-in-law Jaime, Ascensión as a mechanic, Jaime doing what he always did, hanging around doing who knew what and somehow getting himself paid for it, and Lupe was an office assistant to Yoolie and, because she was educated, pretty, and spoke fair English, sometimes Lupe was asked to stand in as a receptionist at the Visitors' Center, as she was scheduled to do today.

But Ascensión had to get Lupe up and to work. Besides the engineers, there would be foreign journalists and maybe even a rich investor or two. Not that any money pumped into Nicaragua by foreign investors would necessarily benefit Ascensión, Lupe, or any Nicaraguan other than a handful of already rich businessmen and politicians. Still, it would be necessary to put on a good show for these foreign *cheles*, and any worker who slacked off on this important day was liable to have their neck wrung like a fat chicken's. So Lupe would be expected not only to show up

6

for work but to be, as the Americans liked to say, on top of her game. Ascensión would be lucky to get her up and into work.

Ascensión gently lifted his wife in his arms—she felt so light—and sat her upright on the bed. "Lupe. You must go to work today. And we can't be late. Because today is an important day, a very important day, you know that, right?"

Lupe nodded listlessly.

"And you know we need the money to keep a roof over our head and, and…to help put food on the table for Blanca and Mauricito."

Ascensión knew that if anything could persuade Lupe, it would be bringing up the welfare of their five-year-old niece and three-year-old nephew. At the same time he knew not to talk about their own baby, David, when Lupe was in such a state. They could only talk about David on her good days, which today was not. And so he would not bring up that she needed to work and be well for the sake of David, because someday, maybe soon, they would be reunited with him and would need to have some money saved to make a good life for him. On good days, dreaming together about that reunion filled Lupe with hope; on bad days, with hopelessness. But in recent weeks, ever since their son's first birthday came and went, the good days had gotten fewer and farther between. In fact Ascensión couldn't remember the last good day Lupe had had since then.

But now she was sitting up on the edge of the bed, mechanically eating the bowl of *gallo pinto*, a mix of rice and red beans, that he'd brought into the room for her. If she ate, the food would give her strength and she'd make it through the day.

"Finish quickly, *amor*, then splash your face. Here, I brought you some water, some to drink and some to wash with." Ascensión gestured towards the small wooden table on which sat a towel and a small bucket of water and a glass of water, both dipped from the barrel that was kept full to use when the water was shut off in the village from 6 a.m. to noon every day. He offered Lupe the glass of water. She set the half-eaten bowl of rice and beans on the floor, took the glass from Ascensión, and drank. Then she stood and stepped over to the bucket and scooped some water onto her face while Ascensión stood behind her and brushed her hair.

"Good, good," he said. "Now here, let's get you dressed, *mi vida.*"

Ascensión pulled off his wife's nightgown and handed her some underclothes and her work uniform, a pair of lightweight khakis and a white polo shirt embroidered with the letters ENEL, for *Empresa Nicaragüense de Electricidad.*

"I've never heard of a man having to dress his wife."

Ascensión turned to see his mother Violeta standing in the doorway, having pushed aside the curtain that served as a divider between the bedroom and the kitchen. Lupe gasped and instinctively tried to cover herself with the clothes.

Ascensión quickly threw Lupe's nightgown back on over her head as his mother entered the bedroom. "*Mamá*, please, can we have *un momentito* of privacy?"

"*Privacy?*" Ascensión's sister Xiomara laughed as she stepped into the room behind her mother. Xiomara rubbed her hands over her seven months' pregnant belly. "Does Lupe think she's still in her big fancy apartment in the United States? Or her father's big fancy house in Managua?" Xiomara's smile removed none of the sting of her words.

"I'm sorry about your *privacy*," said Violeta, "but I have to get at least one of the beds made in here." She gestured towards the other double bed in this bedroom that she and her husband shared with Ascensión and Lupe.

"*Mamá*, Xiomara, *please*," said Ascensión, looking beseechingly at his mother and sister, "we have to get ready for work."

"Work?" Violeta waved her hand towards her daughter-in-law. "This one can't go to work. Look at her, she's too weak. She needs to rest. Let her go back to bed. Here, lie back down," she said to Lupe, "you need to sleep more."

"She's not weak," said Ascensión. "She's strong. Very strong."

Violeta and Xiomara exchanged a look.

"Lupe, you didn't finish your breakfast?" said Xiomara, eyeing the half-eaten bowl of *gallo pinto* on the floor. "Good food that could have gone into the children's mouths? You put it on the floor for the ants to get at?"

"Give it to the children to eat," Lupe said weakly, picking up the bowl and proffering it to her sister-in-law. "There are no ants in it." Lupe flopped back down onto the bed and sat hunched over. Xiomara made a great show of checking the bowl.

"She doesn't like *gallo pinto* anymore," sighed Violeta. "She only likes American food now. I'll have to go look for a box of cornflakes and some American milk at *La Unión*." Xiomara grimaced at her mother's reference to the big, expensive American-style supermarket in the center of León that carried imported *gringo* products and that even the locals who could afford them tended to avoid, preferring to buy their groceries and household needs from among the city's sprawling open-air and covered markets.

"I don't want cornflakes," said Lupe.

"*Mamá*, Xiomara, she doesn't want cornflakes! *Please* leave, we'll be gone in five minutes, you can come in and make the beds then!"

"I can make my bed," said Lupe.

"Yes, yes, when we get home from work," said Ascensión, pulling Lupe to her feet.

"You think I can have this bed sitting all day unmade?" cried Violeta.

"Violeta! Xiomara!" shouted a voice from the kitchen. "Let the *muchachos* get to work! Come out here and feed these *niños*! They're skittering around like little *cucarachas*!"

"Calm down, Nesto, I'm coming," Violeta called to her husband. She shook her head and to Ascensión she said, "Your *papá* is a big *niño* himself."

Xiomara followed her mother out of the bedroom carrying the bowl of Lupe's half-eaten *gallo pinto*.

From just on the other side of the curtain Violeta said, "*Dios mío*, she doesn't want to eat, she doesn't want to work..."

"She doesn't even want her own baby," said Xiomara. "What kind of a mother leaves her baby behind in another country with strangers? I'd give my own life before I'd give up my baby."

Lupe covered her face with her hands.

"*No importa, amor*, never mind," said Ascensión. He lifted Lupe under her arms and tried to stand her up but she was like dead weight and fell back down onto the bed, her body now wracking with sobs.

"I *want* my baby," she wept, "I *want* my baby, I *want* my baby."

"I know, *amor*, I know, but we have to..." Ascensión suddenly gave up trying to lift his wife and instead dropped onto the bed and wrapped his arms around her hunched form. "I know, *amor*, I know," he whispered as he stroked her hair, the tears filling his eyes until they streamed down his face.

Ascensión stepped from the bedroom into the kitchen, closing the curtain behind him. His father Ernesto Guzman sat at the kitchen table, a beer in front of him. On either side of him sat his grandchildren Blanca and Mauricito. The children's mother Xiomara was setting before them bowls of fried plantains that she'd cooked earlier on the propane stove. "Eat," she said to her children. Xiomara's husband Jaime stood leaning against a counter finishing up what was left of Lupe's bowl of *gallo pinto*. Violeta stood over the kitchen counter wiping her eyes with a handkerchief.

After she'd set her children's breakfast before them Xiomara turned back to Violeta and put a hand on her mother's shoulder.

"My little grandson," sniffed Violeta, "with some rich American *chela* instead of here with his father and family where he belongs."

"Don't cry, *mamita*," said Xiomara, "there's nothing we can do about it."

Violeta, seeing Ascensión now standing in the kitchen, rushed to him, wrapped her arms around him and buried her head on his shoulder. "My poor son, my poor son," she sobbed into his shoulder.

"It's okay, *mamá*," he muttered, patting her back.

"*Oye, hombre*," said Jaime, putting his empty bowl on the counter, "you going to work today or no?"

"I'm going," said Ascensión, gently extracting himself from his mother's arms.

"Wait," said Violeta, gripping her son's arm. "What will you tell the boss?"

"What?" said Ascensión.

"What will you tell them at Momotombo? Why Lupe didn't come to work again?"

"Ah, don't worry about it, *mamita*," Jaime chuckled. "They won't do anything. The boss is an American. You know how Americans are." He winked at Ascensión.

Violeta let go of her son's arm with a moan of disgust.

"Come on then, let's go before we miss the bus," said Jaime, taking his backpack down from a nail on the wall.

"You miss the bus, you'll be late," said Xiomara, handing her husband a paper bag filled with his lunch. She added, "No thanks to…" she cocked her head towards the bedroom from which Lupe's soft sobs were ever-so-slightly audible.

"What, she's not going to work again?" said Ernesto from where he still sat at the table. "Anybody who wants to eat around here better work." He shook his head and took a swig from his morning beer.

Ascensión's mother took her son's backpack down from its nail on the wall and put into it the paper bag sitting on the counter. "Here, I made you a nice lunch, *gallo pinto* with eggs wrapped in a tortilla. And some plantains that I fried just the way you like them, good and brown."

"Thank you, *mamá*," Ascensión mumbled, taking his backpack from his mother.

"My poor son," sighed Violeta, kissing Ascensión on the cheek.

"What kind of a wife doesn't fix her husband a good lunch?" said Xiomara.

"Not mine!" said Jaime, patting his stomach. He grabbed Xiomara around her wide waist, pulled her into as tight an embrace as her stomach would allow, kissed her on the mouth and sneaked a quick pat on her backside.

Xiomara feigned annoyance at her husband, swatted his hand and pulled away from him. "Never mind me, go kiss your children."

Jaime kissed Blanca and Mauricito and Ascensión kissed both children good-bye as well.

"Hurry, now, you'll be late." Xiomara kissed her husband again and made a show of shooing him and Ascensión out the door. To Ascensión she said, "Don't worry, we'll take care of her."

Ascensión and his brother-in-law exited the kitchen to the patio where Mauricio still sat smoking.

"Good morning, *abuelito*," said Ascensión.

"What a beautiful day, *muchachos*," said Mauricio, waving his cigarette towards the front yard.

"Keep an eye on the chickens for us, *abuelito*," said Jaime, also calling Mauricio the affectionate term for "grandfather." Jaime cocked his head towards the kitchen. "And keep an eye on the hen house."

Mauricio laughed. "I stay out here and leave the hens in the kitchen to their squawking." To Ascensión he said, "Where's your *chiquita* this morning?"

"She can't get out of bed again." Ascensión sniffled and rubbed the back of his hand across his eyes.

"Again? Well, never mind, never mind. She'll get better. She needs another baby. Give her another baby, she'll be fine."

"What, you two are still here?" said Violeta, who entered the patio from the kitchen carrying a tray on which was a mug of coffee and a plate of *gallo pinto*. She set the tray on the table before Mauricio. "Here, *papito*, eat." To Ascensión she said, "*Now* if you're late you can't blame that wife of yours."

Ascensión and Jaime kissed Mauricio on the cheek then the men headed across the yard towards the dirt path that led to the gravel road where the bus would stop to pick them up to join the other passengers, workers who traveled every day from León and the villages to the Momotombo geothermal plant.

For a while they walked in silence along the dirt path then Jaime said, "*Oye, muchacho,* why don't you tell your *mamita* to lay off your wife?"

"*Oye, maje,*" Ascención shot back, "Why don't you tell *your wife* to lay off my wife?"

Jaime held up his palms. "Oh, no, not me. The only person tougher than your mother is your sister. I don't want Xiomara to cut off my head. Or my..." Jaime cupped his hand around his crotch and laughed. He threw an arm around Ascensión's shoulder. "Aw, what can we do? The Guzman women have *cojones* of steel, and a lot of fire. But they're great cooks and take good care of the little *niños*." Jaime gently poked a finger at Ascensión's chest. "And they take good care of *us, hombre,* so what can we do?"

Of course Jaime was right. Jaime was always right because Jaime always spoke the truth, which was why people found him so damned annoying at times. Still, what he said was true. His mother had always been a good mother to him, the best mother. He recalled how she sat by his bed at night when he was little and afraid of the dark or sick with the *dengue*, never worrying about catching that terrible sickness herself. She worked like a horse, not only for her own family, but she also tended to be a source of expertise, advice, and help on all sorts of problems and needs among the villagers of Krukrulitos.

Everybody loved his mother. And everybody was afraid of his mother. *He* was afraid of his mother. Even his sister Xiomara, strong willed as she was, was no match for his mother, no matter what Jaime thought.

Jaime interrupted his thoughts. "Hey, don't worry about your *mamá* and Xiomara. They're like all women, they like to peck, peck, peck at each other. Your little *Lupita* will get used to it after a while. Pretty soon she'll be as tough and hard as the rest of them."

The thought of that happening sent a shudder through Ascensión's heart.

Chapter Two

Yoolie, *née* Julie Pursglove from Triadelphia, West Virginia, stood outside in front of the small wooden structure that served as her office and took in the landscape of industrial turbines and pipelines, her domain spread out before her, and for a moment wished she were still in the Peace Corps digging irrigation ditches in Burkina Faso.

But the moment was fleeting and passed, as such moments always did. Other than on days like today was going to be, life, Yoolie reminded herself, was good.

She loved waking up every morning and stepping out of her cool cinderblock house, one of a couple dozen in the jungle clearing, to a view of Lake Managua to the south and the majestic volcano Momotombo to the north. She liked waving to her neighbors in the housing area, foreign contract workers like herself, fellow Americans, also Canadians, Indians, Asians, South Americans, the engineers and scientists who worked alongside her at the geothermal fields on the southern flank of the volcano a few miles from the housing area. They all called her Yoolie, everyone here did, even the native English speakers.

She liked socializing with her co-workers, sometimes having dinner with them and spending the evening talking shop. Not all of them, of course; only those who had no problem with her being the chief hydraulic research officer of the geothermal plant, no problem with her being a woman, no problem with her being…who she was. As for the others, well, Yoolie was thirty-eight years old and had learned and accepted years ago, even before she'd left behind Triadelphia and headed for MIT, that she had no control over other people's beliefs or behavior.

She liked her friendly, energetic housekeeper, a middle-aged lady named Rosaria (whom she greatly overpaid) who arrived by taxi every weekday, often laden with food from the market, to cook Yoolie's meals, sweep her house, and wash her clothes by hand, hanging them outside to dry before the afternoon rains arrived.

She enjoyed spending the weekends in León with Cristela, or occasionally having Cristela spend the weekend with her, hiking together through the jungle or sometimes around the volcano, driving ten miles to Las Peñitas to swim in the sea then picnic along the shore, feasting on cheese, tortillas, fresh guava, papaya, and delicious fried plantains, then returning to Yoolie's bungalow to make love while the warm torrents of rain pattered against the clay tile roof.

But those occasions were rare; Cristela could seldom be pulled away for a whole weekend from her work, her heart's calling, caring for the street children of León who ran in packs like the feral dogs who also ran in packs through the city streets, though the children were more troublesome and endangered than the dogs, who knew to keep to their packs and avoid contact with humans. Cristela was the director of *Las Sonrisas* (officially *Casa de las Sonrisas*—House of Smiles—but shortened by everyone and so known locally as *Las Sonrisas*), a group of local women, mostly volunteers, who ran a shelter for the children that provided meals and refuge for them during the day and a safe space on a floor mat to sleep on if needed at night.

The funding for *Las Sonrisas* was provided by *Los Caminadores*, a group of mostly young adult volunteers, mostly adventurous foreigners—though there were Nicaraguans, too, mostly university students—who led tourists on hikes up the local volcanoes, Cerro Negro, Telica, and massive, towering Momotombo. The money *Los Caminadores* charged for the volcano tours they turned over to *Las Sonrisas*.

Yoolie first learned of *Los Caminadores* shortly after she arrived at Momotombo not quite two years ago. She'd caught sight of a line of hikers tromping across the facility and subsequently learned that the *Empresa Nicaragüense de Electricidad*, the Nicaraguan Electric Company, a government entity in charge of all electricity generation, had recently granted the group permission to cut through the Momotombo facility on their hikes up the volcano. And it was an enterprising young Dutch marketing analyst who was doing a stint as a *Los Caminadores* volunteer who came up with the idea of advertising the shortcut across the facility as an added feature of the volcano hike—a tour of the Momotombo Geothermal Fields, he called it—and to charge the tourists an extra fee for it.

The volcano hikes had intrigued Yoolie, and after looking into *Los Caminadores* and learning about *Las Sonrisas*, she was soon taking tourists on day hikes up Cerro Negro on the weekends and sleeping with Cristela. But she would not be taking any hikers up the volcano this weekend. Tomorrow she was going to *Las Sonrisas* to give Cristela a hand. Yesterday in the wee hours of the morning someone had left a sleeping infant in a box outside the doorway of *Las Sonrisas*. This sort of thing happened once in a while and always threw Cristela into a fluttering frenzy, as she normally wasn't equipped to take care of a baby. She'd have to bustle around buying or sometimes looking for the money to buy baby food and diapers. And of course a baby has to be looked after all day and sometimes all night long. Some relative always came around eventually to collect the baby, or else sometimes Cristela was able to return the baby herself after learning from her local sources which family was suddenly missing a baby. But in the meantime Cristela was always stressed out and exhausted trying to manage a baby along with her street kids. And so this weekend Yoolie—little personal interest as she had in children in general and babies in particular—was going to help out Cristela, logistically and probably financially, too.

A couple of workers off in the distance smiled and waved at Yoolie and she waved back. Of all the people she'd met from around the world, Yoolie decided that she liked Nicaraguans the best. She found them friendly, easy-going and sociable, if not above occasionally trying to hit her up for money. They reminded her of Americans, if Americans lived in the poorest country in Central America in a hot, humid tropical climate where half the country was covered in rain forest and it poured every afternoon for half the year. In any case, Yoolie felt more comfortable in hot, wet, poor Nicaragua than in many of the countries she'd lived in or visited—definitely more comfortable than in France, where the Parisians seemed to think it was their patriotic duty to call out to her on the street or from their cars to announce the fact that they could tell she was she was an American (*Voilà l'américaine!*)—though she was occasionally taken for a German (*Voilà l'allemande!*)—or that she had red hair (*Voilà la rousse!*), or that she was tall and big-boned (*Qu'est-ce qu'elle est grande!*), or that she was a tall, big-boned, red-haired American (*Qu'est-ce qu'elle est grande, cette rousse américaine!*) and whom those who knew her called *Zhulie,* the French pronunciation of her name. She frankly preferred the Spanish pronunciation: Yoolie.

But Yoolie was only big compared to the Parisians, who were on average smaller than average Americans. Yoolie was five feet ten inches tall and had weighed one hundred and eighty-two pounds when she'd been in Paris for that international electricity convention five years ago. She'd lost fourteen pounds since arriving in León, where meat, while not exactly scarce if one had the money for it, was far from plentiful. And so she'd become accustomed to eating the diet common among the Nicaraguans of rice, beans, eggs, plantains and fruit, with an occasional piece of chicken.

Still, if Yoolie was taller than the average Parisian, she towered over the average Nicaraguan. And yet the Nicaraguans seemed to have no need to comment on her size or nationality, except to sometimes address her as *chela* or *chelita*—white woman, or young white woman—but, as Yoolie learned, in Nicaragua addressing a foreign woman as *chela* wasn't especially any more disrespectful than addressing her as *miss* would be in English.

Yoolie entered her office and removed her broad-brimmed khaki sun hat and the long-sleeved light-weight sun-protective shirt she'd been wearing over her ENEL polo shirt and hung them on a hook by the door. She slipped off her extra-polarized sunglasses, turned on her ceiling fan, walked to her desk and flipped open her laptop. Today was Friday. She wished it were the weekend already. Mostly she wished this day were over. Still, it was the kind of day there was no escaping from time to time in her job, which on paper was overseeing the development of improved systems for maintaining the constant optimum pressure of the steam wells by ameliorating the linkage between the high temperature subterranean gas phases and the active hydrothermal system beneath. In other words, goosing the volcano to work harder to produce more heat and light. Of course, making heat and light was what the volcano did. Provided the volcano wasn't over-exploited, as Momotombo had been in the past. In the end, as she'd often told herself and some of the more astute among her fellow engineers, the volcano's gonna do what the volcano's gonna do. But of course she'd never say that to the officials of the Nicaraguan Electric Company and she certainly would not say it to the potential investors who were visiting the geothermal fields today. She'd show them the works and then let them assess how much money was to be made from investment in geothermal energy in Central America—though even Yoolie knew there was plenty at this point, and she'd do her part to elucidate this fact to these visitors. Because selling the volcano was, she knew, part of her job. Just not her favorite part.

She was a little nervous, as she always was when the money people came to call. But hopefully the day and the tour would roll out smoothly. Hopefully while showing around these important suits Yoolie wouldn't be accosted by workers frightened by a nest of snakes that had appropriated a patch of the facility on which the *jardineros* had neglected to cut back the ever-impinging jungle growth. Hopefully she wouldn't have to grab a machete and cut back the growth and flush out the snakes herself. (She wasn't dressed for that kind of work today, in her white ENEL polo shirt and clean dress khakis. She was grateful enough she wasn't expected to be mincing around the plant in a skirt and heels, as had been expected of her in some jobs past). Hopefully a couple of starving, desperate *bandidos* wouldn't try to storm the geothermal plant and hopefully she wouldn't have to try to convince them of the lie that there was no cash kept anywhere or on anyone at the facility and then give them her lunch. Hopefully she wouldn't receive a frantic phone call from one of the workers who'd missed the Momotombo bus for any of a hundred heart-tugging reasons, because today Yoolie absolutely could not take off the time to drive into León, or to any of the contiguous jungle villages from which the workers came, to give someone a ride to work. Hopefully the afternoon rains wouldn't come early. And mostly, *mostly*, she hoped her administrative assistant Lupe Guzman would show up today on time and ready to go to work.

Lupe. Smart and capable, but what a problem that girl was turning into. There was something wrong, and Yoolie had been letting her slide, but today… well, Yoolie just hoped Lupe would show up and somehow manage to keep her act together because today Yoolie could not deal with Lupe, her worthless brother-in-law Jaime, or any of the two dozen normally non-momentous problems that could and would be sprung on Yoolie on any given day, probably for the reason that she was the only one who felt compelled to deal with them.

Yoolie looked up from her desk. Through the open door she saw Lupe's husband Ascensión jogging up the hill—without Lupe—towards her office. His face was a study in heart-pumping anxiety.

Yoolie closed her eyes. *Aw, crap,* she thought. This was going to be a day.

Ascensión stood in the doorway, breathless, sweaty, red-eyed. "Yoolie," he panted, continuing in English, though it wasn't necessary as Yoolie was perfectly fluent in Spanish, both conversational and technical. "Lupe, she is sick, she..."

"Uh-huh," said Yoolie, shutting her laptop.

"She will come to work on Monday, she will be better, but..."

"Uh-huh," said Yoolie, glancing at her cell phone to check the time.

"Today I work for her. I can, can...*introducir los datos*...on the computer for you, and I can meet the...*inversores,* and show them Momotombo. My English is even better than Lupe's."

Yoolie sighed. "Yeah, I know, Ascensión." What he said was true. Though he was technically a mechanic he could do all sorts of repairs and diagnostics. He seemed to have a gift for machinery. And he could handle plumbing as well. And he had, on occasion, even done some data entry for Yoolie, he was that smart. He was by far the smartest and most dependable of her workers. In fact recently she'd been laying the groundwork with the powers that be to have Ascensión promoted to foreman. And it was true that his English was better than his wife's, which fact Yoolie figured he was probably trying to impress upon her by carrying on the conversation in his pretty good English. But this wheeling and dealing he'd been pulling over on her lately on Lupe's behalf that she, Yoolie, in truth had been enabling by too often turning a blind eye...okay, things *were* different down here, this was an operation in the middle of the jungle on the slope of a volcano and Central America wasn't Corporate America and the Nicaraguan Electric Company wasn't run like General Electric where Yoolie had spent years in the development of pumped-storage hydroelectricity units used to power commercial and upscale residential heating and air-conditioning systems and felt like she was losing her soul.

But the fact was that today Yoolie needed Lupe and everyone else present and doing their job. She had to make this operation look efficient and profitable to the representatives of Corporate America and to her employers, the suits from ENEL, at least some of whom would notice during their visit that one of their paid employees was again missing and what story could Yoolie tell them this time as to why said employee was missing?

"Look, Ascensión," she said, "today I need Lupe doing *her* job and you doing *your* job, and if—"

"No, no," he cut her off, "I can do her job and my job! I can talk to the *inversores*, and—"

"*Investors*," she corrected him, "and you can't show up in Lupe's place." To herself she finished, *because the Nicaraguan suits liked having a nice-looking prop like Lupe in the reception area dressed in a neat white polo shirt printed with the* Empresa Nicaragüense de Electricidad *logo and crisp khakis to impress upon the American suits how progressive Nicaragua was. Her English skills didn't matter. She was just a prop.*

"Yes, yes, I can," Ascención insisted, "I can meet them, then I come back to your office and work, and then—"

"No, look," Yoolie cut him off, "I need you out on the slope, that generator, number five, needs…" Yoolie stood and waved a hand, "…I don't know, *something*."

"A wire, I'm sure, is always a wire. Is simple. Jaime can do it for me."

"Jaime?" Yoolie laughed in spite of herself.

"Jaime knows how to work. He don't like to, but he knows generators same as me. We worked together at *Reparaciónes León*."

Yoolie shook her head. Her stomach was in a knot. She hated firing people. Especially the wife of her best mechanic. She pulled in a deep breath. "Okay, Ascensión," she said, switching to Spanish to make herself perfectly clear, or so she hoped, "*your* job is to be out on the slope fixing generator number five then reporting back to the machine shack and checking the work order list, and *Jaime's* job is...well, I don't even *know* what in God's name *he* does with himself all day long, and *Lupe's* job is to be down at the reception desk in thirty minutes, and if she's not there in ten I'm calling the front office and telling them to get someone else at that desk *pronto*, and then I'm calling corporate in León and I'm telling them to send someone else up here to help me get this piled-up mountain of data entered before the other engineers come over and chop my head off!" Shoot, she'd been yelling. She didn't usually yell, she didn't like to, but, shoot, that's what she'd been doing.

Ascensión stood there taken aback, wide-eyed. "No, no, don't worry, Yoolie," he said, patting the air. "It's okay, I'll fix the generator, then I'll enter the data for you, all of it, I can do it, then I'll take my work orders, I'll spend the night here with the night crew, and on Monday morning when you come back Lupe will be here, and—"

"No," she cut him off, this time more calmly. "On Monday morning a new assistant will be here. I told you, I'm calling ENEL. Today. I'm sorry, but I can't depend on Lupe anymore. I'm letting her go. I'm sorry. I have to leave. Now."

"Yoolie, wait," he said hoarsely, his large brown eyes filling with tears, "*por favor, por...*" He burst into breathless sobs then stood sobbing uncontrollably.

Yoolie closed her eyes. *Crap*, she thought. *Crap, crap, crap!*

Now Ascensión's hands were folded in supplication. "*Please*, Yoolie, *Please!* For the love of God, please don't fire Lupe! I promise, she will never miss work again, not one day! *Please*, Yoolie!"

"Ascensión, I..." Yoolie looked down. She could already feel her resolve melting in Ascensión's tears.

"Please, Yoolie, please," he sobbed breathlessly. "My Lupe...our baby..."

"What?" Yoolie looked up. "Your *baby*?"

"Lupe...Lupe..." he sobbed. "She's...dying...she's..."

"What? Did you say Lupe is...*dying*?"

Ascensión nodded, his body convulsing with his great sobs.

"Oh, my God," said Yoolie. "Wha...did you take her to the doctor? Is she in the hospital?"

Ascensión shook his head, unable to answer for a moment. When he was able to speak again he put a hand against his chest and said, "It's her heart. Her heart is broken. She lies in bed and cries for our baby boy all day and all night. If she doesn't go to work anymore she'll stay in her bed and cry herself to death." Ascensión put his face in his hand and broke into another round of sobs.

Yoolie felt herself tearing up. "Your baby boy...is he...did he...?"

"No, he didn't die. He is alive. In the United States."

"Wait, what? Your baby is...*in the United States?*"

Ascensión nodded.

Yoolie closed her eyes and sighed. Of course. Of course she was now caught up in what was doubtless a heart-wrenching story and any hope that today was going to roll out any more smoothly or free of drama than any other day immediately dissipated. And now what was she supposed to do about her sobbing chief mechanic and her administrative assistant who was crying herself to death because their baby was in the United States?

"Okay," she sighed. "Can I put you at the Visitors' Center? Can you talk to the investors if any of them ask you a question?"

"Of course," Ascensión said in English, straightening up and recovering himself.

Yoolie scooped up her laptop and a couple of files from her desk and put them into a briefcase. "Let's get into the jeep."

"I can walk, it's no trouble," said Ascensión.

"There's no time. We'll drive."

While Yoolie drove her jeep the quarter mile down the slope to the Visitors' Center she quickly briefed Ascensión. "When we get there I'll have Nico take you back to the storage closet. There are some white polo shirts with the ENEL logo on them and some pairs of khakis. You should be able to find a shirt and pants that fit. Get changed and then come back out to the front. We have about twenty minutes before the suits...uh, visitors arrive. And look, some of the guys from the Electric Company know Lupe and that she's my assistant. They might be expecting her to be there today. If anybody should ask you where she is, say, uh, I don't know...say..."

"I'll say she is somewhere else today."

"Yeah, okay. I guess."

"It will be fine."

Yoolie looked at Ascensión, now smiling his charming smile. He'd actually make a nice-looking prop, too. And his English was good. So long as they didn't mind him not being a female. It would probably be fine.

"Listen, if I put Jaime on that generator you think he can take care of it?"

"Jaime? Oh, sure." Ascensión pulled his cell phone from his pocket. "I'll call down to the machine shack, they'll know where he is now. I'll tell them to send him to the generator. "

"You think it's just that wire again?" asked Yoolie.

"Probably. It's always the wire."

"What about The Squeak?" said Yoolie, referring to the noise, more like a high-pitched moaning grunt, that the generator had begun periodically emitting for the past several weeks and that the crew had christened *El Chirrido*, The Squeak.

"I don't know about The Squeak," said Ascensión. "Nobody knows about The Squeak. It just comes and goes and nobody knows why. It doesn't seem to bother the generator, so nobody knows what to fix. Like you say in the United States, 'If it isn't broke, why are you fixing it?'"

Yoolie smiled at Ascensión's slightly off Americanism. "Close enough," she said.

"But, sure, I'll tell Jaime to check for The Squeak, check the wire, check everything. He can do it."

Yoolie pulled the jeep up to the entrance of the reception center and sighed.

"Yoolie," said Ascensión, switching to English, "You know I don't bullshit you."

"No, Ascensión, you never do." *Which is why I'm trusting you today,* she thought.

"I will make sure the generator is fixed today. Before the rain comes. And I'll get all the data entered for you. Monday morning you will come to work and everything will be good." He hesitated, then added, "And Lupe will be there."

***

It was five-ten pm and Yoolie felt like heading out, going home and indulging in a large celebratory glass of wine that the day was over and the investors had left happy, if heat-addled and drowning in sweat, probably with sounds of coinage jingling in their heads as they hurried back to the Managua Crowne Plaza to bask in the air conditioning.

Yoolie would be happy enough to be sitting in her bungalow in front of her floor fan sipping her *gato negro,* though in a perfect scenario she would stroll, wine glass in hand, down the path from her yard to the shore of Lake Managua to watch a glorious sunset over the lake. The only snag was that there was no glorious sunset to be seen; in this part of Central America the sun dropped quickly like a heavy glowing disc below the horizon while the night fell like a curtain on top of it.

That curtain would drop in one hour, and here in Yoolie's office sat Ascensión at the small table that served as Lupe's desk, still absorbed in catching up on his wife's work. Yoolie was about to remind him that the last bus before nightfall from Momotombo would leave in twenty minutes, or maybe fifteen or thirty—the buses didn't run on a strict schedule—when she saw Jaime standing in her office doorway.

"*Buenos tardes,* Yoolie," he said deferentially, bowing slightly to her. To Ascensión he said, "They told me at the machine shack that you were here."

"Yes, I'm here," said Ascensión without looking up from the computer screen.

"*Hola,* Jaime," Yoolie said. "Thanks for taking care of that generator today."

"No problem," said Jaime, again bowing slightly. "I'm glad to do anything for you, Yoolie, anything you need, you just ask me, I'll do it."

Yoolie had to stifle a laugh. *Yeah, if I could ever find you,* she thought. "So what was it? The wire?"

"Yes, it was the wire, just like Ascensión said. It was easy to fix. I just replaced the wire and it's good as new."

Yoolie shook her head. "It just doesn't make sense, though. Why does that one wire keep dying?" She thought a moment then said, "Jaime, did you by chance take a look at the rest of the generator? To see if anything else was off besides that wire?"

"Oh, sure," said Jaime. "I checked every inch just to make sure."

Jaime, if you're telling me the truth and really checked every inch of that generator then I am unexpectedly impressed with you, Yoolie thought. Then she added, "What about The Squeak?"

"The Squeak wasn't there today. I listened and listened, but no Squeak. Maybe it's gone?"

27

"I don't know," Yoolie sighed.

"Nobody knows," said Jaime with a shrug. "But I checked the generator just like Ascensión told me to, and besides the wire there was nothing else wrong that I could see."

Ascensión looked up from his computer screen. "Maybe it's not the generator," he said.

Yoolie's eyes widened. "Not the generator, you say?"

"Maybe," said Ascensión. "What if the problem was with the turbine? Or maybe the governor?"

"That keeps the turbine from turning too fast," Jaime added in a helpful tone of voice.

"Yoolie knows what the governor is, *muchacho*," said Ascensión.

"No, that's okay," said Yoolie. "It's good to have at least two guys around here who know what a turbine governor is." She thought a minute. "Well, if the governor were malfunctioning, maybe intermittently, and the turbine started getting hot, maybe in one spot...I don't know, I suppose the heat could be hitting the generator in that one spot where the wire is...but that would be pretty..." Yoolie shook her head. "...pretty farfetched. I don't know. And it still wouldn't explain The Squeak."

"Maybe it's just a defect in the generator," said Jaime. "Maybe we have to just keep replacing that wire every now and then."

"Maybe," said Ascensión.

"Maybe," said Yoolie.

"If you were in the United States you would probably just buy a new one," said Jaime.

Yoolie chuckled. "Maybe."

"But here in Nicaragua we cobble things back together. Sometimes with a bicycle wheel or a rusty old garden hoe and some spit." Jaime laughed good-naturedly.

"Yes, we sure do," said Yoolie.

"Maybe you want to get a couple of the engineers to have a look on Monday," said Ascensión. "If they need a crew I can get

28

one together. Meanwhile I'll keep an eye on the generator tonight."

"*Tonight?*" said Jaime.

"You go catch the bus without me. I'm spending the night here."

"Oh, come on, Ascensión," said Yoolie. "It's not necessary for you to spend all night watching that generator."

"That's right, *tio*, I just replaced the wire. It's not gonna do anything anytime soon."

"The weekend shifts will check it now and then like they do on their normal rounds," said Yoolie.

"Okay," said Ascensión. "But after I'm finished here I'll go see if the night crew needs a hand."

"What?" said Jaime. "You're gonna work all night?"

"Not all night. I'll sleep a little on the couch in the machine shack."

"No, no," said Yoolie with a wave of her hand. "Look, you go now and catch the bus with Jaime. Lupe can finish up her work on Monday." *If she shows up,* she added in her mind.

"No, Yoolie, I'll finish here tonight. I'll catch the bus back to Krukrulitos in the morning. When you come in on Monday everything will be caught up." He turned back to the computer screen.

Jaime stood in the doorway and Yoolie stood in her office, both momentarily unsure of what to do.

Ascensión looked up again. "Jaime. You'll look after…?"

"Lupe? Of course. I'll make sure she's okay. And don't worry, I'll make sure the other women don't eat her up." Jaime opened his mouth wide, made a frightening face and raised his hands in the shape of two claws. Then he laughed.

Ascensión smiled wanly at his brother-in-law's joke then he turned back to his work.

But Yoolie sensed that Jaime's quip about the other women eating up Lupe was likely more truth than joke. She knew about extended families living under one roof and she knew about pecking order among groups of females. She imagined that to the women in the household Lupe, wounded and weak, was probably at the bottom of the food chain, and if Lupe was dying of a broken heart she was probably also suffering death by a thousand pecks. Yoolie decided she'd stay and work a while longer, too.

Close to one hour later, with the sun about to drop into the horizon, Ascensión turned off his wife's laptop and shut the lid. "All done," he said. He stood and stretched. "You need me to do anything else?"

Yoolie looked up from her computer. "No, I'm good."

Ascensión picked up his backpack and slung it over his shoulder. "*Buenas noches,* Yoolie," he said. "Have a good weekend."

"Where are you going now?" she asked him.

"Down to the machine shack. I'll see where the night crew needs help."

"Ascensión," she said, "you're only getting paid for one shift."

"It's okay," he said. "I'll do a little extra."

Yoolie sighed. "Ascensión…Okay, how far is Krukrulitos?"

"Halfway between here and León. I could walk, but not in the dark. Maybe I'll walk back when the sun comes up."

Yoolie shook her head. "I'm giving you a ride home. Now."

"No, no, it's not necessary."

"I think it is."

Yoolie began packing up her desk. Ascensión watched her, his eyes luminous and sad.

The exit gate of the Momotombo geothermal plant opened to a macadam road, and as they drove towards Krukrulitos the lights of village houses occasionally shone through the jungle vegetation on either side of the road, which progressively turned from asphalt to gravel the farther one drove from the plant. Far ahead of them the glow from the city lights of León was visible on the horizon.

For the first few minutes Yoolie and Ascensión rode in silence. To Yoolie, now sitting close next to him without the preoccupations of the workday to serve as a buffer, Ascensión's earlier revelation about his baby in the United States hung like a palpable presence in the air between them. Still, uncomfortable as the situation was making her feel, Yoolie preferred not to broach the subject of the baby. After all, other people's personal problems were like sticky spider webs: touch one and you were likely to become enmeshed, and how could one touch a problem as all-consuming as a person's grief over their child without becoming enmeshed?

On the other hand, Yoolie had already touched it, and by extension of Ascensión and Lupe being her employees their problem was in fact her problem and impossible for her to further ignore. Especially since Ascensión had already revealed to her the tip of the story, which Yoolie more than half wished he hadn't. But he had and so how could she now, in decency, show no interest in hearing the rest of the story?

Unless Ascensión didn't want to share any more of the story than he already had. Unless he'd told Yoolie as much as he'd told her in a moment of desperation and only in hopes of keeping his wife from getting fired. Yoolie could probably guess the rest of the story, anyway. It was probably a case of an American adoption. Maybe Lupe had become pregnant before she and Ascensión were married and, unwed mothers being considered socially unacceptable in this country…but then, why couldn't they just have gotten married and kept the baby?

She wouldn't ask any further about the baby, period. It had to be an adoption. How else would the child of a young couple from the Nicaraguan jungle come to be in the United States? Of course she, Yoolie, didn't judge them or care one way or the other, far from it. In fact she felt for them. But she was just as happy not to have to revisit the subject, to leave Lupe and Ascensión to their privacy on the matter. And besides, if Lupe continued missing work—which, in truth, Yoolie suspected was going to be the case—and Yoolie had to fire her, then it would be easier for Yoolie if she didn't know any more of Lupe's sad story than she already did.

"We lived in the United States for almost two years," said Ascensión.

"What?" said Yoolie, roused from her thoughts and needing a moment to comprehend something she wasn't expecting to hear.

"Lupe and me. We lived in Philadelphia. You know Philadelphia?"

"Well, uh, yes. I've been there a couple of times." *How in the world did they wind up in Philadelphia?*

Ascensión then proceeded to tell Yoolie about their flight from Nicaragua across several countries to the U.S. then north, far north of the border to the city of Philadelphia, where they believed—foolishly, in the end—that they might be safe from the immigration police. He told her of the birth of their baby David, of the American couple, a plumber named Silvio and his wife Sally, who befriended them and brought them to the good, clever lawyer who arranged with the immigration judge to grant Ascensión and Lupe voluntary deportation without penalty so that Silvio could apply for a visa for Ascensión to come back and work at his plumbing business. "There's a special visa to hire skilled foreign workers who are badly needed by companies," Ascensión explained. "I can do plumbing as well as anything else, and there's a shortage of good plumbers in Philadelphia, especially plumbers who can speak Spanish as well as English. But Silvio couldn't get this visa for me and a spousal visa for Lupe unless we first returned legally to Nicaragua."

"And you couldn't bring your baby back with you?"

"We left Nicaragua because it was dangerous then with the violent demonstrations and the soldiers in the streets. Anyone could be shot or arrested. My family had lost our business and our house in León. Lupe was a teacher but they stopped paying the teachers. We had to go live with my grandfather in Krukrulitos. My parents, my sister and her husband—that's Jaime—and Lupe and me. We all had to live in my grandfather's house. My sister had one baby and one on the way, and my grandfather was old and we had no money. There wasn't enough food for all of us so Lupe and I left. But I made good money in Philadelphia, enough to send home and help my family. When we had to return, we were afraid to bring our son. We were afraid there wouldn't be work for us here or enough food or that the fighting would break out again and our child would be in danger. We were afraid we wouldn't be able to return to the U.S. Our son is an American. We wanted him to stay there and be safe and well-fed until we could come for him. But now…" Ascensión rubbed the back of his hand across his eyes. "It hasn't been easy."

Yoolie didn't know what to say, or what good saying anything would do in this moment anyway, so she merely nodded and remained silent and hoped to God she wouldn't have to fire Lupe.

Suddenly the village lights and the distant glow of the city blinked off and only the lights of the jeep illuminated the pitch darkness all around them.

"¡Ay, por dios!" said Ascensión. "There goes the electricity!"

"Dang," said Yoolie. "Why so early tonight?"

"Look, León is back on." The glow on the horizon had returned, thanks to the generators that kept most businesses in León running when the electricity went off nightly for several hours, generally starting around 8 pm. It was common knowledge that at any one time only about a third of the residents of León and the surrounding areas paid their electricity bills. This was generally the case throughout the country, and the way the *Empresa Nicaragüense de Electricidad* dealt with the shortfall was with daily or nightly blackouts nationwide.

Off in the jungle patches of light began appearing here and there, houses lit from propane generators, flashlights and candles.

"Will we be able to find Krukrulitos in the dark?" Yoolie asked.

"Oh sure," said Ascensión, "you won't miss Krukrulitos. Look." Up ahead on the right a streetlamp rigged to a tall wooden pole cast light on a wide dirt path off the main road. "Turn here," he said, pointing towards the dirt path. "It's the road to Krukrulitos."

"I like that streetlamp," said Yoolie as she turned her jeep onto the path. "I never noticed it on the road before."

"Some Dutch kids, engineering students, put it up a few weeks ago, Jaime and I helped them. Or maybe they were Swedish. So many foreign volunteers come to the village these days, I get them confused."

Now through the trees there were hints of a brightly lit clearing up ahead. "Is that the village?" Yoolie asked.

"That's my grandfather's farm. Now you can see where Lupe and I live, and our relatives."

"Sure is well lit," said Yoolie. "Do you have a generator?"

"We have a big gas generator. It was the generator we had at *Reparaciónes León*. When the business closed Jaime and I hauled it here from León and we set it up to keep all the houses on the farm lit at night. The streetlamp runs off our generator, too."

A moment later the clearing opened up and the property of Ascensión's grandfather with its family houses and outbuildings came into view, lit up bright as day from the house lights and spotlights in the yards, all empowered by Ascensión's gas generator. Half a dozen adults were sitting on chairs in the Somarriba patio living room while a few barefoot children played on the dirt floor or swung in the hammock. So well-lit was the area that Yoolie could see the outline of Momotombo and the lesser volcanos rising above the trees. It was, she thought, quite a lovely scene.

"Ah, look, there's Lupe," said Ascensión. His face lit up with a smile.

Now Yoolie could see Lupe. She was outside off to the side of the house where the yard sloped downward, unpinning laundry hung on a clothesline, folding the laundry and placing each piece into a woven basket.

"See? She's fine now. Up and bringing in the laundry." Ascensión sounded happy, relieved.

Then as they drove towards the yard a scene played out before them. They saw two small children skip from the patio into the yard. The children snuck up behind Lupe as she was retrieving the clothes from the line and shouted "¡Ay!" then grabbed her legs and waist from behind. Lupe started, then turned and laughed at the sight of the children. She left a piece of laundry half-hung on the line and scooped up both children. She carried them to a nearby bench in the yard and began snuggling and nuzzling them.

A moment later two women, an older one and a younger very pregnant one, stepped out of a doorway onto the patio. They spoke for a moment with the people on the patio then the younger woman caught sight of Lupe playing with the children in her lap and nudged the older one, who shook her head in apparent disapproval. Both women strode towards Lupe. They shooed the children off Lupe's lap and while the older woman spoke animatedly, her face puckered into a frown, her hands gesturing from Lupe to the half-gathered laundry, the younger woman stood next to her rubbing her pregnant belly. Lupe stood and took a few steps towards the clothesline but the older woman waved her away and pointed to the bench. Lupe sat back down. She seemed to crumple, until she sat hunched over, her elbows on her knees and her face in her hands. The two women looked at each other, shook their heads, then proceeded to finish taking down the laundry. The people on the patio by now had become the audience, and they, too, shook their heads, whether in disapproval of or pity for Lupe, an observer could not tell.

Though the jeep was by now still a good hundred feet away from the yard, Ascensión cried out for Yoolie to stop. He jumped from the jeep and ran towards his wife, but he was intercepted by the older woman, who hugged him and buried her head in his chest. While she spoke to him, holding him close, shaking her head and gesturing towards Lupe, Ascensión nodded and patted the woman's shoulder. "*Sí, mamá,*" Yoolie could hear him say, "*Sí, sí, esta bien,*" while over her shoulder he looked anxiously at his wife.

By now the family members on the patio had spotted Yoolie and were waving at her with friendly smiles. Yoolie smiled and waved back then turned her jeep around and headed towards the road that would return her to Momotombo and her house nearby. She stopped just before pulling out onto the main road. She turned off her jeep and sat back and closed her eyes. "Oh boy," she muttered. She pulled out her cell phone. There was service. The cell towers weren't included in the nightly electricity blackout. Yoolie never ceased to be amazed by the quality of the cell service in this country of jungles, volcanoes, rainstorms, rolling utility outages, and relentless poverty. She looked at her phone for a moment then put it down. She picked up her phone again, put it down again, picked it up again. She pulled up Cristela's number then closed it then pulled it up again then closed it. Yoolie sighed. She pulled up Cristela's number and called. In for a penny, in for a pound, as her Grandma Pursglove used to say. Back when her Grandma Pursglove was talking to her. Back when anyone from her family in Triadelphia was talking to her. From nowhere her eyes began to tear up, but only for a moment. "Oh, heck with them all," she said to the jungle around her. She smiled at the sound of Cristela's voice and said, *"Hola, amor, quizás tengo una idea."* Yoolie hoped the idea she was about to propose to Cristela wasn't a terrifically stupid one.

Chapter Three

Ascensión knelt over the large ceiling fan lying in pieces on the yard in front of the house. Blanca and Mauricito squatted on the ground next to him, watching with rapt fascination as he snipped a thin blue wire then proceeded to strip back the plastic coating from the copper. Several other youngsters, children of Ascensión's cousins who lived in the other houses on the property, played and ran around in the yard.

Ascensión looked up at the sound of a vehicle approaching. He was at first startled then hit with anxiety at the sight of Yoolie's jeep. What in the world was she doing back here? And on a Saturday morning, no less. She parked her jeep on the edge of the yard and walked towards him. Ascensión put down his wire snips and stood, wiping his hands on his worn work pants. He waved. Yoolie smiled and waved back. She was dressed in a blue and white patterned sun dress with an unbuttoned silky-looking long-sleeved white blouse on top. She wore a straw sun hat and tan beaded leather sandals. Ascensión had never seen Yoolie dressed in anything but work clothes and boots, her red hair always in a ponytail or clipped up on her head. Today beneath her hat she wore her hair in a French braid. She looked quite pretty. Or maybe it was just the nice clothes that gave that impression. He hoped this wasn't how Yoolie dressed when she came to people's houses to fire them. The thought hit him: Was that why Yoolie had insisted on driving him home last night? So that she could come over today and fire Lupe? Or Him? Or both of them? Why on earth had he led her here? But no, of course Yoolie would never be so underhanded. Would she? She didn't look angry or grave. She looked friendly. But then, Yoolie always looked friendly in the way that Americans generally did.

"*Hola*, Ascensión," she said. She gestured towards the dismantled fan on the ground. "What do you have going on here?"

Ascensión tried to appear calm. He smiled and said, "I'm fixing this fan for a store owner in León. Sometimes our old customers from *Reparaciónes León* bring things here for me to fix."

"Ummm," said Yoolie. "What's the problem with this one?"

"Huh, the same problem as with everything around here. It's old and worn out. But I'll give it some new wires and bolts and get this old *abuelito* back to work."

The children had stopped their playing and were now gathered around Yoolie, their eyes wide and serious. "*Hola,*" said Yoolie, waving to them. "*Hola,*" a few answered back shyly.

"This is *señora* Yoolie," said Ascensión.

"Hola, *señora* Yoolie," a few of them mumbled.

"This is *señora* Yoolie, your boss?" Ascensión's mother Violeta called from the doorway of the kitchen.

Ascensión pretended not to hear, but Violeta hurried over followed by Xiomara, Jaime, Ernesto and old Mauricio, all of whom filed out of the kitchen behind her. On top of his nervousness Ascensión now felt as if he could melt into a puddle of embarrassment.

"*Señora* Yoolie," Violeta said breathlessly, "*buenos días*, welcome. I'm Violeta, Ascensión's mother, this is my father Mauricio, my husband Ernesto, and our daughter Xiomara. And Xiomara's husband—"

"Yoolie knows me," Jaime cut off his mother-in-law, stepping out in front of the group.

Violeta gave Jaime a quick look of disproval then continued smiling at Yoolie and took her hand. "Come to the house and have some breakfast. I've made some plantains, very ripe, and I gathered the eggs from our chickens fresh this morning."

"No thank you, *señora* Violeta," Yoolie replied. "I can't stay long."

"But you'll at least have a cup of coffee?" said Mauricio.

"Yes, of course you'll have a cup of coffee or some orange juice?" said Violeta.

"You should try the plantains, Yoolie," said Jaime. "Nobody makes plantains as good as Violeta's."

"Thank you very much," said Yoolie, "but..." She glanced at Ascensión. "I would like to talk to Ascensión for a moment."

The group had been joined by the rest of the children, as curious as the adults about this *chela* who towered over them all. More Somarriba relatives from the other houses were now sauntering over.

"Of course, of course," said Violeta. "You know my Ascensión is a good worker." Her voice was intense and sincere and she still held firmly onto Yoolie's hand. "You see how he's working all the time." She gestured towards the dismembered fan on the ground. "Even on his day off he's working to put food into the mouths of his family, you won't ever find such a good worker."

"*Mamá...*" said Ascensión.

By now there was a good-sized crowd of friendly looking relatives watching the exchange.

"But I'm only saying the truth, *señora* Yoolie knows this."

"Oh, this is *señora* Yoolie? Ascensión's *jefa*?" asked one of the relatives, a young mother nursing an infant of a few months old as she stood there.

"Yes, this is my boss, Yoolie," said Ascensión.

The family members greeted Yoolie, some of them shaking her free hand.

"*Gracias, mucho gusto,*" Yoolie replied, assuring Ascensión's relatives that it was a pleasure to meet them as well.

"*Señora* Yoolie is a good boss," Violeta said knowingly to her audience, who nodded in agreement. "The best boss," she added. "Ascensión says so all the time."

"And so do I," added Jaime.

This time Violeta smiled indulgently at Jaime, then said with diminished enthusiasm, "Yes, of course, Jaime, too."

"*Gracias,*" said Yoolie. She looked at Ascensión then down at her hand, stilled held captive by Violeta's.

"Everyone knows what a good, kind, person you are, *señora* Yoolie," Violeta added for good measure.

"*Mamá...*" said Ascensión.

"Yes, *mijo?*" Violeta said affectionately.

"Maybe Yoolie would like her hand back."

"Oh, *perdóname,*" Violeta laughed. She released Yoolie's hand.

Yoolie smiled at Violeta then she cleared her throat. "Um..." She looked at Ascensión, who looked at his family.

"We'll go over there and talk," said Ascensión, and he beckoned Yoolie to follow him down the slope to the bench by the clothesline. Yoolie walked with Ascensión while the rest of his family followed behind. Ascensión stopped short and turned around. "*¡Por el amor de Dios!*" he cried at the sight of his family behind him. Yoolie put her hand over her mouth and stifled a laugh by appearing to cough into her hand several times.

"Oh...is this private?" Violeta asked sweetly.

"Yes, *mamá,*" sighed Ascensión.

One by one the family members turned and headed back towards Mauricio's house where they sat or stood on the patio chatting. Some entered the kitchen then returned to the patio with a mug of coffee or a plate of food. Someone turned on the television. The children returned to running around the yard.

Sitting on the bench by the clothesline, Yoolie explained to Ascensión the purpose of her visit.

"What do you think," she asked Ascensión after she'd shared her idea.

Ascensión considered for a moment then pulled in a deep breath. "I don't know. Maybe Lupe would like that."

"Where is Lupe now?" asked Yoolie.

Ascensión hesitated. "She was sleeping a little late today. Maybe she's awake now."

"Right," said Yoolie. "Let's go see."

"I can go ask her," said Ascensión.

"I'll come with you," said Yoolie.

As they approached the patio the family crowded around them.

"Will you have a coffee now?" Violeta asked Yoolie.

"No thank you, *señora*," said Yoolie.

"Excuse me, *mamá*," said Ascensión, trying to get past Violeta, who was blocking his way.

"But where are you going?" asked Violeta.

"Just…inside a moment," said Ascensión.

"What, you want to see our house?" Ernesto asked a little gruffly.

"If *señora* Yoolie would like to see my house, why, she is welcome to see it," said Mauricio proudly. He pulled back the curtain in the kitchen doorway and gestured to Yoolie to enter. "I'll show you my garden as well."

"Thank you very much, *señor*," said Yoolie, "but I'd like to talk to Lupe."

"Lupe?" said Violeta. The others looked at each other and murmured among themselves.

"I think she's still sleeping," said Mauricio. "Lupita?" he called towards the bedroom. "Wake up, *chiquita*. Your boss is here."

Violeta put her hand on her father's arm. "Don't worry, *papá*, I'll go wake her." She looked at Yoolie and shook her head apologetically. "Maybe *now* she'll finally get out of bed."

"I'd like to go see Lupe myself," said Yoolie.

"But she's still in bed," said Violeta.

"It's all right, *mamá*," said Ascensión. "I'll go, too. I'll wake her."

"No, you'd better let me do it," said Violeta, stepping into the kitchen.

"*Mamá*, stop, *please*," said Ascensión, following his mother into the kitchen.

"Stop *what?*" said Violeta. "Do you think she's going to get up for you?"

Xiomara entered the kitchen. "That's right, Ascensión, Lupe doesn't listen to you, she doesn't listen to anybody. You'd better let *mamá*—"

"*Cállense, mujeres*," cried Ernesto from the kitchen doorway. "*Señora* Yoolie wants to talk to Lupe." He moved aside and motioned for Yoolie to enter. "Over there, *señora*, through that doorway. Ascensión will take you." Ernesto gave his wife and daughter an authoritative look. And though the two women looked put out at being told to hush, they nonetheless obeyed when Ernesto motioned them to follow him outside.

Back on the patio Violeta declared to whoever was listening, "I told Ascensión, I *told* him there would be trouble if Lupe kept it up." The women in the room nodded in agreement, though when Violeta looked away several of them caught each other's eyes then rolled their eyes or shook their heads ever so slightly.

Lupe was lying in bed on her back looking at the ceiling. Ascensión entered the room and sat on the bed. She turned her head and reached for his hand. "I'm sorry, *mi amor*," she said, her eyes filling with tears.

Ascensión bent over and kissed her head then stroked her hair. "Are you better today?" he asked.

"I don't feel good," she said.

"You'll feel better if you get up. Time to get up now."

"I can't," she said.

"Lupe, *querida*, you need to get up. Yoolie is here to see you."

"What? Yoolie?" Lupe pulled herself up onto one elbow.

Yoolie pulled back the curtain and stepped into the bedroom. She took in the sight of the two double beds, obviously not both used by Lupe and Ascensión. "*Hola*, Lupe," she said. "How are you?"

Lupe looked at her husband then at Yoolie. "I'm sorry, I wasn't feeling well yesterday."

"But she's better today, right, *amor*?"

"Yes." Lupe lowered herself and lay on her back. "I'm just tired."

Ascensión stood and Yoolie sat down on the bed next to Lupe.

"I'd like to take you out today," said Yoolie.

"I can't," said Lupe wearily. "I'm so tired."

"If you get up and go out with Yoolie you'll feel better," said Ascensión. "Why don't you get up and get dressed and I'll bring you some breakfast?"

"Yes, that sounds like a good idea," said Yoolie.

"I'm not hungry," said Lupe.

"Why don't you go get some food anyway," Yoolie said to Ascensión, "and Lupe and I can talk for a minute." Ascensión nodded and left the room. Yoolie bent closer to Lupe and said, lowering her voice, "Lupe, you've got to get out of here."

Lupe stared at the ceiling.

"Come on," said Yoolie, "we'll go into León."

"I don't feel like shopping."

"Me neither. I have a friend who works at *Las Sonrisas*. You know *Las Sonrisas*?"

Lupe turned to Yoolie. "Where they take care of the street children?"

"Yes. I'm going to go there today to help out. Come with me. Will you?" Yoolie bent closer to Lupe and spoke softly into her ear. "Seriously, do you really want to spend the whole day in this bed, in this house?"

"I…"

44

Violeta poked her head into the bedroom. "Lupe, dear," she said sweetly, "why don't you come into the kitchen and eat with the rest of us?"

Ascensión entered with a bowl of food. "It's okay, *mamá*, I brought some plantains."

Violeta put her hand on Ascensión's arm. "Yes I see that, but let her come and eat with the family." To Lupe she said, "Just get out of bed and come out and eat in the kitchen. Then afterwards you can lie in the hammock and watch the television while Xiomara makes your bed and cleans the room. Won't you, Xiomara," she said to her daughter, who had stepped into the room.

"Of course," said Xiomara, rubbing her back. "You don't have to do a thing. It'll be just like you're at the Princess Hilton Hotel in Managua."

Xiomara and Violeta chuckled and Violeta winked at Ascensión and at Yoolie, who smiled politely then looked at Lupe, whose gazed darted from Yoolie's cool blue eyes to her mother-in-law's saccharine smile to her sister-in-law's smirk to the look of anxiety on her husband's face.

Lupe pulled herself up to her elbow then sat up. "I have to go into León with Yoolie."

"What?" said Violeta. "To go *shopping*?"

"Shopping?" said Xiomara. "Lucky you. If I didn't have two children and so much housework I could go shopping, too."

"No, we're going for work," said Yoolie. She stood and stepped away from the bed.

"Oh?" said Violeta. "On Saturday? What do you need to do on Saturday?"

Lupe threw off the sheet and swung her legs over the side of the bed. "I have to get dressed now," she said breathlessly.

Violeta tsked. "Look how weak she is. Xiomara, you'd better help her up."

"No, please, I'm all right," said Lupe.

"Xiomara, grab some underthings and something nice for Lupe to wear," said Violeta. After a laden pause she added, "for...*work.*"

"I can dress myself, thank you." Lupe gave Violeta and Xiomara a direct look and said, "Go now and take care of Blanca and Mauricito."

Violeta and Xiomara looked at each other with raised eyebrows. "Fine, Dear," said Violeta.

"Fine," said Xiomara.

As soon as the two women left the room Ascensión quickly sat down on the bed next to Lupe. He proffered her the bowl of plantains. "Here, *amor,* eat, quickly."

Lupe ate two mouthfuls of the plantains then handed the bowl back to Ascensión. "I can't," she said.

"But you love plantains," said Ascensión. "And these are so brown and good."

"I'll bring them for later. For lunch."

"But if you're going to work you have to eat something now. What about some *gallo pinto?* Or scrambled eggs? What sounds good to you?"

Lupe laughed weakly. "Cornflakes and milk." She stood up slowly and stretched. "But I'll eat the plantains. Later."

"Great," said Yoolie. "Go ahead and get dressed, pack what you need for the day. I'll wait for you outside."

Back on the patio the Somarriba relatives still congregated, some with cups of coffee.

Violeta set out a plate of plantains still warm from the pan on the patio table. "You should have seen how quick she jumped out of that bed when Yoolie offered to take her shopping in León. One minute she's like a dead leaf, next minute she's up like a rocket."

"That's Lupe," said Xiomara, who'd brought out the coffee pot and was refilling people's cups. "Sick when there's work to be done, fine when it's time to go out."

"Bok, bok, bok," laughed old Mauricio. "You ladies will peck each other down to the feathers."

Jaime and Ernesto laughed and Xiomara said, "Down to the feathers? That doesn't even make any sense, *abuelito*."

"Down to the bone is more like it," said Ernesto.

Violeta waved a dismissive hand at her husband and said, "You don't have to deal with her."

"Of course they don't, Violeta," said fat old *tia* Pilar, whose grandchildren had walked her from her house to Mauricio's while supporting her under her arms. "Do you want me to go in there and crack the whip on that lazy girl for you?"

One of the men whispered to another, "Do *you* want to haul her in there to crack the whip?" The man sputtered on his coffee.

"No, no, thank you, *tia*," said Violeta, wiping her eyes. "She's my cross to bear."

"You say Lupe's going shopping in León today?" asked the cousin who had been nursing and was now bouncing her baby.

"Oh, she *says* it's for work," said Violeta.

"That's what she *says*," said Xiomara.

"But who goes into León for work on a Saturday?" said Violeta. "Xiomara, the plantains are gone, we should make some more, and more coffee, too. Who would like some eggs? Lidia," she said to the woman with the baby, "give me that baby and you sit and rest for a minute."

Violeta and Xiomara went into the kitchen. Cousin Lidia and two other women pulled their folding chairs into a close little circle. Lidia looked around then leaned in close to the other women and said softly. "What's wrong with Lupe going shopping?" One woman took a sip of her coffee and shrugged. "Violeta's always like that to Lupe." The other woman added, "Of course Violeta's always like that. That's what Lupe gets for running off with her precious son." The three women laughed.

Yoolie waited outside with Ascensión behind the house.

"It's beautiful here. Those two palm trees. I've never seen any grow that tall."

"That's *señor* and *señora* Frondosa," said Ascensión. "We think they're so tall because they're so old. They've been here longer than anyone remembers, even my grandfather Mauricio. He loves those trees, my grandfather does. He talks to them. He says he'll live as long as they do."

"Well, those trees still look pretty strong and healthy, so let's hope that's true." She gestured towards the line of volcanoes off in the distance. "Is that Telica? And Cerro Negro?"

"Yes, and the smaller one is El Hoyo. 'The Hole' in English."

"There are mountains where I'm from. The Appalachians. But they're much smaller than these. Much older."

"So you love the mountains?"

Yoolie laughed. "Not the mountains where I'm from. That is to say, I don't much care for anything about Triadelphia, West Virginia."

"West Virginia? That's in the South, no?"

"Yes. Sort of."

"Why don't you like it there?"

"The people there. Sometimes they weren't too…tolerant."

"Ah," said Ascensión. "Sometimes people here aren't too tolerant, either. Maybe it's because we all live so close together." He laughed off the remark as a joke.

"Ummm," said Yoolie. "Ascensión, do you and Lupe share your bedroom with Jaime and his wife?"

"Oh, no," said Ascensión. "We share the room with my parents. Jaime and Xiomara share their bedroom with my grandfather. Except that he never sleeps there. He prefers to sleep on a hammock on the patio."

"So you and Lupe don't have much privacy."

"No, not much privacy for anybody in these houses. But, you know, here people get by without as much privacy as in the United States. When Lupe and I were in Philadelphia we had so much privacy." He smiled. "It was nice. But here when we want...privacy...we take a blanket back into the jungle. There's a nice spot behind my grandfather's cornfield."

Yoolie smiled. "That works. But Ascensión, why don't you build a partition down the middle of the bedroom? You could take a couple of those long pieces of scrap corrugated metal from the machine shack, weld them to a base."

Ascensión rubbed his chin. "I don't know. I don't know if...I'd have to ask my parents. And my grandfather."

"It would be nicer for Lupe. For both of you."

"I don't know. Anyway, lately Lupe hasn't been too interested in...privacy."

"Ummm," said Yoolie.

"I'll go see if she's ready now."

"Okay. And, say, have her pack a bowl and a spoon."

"A bowl and a spoon?"

"Right."

"Okay," said Ascensión.

Yoolie wandered around the yard behind Mauricio's house and among the other houses, chickens, banana palms and small gardens. Against the bright blue sky on the horizon wispy white clouds floated above the gently smoking volcanos along the mountain ridge. Yoolie took in for a few more moments the breathtaking sight of the lofty palm trees in the foreground and the marvelous volcanoes in the background. She then turned and headed back to the family gathering on Mauricio's patio. "Trouble in paradise," she sighed. She arrived at the patio to see Ascensión with his arm around Lupe's waist as if to hold her up. They were encircled by several of the women.

"Lupe, *querida*, are you well?" asked one of the women, caressing Lupe's arm.

"Yes, yes, I'm fine now," said Lupe. "I'm going into León with my boss." She nodded towards Yoolie.

49

"*Que bueno!* If it's no trouble for you while you're in León can you pick up two kilos of rice for us?" the woman asked.

"And we need some coffee at our house," said another.

"Could you bring back some sweets and a bag of oranges for the children?" asked another.

"Well, I..." Lupe looked over at Yoolie.

Yoolie shrugged. "Sure. We can stop at the market."

"All right, then," said Lupe. "Who else needs something?"

Violeta and Xiomara stood in the kitchen doorway watching the circle of happy women around Lupe taking turns typing their grocery requests into her phone.

"We need more plantains," Xiomara said to her mother.

"No we don't," said Violeta, shooting a poisonous look in Lupe's direction before whisking into the kitchen.

Judas Priest, thought Yoolie, who'd intercepted the look Violeta had intended for her daughter-in-law.

Ascensión also saw the hostility towards his wife in his mother's eyes, but immediately blocked it out.

Chapter Four

"No, no, Yoolie, we don't want to shop here," said Lupe as Yoolie pulled her jeep into the parking lot in front of *La Unión* supermarket in the center of León. "The food is fresher and better at the marketplace. And cheaper."

"We can go shopping at the market later. I just need a few things here."

"Oh, of course," said Lupe, thinking, *she needs some American things.*

"You wait here, I'll be right out."

A few minutes later Yoolie returned with a box of cornflakes and a half-liter of milk. "Here," she said, handing the cornflakes to Lupe. "Eat."

"Oh, no, Yoolie," Lupe laughed, "you shouldn't have gone to the trouble." She nonetheless reached into her backpack and pulled out the bowl and spoon that Ascensión had packed for her. She poured herself a bowl of cornflakes and milk and dug in hungrily. "*Ay, que rico!*" she said through a mouthful of cereal. "This tastes so good. Thank you, thank you, Yoolie."

Yoolie watched in amazement while Lupe downed three bowls of cornflakes then drank the remains of the milk from the carton. "*Oye, amiga,* when you said you wanted cornflakes and milk you weren't joking."

"It's all I've wanted to eat for days."

"Hmmm," said Yoolie. "Well, while we're here you'd better buy yourself another couple of boxes and a gallon of milk."

"I wouldn't dare. Violeta and Xiomara would call me a princess. A princess from Managua. Because that's where I'm from. Or an American princess. And all the women would agree with them. Because... see...Ascensión and me, we lived in the United States for a while."

"I know," said Yoolie. "Ascensión told me. Yesterday."

"Did he tell you about...?"

"Your little boy? Yes, he did."

Lupe swallowed hard and spoke with downcast eyes. "I don't think any of them ever liked me all that much. But since we returned from the U.S.—without our baby—they detest me, I know it. They don't blame Ascensión. Only me. They say behind my back that it was my fault, that I didn't want my baby, that I didn't love my baby, as if it was my idea to leave David behind." Lupe looked up at Yoolie, the tears rolling down her cheeks. "Maybe you don't believe me that Violeta and Xiomara don't like me. This morning you saw how kindly they treated me while you were there. They always act that way when someone else is there to see them. And Violeta is very good to her family and very helpful to everyone in the village. Everyone loves Violeta. Including Ascensión." Lupe wiped her eyes with her arm. "And so the other women believe her when she tells them that I'm a bad mother who didn't love her baby or that I'm a spoiled little princess from Managua."

"I know that's not true," said Yoolie. "And I believe you."

"You know I didn't want to leave David. I love our baby with all my heart. It tore my heart out of my chest to leave him."

"Of course it did," said Yoolie.

"But our baby is an American. And we were illegals. We had one close call with American immigration and it was only because of a kind, generous American couple who hid us in their apartment while ICE was going through ours that we escaped. It was then that we realized that we could be caught any day and sent back to Nicaragua without David and then what would have happened to him? And so when this same kind couple got us an immigration lawyer—a good man, a kind-hearted man who made a deal with the judge to allow us to be voluntarily deported so that there would be no stain on our record and we could return someday legally to our baby—we agreed to leave the United States and to leave David behind with our good American friends until we can return."

"You did the right thing," said Yoolie.

"It was so hard to know what to do then," said Lupe. "Now they say I'm a bad mother. And they say that I'm a bad wife to Ascensión and I'm afraid lately that's been true. Ascensión is my husband and I love him and I know he loves me. When we lived in Philadelphia with our baby in our own house and our own life we were so happy. It was the happiest time in my life. But here Ascensión belongs first to his family—first to his mother—and not first to me. When Ascensión grieves his family comforts him. But I don't have a friend in Krukrulitos. And I don't have my baby. Some days I feel as if I don't have anyone or anything at all. "

Sweet Jesus, no wonder you can't get out of bed in the morning, thought Yoolie.

"What about your own family? Your mother? Father? Relatives?"

"My mother died when I was twelve. My father is still in Managua but he hasn't spoken to me nor has the rest of my family since I married Ascensión."

"Wow," Yoolie muttered. *They must be related to my family,* she thought.

Lupe grasped Yoolie's hand. "Thank you, Yoolie," she said.

"What for?"

"For so many things. For not firing me yesterday. For getting me out of bed and out of the house today. But thank you more than anything for believing me. And for telling me that Ascensión and I did the right thing returning to Nicaragua and leaving David in the United States."

"Of course you did the right thing," said Yoolie, though in truth she wasn't sure what the right thing was. "Anyway, what else could you do? As you said, your baby is American and you were in danger of being deported. And it sounds as if David is happy and safe and healthy and in wonderful hands."

"I know all that is true. And deep in my heart I do believe that he is doing well there. And maybe even happier and safer there than he might be here. I'm not sad for David, I'm sad for me and for Ascensión. But I would give my life just to be able to see our baby again. If I could hold him in my arms and kiss him from his head to his toes and watch Ascensión hold him and kiss him and be a loving family again, just for a little while, I believe I would be well. I wouldn't care what Violeta and Xiomara and the others said about me if I could just hold my David again."

Yoolie patted Lupe's hand. "I know. I know."

"I'm sorry I didn't come to work, Yoolie. Some days…I can't do anything. But now I can. Now I'm better. Even though I'm crying I'm much better." She lifted the milk carton to her mouth and tipped back her head to catch the last drops of milk. "That was so good."

That's what happens when you fill your stomach and pour out your heart, Yoolie thought. "Great," she said. "Now you can help me today. I need some things for *Las Sonrisas* and I need you to help me buy them. We don't have time to go to the market, we'll buy them here. Are you all right? Can you help me?"

Lupe rubbed a hand across her eyes. "Yes, I'm all right and I'll gladly help you, Yoolie. Whatever you need me to do."

Lupe had only ever been inside *La Unión* once out of curiosity when she'd been a student at the University and that time she had been overwhelmed by the air conditioning. Her first impression of the American supermarkets—which she'd likewise found to be extraordinarily chilly—had been that they reminded her of *La*

Unión, and now being inside *La Unión* reminded her of being back at a hyper-cooled American supermarket. Even the women who were shopping reminded Lupe of American women: slim, stylish, some dressed in expensive athletic clothes, some with streaks of blonde or auburn in their hair, sporting baseball caps with logos, their ponytails pulled through the back. However these women were likely to be members of the upper crust of León, those who lived on ordinary city streets behind inconspicuous stone facades on the other side of which were luxurious manses with beautifully landscaped courtyards, state-of-the-art interior decorating and servants' quarters.

"Ah," Yoolie sighed, taking in a deep breath as she grabbed a shopping cart. "This place has the best air conditioning in León. Listen, Lupe, I need you to help me get some baby things."

"Baby things?"

"Food, diapers, I don't know, whatever a baby needs."

"Well, I...how old is the baby?"

Yoolie frowned. "Wait a minute." She pulled out her cell phone and punched in a number. "How old is the baby?...About eight months you think?" Yoolie turned from her phone towards Lupe and said, "About eight months." She turned back to her phone. "Okay, *chica,* we'll be there soon."

"Where is the baby?"

"At *Las Sonrisas.*"

"Somebody left their baby at *Las Sonrisas?*"

"They'll be back. Or we'll find them and return the baby. But in the meantime..."

"Yes, of course, the baby needs things. Let's hurry."

They made their way to the baby products aisle where Lupe found the resemblance so close to the same aisle in the American markets at which she'd shopped that she was able to quickly and expertly fill the cart with every baby need: jars of food, boxes of cereal and teething biscuits, cans of formula, bottles, nipples, brushes, bibs, diapers, wipes, ointment, baby bath.

"Phew, I'm sure glad you're here," said Yoolie. She'd gone off to buy a whole chicken, as requested by the *mamita* cook for the children's lunch today at *Las Sonrisas*, but now Yoolie stood by while Lupe grabbed things from the shelf. "I had no idea babies needed all this stuff." *This will be the best outfitted baby in Central America*, Yoolie thought.

"What about clothes?" said Lupe. "And a little blanket to wrap him in. Or her. Is it a little boy or girl?"

Yoolie shrugged. "Cristela didn't say."

Lupe chuckled. "That's all right. Look, here's a package of swaddling blankets, we'll buy that, too." She stopped and turned to Yoolie, the package of blankets in her hand. "But who's paying for all this? Do we have enough money?"

"Don't worry. There's plenty." *Thanks to the good old American Express Platinum*, she added to herself, patting her purse.

***

Once the site of an open-air market located on a street corner, *Las Sonrisas* was mostly a roof-covered patio open to the street on two sides, the other two sides walled with cinderblock, with a hallway opening from the back wall. Off one side of the hallway was a bathroom and a kitchen which opened out to a small yard in which there was a sink with a built-in scrubbing board for washing clothes and a clothesline. Across the hallway from the kitchen was a room, likely once a storage area for the market. Now the room, which everyone referred to as "the room," was sparsely furnished with several pieces of worn, mismatched outdoor furniture, including a cushion-topped wicker sofa, a glider, a coffee table, a card table, and a few chairs. Against one wall were shelves on which were piled books and sheets of paper, blank on at least one side, for drawing or writing. There were canisters of pencils and pens and some basic art supplies, and also a coffee can full of marbles. Against another wall were piled some sleeping mats and light blankets. Though generally the children who dropped in and out of *Las Sonrisas* during the day had some place to call home at night, the room occasionally provided a refuge for a child who might for some reason need a safe place to sleep. Out on the patio there were tables and chairs against the back wall and the side wall, but pushed far enough from the open sides to avoid getting wet during the afternoon rains.

It was during the rains that *Las Sonrisas* would be most crowded. Children caught in the downpour would come squealing down the street, dashing for shelter beneath the patio roof where they'd arrive breathless and laughing and soaking wet.

On this Saturday morning the patio was alive with children. Many of them barefoot, most of them ragged, they nonetheless played hopscotch, jump rope, marbles and games of their own invention. A few boys played soccer in the street in front of the building. Some children sat at the tables and drew. Others hung on a motherly middle-aged woman who was bouncing a squalling baby boy.

When Yoolie's jeep pulled up to the patio some of the children momentarily stopped their activities to look up. One little girl who'd been coloring a picture hopped from the table and ran to the hallway. "Cristela!" she shouted down the hall, "Hurry! Your *amiga* Yoolie is here!"

Cristela came hurrying down the hallway wiping her floury hands on the apron she wore over her tan Capri pants and dark green tee shirt. With her short stylish haircut and out-sized black horn-rimmed glasses Cristela looked as if she belonged more in a business office or a classroom than covered in flour in a run-down building surrounded by street urchins. By the time Cristela reached Yoolie's jeep Yoolie was attempting to open the passenger door without hitting the children who had crowded around, some of whom were already begging with outstretched hands.

"Excuse me, excuse me," said Cristela as she made her way through the children. "Excuse *me*," she said, swatting at the outstretched hands. "You know we don't do that here. Oh, *Dios mío*," she said, hugging Yoolie as she stepped from the jeep. "Where have you been? We're out of baby milk, baby food, baby everything. Luz and Flor were supposed to work today but Luz's cousin is sick and Flor's husband was being *un idiota,* and I sent Maria out to look for some more baby things, now *I* have to make the lunch, the baby wants to be held every minute, I was up half the night with him..."

"...and I was up the other half," said Rafaela, who joined the other women, still bouncing the baby.

"...this angel," said Cristela, giving Rafaela a kiss on the cheek, "for the past two nights she's stayed the night with me. Yoolie, did you bring diapers? Yesterday Maria brought some old cloths to use—oh, where *is* she?—but this kid, he runs through them like a hurricane!"

"Yes, that's what they do," said Rafaela.

"*Calmate,* Cristela," said Yoolie. "Call Maria, tell her we have everything we need."

"She doesn't have a cellphone," said Cristela. "She was going to her sister's for more supplies. Her sister has a baby."

"Her sister has a houseful," said Rafaela.

Lupe meanwhile was reaching into the back seat of the jeep and fetching the baby supplies.

"Cristela, Rafaela, this is Lupe," said Yoolie. "Lupe, Cristela and Rafaela."

"*Mucho gusto,*" Lupe called over her shoulder. Her eye was immediately caught by the baby in Rafaela's arms. "Oh," she said, setting the shopping bags on the ground and reaching for the baby, "look at him, oh can I hold him?"

"Gladly," said Rafaela. "I've been holding him all morning. He wants to be held all the time. Here, take him. He needs a change."

"Oh, oh, oh," Lupe cooed, holding him close. "Shhh, shhh." She kissed his sweaty, slightly acrid-smelling hair and looked into his deep brown, almond-shaped eyes. "He isn't eight months," she said. "He's not more than six at most. Does he have a name?"

"We named him Pablito," said Rafaela.

"Pablito, Pablito," she cooed. She smiled at him and he stopped whimpering and smiled back at her. She spoke to him in the sing-songy voice that mothers use on babies. "Yes, Pablito needs a change, doesn't he? And a little bath, too, doesn't he?" She sniffled and rubbed her eyes with her hand then looked up at Rafaela. "Is there somewhere I can wash him?"

"Down the hall in the bathroom sink," said Rafaela.

"Do you think he's hungry, too?" asked Lupe.

"We gave him a mashed banana this morning. He's probably pretty hungry now. Did you bring some food for him?"

"Yes, and some formula, and…" Lupe looked down and saw the children rummaging through the bags of baby things.

"Okay, okay," said Cristela, stepping over and retrieving the bottles and other things that the children had taken from the bags and were now turning over in their grimy hands.

Lupe chuckled. "*Con permiso*, could I trouble someone to wash these bottles?"

"Of course," said Cristela over her shoulder while she shooed the children back to the patio. She then turned and hurried towards Lupe, speaking as she walked. "I'm trying to make the lunch, and Rafaela probably wants to sit down for a minute…but Rafaela, *amor*, could you sit in here and keep an eye on the *niños*? And Maria's not here, but Yoolie is, so I'm sure she could wash the bottles, and you're taking the baby, Lupe…wait…*Lupe? Lupe Paloma?* From the University? Is that *you?*"

"*Profesora Gutierrez?*" The two women looked at each other for a moment then hugged as well as they could with the baby between them. "When Yoolie said her friend was Cristela, I never dreamed it was *you!*"

"And I never guessed Yoolie's Lupe was Lupe Paloma, my little education student."

"From when you were on the faculty at the Teacher's College?" asked Yoolie.

"Yes, and Lupe, you call me Cristela from now on. But I have to get back to the kitchen or lunch will never be ready in time, so…"

"Of course," said Lupe, but then she reached again for Cristela and buried her head in her former teacher's shoulder.

"*Esta bien, cariño, esta bien,*" Cristela said softly, rubbing Lupe's back. She glanced at Yoolie, who sighed and shook her head slightly.

"I'm sorry," sniffed Lupe, stepping back from Cristela. "Just for a minute I was remembering being back in school, when I was so happy and…" She again rubbed her eyes with the back of her hand. "…so young."

"You're still young, *chiquita,*" said Rafaela. "What's this?" she asked, pulling from the grocery bag the package of chicken Yoolie had brought from *La Unión*.

"Cristela said Maria wanted some chicken for the *gallo pinto,*" said Yoolie.

Rafaela held it away from her with both hands as if examining a strange object, frowned, then sniffed it through the plastic wrap. "Is it fresh?"

"It has a date on the package," Yoolie said sheepishly.

"*¡Madre mia!*" cried Cristela, wringing her hands. "Where *is* Maria?"

"I'm here, I'm here," cried Maria, breathless from running. She was a chubby, pregnant, hard-working teenager whom Cristela had hired to cook *gallo pinto,* tortillas and whatever else Cristela could scrounge together for the daily meal at *Las Sonrisas*. In one hand Maria carried a crocheted bag with some baby clothes and in the other she held a small baby bottle full of milk.

"Maria, *amor,* where have you been?" said Rafaela, giving the girl a kiss on her forehead. "Cristela *se vuelve loca,* and look, Yoolie bought *this* from *La Unión*…"

"From *La Unión?*" said Maria, still a little breathless from being pregnant and having run from her sister's house. She looked closely at the chicken in Rafaela's hand then accusingly at Yoolie. "Is it *fresh?*"

Lupe found herself trying to suppress her laughter and amazement at seeing these women, one of them a young girl, take to task her university professor and her American boss.

"Well, give it to me," sighed Maria. "Here," she said, handing the bottle of milk to Lupe. Then she added, "I'm Maria."

"Hello, Maria, I'm Lupe," said Lupe, taking the bottle.

"Have him drink it right now while it's fresh. It's from my sister."

"From your sister?" Lupe hesitated, holding the bottle away from the baby, who began whimpering and reaching for it.

"From her..." Maria cupped her breast.

"*Oh.*" Lupe gave Pablito the bottle and he began drinking thirstily. "He likes your sister's milk," she chuckled.

"Your sister filled that bottle with her milk?" said Rafaela.

"That's why I took so long," said Maria.

"Your sister is very kind and generous," said Lupe, smiling down at Pablito.

"She has plenty," said Maria. "Do you need me to take him?"

"Lupe knows what she's doing," said Cristela. "But I need you to take care of that chicken so he'll be ready for lunch."

"And she needs you to take over making the tortillas," laughed Rafaela, pointing to Cristela's flour-covered apron. "Or else there will be flour all over the place."

Maria put a hand against her hip and eyed Cristela disapprovingly. "Looks like there already is. Here are some clothes for Pablito. I'll bring them inside. My sister needs them back." She gently petted the baby's head. "After his mother comes back for him." Maria rubbed her stomach. "I would never give up my baby."

"Of course you wouldn't," said Lupe, with a catch in her throat. "No mother would. If she had a choice."

"Even if my family kicked me out. Even if Marcus never comes back to me."

"He will, *chiquita*," said Rafaela. "They always do."

"Marcus won't," said Maria. "He has a new girlfriend now. And he'll leave her, too, when she's like me." Maria rubbed her stomach again as her eyes glistened with tears. She stroked Pablito's cheek. "That probably happened to his mother, too."

"Oh, let's forget about those men and get lunch ready for these children," said Cristela. "Yoolie, wash the baby bottles and take care of," she gestured towards the bags of baby things, "...all that. Lupe, *amor*, take care of the baby, and, let me see..."

"I'll give him a bath and some clean clothes and some lunch. Then I'll try to get him down for a nap."

"*Sí, sí, fantastico*," said Cristela distractedly. "Rafaela, *mi ángel*, do you need to rest a little?"

"Yes, but I'll sit on the patio and keep an eye on the...*Cesar! Felix!* You leave those girls alone! Do I have to give you a smack in the head?" Rafaela called to a couple of laughing boys who were attempting to sabotage a game of jump rope to the dismay of several squealing girls.

"And Maria, *cariño*, please liberate me from the kitchen," said Cristela. She undid her apron, shook out the flour, slipped the apron over Maria's head and tied it around the girl's wide waist. She then gave her a kiss on the cheek. "Never mind that boy. You'll be a wonderful *mamita*, you know that, right?"

"I know," sniffed Maria, straightening her apron and marching back to the kitchen with the chicken.

***

After the last of the *gallo pinto* with chicken had been scraped from the pot and the last child fed, Maria, Rafaela and Yoolie were finishing the dishes and cleaning the kitchen while Cristela read to a group of the children on the patio as the sun began shining through the final drops of the afternoon rain.

"She ate one bite, maybe two," tsked Rafaela, looking at an almost-full bowl of beans and rice.

"She ate three tortillas, though," said Maria.

"*Three tortillas? Santo Minguito!*" said Rafaela.

And half a box of dry cornflakes, thought Yoolie, who'd retrieved the leftover cornflakes from the jeep for Lupe at her request.

"Here, you eat this so I can wash the bowl," said Rafaela, handing Lupe's leftovers to Maria.

"Maybe Lupe wants it now," said Maria.

"No, you eat it," said Yoolie. "I'm sure Lupe doesn't want it." *Not after all those tortillas and cornflakes,* she thought.

"Where is she?" said Rafaela. "Still in the room rocking the baby?"

Yoolie stepped across the hall and stuck her head into the room then returned to the kitchen. "She fell asleep on the glider rocking Pablito," said Yoolie. "They're both sound asleep."

"She can't put him down," said Maria through a mouthful of *gallo pinto.* She and Rafaela exchanged a glance, each nursing the same suspicion. They lived in a world where women lost babies every day.

"Well, she knows how to take care of a baby," said Rafaela. Maria nodded.

"And thank God for that," said Cristela, stepping into the kitchen followed by two little girls who clung to the hem of her shirt. She set a pile of children's books on the counter. While she spoke she hugged the girls close to her on either side. "I wish Pablito's *mamá* was half as attached to him. If she doesn't come for him by tomorrow I'm going to have to…Maria, did you ask your sister if she knew of anyone in town who's missing a baby?"

"She's asking around," said Maria. "She wants her diapers and baby clothes back."

"Do you think your sister would take Pablito for the night?" Cristela asked.

"If she does she'll want me to stay and take care of him and I'm too tired," said Maria with a yawn.

"Rafaela..." said Cristela.

"I can't stay the night again with you and I can't take him home," said Rafaela, also yawning. "In fact I have to go home pretty soon. I've been here since yesterday and if I don't come home and fix my husband some food he'll go to his mother's house and never come back again. Yoolie, it looks like you'll be helping Cristela with Pablito tonight."

Yoolie groaned.

"Unless," said Maria, "you can get Luz or Flor or one of the others, or..."

At that moment Lupe entered the kitchen with Pablito in her arms. The four women looked at her then at each other.

Chapter Five

That evening just before sunset Yoolie's jeep returned to Krukrulitos laden with groceries from the market, but interest in the groceries was eclipsed by the arrival of Lupe with baby Pablito.

Was that Lupe and Ascensión's baby? Had their baby been returned to them from the United States? Was that what Lupe's trip into León had really been all about? The complete illogic of such speculation did not nonetheless keep it from quickly spreading from the first relative who sighted Lupe and Ascensión with Pablito to all the other relatives on the property and from them to the rest of the village at large. The rumor was soon enough put to rest, but not for days, and not before half the village had stopped by, by which time Pablito had been returned to his mother and that rumor had in any case already been trumped by a much more compelling drama that would soon be radiating from Mauricio Somarriba's household.

Lupe had called Ascensión in advance to tell him about Pablito, and so he was watching and waiting for her on the patio. As soon as he sighted the jeep coming down the path towards the yard he ran to it.

"Here, give him to me, *amor*," said Ascensión, opening the door of the jeep for Lupe and taking the baby from her arms then kissing her forehead. "So this *pequeñito* is staying with us for a while?" He smiled at Pablito and put out his finger for the baby to grab with his chubby fist.

"Just for a day or two," said Yoolie, exiting the jeep. "Until we can find his mother."

"It should be all right if he stays with us, don't you think, *mi amor?*" said Lupe.

"Of course," said Ascensión. "Xiomara can watch him, or one of my cousins will."

"I hope Violeta doesn't mind."

"*Mamá*? No, no I'm sure she won't mind. You know she loves babies."

"Yes, of course she does," said Lupe. *It's only me she hates*, she thought. "By the way, I brought your *mamá* some more plantains from the market."

"That was good, *amor,* we're all out of plantains."

"That's what I thought. And for me...*con permiso,* Yoolie," she said, reaching into the back of the jeep, "let me get the cornflakes."

"Cornflakes?" laughed Ascensión, bouncing Pablito, falling unconsciously into an old habit and giving him a kiss on the forehead.

"We stopped at *La Unión* this morning for baby things," said Yoolie, "and I bought a box of cornflakes and some milk for Lupe since that's what she was craving."

"I ate almost the whole box, *amor,* and I drank all the milk, I was so hungry and it tasted so good. Then I finished the rest for lunch. With three tortillas."

"Cornflakes and tortillas for lunch?" Ascensión laughed again and Lupe laughed with him. His heart felt so light at this moment, holding this baby in his arms and seeing his wife happy, the old sparkle returned to her beautiful dark eyes.

"So anyway," Yoolie continued, "later in the day I drove Lupe to the market for the groceries and after the market we stopped again at *La Unión*..."

"...And I said 'Yoolie, *why* are we stopping at *La Unión* again?' because we'd just been to the market. And Yoolie said, 'I only need one more thing.' And look what she bought!" Lupe reached into the jeep and pulled out two more large shopping bags filled with three large boxes of cornflakes and three half-gallons of milk.

"*What?*" laughed Ascensión, as Lupe held open the bags for him to see.

"I bought them for her as a thank you for helping today at *Las Sonrisas*," said Yoolie. "And for watching Pablito."

"Cornflakes from *La Unión*?" Ascensión laughed again. He shifted Pablito to one arm and put the other around Lupe's waist. "Is my wife now a fancy lady?" He pulled her close for a kiss.

"Very fancy," Lupe giggled and kissed him back. "And how crazy, but I think now I'm going to eat more for dinner. Maybe Blanca and Mauricito would like to try some, too. And maybe Grandfather Mauricio. We have plenty. Maybe everybody would like to try some."

"Maybe," said Ascensión. He hugged Lupe closer and nuzzled her hair for a moment.

"Well," said Yoolie, "I guess we want to unload these groceries from my jeep."

"Oh sure, here," said Ascensión, handing Pablito back to Lupe. "I'll get the groceries, why don't you bring Pablito into the house and introduce him to the family, and—here, can you carry the milk, too? It should be refrigerated right away."

"Ascensión," said Lupe as she reached with her free hand for the bags holding the bottles of milk, "have you told them yet? Your *mamá* and Xiomara and the others? Do they know about Pablito?"

"No," Ascensión said a bit sheepishly. "No, I wanted to wait until—"

"Ascensión!" called Violeta from the kitchen doorway. "What in the world is going on out there?"

A moment later Violeta was hurrying across the patio and the yard followed by Xiomara and Jaime and the children and Ernesto. Old Mauricio, who'd been out back working in his garden, came walking slowing around to the front of the house, followed by members of the other households who by now had caught wind of the activity going on in Mauricio's yard and had already passed on the word from one house to another and, via cellphone, to the rest of the village.

Jaime tried to sidle up to Ascensión and Lupe, having an inkling that his brother-in-law—not to mention his brother-in-law's wife—might end up welcoming the moral support of a friendly presence, but he was jockeyed back by the women pressing in close to coo over the baby between peppering Lupe with questions about him. Jaime then meandered over to Yoolie, who was leaning against her jeep, arms crossed, watching the scene before her. Her presence, in the excitement over the baby, had hardly been noticed.

"*Que tal*, Yoolie?" said Jaime, leaning against the jeep next to her.

"I'm good, thank you," said Yoolie. "Just waiting for people to come and pick up their groceries."

Jaime laughed. "That baby's more exciting than groceries."

"I see," said Yoolie. "Jaime, help me unload this stuff, we can just put it on the ground, then they can get it when they're ready."

"Sure," said Jaime. "What's this? Bags from *La Unión*?" He looked into the bags of baby things. "That's gonna be one fancy baby," he laughed. "Maybe I better take these baby bags right to the house before the women notice them, or else there will all kinds of squawking. I'll stash them in Lupe's room."

"Good idea," said Yoolie. "Thanks."

"Certainly," said Jaime. "I'm always glad to help you, Yoolie, you know?"

"Sure," said Yoolie. *Yeah, sure you are, as long as it doesn't involve any work,* she thought. Still, she was grateful for Jaime's help in this instance.

Once it became clear that this baby in Lupe's arms was not hers and the story was told about how he arrived at the Somarriba household, the cooing women who encircled Lupe and asked to hold the baby were careful while in her presence not to wonder aloud or voice their indignation over the child's mother leaving him. Except for Violeta.

"Here, give him to me," said Violeta, taking Pablito from the woman who had previously taken him from Lupe. "What kind of mother could leave behind her precious baby?" she asked, nuzzling his cheek and shaking her head.

"I imagine a young desperate one," said Lupe. "Maybe a young girl left by the baby's father and cast out by her family."

The group went suddenly silent. This was the first time anyone had ever heard Lupe speak up to her mother-in-law, and the more perceptive among them knew that Lupe had just set a trap for herself that Violeta would surely spring. Lupe glanced at Ascensión and noticed that he seemed to be studying the sky. All the men seemed to be studying the sky or something else off in the distance.

"Yes, maybe if a girl were young and desperate," said Violeta. "But of course no woman who had a husband and a family waiting with open arms would think of doing such a thing. Lidia," she said to the young mother of the nursing baby, "could you abandon your dear baby on the doorstep of strangers?"

Lidia looked uncomfortable and dared not look at Lupe, but she shook her head.

"What about you, Xiomara, could you give away little Blanca or Mauricito?"

"I'd die first," proclaimed Xiomara dramatically, gathering her two children who were playing nearby and smothering them with kisses.

"Any of you mothers?" said Violeta to the group. "Could any of you give up your babies?" The women glanced at each other, some shaking their heads, some murmuring "no," no one wanting to cross Violeta, no one wanting to look at Lupe, everyone wishing for this scene, which was creeping across the line from uncomfortable to excruciating, to end.

"*Oye*, come and get your groceries, everybody," called Yoolie, who'd also had enough of watching Violeta's not-too-subtle torment of Lupe.

"Yes, yes," said Ernesto with a wave of his hand, "we all know what wonderful mothers you women are, no need to stand around wagging your tongues about it all night while your husbands starve to death. Get your groceries, *señoras*, then go home and make us some dinner!"

"Yes, all you beautiful *señoras* get your groceries and go home and make us some dinner," said Mauricio good-naturedly, likewise with a wave of his hand, "and bring the little *niño* to the house, Violeta, and give him some food, too."

Now grateful for an excuse to leave, the Somarriba relatives either headed to Yoolie's jeep for the groceries they'd requested or to their own houses to fix dinner.

"Here, don't forget your plantains," said Yoolie, proffering the bunch to Lupe then dropping them into one of her grocery bags.

"*Mamá,* Lupe bought you some more plantains at the market," said Ascensión, smiling widely, hopefully, at his mother and at Lupe.

"Oh she did?" said Violeta pleasantly. "Well then, they're her plantains, she can cook them how she wants. Ascensión," she said in a tone of disbelief, "what are those that you're holding? Are those…*bags* from La Unión?" She balanced Pablito on her hip and held him against her with one hand while with the other she reached into one of Ascensión's bags and pulled out the box of cornflakes and held it up. "*Cornflakes?*" She looked into Lupe's *La Unión* bags, saw the bottles of milk, then stared at Lupe with eyes filled with such malevolence that Lupe gasped and quickly stepped back, for one fleeting moment under the illusion that she was staring into the eyes of a viper. "You won't eat the good food that I cook? You have to go *La Unión* and spend money on *this*?" She dropped the box of cereal back into the bag.

"No, no," said Yoolie, trying to sound conciliatory, "Lupe didn't buy the cereal or the milk. I bought them for her because she—"

Violeta cut Yoolie off. "¡*Válgame dios*, Lupe! *Señora* Yoolie, your *boss*, has to buy you cereal and milk? Food for little babies?" She turned to Yoolie and said, "I apologize for my daughter-in-law, *señora* Yoolie. She's a grown woman, you should not have had to buy her this baby food." She shot Lupe a look of exasperation and looked at Yoolie with the sad smile of a long-suffering martyr.

The chief hydraulic research officer of the Momotombo geothermal plant, who had the previous day dealt with powerful international investors, now found herself dumbfounded in the presence of this velvet tyrant of a matriarch. All she could think of to say was, "In the United States everybody eats cereal and milk. Not just children. It's nutritious. And Lupe didn't ask me to buy it for her."

"Of course, of course," Violeta chuckled indulgently with a wave of her hand. "We won't worry about it." To Lupe she said, "Here, give me those bags and you take him."

Lupe did as she was told, mechanically exchanging the shopping bags for Pablito, once again cowed and tongue-tied by her mother-in-law, her face burning and half paralyzed with humiliation in the presence of Yoolie. Her stomach began to ache. She looked at Ascensión, willing him to somehow deliver her. But in his face she saw the look of a guilty schoolboy terrified of getting into trouble and she knew there and then that her strong, dependable husband, the brave man who had once made her brave enough to flee with him two thousand miles across treacherous territory, the man who gave her the courage to leave their home for a strange country and the courage to return, the man whom she'd believed would defend her against any harm, would never defend her against his mother. Nobody would. And she knew at that moment that she was as alone in the world as the poor unwanted foundling whom she held in her arms.

Violeta turned away from Lupe after shooting her one more quick, terrible look. "*Señora* Yoolie," she continued with a friendly smile, "please stay for dinner. I've made a frittata with cheese, black beans and potatoes. And corn from my father Mauricio's garden." She held up one of the bags of cornflakes. "I would hate for you to think that this is the kind of thing I would serve in my house."

"No, it's fine, I like cornflakes, myself," said Yoolie, wishing to say something in defense of Lupe. "I often eat them for dinner," she lied.

"Oh, we know how you Americans love your cornflakes," Violeta chuckled good-naturedly. "Come in for dinner, then, you can have a bowl of cornflakes. That is, if Lupe will share them."

"Oh, no, thank you, I have to go," said Yoolie. "Lupe, Jaime brought the things for the baby to the house."

"Thank you, Yoolie," Lupe said hoarsely. "I have to go now." She turned and began walking towards the house, holding Pablito close.

"Lupe, thank you so much for helping today and taking care of Pablito," Yoolie called after her. She had the desire to lay it on thick in Violeta's presence. "You've been a real lifesaver. I don't know how we would have gotten by without you. I'll call you when we find Pablito's mother. We should find her soon." Lupe continued walking away as if she hadn't heard. Yoolie called, "I'll see you on Monday at work?"

Lupe turned her head halfway and nodded, then quickly turned back and hurried away, soon disappearing behind the house, holding Pablito close, kissing his head, and doing her best to hold back tears of anger, shame, and sorrow.

72

***

"What's wrong with this food?" Violeta asked of her family as they sat around the kitchen table eating the egg frittata, corn and tortillas she'd prepared for their dinner.

"What's wrong with it?" said her husband Ernesto through a mouthful of frittata. He looked over the food on his fork and on his plate. "Nothing, *mi vida*." He loaded the forkful of food into his mouth. "Ummm." He gave his wife a wink and a thumbs up.

"That's true, Violeta," said Mauricio to his daughter. "Nobody makes a frittata like yours."

There were murmurs of agreement around the room.

"What do you think, Ascensión?" Violeta said to her son in a quavering voice. "Is there something wrong with this frittata I made for the family?"

"No, of course not, *mamá*," said Ascensión. "It's a wonderful frittata. A delicious frittata." But Ascensión by now knew that this was not about the frittata. It was with a sinking feeling that he recognized that tone, the tone that communicated to him from his childhood even to this day that he'd said or done something so unspeakable that it was going to make his mother cry. And sure enough, a moment later tears filled her eyes.

"Then why won't your wife eat what I cook? Is my food not as good as what her servants cooked for her when she was a rich doctor's daughter? Does she think my food is poison?"

"No, of course not, *mamá*," Ascensión said with a catch in his voice. "She doesn't think that."

"Is this house too poor for her now? That she won't even come in and sit with us anymore?" Violeta gestured to her family sitting around the table. "She came into the house carrying that baby as if it were her own, changed him, grabbed food and a bottle for him then went back outside into the dark, as if we were such bad people that it would poison him and her, too, to breathe the same

73

air!" Now the tears were streaming down Violeta's face and she sobbed into her hands.

Xiomara's children began to cry but instead of comforting them their mother rose from her seat at the table and hurried over to her own mother. "Don't cry, *mamita*, we all love you, we all love your cooking, never mind about her. Blanca, Mauricito, come over and hug *abuelita* and give her some kisses."

Ascención felt as if he were going to cry, too. "*Mamá*," he said, "it's not that Lupe doesn't like the family."

"Oh, I know," sobbed Violeta as her grandchildren climbed into her lap and began kissing her cheeks. "It's only me she hates."

"She doesn't hate you, *mamá*," said Ascensión. "Lupe doesn't hate anybody."

"No, she just thinks she's better than us," sniffed Xiomara.

"Look, look," said old Mauricito patting the air with his palms. He turned to Violeta. "Didn't I warn you, *mija*," he said to his daughter, "that you needed to be gentler with this *chiquita?*"

"I said the same thing," said Ernesto. "You women keep it up, maybe she won't come back."

"I said that, too," added Jaime, shoveling the last forkful of frittata on his plate into his mouth.

"Oh, Jaime, you always talk too much," Xiomara snapped, grabbing her husband's empty plate and passing it down the table. "Give Jaime another slice of frittata, just a small one this time, and another tortilla."

"Ah, *mi vida*," said Jaime, pecking Xiomara on the cheek, "you're a wife fit for a king."

"Of course, she'll come back," said Violeta, returning to the subject of Lupe and daubing her eyes. "When she gets hungry."

"I myself wouldn't blame her if she decided to stay outside from now on," said Ernesto. "Just wait, *abuelo*," he said to Mauricio with a wink, "she'll want to sleep outside in your hammock and you'll have to sleep in the house with the children or in the pen with chickens and pigs."

Mauricio laughed. "Come here, you two," he said to Blanca and Mauricito. The children climbed down from Violeta's lap and snuggled next to their great-grandfather, who put and arm around each of them. "Better sleeping out with the chickens and pigs than inside with this noisy bunch." He gave each child a kiss on the head. "You see, little Lupita, she has her fine education, but she's not tough and strong like you village women. She's much softer and weaker."

"She *is* tough," said Ascención, his eyes filling with tears. "She *is* strong."

Ascención's family burst out laughing but their laughter turned into sympathetic *"Awww's"* when they realized that he was rubbing his hands across his eyes.

"Aw, *mijo*," said Violeta, "now she's making you cry."

"It's not her," Ascención mumbled.

"What do you mean, it's not her?" asked Violeta.

"He means," Jaime spoke up, "it's…" He made a wide circular motion with his finger indicating the family members sitting around the table. He shot Ascención a sympathetic look.

"Us?" said Xiomara.

Violeta turned to her son. "What?" she chuckled. "You don't mean your father and grandfather's teasing?"

Ascención looked down at his plate, his mouth a thin, angry line.

"What's going on?" asked his father. "You were never so sensitive before. We're a family, can't we even joke around the dinner table like we always have done?"

"Is it our fault she won't come in and join us for dinner?" said Xiomara. "She won't join us for breakfast, she won't join us for dinner…That's what's causing all the tension in this house."

Violeta caught her daughter's eye and shook her head and quietly shushed her. She stood up from the table and stepped over to her son and rubbed his shoulders. "Never mind, *querido*, you know we all love you." She bent over him and kissed his cheek.

"And of course we love Lupe, too. You know we all try our best. Tell her to come in and eat with us."

Ascensión stood. "I'll bring her some food."

Violeta raised her arms and shook her head in exasperation, but then she again placed a hand on Ascensión's shoulder. "No, you stay here and finish your dinner. I'll bring her out a plate of food."

"No, thank you, *mamá*, I will."

"Sit and eat," said his father Ernesto. "This is between the women. Let your mother handle this."

"That's right," said Violeta, both hands now firmly pressed on her son's shoulders. "You worked hard today, you need to sit now and eat your dinner. With your family. And I need to talk to Lupe. Xiomara," Violeta said to her daughter, "get up please, Dear, and fix a plate for Lupe." To Ascensión she said, "Don't worry, *mijo*, I'll be very gentle and good. She and I will work this out between us."

Ascensión obediently sat back down and watched as his sister rose from her seat at the table, shaking her head and reaching for the plate that had been set at the table for Lupe. But before she could fill it with food Ascensión said, sheepishly, "Lupe wanted a bowl of cornflakes for dinner."

"Ah, that's what this is all about," said Violeta, "she wanted those cornflakes!"

"What cornflakes?" asked Ernesto.

"She sent *señora* Yoolie to *La Unión* to buy her cornflakes and milk." Violeta opened a kitchen cupboard to reveal the boxes of cornflakes.

"*Mamita*, what is cornflakes?" asked Blanca.

"Cornflakes is food for whiney little babies," replied Xiomara. "Really, *mamá*, she asked her boss to buy her cornflakes?"

Violeta nodded.

"Lupe didn't ask Yoolie to buy those cornflakes," said Ascensión, "she only said—"

"But *tía* Lupe is not a baby," Blanca interrupted. "Why does she want to eat cornflakes?"

"If Lupe wants cornflakes for dinner then why doesn't she just come in and get herself cornflakes?" said Ernesto, ignoring Blanca's question. "*Dios mío,* does she think we'll have her arrested for eating cornflakes?"

Violeta sighed. "I've given up trying to figure out what that girl thinks." She took down a bowl from the cupboard and filled it with cornflakes and milk from the refrigerator. She grabbed a spoon from the drawer and stuck it into the bowl of cereal. "But if this makes her happy, fine. I only want to make everybody in this family happy."

***

Lupe sat in the brightly lit yard on the bench by the clothesline. She'd held Pablito on her lap and fed him his dinner, jars of baby food carrots and bananas, and he'd fallen asleep in her arms drinking his bottle.

She closed her eyes and sat back against the back of the bench. She felt better now. When she'd entered the kitchen earlier, still stinging from the humiliating scene in front of Yoolie, the permeating smell of cooked egg combined with the sight of the frittata that Xiomara was dishing out to the rest of the family had made her stomach turn. And so she'd hurried to her bedroom where she found the *La Unión* bags of baby things that Jaime had left there, quickly changed Pablito, and filled one of the bags with baby food, formula, and a bottle. Then she rushed from the house, so nauseous that she feared she might not make it outside without retching.

Ascensión had gotten up from his seat at the table and called after her. "Are you all right?"

"Yes," she'd called over her shoulder. But she wasn't all right. Now, though, she felt better. Hungry again, even.

"Lupe."

She opened her eyes to see Violeta standing over her, smiling, holding out to her a bowl of cornflakes and milk. She shifted Pablito on her lap and took the cornflakes from Violeta. She looked at the cereal for a moment, then threw the bowl at Violeta, unable to repress her laughter as the milk and cereal dripped down her mother-in-law's shocked face.

But that scene only happened in Lupe's imagination and Violeta still stood smiling over her. She set the bowl of cornflakes on the bench next to Lupe then opened her arms. "Give me the baby," she said. "He can sleep in the crib in Xiomara's room." And because Lupe was now bone-tired from holding Pablito all day she handed him to Violeta. "Now eat," Violeta said, nodding towards the cornflakes. Then she turned and walked back to the house carrying Pablito. And because she was now ravenous Lupe took the bowl of cornflakes and wolfed it down.

After she finished the cornflakes and had drunk down every drop of milk she dearly wanted more. But she didn't dare return to the kitchen and help herself another bowl. She knew that as long as she lived in that house she would never feel free to help herself to what was hers.

Chapter Six

Next door to the former open-air market that was now *Las Sonrisas*, and sharing a wall with the old market, there was a long, narrow house that used to belong to the family that owned the market and now belonged to Cristela. Through the front door one entered the living room then passed into a hallway that opened on the left to a bedroom. Across from the bedroom for a space of about eight feet, there was no wall separating the house from the outdoors, and the hallway opened directly out to a small walled garden, making the garden part of the house, a common construction in the houses of well-off Nicaraguans. Or, in larger houses and buildings, there might be an open courtyard in the center of a room.

A wide hammock had been hung from the hallway ceiling next to the garden by the original owners of the house with the idea that it would be especially pleasant in the afternoon to lie in the hammock and watch the rain fall in the garden. Off the hallway on the other side of the garden was a small bathroom with a skylight overhead, and the hallway ended in a kitchen. Just outside the kitchen there was a table pushed against the hallway wall, and around the table were three chairs. Three more chairs stood across from the table against the opposite wall. There were two doors in the kitchen: a side door that led to the kitchen of *Las*

Sonrisas and a back door that opened to another small garden at the back end of the house.

At this moment Cristela and Yoolie lay gently swinging in the hammock entwined in each other's arms, the fragrant night aroma of tropical plants wafting in from the moonlit garden.

"That poor girl," said Cristela. "Her mother-in-law sounds almost as bad as mine."

"Ha, I can't imagine a worse mother-in-law than *señora* Violeta."

"Ha, you never met mine. Though in fairness, I suppose my husband's mother had every right to hate me after I left her spoiled little prince of a son for a woman and brought disgrace to the family."

"Ah. And where is this woman now?" asked Yoolie.

"She went back to her husband. He had too much money for her to give him up."

"Did she break your heart, *mi amor?*"

Cristela laughed. "For five minutes, maybe." She kissed Yoolie's forehead.

"See," said Yoolie, "that's what's so sad about Lupe, and so stupid of her mother-in-law. Lupe truly loves Ascensión. And he loves her. But Violeta is making life miserable for both of them, really."

"That's what they don't see, mothers like Violeta and Marlene."

"Marlene?"

"My mother-in-law. Who didn't only start hating me after I became a bad wife. She hated me even back when I was a good wife to her son. When I was a wonderful wife. And he was an awful husband."

"But are you *sure* you were a wonderful wife?" Yoolie teased.

"I was such a wonderful wife, I could have won an academy award in Hollywood for best actress."

"So why did your evil mother-in-law hate you so much?"

"Ah, that's my point," said Cristela. "Why was Marlene so unkind to me when I cared so much for her son? Why is Violeta so unkind to Lupe when Lupe cares so much for *her* son? What more could a mother ask for in a daughter-in-law than someone who loves and cares so dearly for her son?"

Yoolie stroked Cristela's hair. "I'm sorry she was so mean to you."

"Oh, it's all right. In the end, she made it easier to leave. If she had been kind I suppose I'd have felt at least a little badly about leaving her awful son. In fact, if he'd been a loving husband and she'd been a kind mother-in-law, who knows, maybe I would have felt too badly to leave at all. I'd still be married and earning my academy award for Best Wife. So I guess I'm glad they made it so easy for me to leave."

"But still," said Yoolie, continuing to gently stroke Cristela's hair.

"Just be glad you never married and had to deal with a mother-in-law," said Cristela.

"I'm *very* glad I never married and had to deal with a mother-in-law. All I had to deal with was my mother. And my father. And my brother. And my aunts, uncles, cousins, grandparents and everybody at the Whitehall Road New Life Evangelical Church."

"Where your family are the ministers."

"Right. My mother is the music minister, my brother is the youth minister, and my father is an honorary minister because he donates so much money to the church. And I brought disgrace to my whole family, too. Cheers."

Cristela sighed. "It's not easy for any of us."

"Oh, it's not so bad now."

Cristela smiled. "It's never bad when it's you and me, *querida*. Let's go to bed now."

The following morning Cristela and Yoolie were sitting at the hallway table finishing up their breakfast of fruit, scrambled eggs, tortillas and coffee when there was a banging on the kitchen side door.

"*Caramba*," said Cristela. She unlocked the kitchen door. "Rafaela? You're not at church? You're here already?"

"Yes, and I'm not the only one. I was on my way to church when I passed by *Las Sonrisas* and I saw a girl and her mother standing on the patio looking around. They're looking for a baby boy."

"I'll be right out." She turned to Yoolie. "They're here for Pablito."

"I heard."

"Can you drive them to Lupe's and back?"

"I'm at your service all weekend, *amor*."

***

The girl looked to be about twelve though her mother said she was fifteen. She was scrawny, with long hair in a loosely done braid and wearing a faded, ill-fitting pink checkered dress with a frayed hem. On her feet she wore a pair of worn sandals. Whenever she was asked a question her mother smacked her in the back of the head, as if the girl were a slightly glitched appliance that needed a smack each time to get it working. The mother, a squat woman who appeared to be in her mid-thirties, looked exasperated with her daughter. However both mother and daughter seemed pleased to go for a ride to the jungle in Yoolie's jeep.

When they arrived at the Somarriba household old Mauricio was sitting outside at the patio table with a child on his lap and several others playing at his feet. He stood when he saw Yoolie's jeep, smiled and waved her over.

"Most of the family is at church," he said, taking Yoolie's hand, "But Lupe is inside feeding Pablito. She'll fix you some *nacatamales* my daughter Violeta made this morning with cassava from my garden and fresh corn bread.

The woman and her daughter exchanged an expectant glance at the offer of food, but their faces fell when Yoolie declined.

"No thank you," said Yoolie. "We can't stay, we just—"

Mauricio cut her off. "These *señoritas* will come in and have a little breakfast, won't you?"

"*Gracias, señor,*" said the woman with a small curtsey, then she smacked her daughter's head.

"*Gracias, señor,*" said the girl with a curtsey.

"They're here to take Pablito," said Yoolie. "This is his mother and grandmother."

"His name isn't Pablito," said the girl, "it's Hernandito," and this time she ducked before her mother's hand could connect with the back of her head.

Mauricio led them into the kitchen where they found Lupe and Ascensión sitting at the table next to each other, Ascensión holding Pablito—now Hernandito—on his lap while Lupe spooned baby food from a jar into his mouth. Yoolie regretted having to intrude on this quiet, finally peaceful domestic scene.

"*Oye, muchachos,*" cried Mauricio, "The *niño's mamita* and *abuelita* have come to take him home."

Lupe and Ascensión looked over at the group standing just inside the kitchen doorway: a ragged-looking woman, an equally ragged girl, Mauricio and Yoolie. Ascensión and Lupe looked at each other then back at the group. The mother curtseyed then drew back her hand to hit her daughter's head but thought better of it in front of these people. It wasn't necessary anyway, as the girl followed her mother's suit and curtseyed without being hit.

"Oh," said Lupe.

"*Hola,* Yoolie," said Ascensión.

"*Hola,* Ascensión, Lupe," said Yoolie.

The group stood in awkward silence for a moment, then Mauricio said, "Give them their baby, then fix them a plate of *nacatamales*. And cut them some corn bread."

"Oh," said Lupe. "We were feeding him…" She hesitated only a moment longer, then she lifted Pablito from Ascensión's lap and brought him over to the girl, who looked unsure what to do next until her mother nudged her to take her baby from Lupe.

"His name is Hernandito," said the girl as she took the child into her arms.

"That's a nice name," said Lupe.

"He's a good little *majito*," said Ascensión. "He's been eating like a little horse."

"This is my husband, Ascensión," said Lupe. "And I'm Lupe." She gestured towards Mauricio. "This is Grandfather Mauricio."

Mauricio bowed deeply to the girl and her mother. "*Mucho gusto, señora* and *señorita*. Now I'll go back outside to my own little *nietos*. That's my job now," he chuckled. "I watch *nietos*." Mauricio took Yoolie by the arm. "Come outside and talk with me while I watch my grandchildren, *señora* Yoolie." Yoolie walked with Mauricio out onto to patio.

"What's your name?" Lupe asked the girl.

"I'm Preciosa," said the girl, slightly curtseying with the baby in her arms.

"I'm Linda," said her mother, also curtseying.

Lupe shepherded Preciosa and her mother to the table and sat them down. She set the jar of baby food and the spoon on the table in front of Preciosa. "Here, you can feed him. It's mango and banana. He likes it."

Lupe and Ascensión went into the bedroom to gather up the baby supplies, but as soon as they were on the other side of the curtain Ascensión took Lupe into his arms. "It will be all right, *querida*."

"I know, *amor*," she said, laying her head against his chest. She closed her eyes for a moment. When she opened them she could see Preciosa and Linda in the kitchen through an opening in the curtain. She saw Preciosa dip the spoon into the baby food jar. The girl looked around then put the spoon into her mouth. She scooped out another spoonful, but before she could get it to her mouth her mother grabbed the girl's wrist and twisted it towards herself and forced it into her own mouth.

Lupe pulled away from Ascensión's chest and moved closer to the opening in the curtain. "Look at this," she whispered and pulled him to the curtain. The two watched as Preciosa quickly spooned out the remainder of the baby food, taking turns feeding herself and her mother.

"Now," said Linda, reaching to unbutton the top of her daughter's dress.

Preciosa swatted her mother's hand away and finished opening her dress. Then she put Hernandito to her breast.

Ascensión put a hand on Lupe's shoulder. "There's nothing we can do, *amor*," he said.

Lupe reached up and laid her hand over his. "I know," she said, blinking back tears.

They sat on the bed together for a while, then they brought two *La Unión* bags full of baby things to the kitchen and set them on the floor next to Linda and Preciosa. At the sight of Lupe and Ascensión Preciosa pulled the baby from her breast then fumbled to button her dress.

"Ah, look at this," said Linda excitedly to her daughter, picking up one of the bags and lifting out baby items. Preciosa reached for the bag on Linda's lap and began riffling through it before her mother swatted the girl's hand away.

Lupe cleared her throat. "Yoolie will take you home now."

"Here, I'll help you carry the bags to the jeep," said Ascensión.

But neither Linda nor Preciosa made a move to rise from their seats. The two looked at each other, then Linda said, "The *señor* said there would be *nacatamales*."

Lupe and Ascensión exchanged a glance. Ascensión shrugged and nodded.

"Oh, of course," said Lupe. She stepped to the stove and lifted the lid of the over-sized pot inside of which were the gently simmering *nacatamales*, circles of steamed corn dough folded around a filling of chicken, rice, tomatoes and vegetables, wrapped in a plantain leaf and simmered for several hours. "But I don't know if they're done."

"Of course, they're done." Mauricio had stepped back into the kitchen and was now standing next to Lupe over the pot. "They've been cooking since before the roosters were up." He pointed into the pot. "Give them those two nice big ones. And don't forget the corn bread."

"All right," said Lupe. She took two plates from the cupboard and scooped out two *nacatamales* from the pot. She cut two squares of corn bread from a pan sitting on the counter next to the stove. She served each woman a plate of food.

Ascensión picked up the two *La Unión* bags. "I'll bring these out to the jeep," he said.

"I'll help you," said Lupe, taking one of the bags from Ascensión and following him out of the kitchen.

Yoolie was still waiting on the patio.

"They're eating *nacatamales*," said Lupe as she passed by Yoolie.

"Oh," said Yoolie, glancing at her phone.

Back in the kitchen Mauricio sat at the table next to Linda and Preciosa, bouncing Hernandito on his lap while they ate. "Are the *nacatamales* good?" asked Mauricio.

"Mmmm, *perfecto*," said Linda. Preciosa nodded in agreement.

"Nobody makes *nacatamales* like my Violeta," he said proudly. "And her cornbread?"

"Mmmm." The women nodded.

"Ah, I hear the church bus," said Mauricio, picking up the sound of the small school bus driven by an elderly nun that transported the packed-in residents of Krukrulitos to and from the next village over for Sunday Mass. Soon Mauricio could hear his family on the patio talking to Yoolie. He heard Violeta say in a raised voice, "The *nacatamales?*" The tone of his daughter's voice when she said the word gave Mauricio an uneasy twinge that perhaps he should not have been so quick to give away to these ragged strangers the delicacy that she had risen before dawn to make as a treat for her family. When Violeta entered the kitchen with the rest of the family she gave the two women who were scraping their plates clean a warm smile, but in the second before the smile Mauricio detected in his daughter's eyes a flash that he knew well.

"See?" he said, "Lupe gave our guests a plate of your delicious *nacatamales.*" He then stood, handed Hernandito back to his mother and headed out the kitchen doorway.

"She did? Well, I hope the *nacatamales* are good," said Violeta pleasantly.

"Delicious," said Linda.

"Delicious," repeated Preciosa.

Yoolie stepped into the kitchen followed by Lupe and Ascensión. "Ready to go home?" she said.

The mother and daughter looked around the room and, no one telling them to do otherwise, they stood.

"*Gracias,*" said Linda with a curtsey.

"*Gracias,*" said Preciosa, also curtseying.

"Wait a moment," said Violeta, stopping the two women as they headed towards the door. She pulled three small paper bags from a drawer. She took a bowl of plantains from the refrigerator and deposited a scoopful of plantains into each bag. "Here," she said, giving one bag to Linda, one to Preciosa and one to Yoolie. "A little treat for later." She then wrapped her arms around Preciosa and kissed Hernandito on the head. "God bless your precious little one."

During the ride back to León Linda and Preciosa gobbled their plantains so as not to have to share with the houseful of family members with whom they lived in their wood and corrugated metal hovel. "Such a nice *señora*," said Linda through a mouthful of plantains.

"Yeah," Yoolie mumbled.

Back at the Somarriba house Lupe stood in front of the stove scooping *nacatamales* from the large pot, placing one on a plate then passing the plate to Xiomara, who added a square of cornbread to each plate before passing the plates two at a time to Violeta, who then slammed the plates down on the table. Around the table sat Ernesto, Jaime, Ascensión and the children, Mauricio having opted to have his lunch brought out to him on the patio.

"Stop slamming those plates, woman," Ernesto said to his wife.

"Stop slamming the plates, *abuelita*," said Blanca, putting her hands over her ears. Mauricito copied his sister and put his hands over his ears, grinning.

"*Mamá*, what's wrong?" asked Ascensión.

"Ask your wife," snapped Violeta.

Lupe stopped in mid-scoop and turned to Violeta. "Me?" she asked.

"For God's sake, Lupe, will you pass me the plate?" snapped Xiomara.

Lupe returned to scooping and passing, confused as to why she was supposed to know why Violeta was slamming down the plates.

"Why are you women so grouchy today?" said Ernesto.

"You would be, too, if you'd been the one who was up with that crying baby last night," said Xiomara.

"I'm sorry, Xiomara. You should have brought Pablito to me," said Lupe.

She shot Lupe an irritable look. "Here, take this plate back and put on another *nacatamal*, Jaime will eat two."

"You know me so well, *mi amor*," said Jaime, blowing his wife a kiss.

After all the plates were filed and everyone was sitting around the table unwrapping the banana leaves Violeta said petulantly, "I was up at five am making these. *Nacatamales* and cornbread are a lot of work, you know."

"Ah, that's why you're grouchy," said Ernesto.

"Ummm," said Jaime, taking his first mouthful and closing his eyes in relishment. "These *nacatamales* are a masterpiece. No wonder they took so long to make."

"*Mamita*, next time you decide to make *nacatamales* for lunch wake me up to help you," said Xiomara. "Then you won't have to get up so early."

"You have two small children to take care of and the one you're carrying around in your belly all day. Of course I wouldn't wake you, you need your sleep."

"Ha, I wish you would have told that to Pablito last night," said Xiomara, shooting Lupe another look of annoyance.

"I would always get up and help you, *mamita*," said Ascensión.

"I know you would, *mijo*," said Violeta tenderly, reaching across the table to pat her son's hand.

"Or you could have woken me up," said Lupe. "I could have helped."

The whole table laughed except for Ascensión. Jaime started to laugh but quickly stopped himself.

Lupe felt her face burning. "I know that I wasn't feeling well for a few days. But I'm fine today."

"In that case I *should* have woken you up to help me make the *nacatamales*," said Violeta. "Maybe if you had done a little of the work you wouldn't have been so quick to give them away to those two…" Violeta waived her hand, unable to find the words to describe the two women who'd eaten her family's food.

"*What?*" said Lupe.

"If you had to feed them, why didn't you give them the left-over plantains? You saw how happy they were with the plantains I gave them. Or you could have made them some scrambled eggs. Or given them your precious..." She practically spat the word, "...*cornflakes!* They didn't need the *nacatamales* that I made for this family, and now there's just barely enough for lunch and some dinner for us tonight. Really Lupe, with that college degree sometimes you just *don't think!*"

"But...I didn't...it wasn't," Lupe stammered. "It was Mauricio who offered..." she looked to Ascensión for support of this fact but his head was bent over his plate and he seemed as absorbed in his lunch as the other men sitting around the table.

"Oh, that's right, blame poor old *abuelito*," Violeta snapped.

"I'm not blaming...*Ascensión*," Lupe entreated her husband.

Ascensión looked up from his plate. "*Mamá*," he said, "please let it go, okay?"

"Yes, let it go," said Ernesto.

"Fine," sniffed Violeta. She was silent for a moment then she added, "After all, I suppose her family's food isn't the worst thing she's ever given away."

Lupe rose from the table, grabbed her plate and dumped her untouched *nacatamal* back into the pot on the stove and tossed her half-eaten square of corn bread back into the pan.

"There," she said, "now there's enough!" She ran off to the bedroom and yanked the curtain shut behind her.

"Now you've done it," said Ernesto to Violeta.

"But all I said was..."

Ascensión pushed away from the table and hurried after his wife but as he passed by his mother she reached out and grabbed his arm. "Wait, *mijo*," she said. "Let her be."

"*Mamá*, let go," said Ascensión.

"*Válgame dios*," said Ernesto, "can't a man eat in peace here? Yes, let her be, let her cool down." He looked at his wife and daughter. "All you women need to cool down. You're all worse than a bunch of she cats in heat."

"Ernesto," said Violeta, still holding onto Ascensión, "don't use such language in front of the children."

"Are the cats hot, *abuelo?*" Blanca asked her grandfather.

"Yes, *pitu,* when they go *wroww, wroww, wroww,*" said Ernesto, winking at his grandchildren. He waved his fork and motioned for Violeta to release Ascensión's arm and for Ascensión to go sit back down at the table. Then he stabbed his fork into his *nacatamal.* "Ummm," he said through a mouthful of food. "Delicious."

"Ummm," said Jaime in agreement.

"Yes, *mamá,* these are the best *nacatamales,*" said Xiomara.

"Ascensión, *querido,*" said Violeta, "why are you still standing here? You sit down now and finish your lunch before it gets cold. We aren't in the U.S., we don't have a microwave oven to heat things back up when they get cold." She chuckled, and the rest of the table chuckled along with her.

"Why don't we have a microwave oven, *abuelita?*" Blanca asked her grandmother.

"Ask your *abuelito* why we can't have one," said Violeta, giving her husband an inquiring look.

"Because we aren't in the U.S.," said Ernesto

"*Oye,* Ascensión," said Jaime, "if we bought a microwave could you rig up the electrical for us?"

"Huh?" said Ascensión. He was still standing by the table with his eyes on the bedroom curtain, caught up in anxious indecision.

"Will you *please* sit down like *mamá* asked you?" said Xiomara. "It's annoying with you standing there like that."

"That's right, she'll be back out when she's ready," said Violeta. "Maybe working at the stove was too tiring for her. She's probably lying down on her bed."

"Maybe she wasn't hungry," said Jaime.

"I know she doesn't like my cooking," said Violeta. "How she just threw that *nacatamal* that I worked so hard on back into the pot..." She sighed and shook her head.

"And the way she wasted that good piece of corn bread," said Xiomara. "So wasteful. And rude."

"Don't worry about that piece of cornbread, I'll eat it," said Jaime.

"Maybe she wants that cornbread," said Ascensión, still standing watching the bedroom curtain. "I'll ask her if she wants it." He was headed towards the bedroom when Lupe came rushing out, her backpack and purse slung over her shoulder and a cloth shopping bag in her hand.

"Lupe, where are you going?" said Ascensión, trying to catch his wife as she dashed by him. She stopped at the cupboard and retrieved her boxes of cornflakes then at the refrigerator from which she grabbed the remains of her bottles of milk. She tossed the items into the shopping bag.

"Ah, going on a picnic, are you?" asked Ernesto.

But Lupe headed out the door without answering while Ascensión followed after her.

"Where is *tia* Lupe going?" asked Blanca.

"Never mind," said Xiomara. "Eat your *nacatamales*."

"So much drama," said Ernesto through a mouthful of *nacatamal*.

"With that one it's nothing but drama," sighed Violeta.

Ascensión caught up with Lupe and planted himself in front of her. When she tried to pass him he grasped her arm. "Stop. Stop."

Lupe's face was aflame and her eyes flashed but she said nothing.

"Listen." Ascensión released her arm. "I know you don't like my mother or my sister, but—"

"*I* don't like *them?*" she cut him off. "Ha!" Her chest heaved in anger.

"I mean, because of the things they say…sometimes."

"*Sometimes?*" She laughed bitterly. "Now *you* listen. Your mother and sister treat me badly. Not sometimes. *All* the time. And why? Have I ever once been hostile or unfriendly to either of them? Have I ever talked back, even to defend myself? Have I ever gotten angry?"

"No, *amor*, but—"

"Well, I'm angry now! And you know what? I don't blame your mother. Or your sister. I blame *you*."

"*Me?*"

"Your sister treats me the way she does because your mother allows her to. And your mother treats me the way she does because *you* allow her to."

"But…you know I can't control my mother's behavior."

"Oh yes, you can. You could tell her not to speak to me the way she does. You could tell her that you won't tolerate her being mean to your wife. You could speak up for me! You could tell her to behave herself, for God's sake!"

"I can't say that to my mother," said Ascensión.

"Why not?"

"Because…because…she's my *mother!*"

"Fine," Lupe cried, "you can go sleep with your mother!" She stormed off towards the back of the house.

"Don't you talk about my mother that way!" Ascensión shouted after her.

She looked back at him. "You let your mother talk to *me* that way!"

Ascensión tromped over to the bench by the clothesline and plopped himself down. *Lupe* was angry? *She* was angry? And she blamed *him*? Wasn't he always trying to soothe her, comfort her, protect her? Did she have any idea how he'd been protecting her at work, doing her work for her, practically getting down on his knees to Yoolie? Did she have no idea how stressful all this was for him? And did she really expect him to chew out his mother, his *own mother?* His mother who loved him and cared for him, cared for the whole family? Could Lupe not even *try* to understand his mother's feelings? Or *his* feelings? A tear rolled down his cheek. Did Lupe not realize that his heart was breaking as much as hers over their son? Did she not realize that he didn't have the luxury of staying in bed all day crying, of not eating, of not sleeping, of not working? Did she not realize that his mother comforted him? *But not her,* a voice in his head interrupted him. *Your mother blames her for giving up your child. But you she doesn't blame,* said the voice. *And you never told your mother that it was your idea to leave David behind with your American friends, never explained to her that you'd had no choice. You never told her that Lupe had collapsed to the ground outside the immigration courtroom. That David had to be pulled from her arms as you left for the airport. No, you couldn't tell your mother that. You could not bear her being upset with you. Because you are as afraid of your mother as you love her.*

He looked up and saw Lupe riding her bike from behind the house towards the dirt path that led to the main road, her backpack on her back and her purse and shopping bag tossed into the basket attached to the front of her bike. Ascensión ran towards the path and intercepted her, blocking her way.

"Lupe," he said breathlessly, "stop." She stopped her bike in front of him and he grabbed the handlebar. "Where are you going?"

"Let go of my bike!"

"*Dios mío,* would you calm down? I know my mother has been—"

"It's not just your mother," she cut him off. "It's your whole family. They all make fun of me because I've been sick and sad. They feel no kindness for me. They hurt me. But they forget that it was *me* who kept them from starving and being put on the street when they lost the business in León. *I* worked, *I* put the food in their mouths, and I *still* work, I *still* support this family, my paycheck *still* goes to them! Well, that could change! See if they'll be laughing then!" She pulled his hand off the handlebar and rode off.

Ascensión began running towards her and calling to her, but she ignored him and rode on.

"Ascensión." He turned to see Mauricio walking slowing towards him. When the old man reached him he said, "Let her go. She'll come back when she's ready."

"But where will she go?"

His grandfather shrugged. "Maybe she doesn't yet know."

But Lupe knew exactly where she was going.

Chapter Seven

Cristela dished out the beans and rice while Lupe added a scoop of plantains to each plate. Yoolie and Rafaela carried the plates out to the tables on the patio where the children sat waiting for their lunch.

"Are the rest of the plantains almost ready?" Lupe looked over her shoulder at Maria who stood at the stove frying up the last of the plantains.

"Here, they're all done," said Maria. "This is the last of them."

"No, no, Maria, don't lift that heavy pan," said Lupe. She brought her bowl over to Maria and set it on the stove. She patted Maria's pregnant belly and smiled. "You're carrying enough these days, *mamacita*."

"Is that all the plantains?" asked Cristela.

"All that I cooked," said Maria. "Should I make more?"

"I can slice them if you want," said Lupe.

Cristela looked from the pot of beans and rice to the bowl plantains. "Yoolie, how many more children need to eat?"

"Four more," said Yoolie, returning to the kitchen followed by Rafaela.

"Four more children then four of us," said Cristela. "Try to stretch it out. Lupe, will there be enough plantains for everybody?"

"Oh, yes, plenty, we won't need any more, Maria."

"Thank the Holy Mother," said Maria, "my feet are tired."

***

Though she had been surprised when Lupe had suddenly whisked into the kitchen, Cristela had been too busy to question her, being once again short-handed and behind with serving the children lunch. So she had put Lupe to work, even as she wondered what the girl was doing here again. After lunch Lupe stayed to help clean the kitchen then to help with the children.

Now Cristela stood next to Yoolie in the doorway to the patio, both of them watching Lupe sitting on a chair in a corner of the area reading a book to a group of children who sat on the floor encircled around her.

Cristela leaned her head in close to Yoolie's, her eyes still on Lupe. "What's going on with your little assistant?" she said softly.

"I don't exactly know," Yoolie replied softly, also looking straight ahead at Lupe.

"Did she run away from home? She brought her backpack and her cornflakes."

"I wouldn't blame her if she did," said Yoolie. "Except that I don't want to be in charge of her now."

"Maybe we should ask her?" said Cristela.

Yoolie sighed. "Yes, maybe we should."

After Lupe finished reading her book and the children had dispersed to find some new diversion, the two women approached her. They exchanged a glance then Cristela spoke.

"How is it going, Lupe?"

"Fine, but..." Lupe yawned. "I'm tired out."

"Working here with all these kids will do that to you," said Cristela.

"Not to mention that you took care of Pablito all morning then rode your bike all the way from Krukrulitos," said Yoolie.

"I know," said Lupe. She yawned again. "Maybe I could go into the room and lie down on the sofa and close my eyes for a few minutes?"

97

"Go ahead," said Cristela. "But you know that the children will be running in and out of the room. It won't be quiet."

"Oh, I don't mind the children."

Cristela and Yoolie followed Lupe with their eyes as she walked down the hallway towards the room. Cristela shrugged. "I guess we'll ask her when she wakes up."

Two hours later Yoolie gently shook Lupe's shoulder. "Lupe. Wake up, I'll give you a ride home."

"What?" Lupe said groggily, pulling herself up onto her elbow.

"It's time to go home."

Lupe sat up quickly. "No, I'll stay and help Cristela with the children."

"Cristela closes Las Sonrisas at five. She wants the children to go home before dark."

"I'll talk to Cristela," said Lupe. She stood up.

"Don't you want a ride home?"

"No, thank you, Yoolie, I'm all right."

"Cristela's in the kitchen fixing a scraped knee."

Lupe and Yoolie crossed the hallway to the kitchen where Cristela held on her lap a sobbing little girl who looked to be about five years old. Rafaela was attempting to daub the girl's dirty bleeding knee with a wet rag, but every time she touched the skin the child shrieked and pulled away.

"Here, give her to me," said Lupe, whisking the girl up from Cristela's lap. "What's your name?" she asked the child.

"A-A-Agna," she sobbed.

"Agna? What a pretty name."

Agna smiled through her tears. Lupe balanced Agna on one hip and with her opposite hand she held up the child's hurt leg. "Tsk. Look at this little knee. Have you ever seen such a boo boo?"

"No," said Rafaela and Cristela, both of whom were happy to have handed over to Lupe the task of dealing with the squealing child, whose crying had now simmered down to a sniffle.

"Hmmm," said Lupe, closely inspecting the scrape. "I think this knee needs a princess wash. What do you think, everybody?"

Everyone in the room agreed, including the little girl, who nodded seriously. "We also need a bandage for this knee to keep it clean. Do we have a bandage?"

"We have a Band-Aid," said Cristela.

"Can someone run to the pharmacy and buy a package of big bandages?" said Lupe.

"I'll do it," said Rafaela.

"My backpack is in the room on the top shelf," said Lupe. "Take out my wallet and take some money."

Rafaela looked astonished at Lupe's instructions, but on her way out of the kitchen she took Lupe's face in her hands, gave her a quick kiss on the cheek then hurried off to the pharmacy.

Lupe set the child on the sink counter with her feet and legs in the sink. She ran the water until it was warm, then splashed the water over her knees, legs, and feet. Dirty rivulets ran down the girl's legs. Lupe lathered up her hands with the bar of soap on the sink then ran her lathered hands gently up and down the little girl's legs, being especially careful over the scraped knee.

"Doesn't that feel good, *amorcito?*" she cooed. "Doesn't that make you feel like a princess?"

The little girl nodded. Lupe washed the girl's hands, arms and face as well, then dried her off with a kitchen towel and lifted her down from the sink. "If you want you can sit here in the kitchen and wait until Rafaela returns with a bandage for your knee."

By now a small crowd of children had gathered at the kitchen door. A little girl who looked a year or two older than Agna came up to Lupe and said, "Agna is my sister and I need to be washed, too."

Lupe laughed and hoisted the girl up to the sink and washed her, too. Soon there was a line of children waiting to be washed at the sink by Lupe.

"Lupe," said Cristela, "I'm trying to close up and get these children home before dark."

"I'll be quick," said Lupe. "I'll take one minute with each. But are there more towels?"

Cristela sighed and went to the room where there were a few towels and rags stacked on one of the shelves. Yoolie followed out behind her.

"Looks like your assistant is upstaging us all," said Cristela as she reached for the towels.

"Or else she's just full of energy from that two-hour nap," said Yoolie.

"*Fantastico*," said Cristela. "But she has to leave so *I* can go home and take a nap."

"So let's go flush out our little mother hen and her chicks. Then I have to leave, too, Cristela."

"What, you can't stay?"

"I'm thinking about that generator."

"What generator?"

"One of the generators. Number five. I think it's okay. I think it was just a wire, but…"

"…but maybe you need to swing by on a Sunday night and check it? Make sure it's okay? Pat its head and give it a little kiss and tuck it in?"

Yoolie laughed. "Exactly."

"Fine," said Cristela. "Go spend the night with your generator. But first we take care of the hen and the chicks."

"Wait," said Yoolie, gently grasping Cristela's arm. "You know I would rather spend the night with you."

"I know," said Cristela. She cocked her head towards the kitchen. "Let's go."

In the kitchen Rafaela, who had returned from the pharmacy with the bandages, was tending to Agna's knee while Lupe was washing a child at the sink with several more lined up for their turn.

"Oh good, some dry towels," said Lupe.

Cristela set the stack of towels on the table, grabbed a towel, then began briskly drying the legs and feet of the little boy who had just been washed. She then set him on the ground and told him, "Now time to go home. Agna, all better now?" she said to the girl with the bandaged knee. "Time for you and your sister to go home."

"Time for everyone to go home to their own *mamitas*," said Rafaela, making a shooing with her hands towards the children.

The children still in line to have their legs washed protested.

"All right, all right," Lupe laughed. "I'll get you all." To Cristela, Yoolie and Rafaela she said, "Why don't you all go home?" She lifted another child to the sink and began washing their legs. "I can finish up these children. Then I can lock up. You can leave me the key."

Cristela, Yoolie, and Rafaela looked at each other.

"No, we'll wait," said Cristela, drying the legs of the most recently cleaned child.

When all the children were washed, dried and shooed from *Las Sonrisas* Rafaela gathered up the wet towels. "I'll drop these off with Flor. She hasn't been here for days so she can wash them at home."

"No, leave them with me," said Lupe. "I'll wash them here tonight in the yard out back and hang them on the clothesline. They'll be dry by morning."

"Lupe, listen," said Cristela, speaking slowly as if to a child, "we're all going home now."

"Gather your backpack and bike," said Yoolie. "I'll give you a lift home."

"And I'll bring these to Flor," said Rafaela, lifting the towels in her arms.

Lupe pulled in a deep breath. "Cristela, can I stay here for the night? Maybe a few nights? I can sleep in the room. I'll keep an eye on the place for you. I'll lock the door before I leave for work," here she looked at Yoolie, "and I could hide the key under the table leg on the patio."

Yoolie and Cristela again exchanged a look.

"Aha, Lupita, so you *did* run away from home," said Cristela.

Lupe looked taken aback for a moment, then she spoke. "Yes, I ran away, but not from home. I ran away from a place that was making me sad and sick." Her eyes filled with tears. "You see, I have no home now. But it's all right. For now I just need a place to sleep at night."

Yoolie looked aghast. "Lupe, what are you saying? You've...you've left Ascensión?"

A tear began trickling down Lupe's cheek. She wiped it away with the back of her hand. "A hundred times in our marriage his mother has forced him to choose between herself and me. And every time he's chosen her. Not because he doesn't love me. But because he's afraid of her. Everybody is afraid of Violeta." Lupe chuckled sadly through her tears. "I'm afraid of her myself. People are not only afraid of her anger. They're afraid of standing up to her because whenever anyone does she crumbles and plays the most pitiful victim and no one can stand to see her suffer that way, either. Because they all love her, too." Lupe wiped away another tear. "But, you see, nobody is afraid of me. And, except for Ascensión, nobody loves me much, either. And it doesn't matter whether or not Ascensión loves me, because he can't stand up to his mother. But never mind. I'll be fine. I just need a place to stay for a while. And I'll help with *Las Sonrisas* any way I can."

Cristela wrapped her arms around Lupe and kissed her forehead. "Of course you can stay here, *cariño.*"

"Thank you, Cristela," she sniffled.

Yoolie sighed. *Shit,* she thought. She cleared her throat. "Lupe..."

Lupe pulled away from Cristela and turned to Yoolie. "I know I need to be at work tomorrow and every day. And from now on

I promise I will be. After all, the bus runs from León to Momotombo."

"And what about Ascensión? What about having to take the bus with him? What about seeing him at work?"

"I'll be all right. And you know Ascensión. He takes his work seriously."

Yes, and he kept you from getting fired a few days ago, Yoolie thought.

Rafaela, who'd been standing in the background and who still held the armful of damp towels said, "But what will you eat, Lupita?"

"Don't worry, Rafaela, I brought my cornflakes with me and I put some milk into the refrigerator."

"Cornflakes and milk?" Rafaela said disparagingly. "Huh, never mind eating that *chela* food, it's not healthy." Suddenly aware of Yoolie, she said, *"Perdóname,* Yoolie."

Yoolie chuckled. "No offense taken."

"Yes, why should Yoolie take offense?" said Cristela with a wink. "She's the whitest *chela* in León."

"Maybe in Nicaragua," said Yoolie.

"Maybe in the world," said Cristela.

Rafaela laughed. "You see, Lupe? You eat cornflakes you'll end up as white as Yoolie."

Lupe smiled. "I wouldn't mind if I ended up as smart as Yoolie as well."

"Ah, you see," said Cristela, "this girl knows how to flatter her boss."

"No, it's true," said Lupe.

"Yes, yes, but let's not embarrass Yoolie anymore," said Cristela.

"Yes, I agree," said Yoolie, who was starting to feel slightly awkward and by no means comfortable with the whole situation.

Lupe took the towels from Rafaela. "I'll take care of these. And don't worry about me, Rafaela, I can go to the market and buy myself some more food." To Cristela and Yoolie she said brightly, "So then? Anything else I should do here tonight?"

"I live next door," said Cristela. "That side door in the kitchen leads to my house. If you need me, if there's an emergency, you could bang on that door."

"I would certainly never disturb you, Cristela."

"Good," said Cristela with a smile. "Here's the key to *Las Sonrisas*. And fine, leave it under the table leg when you leave for work tomorrow."

"Will you be all right?" asked Yoolie.

"Yes, of course," said Lupe with a smile.

But after the women had left and she was in the back yard scrubbing and hanging the towels while the tears streamed down her cheeks she wondered if she really would be all right.

Chapter Eight

The sun would be setting soon. Ascensión glanced at his cell phone again. There was still no message from Lupe. He'd been worried all afternoon, but now he was worried sick.

"You talk to Lupe yet?" Jaime joined Ascensión in the front yard where he'd been standing, looking alternately up at the sky and down at his cell phone.

"No," said Ascensión. "I've got to call her."

"Why didn't you call her already? She's been gone all afternoon. Are you playing games with her, *maje?*"

"No, no. I wanted to call her, but *abuelito* and *mamá* and *papá* and Xiomara kept telling me, 'Don't call her, let her go, let her call you, she'll be right back.' And now…"

"…it's almost dark and you don't know where your wife is. If my wife left me I wouldn't listen to what anybody said, I'd be out looking for her long ago, *maje.*"

"Jaime!" Xiomara called impatiently from the house. "What are you doing standing around out there? Come in here!"

Jaime rolled his eyes. "Well, maybe on second thought I'd let her go for a while." He patted Ascensión on the shoulder then called to his wife, "Coming, *amor.*"

As soon as Jaime returned to the house Ascensión dialed Lupe's number. *Please answer, please answer, please answer,* he prayed to his phone.

Lupe looked at her phone screen and her heart fluttered. She felt so alone, so sad, she wanted so badly to hear the sound of his voice. But what if the sound of his voice made her change her mind? She waivered indecisively, her thumb hovering over the screen while her phone continued playing its twinkly ringtone. As soon as the ringtone stopped it hit her: *Dios mío,* He has no idea where I am! He's worried! Of course I have to at least let him know I'm all right! When her phone began twinkling again she immediately picked it up.

"Hello, Ascensión," she said coolly.

"Lupe? Lupe, where are you?"

Yes, he sounded worried. Lupe felt a twinge of guilt. "I'm all right," she said.

"But…where are you? Where did you go?"

"Don't worry. I'm fine. I'm staying with a friend."

"A *friend*? *What* friend? Where are you? *Lupe, where are you?*" He was hit with the thought—completely irrational but no less terrifying—that his wife could be with another man.

He sounded frantic. She had to tell him. *"Las Sonrisas."*

"Las Sonrisas? Where you went to work yesterday?"

"I went to work there today, too."

"Why didn't you tell me that's where you were going? Why didn't you call me? When are you coming home?"

He was breathing so heavily that Lupe feared he might pass out. Or start to cry. Still, she had to tell him. "I'm not coming back. I'm staying here."

"What? What do you mean?"

"What I just said."

"No, but I don't under…"

"Cristela is letting me sleep on a couch here…until…" Lupe left the sentence unfinished.

"Until *what*? Cristela *who*?"

"I'm not coming back to Krukrulitos. Ever."

"No, but I don't..." Ascensión stopped. But of course he understood what she meant. She meant what she'd said. She meant that she was staying at *Las Sonrisas*. That she wasn't coming back. Ever. She meant that she'd left him.

"Don't worry," she said. "I'll be all right. Good-bye, *mi amo*...Ascensión."

"No, Lupe, Lupe, no..." Ascensión moved the phone away from his ear. He stared at the phone's blank screen for a moment. What had happened? He closed his eyes and tried to think despite the pounding in his brain, to find the connection between and put into some order all the separate things that had happened that together made this one thing happen. Yesterday and the day before he'd had to pull Lupe out of bed, dress her, force her to eat. Today she left home. Left him. His head began swimming. He had a strange sensation of being not himself, of being detached from reality. He needed to do something...but what? He'd call her back, but...he felt confused, paralyzed, weighted down by something that made it too hard to think, too hard to move.

"Ascención! Come for dinner!"

He turned around to see his mother standing on the front porch gesturing for him to come, smiling. Smiling as if all were well. Calling him for dinner as if it made no difference that his wife rode off on her bicycle this afternoon and still wasn't back. As if it didn't matter, as if he could come in and eat dinner all the same. As if he weren't falling apart, as if his heart weren't breaking.

"Ascención!" his mother called again.

He didn't want to go inside to his family. But he didn't know where else to go.

Mauricio was sitting at the table on the patio with the two children, who were eating their dinner with their great-grandfather. As Ascensión passed by the old man grabbed his hand. Ascensión patted his grandfather's hand and kissed the old man's cheek. He kissed each child on the head. When he entered the kitchen the adults were already sitting around the table, their plates filled with the *nacatamales* left over from lunch. Ascensión approached the table then stopped, not knowing whether to go forward or to leave. Everyone was still, looking at him. Ascensión noticed that there was a place set for him but not for Lupe.

"Well?" said his father.

When Ascensión didn't reply his mother said, "What you father is asking you is, have you heard from her?"

"Yes," said Ascensión.

"Where is she?" asked his sister Xiomara. "Not coming home for dinner?"

"No," said Ascensión. "She's not coming home for dinner."

"She must not be hungry," said Ernesto, digging his fork into his food. "Not like the rest of us."

"*Santa Maria,*" said Violeta, "when it isn't one thing with that girl it's another! She wasn't bad enough before, now this." Violeta sighed. "Well, where is she now?"

"She's gone. She says she's not coming back here. Ever."

"*What?*" cried the family in unison.

"Why are you all so surprised? You made her sick with your meanness, and now you've driven her away!"

"Us?" said Violeta.

"*You, mamá, you.*"

"Me?" Violeta's eyes filled with tears.

"*You, mamá,* and *you,* Xiomara. You treat Lupe badly, not sometimes, *all* the time. And why do you do that, *why?* Was she ever once hostile or unfriendly to either of you? Did she ever talk back, even to defend herself? Did she ever get angry?"

Xiomara sat drop-jawed while Violeta began softly sobbing.

"But not just *mamá* and Xiomara. It's this whole family! You all made fun of her because she was sick and sad. You accused her of giving up our baby when it wasn't true. You hurt her, you showed her no kindness. But you forget that it was Lupe who kept us from starving and being put on the street when we lost the business in

León. *She* worked, *she* put the food in our mouths. And she *still* works, she *still* supports us, her paycheck *still* comes to us. But now she's gone, so maybe that will change. Will you be laughing at her then?"

Violeta's sobbing stopped short and she gasped. "Oh, she wouldn't do that!"

Ernesto said to his wife and daughter, "Now you women see what all your peck, peck, pecking has done? How many times did I tell you to leave that girl alone?"

Ascensión rushed from the kitchen past his grandfather and niece and nephew. He ran down to the bench by the clothesline and buried his head in his hands, sobbing. Violeta got up from the kitchen table to follow after him, but Mauricio stood and stopped her at the door.

"Let him be, *mija*," he said to his daughter, taking her by the arm. "Let him calm down. Let everyone calm down. Go back inside and eat. You need to eat. Everyone needs to eat."

"Yes, *papá*," she said obediently as a little girl, and she returned to the kitchen to eat and cry.

After a few minutes Jaime exited the kitchen with two plates of food.

"He's down there," said Mauricio, pointing in the direction of the clothesline.

Jaime sat down on the bench next to Ascensión, who still sat with his head in his hands. Jaime nudged Ascensión and proffered him one of the plates of food but Ascensión looked up briefly and shook his head.

"Come on," said Jaime, "at least take it."

When Ascensión made no move to take the food Jaime shrugged and set the plate on the bench.

Jaime dug into his *nacatamal*. "You know, *muchacho*," he said through a mouthful of food, "that was good, what you said in there."

Ascensión looked up at his brother-in-law.

"Maybe you should have said it a little sooner, though."

"She left me, Jaime." Ascensión rubbed the back of his hand across his eyes.

"Are you sure?"

"She said she's never coming back here."

"So is it you she left? Or your family?"

Ascensión opened his mouth as if to speak, then closed it again.

"Here," said Jaime, handing Ascensión the plate of food. "Eat while you think about it."

Ascensión suddenly realized how hungry he was. He shoveled a few forkfuls of food into his mouth. "But what do I do, Jaime?"

"What do you do? If she won't come back here, you better go to her."

"What do you mean? I should move out, too? Leave my family?"

"You did it before."

Ascensión ate a few more mouthfuls of food, looked off into the distance for a few moments, then turned to Jaime.

"But when Lupe and I left for the United States, that was different. Now if I tried to leave...my family, they would..." Ascensión shook his head.

"Ha, yes it was different then, all right. Back then when we were all starving your family was thrilled to see you move out. They practically kicked you out the door."

"That's harsh, *maje*," said Ascensión. He continued eating.

"Yeah, well, you could do it again, you know. Move out."

"More room for you," said Ascensión.

"And my little *majito* on the way."

Ascensión sighed. "But what would my *mamá* say? If I moved to León with Lupe?"

Jaime laughed. "How far is León from Krukrulitos? A thousand miles?"

"It might be if I left."

"If you left your *mamá* for your wife?"

Ascensión put his head back into his hands.

"Oh, come on, *tio*. You know your *mamá*. After a while she wouldn't mind." Jaime laughed. "As long as you keep sending money. Seriously, you know your *mamita* and your wife can't live in the same house, right?"

"I think you're right, Jaime. But...Lupe was so angry with me today. I don't think she's ever been angry at me before." His eyes began to tear up again.

"Like Momotombo."

"What?"

"Momotombo. Quiet as a church for years. Then one day, suddenly..." Jaime put his fingertips together then threw open his hands. "Pshhhh!"

Ascensión shook his head.

"But hey, a volcano shoots off hot but not for very long, and today is today and tomorrow is another day. Don't call Lupe tonight. Give her a little time to miss you. You'll see her tomorrow at work. You'll talk then."

"Right. You're always right."

"Of course," Jaime chuckled. Then his expression turned serious. "But *tio*, when you said that your family was mean to Lupe...you didn't mean me, did you?"

Ascensión patted his brother-in-law's back. "No, *maje*. Not you." *You may be lazy and sometimes annoying*, he thought to himself, *but you're not mean.*

The sun had set and the spotlights lit up the yard. Some relatives from the other houses had gathered on the patio. The television was on, but there was little attention being paid to what was playing on the screen, the turbulence in Violeta's household providing a much more compelling drama.

Xiomara was passing around a plate of left-over cornbread and filling everyone in on Lupe's flight and Ascensión's outburst during dinner. Now and then people would glance over down the slope to the bench by the clothesline where Ascensión sat with Jaime.

"He'll be all right," said Xiomara in a hushed voice to the circle of women around her. "Jaime's with him. But poor *mamá*." She cocked her head towards the kitchen. "She's in there crying her eyes out. The things Ascensión said to her. To her, to me, to his whole family. Well, *mamá* knows it's all Lupe's fault, otherwise Ascensión would never have talked to us that way."

Old *tia* Pilar sat in one of the wooden chairs, a grandchild sitting close on either side of her to support her in case she wished to stand. "Ascensión was always such a good boy," she tsked. "But he'll apologize to his mother or else he'll be in trouble with me!"

"Don't worry yourself, *tia*," said Xiomara. "Here, have some corn bread."

"Look, he's coming," said one of the relatives. All heads turned to Ascensión and Jaime, who were walking back to the house. Xiomara set down the plate of corn bread and watched them approach, her hands on her hips, a stern expression on her face.

When they reached the patio Ascensión tried to pass by his sister but she grabbed him by the arm. "*Mamá* is in the kitchen crying her eyes out."

"I'll talk to her," said Ascensión.

But Xiomara still held onto her brother's arm. "What about what you said to me?" she snapped.

"I'm sorry, Xiomara," he said, but he sounded distracted.

Xiomara let go of his arm. "Here, give me those plates," she said, snatching from Ascensión and Jaime their dirty dinner plates. She turned and whisked away to the kitchen, turning back to give her brother one more disapproving look before disappearing into the kitchen.

Ascensión stood for a moment surrounded by the relatives who looked at him in silence. He moved by them and entered the kitchen. They followed in after him.

He found his mother sitting at the kitchen table, not crying her eyes out but red-eyed and looking weary. Ernesto and Mauricio sat at the table with her. Some of the relatives took up the available seats while the others stood around. *Tia* Pilar's grandchildren settled her into one of the chairs then stood on either side of her. Jaime jockeyed himself as closely to Ascensión as he was able, as if by standing close to his brother-in-law he might give him some moral support.

"Ascensión," said Violeta.

"*Mamá*, I'm sorry," he said.

Violeta raised a hand. "Never mind," she said gently. "Where is she?"

"In León."

"*León?*" said Violeta. "Who is she with?"

"She's at *Las Sonrisas*. She says she's staying there. Until..."

"Until *what?*" said Violeta.

"I...don't know," said Ascensión.

"Ha, is that what that place is?" said Xiomara. "A hotel for women who abandon their husbands and families?"

"Well, she's gone now," sighed Violeta, "and that can only be for the better."

"No, *mamá*, I'm going to—"

"Your *mamá* is right," Ernesto cut him off. "There's been no peace around here lately. Now we can have some peace. But there's something you have to do. Very important."

"I'm going to her, that's what I'm going to do."

Violeta threw her arms into the air. "*¡Madre de Dios!* The woman *left* you!"

Ascensión pulled in a deep breath. "She didn't leave me. She left you."

"Is that so?" said Violeta. "I don't see her here with *you*." She made a show of looking around, as if for Lupe.

"That girl has no sense of family," said *tia* Pilar. "Xiomara, Dear, will you get me a cup of coffee?"

"Of course, *tia*," said Xiomara. "She has never fit in well. She came from such a rich family, she always thought she was better than us."

"No, she didn't think that," said Ascensión.

"It doesn't matter what she thought," said Violeta, sounding exasperated. "What matters is that she's gone, and what it means for this family." She smacked her hand on the table for emphasis.

"What are you talking about?" said Ascensión.

"What you said," said Ernesto. "About her keeping her paycheck from the family now that she's gone."

There was a collective gasp and some murmuring among the relatives in the room as they suddenly realized how Lupe's leaving could affect them all if there were less money in the collective pot. "Would Lupe do that?" they pondered. "Would she keep her paycheck from the family?"

"*I* don't know!" said Ascensión, looking around the room. "Is that all you're worried about?"

"No, of course that's not all," said Violeta. "Her name is on your bank account—the family's bank account—right?"

"Yes," said Ascensión, feeling a queasy sensation over where this conversation might be heading.

"You have to close that bank account right away," said Ernesto. "Take out all the money before she does."

There was another round of gasping and muttering among the relatives. "Oh, Lupe wouldn't do that, would she?" they wondered.

"Of course she wouldn't," said Ascensión.

"Well, you do it before she does," said his father.

"Lupe would not do that! *I* would not do that!"

"Calm down, *mijo*," said Violeta, taking her son's hand. "We just mean, if she doesn't want to be part of this family, then she should not be allowed to spend our money."

"It's her money, too," said Ascensión.

Tia Pilar waved a hand dismissively. "*Caramba*, those two spent too much time in the United States. But maybe after you close out her bank account you could talk to your American boss and have Lupe's paycheck sent to your account. You see how fast she would come crawling back to this family." She turned to one of the grandchildren sitting next to her. "Go and get me another piece of corn bread, *querida*."

"Look," said Ascensión, "I'm not closing Lupe's and my bank account."

"You mean *your family's* bank account," said Violeta.

Ascensión pulled in a deep breath. "If Lupe wants to live in León, then I'm going to go and live in León with her."

This time it was a chorus of shocked cries that filled the room.

His father sprang from his seat. "What? You want to live in *León? By yourself?*"

His mother also sprang from her seat. "You want to *leave? Leave your family?*" She then had to sit back down, as if overcome by the thought.

"Don't talk such nonsense," said his father. "Why in the world would you leave Krukrulitos?"

"Ummm...because his wife's in León?" Jaime ventured.

"Oh, Jaime, keep out of this!" cried Xiomara. "Why would you say such a thing?"

"Sorry, *muchacho*," Jaime whispered out of the side of his mouth into Ascensión's ear.

"Look," said Ascensión, "You need more room in this house, with Jaime and Xiomara's little one on the way..."

"What do you mean?" said Mauricio. "There's plenty of room in this house. It's the biggest house in the village." He looked around the room and his relatives nodded and muttered their agreement.

His father chuckled. "Of course, you lived in the United States, now you want to live like a rich American, have your own house. Fine. There's plenty of room for another house on *abuelito's* land, right *abuelito?*"

"Yes, yes, plenty of room," agreed Mauricio. "No need to move away from your family."

"You move to León, it would be money for an apartment, money for this, money for that." Ernesto gave a dismissive wave of his hand. "I'll tell you what, you can build a house here, out in the back, out by the cornfield. Then if you want you can tell your little…" here he gave another dismissive wave of his hand "…she can come back."

"As long as she doesn't have to live in the same house as the rest of us," said Xiomara.

"But only if she apologizes to the family and stops all her nonsense," said Violeta. "No more sleeping all day, no more spending all your money on…" she spat out the word, "…*cornflakes*."

"Stop it!" Ascensión cried. "I don't even know if Lupe will come back to me in León, let alone here!" His eyes began to fill with tears again.

"Fine, if she won't come back to you here then let her stay in León," snapped Violeta. "You close out her bank account, get her salary sent to you, and let her crawl back to you when she's good and hungry. Or let her go back to her father. Or live on the street."

"No, no!" Ascensión began sobbing into his hands.

"Aw, *mijo, mijo,*" cooed his mother. She stood up and stepped over to him, wrapping her arms around him and rubbing his back.

"Oh, stop your crying, boy," said his father. "No need to cry over this woman. You'll find yourself another one. Plenty of fine women out there looking for a good man. Listen, *mijo.* You can live without that woman. You can live without any woman. But you can't live without your family."

There was a murmur of assent around the room.

"It's true," said *tia* Pilar. "This isn't the United States, after all."

Another murmur of assent.

"I'll tell you what," said Ernesto, "That *chiquita* wants to fly away, you'll let her fly away and you'll forget about her. You'll be fine, you'll see. You'll stay in Krukrulitos, we'll build you a house. Made of cinderblocks, just as nice as *abuelito's* here. Right, *abuelito?*"

Mauricio smiled proudly.

"You know what else? You can buy a car, what do you think of that? A jeep, an SUV. To drive to León, maybe even drive to Managua sometimes." He looked around the room. "It's about time this family had a car, eh?"

His question was answered with whoops of happy agreement by the relatives, who then murmured excitedly among themselves about the shiny new vehicle in which each of them imagined themselves riding to León or even Managua sometimes.

"Won't that be wonderful?" Violeta crooned to her son, still holding him and patting his back as if he were a small child. "You'll have a good house and a good car and you'll be here with your family that loves you."

Some of the relatives gathered around closer to Ascensión and murmured words of cheerful reassurance about all the good things he had and all the good things to come, as if the happy ending to this story had now arrived.

But at this moment Ascensión didn't want a house, a car, or his family. All he wanted was Lupe, their son, and the life they once had.

***

Darkness had already fallen as Yoolie drove her jeep along the macadam road from León towards the Momotombo geothermal plant. She was a bit annoyed with Cristela for allowing Lupe to stay at *Las Sonrisas*. Now, as Yoolie's Grandma Pursglove would say, Lupe was Cristela's Little Red Wagon. Which made Lupe, by extension, Yoolie's Little Red Wagon. Yoolie sighed. Aw, hell, why was she blaming Cristela? Wasn't it Yoolie who had brought Lupe to *Las Sonrisas* in the first place? Who had bought her cornflakes? Who had been cutting her breaks like crazy at work? Was Lupe not already Yoolie's Little Red Wagon?

And would she really have expected Cristela, her golden-hearted Cristela, to turn poor Lupe away? Would she, Yoolie, have turned Lupe away at this point? Maybe in truth we were all each other's Little Red Wagon. Maybe that's what it was to be a human. And definitely what it was to be in love.

Now Yoolie was annoyed with herself. Was it really all that important that she stop by Momotombo and check the generator? Couldn't she have let the damn generator go until morning and stayed the night with Cristela? It wasn't as if Jaime hadn't done the repair on the generator on Friday. Though how thorough a job she couldn't say, knowing Jaime. Which was probably why she *should* have a look herself. On the other hand it wasn't a particularly complicated repair. Important, but not complicated. And it wasn't as if there wasn't a night crew there to keep an eye on things. *They* should be checking on all the generators. *Should* being the key word.

Yoolie yawned. She felt so tired. Sprinting around after a bunch of kids all weekend was much more tiring than spending the weekend hiking up and down a volcano. Up ahead spotlights showed the silhouettes of the geothermal plant and the slope of the volcano in relief against the dark. She drove up to the well-lit entrance and stopped at the gate. The security guard approached her jeep, a young man whose name badge identified him as *José* and a face she didn't recognize. José, however, knew who Yoolie was.

"Good evening, *señora* Yoolie," said José.

"Good evening, José. Wait a minute, I have my badge right here." Yoolie began rifling through her backpack.

"Oh, no need, *señora*," said José. He stepped back and waved her through.

Yoolie's first impulse was to remind the guard that he should never let anyone through the gate, no matter who, without first checking their ID. But then how many red-haired *chelas* with a Momotombo permit pasted to the windshield of their car were there likely to be in these parts?

Yoolie pulled her car through the gate then stopped. Did she really need to go in?

"*Oye*, José," she called to the guard, who returned to the car window.

"Yes, *señora* Yoolie?"

"How is it going? Everything quiet?"

"Yes, *señora*. Very quiet."

"No problems with the generators?"

The guard looked unsure, but he said, "No, the generators are fine, I think."

Yoolie realized the pointlessness of asking the gate guard what was going on with the generators, and she knew she was merely looking for an excuse not to have to spend an hour at the plant tonight. Still, if there was any serious problem he surely would have heard about it from someone on the night shift. But what was she thinking? If there was any serious problem *she* surely would have heard about it from someone on the night shift. The heck with it.

"Okay, thank you," she said. Then she pulled far enough inside the gate to make a U-turn and exited back out onto the macadam road from where she soon turned off onto the road that led to her housing area. As she settled into her bed, bone-tired, the whirring of her room fan lulling her off to sleep, she felt glad that she'd made the decision to skip inspecting that generator.

By the following dawn, soon after she'd been jarred awake from a deep sleep by the ringing of her cell phone, she'd be regretting that decision.

Chapter Nine

Ascensión sat at the kitchen table picking at his breakfast while his family chattered around him. His mother entered the kitchen from his bedroom carrying two *La Unión* shopping bags now filled with clothes and a few other items.

"Here," she said, setting the bags on the floor near him. "You can give these to Lupe at work."

"*If* she shows up for work," said Xiomara from where she stood at the stove stirring a pot of rice and beans.

"Of course she has nobody to pull her out of bed now, so we'll see," said Violeta.

"*Mamá*, Xiomara, please," Ascensión muttered.

"That's right, don't torment the boy," said Ernesto from where he sat at the table across from Ascensión.

Violeta threw up her hands, palms outward in a *don't shoot* gesture. "Only trying to help," she muttered in a wounded tone.

"Huh," Xiomara mumbled as she scooped out a bowl of rice, topped it with a sunny side egg and brought it to Jaime, who also sat at the table.

"Thank you, *mi amor*," said Jaime. Then he added, for good measure and to sweeten the mood in the room, "Nobody eats like we do here in this house."

"That's true," said Ernesto, deeming it wise to follow Jaime's lead.

Violeta, somewhat placated, sighed. "Ascensión, *mijo*, you have to cheer up." She put her hands on her son's shoulders.

"Give him time." Everyone turned to see Mauricio standing in the doorway.

"Ah, *abuelito*," cried Violeta. "Here's your breakfast sitting on the counter! How did I neglect to bring it out to you?" She grabbed the tray of food and whisked by Mauricio and out the kitchen door. "Come out to the patio now and eat."

"Life will go on, you'll see," said Mauricio before heading back out onto the patio to eat his breakfast.

Violeta returned to the kitchen followed by several villagers, a few men, a few women, some carrying babies or toting children, who'd walked over early in the morning to catch up on the gossip that had been percolating over the weekend throughout Krukrulitos about the Somarriba family.

"No, the baby wasn't Lupe's," Violeta explained. "It belonged to some little...*fulanita*," she threw up her hands in irritation, "...who tried to give it away."

"*Oh, Dios mío, que terrible,*" the neighbors mumbled among themselves.

"And Lupe brought the baby *here?*" asked one of the village women.

"Yes, do you believe it?" Xiomara chimed in.

"Then," continued Violeta, "when the mother showed up—she was just a little girl herself—with her mother to collect the baby, they about ate us out of house and home before they finally left!"

"*Mamá,*" said Ascensión, "they didn't eat that much."

"And then we heard Lupe ran away," said another. "Ah, poor Ascensión."

"I'm fine," muttered Ascensión, wishing all the neighbors would run away, but knowing better than to think they might.

"Well, *muchacho,*" chuckled one of the men, clapping him on the shoulder, "don't worry, you'll have another woman soon. As soon as word gets out the women will be flocking around you like geese."

"That's what I told him," said his father. "Like *geese*."

"I don't *want*," Ascensión started to say.

"He doesn't *want*," his mother cut him off.

"Oh, he will," his father cut his mother off, "just give him some time." His father took a drink of his morning beer then dug into his egg-topped rice.

"Would everybody please," Ascensión started to say.

"I heard the family is buying you a jeep," one of the women cut Ascensión off.

"A jeep?" said one of the men. "*Oye*, Ascensión, you want a good woman? I'll trade you Conchita for that jeep. I'll throw in the *niños*, too."

Conchita jabbed her laughing husband with her elbow, then joined the rest of the room in the laughter.

From there the room broke into a gaggle of good-natured jokes, sympathy, advice, and prying questions, always several people talking at once, everyone gesticulating, Ascensión trying to no avail to make them stop, until he finally stood and shouted, "Will everybody *please*—"

"Ascensión!" Jaime cut him off.

"I said, WILL EVERYBODY *PLEASE*—"

"ASCENSIÓN!" Jaime shouted, cutting him off again, pushing Ascensión's cell phone across the table at him. "Answer your phone, *hombre!* It's Yoolie."

"What?" Ascensión reached for his phone, put it to one ear while he covered the other, and hurried from the noisy kitchen out onto the patio. His family and neighbors were suddenly quiet as they followed after him. However there was little information to be picked up from listening in on Ascensión's call, only his intermittent exclamations of "What...? How bad...? When did they...? Yes, yes, of course...Yes, I can be at the road in fifteen minutes."

After he hung up Ascensión looked at the semi-circle of wide-eyed people around him, reading the question in their expectant faces.

"I have to leave for work," was all he said.

Ascensión hurried into the house followed by his mother and Jaime while the rest of the crowd stayed on the patio to discuss what this emergency might mean.

"Why do you have to leave already?" said his mother. "Why do you have to be at the road in fifteen minutes? You don't have to leave for the bus for at least half an hour. You haven't finished your breakfast. I don't have your lunch made."

"What is it?" asked Jaime.

Ascensión reached for his backpack from its hook on the wall then turned back to Jaime. "Generator five."

"Oh, *mierda*," Jaime gasped, then he quickly apologized to his mother-in-law.

Violeta ignored Jaime but grabbed Ascensión by the arm. "What is it, *mijo*?"

"I have to go, *mamá*. Yoolie is sending a jeep to pick me up at the road."

"Wait, Ascensión," said Jaime. He looked as if he might start to cry.

Ascensión cocked his head for Jaime to follow him, and the two of them hurried out the door, Violeta behind them.

"Wait, *mija*," said Mauricio as Violeta passed him while weaving through the group on the patio and following after Ascensión and Jaime.

Violeta stopped and turned to her father, who was sitting in his wooden chair. "What is it, *papá*?" To Xiomara, who stood nearby, she said, "Get *abuelito* whatever he needs. I have to-"

"No, *mija*," Mauricio cut her off. "I don't need anything. Come here."

Violeta looked from her son, now standing in the yard with Jaime, back to her father. "What is it, *papá*?"

"Come here," said Mauricio.

Violeta looked again to her son, but turned and obediently walked back to her father.

"What, *papá*?"

Mauricio smiled at his daughter. "Did Ascensión ask you to follow him out to the yard?"

Violeta was momentarily taken aback. "Well…I'm his mother. Of course I need to know what's going on with my son."

Mauricio nodded. "I'm sure you'll find out soon. We'll all find out soon. You stay here for now." He reached for his daughter's hand, and though she dearly wanted to pull away and follow after her son, she did as her father told her.

While the relatives and neighbors watched from the patio, Ascensión and Jaime hurried across the yard, stopping when they reached the dirt path. The group continued watching as the two spoke excitably, everyone quiet and straining to hear what was being said, but able to make out nothing above the noise of the children playing in the yard.

When they were far enough away from the patio Jaime grasped Ascensión's arm. "What happened to the generator? Am I in trouble? I fixed the wire, I swear!"

"Calm down, *maje*," said Ascensión. "Yoolie doesn't know what's wrong with the generator, except that early this morning it was smoking and now it's dead."

"*Dead?*"

"A section of León has been without electricity for a few hours."

"*Oh, Dios mío.*" Jaime let go of Ascensión's arm and rubbed the sweat that had broken out on his forehead. Then he said, "Well, maybe it doesn't matter. Maybe they'll just think the electricity was being turned off in their neighborhood at a different time than usual."

Ascensión gave a short humorless chuckle. "Maybe. It's in the *Barrio San Mateo.*"

"Oh great. *San Mateo*. Where the rich people live. It's going to matter."

"They're probably blowing up the phone lines of the *Empresa de Electricidad*."

"Huh, the *Empresa de Electricidad* probably wants Yoolie's head on a platter." Jaime swallowed hard. "I hope Yoolie doesn't want my head on platter."

"Right now Yoolie's got her own head to worry about," said Ascensión.

"If only it had taken out the *Barrio Villa Democracia*," said Jaime, citing one of the poorest neighborhoods. "If there's no electricity there nobody cares."

"Ha, that's true," said Ascensión. "But Yoolie wants me to open the generator and figure out what happened."

"*Maje,* don't let Yoolie fire me, okay?" Jaime's eyes began to tear up.

"*Maje,* she didn't say anything about firing you. But look, just be sure and make yourself useful today. And make sure Yoolie sees you working. Make sure *everybody* sees you working today."

"Sure, sure. But you'll put a good word for me, right? You'll know what to say."

"Of course."

"Thank you, thank you."

Jaime hugged Ascensión, who gave his sniffling brother-in-law a pat on the back. "And Jaime," he said hesitantly, "if you...if you see...Lupe...tell her..."

"What do you want me to tell her?"

"...tell her...I don't know. You'll know what to say."

Now it was Jaime who patted Ascensión's shoulder. "Of course, *maje*."

Then Ascensión was hurrying off down the dirt path towards the gravel road where the jeep would soon be arriving to take him to Momotombo.

Jaime quickly wiped his eyes then headed back to the patio where the relatives and neighbors still gathered on the patio stood watching him. They'd been excitedly discussing what Ascensión's hasty exit could mean. Some trouble at Momotombo? Was it the volcano?

"What did Ascensión say to you?" asked Violeta. "Why are you so upset?"

"It's one of the generators," said Jaime. "It's stopped working."

This revelation sent another round of buzzing among the group.

"You're that upset about a generator that's stopped working?" said Ernesto.

"*Papá*," said Xiomara, "you know how seriously Jaime takes his work."

"Thank you, *mi vida*," said Jaime, and, still a little rattled, he put his arms around his wife and buried his head against her shoulder.

"It's all right, *amor*," said Xiomara, patting her husband on the back. "Come inside and finish your breakfast."

Violeta shook her head and sighed and Ernesto rolled his eyes.

Violeta looked around at the people on the porch. "You see how important my son is?" she said with just a hint of imperiousness, as if she were royalty addressing her subjects. "The generator shuts down and he's the one they call." And, as if they were indeed her loyal subjects, her relatives and neighbors nodded and murmured their assent. Violeta's eyes suddenly widened and she dashed into the kitchen. She came back out carrying the two *La Unión* shopping bags of Lupe's things that were still sitting on the kitchen floor. She hurried across the yard until she reached the dirt path then she called, "Wait, Ascensión," holding up the bags. After a moment she lowered the bags, turned around and returned, still breathless, to the house.

"Maybe our son isn't yet ready to send her packing," said Ernesto, putting a hand gently on his wife's shoulder. Violeta began sniffling softly.

***

Ascensión had never seen Yoolie looking so rattled. In fact, he'd never seen her looking rattled at all. Well, at least until last Friday when the big-shot foreign *cheles* were about to arrive and Lupe hadn't shown up for work. She'd looked a little rattled then. This morning, though, she definitely looked much more rattled. The jeep she'd sent to pick him up deposited him at the generator site, where Yoolie stood tapping a pen against a clipboard. With her were some engineers and night crew workers who were on the last hour of their shift. The workers were talking and gesticulating while Yoolie nodded, blinked, shook her head, took notes and sighed. The other engineers were not so attentive to the workers as Yoolie was. Rather, they looked around or at the generator or at each other, making comments to each other and shrugging. They stood back a little behind Yoolie, as if to demarcate that, though they were present, they were in no way to be considered the responsible parties in this situation.

"*Oye*, Ascensión," Yoolie called when she caught sight of him stepping out of the jeep. She waved her clipboard in a gesture for him to hurry over. As Ascensión approached he could hear her asking the men if any of them had heard any squeaking from the generator during the night. The men looked and each other, shrugged, shook their heads.

Ascensión was intercepted by the head geologist, a handsome, perennially annoying Argentinian who liked to lord his authority over others even though he was himself mediocre at his work. "Do you know anything about this, Ascensión?" he asked.

"No, *señor*," said Ascensión.

Yoolie ignored her colleague and stepped in front of him as if he weren't there. To Ascensión she said, "Can you gather a crew to rig this thing back together and get it working so we can at least get the electricity back on in the *Barrio San Mateo?*"

"Certainly, Yoolie," said Ascensión. "But the morning shift won't start arriving for another hour. I'll leave a message at the machine shack to send over Francisco and Diego as soon as they arrive, and a few more. In the meantime a couple of these *muchachos* from the night shift can help me get things started."

"Fine," said Yoolie. *And you, my man, will get a promotion to foreman out of this,* she thought.

"The *Barrio San Mateo?*" snickered one of the workers behind his hand to the other workers. "I'll bet they're jumping through their asses at the *Empresa de Electricidad.*"

The men laughed and the Argentinian geologist spun around to face them. "This is not a laughing matter," he huffed. "And *you,*" he said to Ascensión in an imperious tone, "should not be calling your boss by her first name." He looked around at the other workers. "None of you should. To you she is *señora* Pursglove." He looked at Yoolie as if he expected her to thank him for his chivalry on her behalf even though he'd butchered her last name which was, in fact, difficult to pronounce in Spanish.

Yoolie had a strong desire to tell him to shove it in his pie hole, but knowing what a bad idea this would be even if she could figure out how to translate that particular West Virginia-ism, she instead looked down at her clipboard and began doodling as if she were jotting down some notes. "It's fine, Alejandro," she said without looking up from her clipboard. She doodled for a few moments while considering how to handle the awkward dynamic that she knew had now been created between herself and her workers by that idiot Alejandro. She decided to make a spur-of-the-moment decision. She looked up from her clipboard and took Ascención aside. When they were out of earshot of the others she said, "As of this moment I'm promoting you to foreman if you want the position. It will involve a substantial pay raise and more responsibility, though frankly I've often seen you take a foreman's responsibility in the past. But we can discuss the details in my office later. If you're interested. Are you interested?"

Ascención looked momentarily stunned, then he replied, "Uhhh…yes."

"Good. I need you to start right now."

"Of course, whatever you need me to do, Yool…" Ascención glanced over at Alejandro. "…*señora*, uh…"

"Oh, cut it out, Ascención. Just go ahead and get that crew on the generator. The engineers will be hanging around, as well."

"Yes, okay. And thank you…" Ascensión glanced again at Alejandro. "…Yoolie."

"One more thing," said Yoolie. "You'll need to get yourself a car. A jeep, probably, or an all-terrain."

"I can get one," said Ascensión.

"Tell you what," said Yoolie, looking around then switching to English. "There are a couple of used four-by-fours in the fleet. They're still in pretty good condition, maybe a little rust along the bottom."

"Yes, I know those trucks," said Ascensión. "I've driven them."

"ENEL is going to sell them off or scrap them in a couple of weeks and replace them with Toyotas. I'll arrange to sell one to you. Maybe I can even finagle them into letting me give you one. I'll see."

"*Finagle?*"

"Oh, finagle means, uh…"

"*Negociar?*"

"That's right," said Yoolie. "But kind of…" She held her hand out palm down and did a *maybe, maybe not* motion.

Ascensión laughed. "Okay, now I know a new word. Thank you, Yoolie."

"You're welcome."

"Wait, Yoolie," said Ascensión as Yoolie turned to leave. She turned back to him. "Is this Jaime's fault?"

Yoolie pulled in a deep breath then blew it out. "I doubt it. It looks like the wires are blown again, but what's been making them blow in the first place? There's got to be something else wrong."

"Like we were saying on Friday."

"Right. Somebody has to go in and take the whole damn thing apart, turbine, coupling, cylinders, everything, while we keep the generator running with...rubber bands or chewing gum, or something."

"Don't worry, Yoolie, we will get the generator running again. But what about Jaime? He's not in trouble, then?"

Yoolie sighed again. "No, Jaime's not in trouble. I am."

They returned to where the workers and engineers still stood and Yoolie announced that Ascensión was going to start immediately putting together a crew to work on the generator. "You all only have an hour or so left, but maybe a few of you can hang around here until the end of the shift and give him a hand rigging something together so we can get the electricity back on in León." Two of the men raised their hands to volunteer. She nodded at them. "Mario? Albin?"

"Sí..." Both men glanced at Alejandro, who stood scowling, then finished with, "*señora...*"

Yoolie made a horizontal cutting motion with one hand. "Yoolie," she said. "Just Yoolie, okay?"

As Yoolie and a few of the engineers walked up to the generator to have another look Alejandro sidled up next to her and said, "You should not allow those men to address you that way."

Yoolie looked up at the useless generator and began drumming her pen against her clipboard. "It's fine, Alejandro," she said in a flat tone without looking at him. "But have a look at that damned volcano, would you?"

***

Jaime felt better after Ascensión's call telling him that he wasn't in trouble over the generator. Still, he was less cheerful than usual as he rode the bus to Momotombo holding onto the two *La Unión* shopping bags of clothes and things that Violeta had ordered him to give to Lupe at work. It would be a chore toting the bags up the hill from the front gate to Yoolie's office. Jaime generally disliked physical exertion of any kind and he had already hauled the bags from the house to the bus stop.

But more troubling to Jaime than the thought of having to haul the bags yet again was the thought of having to be the one to give them to Lupe. Jaime imagined walking into Yoolie's office. (He likewise had no desire to have to face Yoolie, in case she might, in spite of Ascensión's assurance, still think that he was somehow to blame for the problem with the generator). He could see Lupe looking up from her desk in bewilderment as he walked in and then set at her feet the *La Unión* bags that she had brought home, now returned to her filled with her own belongings. True, it was Lupe who had run away from home. Still, she was bound to feel hurt. He pictured the sad look on her face. Poor Lupe. Jaime hoped she would not think that it was his idea to kick her belongings out of the house. He hoped maybe Lupe wouldn't show up at work today after all.

Jaime breathed a sigh of relief when he found neither Lupe nor Yoolie in Yoolie's office. At first he thought that Lupe must have stayed home from work again, but then he spotted her backpack hanging on a hook behind her desk. She must have stepped out, but she might be back soon, any minute, as might Yoolie. Jaime set down the bags by Lupe's desk. He wondered if he should leave a note, decided against it, and hurried out of the office and back down the hill to the machine shack. He clocked in for work and then, after looking around to make sure that he'd caught no one's eye, he sauntered off to sit behind a storage shed to rest for a little minute or two.

***

Lupe noticed the *La Unión* bags as soon she returned to her desk after having accompanied a pair of ENEL officials from to the site of the broken generator. The two men appeared to be in a bad mood, but not so bad that one of them didn't remark how pretty she looked in the company uniform while the other provided the punchline that she'd look even prettier out of uniform. When Lupe neglected to giggle or even smile and made a point of flashing the wedding band still on her finger the man added, "Of course, I meant you'd look prettier wearing a nice dress, *señora*."

But what did Lupe care what nonsense those stupid suits—as Yoolie referred to them—spouted? Surely they had other things on their minds and so did Lupe. It must have been Ascensión who dropped off these bags filled with her clothes and a few other things. Fine. She would need them, after all. But still. It was over with Ascensión and his witchy mother and sister and his overbearing family whom he'd chosen over her, and she was never again going back to that house, but still. And if after having spent the night alone on the old couch at *Las Sonrisas* she had woken up this morning feeling somewhat differently than she had the day before in the heat of her anger at her husband, well, it wasn't as if she were expecting him to run from his family and rush to her, take her in his arms, tell her that he would never let her go, that he'd do anything, anything, anything...but still. But still she hadn't been expecting him to toss her things as if they were trash into those *La Unión* shopping bags. The bags that she had brought home and that she and Ascensión had happily carried into the house together along with little Pablito, happily until his mother grabbed away their happiness and forbade them to be happy like she always did. And Ascensión had allowed her to, like he always did.

But still, Lupe had seen him off in the distance when she dropped off the suits at the generator site and she thought he had looked over and seen her, too. She thought he had smiled at her. She had smiled back. But that would have been after he'd left the bags of her things and before she found them. She felt a great, hollow ache ballooning to fill up her whole chest, making it hard to breathe. She felt sick to her stomach.

She reached into her backpack and retrieved a handful of the cornflakes that she had brought along for lunch. She threw the dry cornflakes into her mouth. Fine. She had made her decision and Ascensión had made his. She now had to accept that it would take her some time to get used to the new life she'd stepped into. Bicycled into. She riffled absently through the bags: clothes, mostly; shoes, some hair clips, her make-up, her soap. No note of any kind. But then, why would she think he might have left her a note? What did she think he might want to say to her while ridding every material memory of her from his life? No, there was no need for a note. The lack of a note was a message in itself. In one of the bags she felt something round wrapped in a cloth. She pulled it out and uncovered a small glass snow globe in the center of which was the word LOVE formed in block letters, red on the front, blue and green on the sides, the letters forming a block with the L and O sitting on top of the V and E, and the O slanted away from the L. It was a replica of a famous sculpture in downtown Philadelphia that had so delighted her and Ascensión when they'd seen it on their first visit to Center City, as the locals called that part of Philadelphia. Lupe recalled how Ascensión had surprised her with the snow globe on the day they brought David home from the hospital. She remembered how they used to shake it for David when he was a few months old. How he'd giggle. She remembered wrapping the snow globe and packing it into their suitcase, their only memento of that life they'd left behind to return to this one. And since they'd returned to life with Ascensión's family in Krukrulitos the snow globe had stayed wrapped in its cloth in the back of a drawer. Until now, when Ascensión returned it to her, this souvenir of their once-upon-a-time love and happiness. Tears rolled down her cheeks as she re-wrapped the globe and placed it gently back into the bag. If she still wasn't yet exactly sure where her heart was moored, she at least knew where Ascensión's was: in Krukrulitos with his terrible mother.

***

Ascensión had intended to call Lupe at work as soon as possible, but the possibility didn't materialize until the day was over. He and his crew had worked all day on the generator, even donning their weatherized gear to work through the afternoon rains. They still weren't sure why the generator had blown, but a couple of the engineers suspected that the problem might be in the turbine. Or one of the components that drove the turbine. Yoolie had even pressed *señor* Alejandro to run a scan of the volcano's subterranean activity, but of course *señor* Alejandro did not like being pressed, probably least of all, Ascensión guessed, by a big American *chelita,* as a group of the workers once overheard Alejandro refer to Yoolie behind her back.

No matter, they'd gotten the generator up and running again. It seemed to Ascensión that whatever was ailing this powerful machine was like some mischievous invisible imp that came when the mood struck it, did its damage, then disappeared without leaving a trace. Maybe the problem, whatever it was, had been taken care of with today's repair. Now Ascensión had his own problem to take care of.

He had hoped to meet up with Lupe on the bus back from Momotombo, just as they used to. Maybe, as Jaime had suggested, after having had a night to herself to cool down, maybe even to miss him, maybe Lupe would at least talk to him. No, *listen* to him, that's what he needed, for her to listen to him. He was bursting to tell her about the drama with the generator. But of course she already knew about the generator, Ascensión had even caught a glimpse of her bringing those corporate bigshots from the *Empresa* to the generator site. He had smiled at her and swore he saw her smile back. He couldn't wait to tell her about his promotion, the pay raise he would be getting, starting today already. He couldn't wait to tell her that he was going to get a truck. Mostly he wanted to tell her that he was moving from Krukrulitos, joining her in León, they would rent an apartment together, start their life over the way they should have started it when they'd returned from the United States. Of course back then they had needed to live with the family for a while, it had been necessary at first, especially before they had found their jobs at Momotombo. But now it was different, now was the time for them to move out together, as Jaime had made clear to him. But of course they'd need to stay with his family for a just little while yet until they found an apartment. Hopefully he could talk Lupe into staying in Krukrulitos just a little while longer. Maybe he could even put up a divider in their bedroom as Yoolie had suggested.

Except that he'd have to ask his parents first. He'd have to ask them if he could put a divider in the room dividing his and Lupe's space from theirs. His father would snort and wave off his plan as some sort of American nonsense. Xiomara would roll her eyes and snigger. His grandfather Mauricio would smile. And his mother…he didn't want to think about how his mother would react. Well, that wasn't important. He and Lupe would have their truck and find their apartment soon. He couldn't wait to tell her.

When he arrived at the bus stop she wasn't there. There was the usual crowd of workers returning home for the day, but Lupe wasn't among them.

"*Oye, maje*," said Jaime, coming up behind him. "You looking for someone?"

"Lupe," said Ascensión. "I don't see her here." He looked around him again.

"Oh, yeah." Jaime looked around him again. "I don't see her here either. Maybe she took an earlier bus. Or maybe she's waiting for the later bus. Or maybe Yoolie is driving her home."

"Yoolie? Why would Yoolie drive her home?"

"Maybe because otherwise Lupe would have to carry those bags. They are a little heavy."

"Bags? What bags? What are you talking about, Jaime?"

"You know, those bags full of her clothes and things that your mother packed for you to take to her this morning."

"But...I didn't take those fucking bags!"

"Well..."

"Well, what, Jaime?"

"Your *mamita*, she made *me* take them."

"*What?*"

"She *made* me, *maje*, you know nobody says no to Violeta, and I had to haul them all the way to the bus stop, then all the way up the hill to Yoolie's office, and I had to hold them on my lap the whole way on the bus, too."

"What did Lupe say when you brought them to her?"

"Nothing, *maje*, she was out of the office."

"So you just...left them there?"

"Yeah, I just left them there. What else could I do?"

"*Mierda*," Ascensión muttered.

"Sorry, *hombre*. What else could I do?"

"You could have..." Ascensión sighed. "I don't know. I have to call Lupe."

***

At that moment Yoolie was in fact driving Lupe and her bags home, or to her home such as it was, the couch in the room at *Las Sonrisas*. Although today had been a long, stressful and exhausting day—or maybe because it had been—Yoolie had a strong desire to see Cristela and to be with her for a while. What she really yearned for was to lie silently in the consolation of Cristela's arms. It had been a hard day. Maybe she'd spend the night.

Driving Lupe home had been Yoolie's excuse to see Cristela. Or maybe seeing Cristela had been her excuse to drive Lupe. In any case, here she was driving poor Lupe laden with her sad paper shopping bags full of her things that were left for her without a word. But when would Ascensión have left them? As far as Yoolie knew, he was out at the generator for most of the day, as was Yoolie herself. Well, somehow the bags had shown up at Lupe's desk. "They're my things," was all Lupe had said about them. After work she had insisted that she didn't need a ride home, that she would take the bus back to León, and only relented when Yoolie told her that she needed to drive into León, anyway. That was true. She needed to see Cristela.

Though Lupe sat next to her in the passenger seat, Yoolie kept her eyes straight ahead on the road. "I don't know where you're going to keep those bags at *Las Sonrisas*," she said. She considered a moment, then added, "Maybe there's room in one of the kitchen cupboards."

"There's not much of value," said Lupe. "Some clothes. Some shoes."

In this country people fight over clothes and shoes, Yoolie thought, but kept silent.

"Do you think Cristela might know someone in León with a room to let?" asked Lupe.

"You can ask her," said Yoolie.

"A place close to *Las Sonrisas* would be nice. I want to work there on my days off."

"Ummm," said Yoolie.

"And I want to thank you, Yoolie, for bringing me to *Las Sonrisas*. I feel like being there...being around those children, taking care of Pablito..." Here Lupe smiled, "or Hernandito...I feel like this saved my life. And will continue to save my life. I yearn to be around these children. I wish I could work with them every day."

"Ummm," said Yoolie.

"And it's thanks to you," said Lupe.

"Ummm," said Yoolie. *Yep, thanks to me,* she thought. *I created this situation, and however it plays out, I own it.*

Lupe's phone began ringing. She glanced at the screen then pressed the "sleep" button to cut off the ringing and send the call to voicemail. A few moments later the phone rang again. She again cut off the call. When the phone began ringing a third time Lupe pressed the "mute" button.

"Sounds like somebody is trying to get ahold of you," said Yoolie.

"Yes," Lupe sighed. "Although I don't know why." She glanced again at the screen of her now silently ringing phone, sighed again, and answered. "I can't talk," she said, "I'm with Yoolie."

"What, you're still at work?" said Ascensión.

"I'm sorry, I can't talk right now."

"But when can you talk to me?"

"I have to go now."

"I need to talk to you, Lupe. Will you call me back as soon as you can?"

Lupe hesitated a moment. "No. Good-bye."

Lupe was determined not to cry in front of Yoolie so she stared straight ahead in silence. Yoolie, for her part, was happy to stay out of the details of whatever conversation Lupe had used Yoolie as an excuse to get out of. They drove the rest of the way to León in silence while Ascensión rode the bus back to Krukrulitos also in silence, his plans now coalesced into an indistinct, greyish blob that settled like a weight on his heart.

After dinner that night, while some of the family members from the nearby houses sat or stood around on Mauricio's patio watching television, Ascensión sat alone on the bench by the clothesline. Violeta stood by the edge of the patio, watching not the television but her son sitting off by himself again.

"*Madre cariñosa de Dios*," she said. "Look at that boy sitting off by himself again. And he hardly spoke two words to us at dinner."

"Give him time, Violeta," said one of the women. "He won't get over this in one day."

"Ernesto," Violeta said to her husband, who was intent upon what was happening on the television screen, "go down there and talk to our son."

Ernest looked over at his wife. "If he wanted to talk he wouldn't be off by himself," he said, then he turned back to the television.

"But he shouldn't be off by himself," said Violeta. "Someone should go talk to him."

"Someone should give him some peace and quiet," said Ernesto.

Xiomara lay in one of the hammocks, her two children snuggled on either side of her. "Jaime," she called to her husband, who was among the group in front of the television.

"What is it, *mi amor?*"

"Go down and talk to Ascensión."

"But he didn't want to talk to me today on the bus. And he didn't want to talk at dinner."

"He doesn't want to talk now," said Ernesto.

"I agree with Violeta and Xiomara," said one of the women. "One of you men should go and talk to him."

The woman's husband replied, "What, you think he's like you women who need to talk all the time?" His remark drew a laugh from the other men.

"It's not funny, Rodrigo," huffed his wife.

140

"Who says it's funny?" said Rodrigo.

"She's right," added another woman, "it's no laughing matter."

"Nobody's laughing," added another of the men. "We're just talking, you know, talking?" With his hands he made a gesture of two talking mouths.

From there the patio burst into a cacophony of voices, each giving an opinion on the matter, while hands gesticulated for emphasis.

Jaime hauled himself up from his chair. "*Calma, calma,* everybody. I'll go down and talk to him."

"Wait, maybe I should go," said Violeta.

"Better if Jaime goes," said Ernesto.

The group nodded and murmured their assent at the idea. "Yes," they said among themselves, "better if Jaime goes."

"Bring him a beer," one of the men suggested.

"Yes, he'll feel better with a beer," agreed another.

"No," said Violeta. "He mustn't turn to drinking over this woman."

"Just one won't kill the boy." Everyone turned to old Mauricio. He waved towards the kitchen. "Get him a beer, Jaime. But only one."

Jaime headed down the slope to the bench by the clothesline with two beers in his hands. He sat down next to Ascensión. "Here, *maje,*" he said, handing Ascensión one of the beers. Ascensión shook his head. In the shadowy glow cast by the yard lights Jaime could see that Ascensión had been crying. "Have a little drink. *Abuelito's* orders," he chuckled. He nudged the beer at Ascensión. "Just one, though." Ascensión took the beer. The men drank in silence for a few moments.

Ascensión sniffled and wiped his eyes with the back of his arm. "How did all this happen to Lupe and me?"

"Things happen," said Jaime. "Things go wrong. Then you fix them. Like the generator today."

Ascensión laughed a little in spite of himself at Jaime's comparison, but then he said. "Yes. Like the generator."

"Sure," Jaime continued. "Just like that generator. People, relationships…a lot of moving parts, you know?" He rotated his hands in opposite directions in imitation of an engine.

"I no more know how to fix what's wrong between Lupe and me than I know how to fix what's wrong with that generator."

"So you try this and that," said Jaime.

"How can I try anything when she won't even talk to me?"

"Maybe not today. But she will." Jaime took a drink of his beer and considered a moment. "You know what, *maje*? Don't call her anymore. Go see her. Is she still staying at that orphanage in León?"

"It's not really an orphanage, it's…well, I don't know if she's still there. I don't know where she is."

"So you should go there and find out. If she's not there they will at least know where she is."

"Right, right," said Ascensión. "I'll go there. I'll call there in the morning and ask if she's there. Then I can go after work."

"Or if you're careful, maybe you can run into her at work. Or at the bus stop. At the bus stop would be better than at work."

"Yes, maybe," said Ascensión. "But I have to be careful."

"Ummm," Jaime agreed. "I know. You could try sending her an email explaining everything."

"What if she deletes it?"

"What about leaving a note for her on her desk? You could give it to Nico and have him drop it off."

"What if she rips it up when she realizes it's from me?"

"Then you leave her another one. Leave her one every day. She'll eventually open it. You'll see. Or wait. Don't just leave her a note. Give her a present. A nice one. Something to make up for those bags of her clothes you left her."

"*You* left her!"

"Hey, it wasn't my fault, *maje*. I told you, your *mamita* made me do it."

"Whatever," said Ascensión.

"But you can make it right. Give Lupe a nice present. Something she'd really like. Maybe something she really wants. Something that would make her happy."

Ascensión sighed. "There's only one thing in the world Lupe really wants that would make her happy. And that's not..." Ascensión smacked his head. "*¡Vaya!*"

"What?"

"Of course!" Now he smacked his knee. "Why didn't I think of this sooner?"

"What?"

"I have it!" Ascensión put down his beer and grabbed Jaime by the shoulders. He planted a kiss on his bewildered brother-in-law's mouth. "You're a genius, *maje!*"

The relatives had been watching Jaime and Ascensión from the patio, trying to decipher the substance of their conversation. There was a gasp when Ascensión grabbed Jaime by the shoulders and kissed him full on the lips. As Jaime trekked back up the slope the group stood in suspense, then crowded around him when he arrived at the patio.

"I don't know," Jaime replied to their barrage of questions. "He says he needs to make a phone call."

Part Two

The Americans

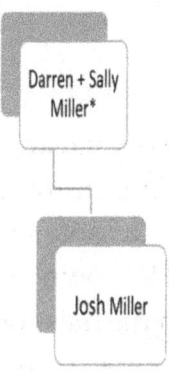

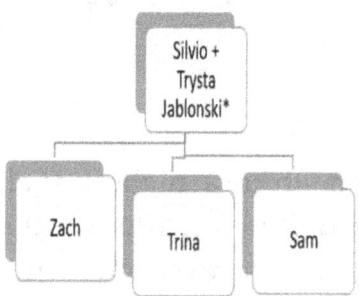

*Trysta divorces Silvio. Trysta marries Darren. Silvio meets Sally, they fall in love and marry.

*Darren divorces Sally. Darren marries Trysta.

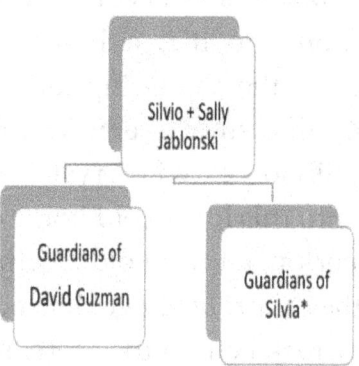

** Trysta divorces Darren. *Trysta is the mother of Silvia.

Chapter Ten

It was nine-thirty at night and Sally Jablonski was exhausted. And hot. Married to a master of residential plumbing, heating, and cooling, and here she was in the middle of a hot summer sweltering to death in her own residence. Her own chaotic residence. She stood in the family room taking in the mess of toys, books, puzzles, sports equipment, ballet shoes, cups, dishes, not to mention a bottle, a binky, a blankey, and other assorted evidence of the three-ring kid circus that life around here had devolved into since she, Silvio, their blended family of his kids, her kid, Silvio's ex-wife Trysta's baby, and their little Nicaraguan moved into this lovely old home on this lovely old street in lovely old Somerton, a lovely old Northeast Philadelphia neighborhood which they'd probably get kicked out of if anybody could see the unholy wreck behind the pretty stained wood front door with the cut-glass window that Silvio had installed last week.

At least the babies David and Silvia were asleep, finally, but the little kids were still out back running around and twelve-year-old Zach was up in his room, hopefully not brooding.

Geez, what little slobs Silvio's three kids were. Not that her son Josh was a whole lot better these days. Since they'd moved in with Silvio's wild brood he'd gotten less neat and more rough-and-tumble, which was, Sally surmised, probably a good thing, Josh having always been such a shy, quiet little guy. And now that

146

David had started toddling—he'd found his feet the day after his first birthday— there was no doubt he'd soon be rolling along with the rest of them. Sally smiled. David was such a little doll. An easy-going baby, good-natured like his daddy Ascensión—he'd likely grow up to be just as charming—and sweet and affectionate like his mother Lupe. He was also gifted with Lupe's wide, gorgeous brown eyes.

Poor little guy, thought Sally, having been separated from his parents like that. But on the other hand, *he* actually seemed none the worse for wear. The other kids doted on David—passed him around like a little football—and she could see that he was developing a special attachment to eight-month-old Silvia, Trysta's fatherless daughter whom Trysta had left in Sally and Silvio's care when she took off to find herself.

So no, it wasn't David who was suffering. It was rather poor Lupe and Ascensión, down there in the jungle, waiting for a work visa for Ascensión so that Silvio could hire him on at his business, Quick and Reliable Plumbing, with Lupe tagging along on a spousal visa. But in the meantime there they were without their child, and here she was with their child and five more besides and about going crazy. Well, it was what it was.

Sally decided to take a quick swipe at straightening up before Silvio got home, but after picking up a bowl and staring into the dried cereal stuck to the bottom she ran her arm cross her damp forehead and muttered, "Why the hell am *I* doing this?" She crossed the hallway to the foot of the stairs and called up, "Yo, Zach!"

She heard a door open. "What?"

"Come on down. You guys have got to pick up your stuff before your dad gets home."

"It's not my stuff," Zach called down.

"It's not my stuff, either," Sally called up, then she heard the bedroom door close again.

At that moment the back door slammed open and Sally heard the tramping of feet amid shrieks of laughter. A moment later her seven-year-old son Josh came running into the room followed by his stepsisters, ten-year-old Trina and almost-eight-year-old Sam, the three of them breathless and sweaty.

"Mom, we're thirsty!" cried Josh.

"We're thirsty, Mom," cried Sam. "We want some ice-cold lemonade!"

Sally sighed and headed for the kitchen followed by her bleating little flock.

"I'm *hot*," whined Trina, tilting her head and slumping her shoulders in a pose of pre-teenage long-suffering before posting herself in front of the fan whirring in a corner of the kitchen so that the breeze blew directly into her face.

"Okay, you know what?" said Sally, "You know where the lemonade is and you know where the ice is and you know where the cups are."

"But I can't reach the cups," said Josh.

"Trina," said Sally, "get cups for Josh and Sam."

"*Fine,*" Trina huffed as she moved away from the fan then swung open the cabinet door. "Mom, there are no clean cups left!"

Sally felt a ping of irritation that was overruled by the warm squeeze she felt in her heart each time Silvio's children called her "Mom." They might be a pack of wild slobbering puppies, but there was no denying that Trina, Sam, and underneath his cool exterior Zach, too, were likewise friendly and affectionate slobbering little puppies. But boy, could they use some housebreaking. Sally pulled from a cupboard three paper cups which she lined up on the kitchen counter then filled with ice and lemonade.

As Sally handed around the cups of lemonade she said, "There are no clean cups because half the cups in this house are sitting around the family room in front of the TV. Here, drink up fast then march yourselves into the family room and put away your stuff."

"But we can't do it now," said Trina. "It's too late. And it's too hot. And it's bedtime."

"Yeah," said Sam, breathless from her long pull of lemonade, "it's time for you to put us to bed."

"Oh, for crying out loud," said Sally.

"Well, it *is*," said Trina, the soul of young self-righteousness. "It's way past our bedtime. It's almost ten o'clock. We're *tired*."

"You need to put us to *bed*, Mom," said Sam.

"Okay," said Sally. "Here's the deal. Trina, you just turned ten. From now on it's your job to put yourself and Sam to bed."

"*What?*" Trina shrieked.

"That's right," said Sally. "From now on that's your job. And you both take a shower first, you hear? You're as sweaty as a bunch of…soccer balls."

The children laughed and Josh said, "*Mo*-om, soccer balls aren't sweaty!"

"They are when they've been rolling up and down the yard like you guys. Now upstairs, girls. Showers and bed. You can turn on the fan in your room and I'll be up to tuck you in pretty soon. And for goodness' sake, be quiet, don't wake the babies."

"Am I gonna get paid?" said Trina.

"*Paid?*" said Sally.

"For putting Sam to bed."

"If Trina gets paid then I want to get paid!" cried Sam.

"No fair!" cried Trina. "Why does Sam get paid if I have to do all the work?"

"For *cooperating*," Sam replied.

Sally pushed back her hair with both hands. "Look, we'll talk about payment plans tomorrow, okay?"

"What about me, Mom?" said Josh.

"Zach can put you to bed."

Josh gave a whoop of joy as Zach entered the kitchen. "I have to *what?*"

"Put me to bed," said Josh, running up to his stepbrother and hugging him around the waist.

"It would be a big help to me, Zach," said Sally.

"Yay," said Josh, tugging Zach left and right while Zach laughed in spite of himself.

"So could you please take him up, give him a shower—or in the downstairs bathroom, I don't care—and get him into his bed? Please."

"*Fine,*" Zach sighed. "At least it will be better than putting the girls to bed like Trysta used to make me do."

"*Trysta?*" said Sally. "What happened to 'Mom?'"

"You're his mom, now," said Josh, pulling Zach out of the kitchen. "C'mon, Zach." He stood on his tiptoes and whispered into Zach's ear, but loudly enough that Sally could hear, "After my shower you and me can play some video games in my room."

Sally purposely ignored what she heard but called After Zach, "She's still your mom, too, you know." Nonetheless she felt that same warm squeeze and not a little satisfaction.

After a moment of whispers and hushed giggling the children reappeared in the kitchen and, Josh included, shouted in unison, "Okay, Sally!" Then they ran off and up the stairs laughing.

"What?" Sally called after them, laughing. She shook her head, still chuckling. She supposed there were worse things in the world than having to pick up after a pack of slobby but good kids who called her "Mom." Or at least most of the time. Even little Silvia had started calling her "Ma." The only exception was David, who called her "Didi." He tended to call everybody "Didi" these days. Of course this had been Sally's doing. She'd always referred to herself in front of him as *"Tia* Sally," shortened to *"Tia,"* Spanish for aunt. "Didi" in baby talk. Now Sally was Didi, Silvio was Didi, his foster siblings were Didi, everybody was Didi. Except that more recently he had started from time to time calling her

"Mama," Silvio "Dada," and the other family members by his new babyfied version of their names. Sally often showed David pictures on her phone of his parents and referred to them as "*mamá*" and "*papá*." She tried Facetiming Lupe and Ascensión a few times to show David his "*mamá*" and "*papá*" in person, but the connection was always so bad that the images and sounds barely made sense to Sally let alone the baby. Well, she was probably just confusing the poor kid with all this "*mamá*" and "*papá*" and "Didi."

But then how would it be for David when his parents finally returned? *If* they returned. Sally immediately whisked that thought out of her mind. Of course they would return. Of course they would. And in the meantime it was what it was and she was doing what she could.

She began gathering up the dirty dishes in the family room. She wished Silvio didn't have to work so late. But of course all those long hours were what brought in the money to pay for this nice big house and to support their nice...Sally sighed... *big* family. And it wasn't like she had to work anymore, though she did kind of miss her old job at Zarnecki and Young, especially her old boss and wonderful friend Joanne. She needed to call Joanne. It had been a while. Still, what in the world would she do without Joanne, who'd become like a second mother to her? Or, for that matter, what would she do without her own mother, who, never mind her overly religious schtick and her sometimes maddening propensity for high-octane smother-mothering, would be there for Sally, Silvio and the kids at the drop of a nickel to deliver whatever they happened to need at the moment, whether it was groceries, babysitting, some household help, or sometimes just some high-octane smother-mothering?

And then there was Silvio's big, cheerful Italian mother, who since their marriage had become like a third mother to Sally. And heck, even Trysta's mother stepped up to the plate to lend a hand and was always happy for any occasion to see her grandchildren.

Or maybe for any occasion to get away from the Gunnery Sergeant, as Sally and Silvio had christened the ex-Marine bruiser she was married to, Trysta's father. No wonder Trysta became so adept at playing the damsel in distress, at wrapping men around her little finger. She must have gotten oodles of training growing up and watching her mother, who reminded Sally of an aging Barbie doll, use her womanly wiles to negotiate her due as her husband's subject and protectorate.

But even Trysta's father, angry and bewildered in his inability to accept that his Barbie-doll daughter had turned into a goddamn dyke, as he described the tragic situation, appeared to love Trysta's children, and even her children's stepsiblings, in his own drill-sergeant kind of way. In fact Sally decided that she wouldn't mind if Trysta's drill-sergeant father were here at this moment to whip her little troops into some action on a clean-up operation of this disastrous family room.

And then there was her ex-husband Darren. Poor Darren. He seemed kind of lost at sea these days. Still, Sally had to give him credit. His child support payments for Josh now arrived on time and to the dime, and not only did he never miss a visitation with their son, but at least every other week he showed up for dinner with pizza and ice cream in tow for the whole family. In truth, Sally wished Darren wouldn't hang around quite so much or make himself quite so at home, but then Darren never did things in half-measures, and besides, where else did the guy have to go? Fortunately Silvio was being a good sport about Darren—so far—but then it didn't hurt that Darren made himself available for babysitting duty as well.

It positively amazed Sally to see how good Darren had become at handling Trysta's kids. The girls called him "Daddy Darren" and halfway minded him and he and Zach peacefully co-existed. He'd even become an old hand with the babies. Whoever would have thought Darren Miller would end up being so good with kids? Or that he'd become such a responsible father? All it took for this great transformation, Sally mused, was losing his job, his home, two marriages, his have-it-all fever dreams, and escaping by the skin of his teeth from Angelo Barbieri, the South Philadelphia salvage yard thug—and, coincidentally, a distant ex-relative of Silvio by former marriage—who'd roped Darren by the nose into a real-estate money-laundering scheme. Darren was lucky the FBI valued him more as an informant than as a catch or he'd now be sitting in prison next to Barbieri. Maybe that's why Darren liked to spend so much time at Sally and Silvio's house. Maybe even with Barbieri behind bars he still felt jittery being alone.

In any case Darren's old cocky self-centeredness—or was it self-centered cockiness?—had been knocked down a good dozen pegs from when he was a young star shooting up through the corporate galaxy, constructing fabulous properties in his mind out on the Philadelphia Main Line and on beaches in Mexico, grabbing what he wanted, leaving behind what he no longer did. To think of the bitter tears Sally had cried over Darren after he left her for the bosomy blonde sexpot of a receptionist who in turn left her husband for Darren, said sexpot being one Trysta Jablonski and her husband being Silvio Jablonski, the plumber who showed up at Sally's house one day to fix her broken toilet.

Now Sally could smile when she remembered the day she met Silvio. But at the time it had felt like the worst day of her life. She had recently gone from being the happily married wife of an up-and-coming broker with a high-end Philadelphia commercial real estate firm to a financially and emotionally struggling single mother living in a cardboard shoebox of a condo on the Roosevelt Boulevard in Northeast Philly with a sad little boy and a broken toilet. Brimming with woe and resentment, she had called some plumbing outfit she'd found online called Quick and Reliable, then she went off like a volcano on the plumber when he handed her what she considered to be an exorbitant bill for the job. The plumber, one Silvio Jablonski, who gave off a vibe of being not a little woeful and resentful himself, nonetheless made right the situation in regard to the bill. In fact, he made the situation more than right. After they came to the shocking—and shockingly humiliating—realization that their ex-spouses were married to each other, Silvio tore up the bill, stating that they were exes-in-law and he wasn't required to bill family.

How weird that day had been. That was also the day that she met her Nicaraguan neighbors—undocumented Nicaraguan neighbors, she'd soon find out—Lupe and Ascensión Guzman and their baby David. She'd had to knock on her neighbors' door to ask to use their toilet while she waited for the plumber. Sally chuckled at the memory. Maybe *that* hadn't been awkward and weird. And yet how much weirder had her life become since that day. Weirder and exponentially better. Since then she and Silvio had fallen in love and married. Silvio had inherited Quick and Reliable from his Uncle Bud. She and Silvio had befriended Ascensión and Lupe and their lives became more and more involved, more and more intertwined, one favor begetting another, then another, then another, every action bringing an equal and opposite reaction, until they all landed in the office of Charleston Tilley, an immigration lawyer with a social conscience. It was Mr. Tilley who helped the Guzmans attain from a sympathetic judge a voluntary deportation grounded on Silvio's commitment to seek permanent labor certification for Ascensión. And she, Sally, had become mother to Ascensión's and Lupe's child. And to Trysta's child. And to Silvio's children. And her own child, her Joshua, was thriving in this big messy patchwork of a family. All from a broken toilet.

As for Darren, just as Sally's low fortunes began to ascend, Darren's began rolling downhill and likely hit bottom when Trysta, the heartbreaker who racked up more husbands, lovers, and kids than even a promiscuous Mary Poppins would know what to do with and for whom Darren had dumped his marriage to Sally, turned out to be a lesbian in hetero-sexpot's clothing.

Upon making this self-revelation Trysta had subsequently shorn her long, luxurious blond locks and thrown off her body-hugging clothes. She now marched around in an army jacket, baggy thrift-store fatigues and Doc Martens while she pursued an IT degree. And probably other women.

"And me, I'm pursuing kids and dirty dishes," Sally mumbled.

She wondered if Darren would ever get married again. Now that he'd broken away from Angelo Barbieri and had managed to calm his financial troubles his new real estate management business seemed to be sprouting and apparently he was still doing some contract work for Highland and Erskerberg. So he had a little money in his pocket. And a nice loft out by Drexel, though at the moment he obviously preferred Sally and Silvio's insane asylum. Still, Sally guessed that he'd probably take up with a new lady one of these days. Once he'd recovered from his current state of PTSD. Who knew, maybe he'd even try for another round of marriage. Hopefully next time he'd choose a little more wisely than last time.

In retrospect, Sally ruminated as she grabbed the broom to sweep up a trail of crumbs from the kitchen floor, she and Darren had probably gotten married too young. He was just out of college and she was still a college student, soon-to-be college drop-out, soon-to-be pregnant college drop-out working as a bottom-of-the-rung office assistant. But then that was where her friendship with Joanne blossomed, so that was a good thing. But being shackled to a dead-end office job without a college degree wasn't such a great thing. But then it was Joanne who had talked her off a ledge a finity of times after Darren left her, and also Joanne who encouraged her—make that kicked her butt—to go back to school, which was good. But then she'd recently dropped out again after she'd acquired this big house and this houseful of kids. Who loved her. And each other. And who she loved and wouldn't trade for anything, even at moments like this.

"So quit bitching and count your goddamn blessings," she murmured to herself as she unloaded the clean dinner dishes from the dishwasher and loaded the dirty family room dishes.

She swung by the downstairs bathroom to splash some water on her face then headed back to the family room. She plopped down on the couch for a moment and once again surveyed the mess. *My kingdom,* she thought with a sigh. *I mean, my queendom.* Where to begin? She heard the patter of feet on the stairs and a few moments later there was Josh in his pajamas scampering towards her. When he reached the couch he took a little leap and landed on her lap.

"*Ooof,*" said Sally, wrapping her arms around him. "What, finished with your shower already?"

"Yep. Smell?" He put his damp hair close to her face.

"Ummm," said Sally, sniffing. "Smells clean, all right."

"The girls were gonna yell down the steps for you to come up and tuck us in, but I told them not to because they would wake the babies."

"You did good. Thanks, Honey."

"I told them I would come down and get you instead."

"You did extra good." She hugged him close and kissed his head. "Do you like our new house?"

"I *looooove* our new house. I hope we live here forever. Can we live here forever, Mom?"

"As long as you want, Babe."

Josh laid his head against his mother's chest and she stroked his hair. "I want to live here forever," he said. He yawned and closed his eyes.

"But hey, no falling asleep down here. Come on, let's go tuck everybody in."

"Will you do me first?"

"Sure, Babe."

Fifteen minutes later after everyone was kissed and tucked in for the night and the babies checked—both sleeping soundly so far, thank goodness—Sally returned downstairs. She wished Silvio were home. She wanted to go to bed herself but she also wanted to wait up for him. She returned to the family room, determined to straighten up at least a little before Silvio arrived home. She picked up a baby blanket and a stuffed dolphin. She looked at the items in her hand. The blanket needed to go into the wash and the dolphin was pretty grody, too. She wondered if she could throw this dolphin into the wash as well. She sat back down on the couch, dropped the blanket into her lap and studied the label on the stuffed dolphin. Yep, machine washable. Thank God for small favors. She looked around the room. What else needed to be gathered for the wash? She sat back and stretched out her legs. She'd get back to the family room in a minute.

"Hey."

Sally opened her eyes to see Silvio standing over her, smiling.

"Oh, geez," she said, sitting up, "did I fall asleep?"

"With your blankey and dolphin," he said.

Sally looked at the dolphin she still clutched and the blanket in her lap. "Oh, geez," she laughed.

Silvio sat down next to her and put an arm around her. "How was your day?" he asked, then kissed her forehead.

"Hot. And all this." She spread out her arm to the room. "How about you? How come you're so late?"

"A whole lot of evening calls. Air-conditioner emergencies. The heat, you know?"

Sally laughed. "As a matter of fact, I *do* know."

"Hey, yeah, I'm sorry. But our new A.C. unit finally arrived—I mean, this old house, we had to special order, I told you, right, about having to special order?"

"Yeah. The joys of an old house."

"It'll be like new when we're finished with it."

"I'll be happy with a working air conditioner, thank you."

"Right. Kevin and Jarrod will be over first thing tomorrow to install it. You'll be cool by noon."

"Hallelujah," said Sally. "I hope they can find their way to the basement through this mess."

"Don't worry about the mess. Speaking of which, the kids all asleep?"

"I guess. I don't hear any more noise," said Sally.

"How were they today?"

"Aw, they're good, Silvio, they really are. I just wish they wouldn't leave their stuff all over the place."

"Look, the problem is, they don't know where to put everything. We've only been here a couple months. We haven't even gotten all the boxes unpacked. Or the shelving up. We're nowhere near organized yet."

"Who's got time for organized? I'm happy to deliver clean clothes and food on the table. Oh, and then there's delivering everybody to their swimming lessons, and summer soccer, and summer dance lessons, and…all right, seriously, do they really need all this summer this and summer that all summer long?"

Silvio shrugged. "You tell me, Mom. The choice is yours."

Sally sighed. "So Kevin and Jarrod are coming with the A.C. tomorrow?"

"Yep. And I'm taking the day off to oversee."

Sally perked up. "You are? The whole day?"

"And the day after, too. And I'm taking the weekend off, too."

"The whole weekend?"

"I'll be yours for the whole forty-eight hours."

Sally wrapped her arms around him and kissed him then laid her head against his chest.

"I'll tell you what," said Silvio, stroking her hair, "How about if we see which relatives we can round up to come over on Saturday and help us organize?"

Sally sat up and she and Silvio disentangled. "Seriously?"

"Why not seriously?" said Silvio.

"That would be phenomenal. I think there's only one soccer game on Saturday. Maybe two. And Josh's tee-ball workshop."

"Okay, we'll sort out the tee-ball and the soccer and whatever else."

"We could try to get the Gunnery Sergeant over here to manage the operation."

"You mean Trysta's father?" said Silvio. "Huh, you pay a price with that guy."

"Well, yeah. But then, you get what you pay for, right?" said Sally.

"I guess," said Silvio. "But okay, I'll call the Gunnery Sergeant and Trysta's mom. And my mom, and my dad, if he doesn't have to work at the post office."

"And I'll call my mom. And maybe Joanne and her husband Ponti. And what about…never mind."

"Who?"

"Aw, never mind," said Sally.

"No, who? Darren?"

"Well, yeah, I was thinking Darren, but…"

"Hey, I don't care if Darren shows up. He practically lives here. Heck, you know Darren, he's likely to show up uninvited anyway like he always does. Only Trysta's father…" Silvio shook his head. "Putting Darren in the same room with the Gunnery Sergeant is like waving a red cape in front of a bull."

"Yeah, he still can't abide Darren," said Sally. "It's like he thinks Darren's somehow responsible for his daughter turning lesbian." Sally started laughing then Silvio joined in. "Aw geez, I don't know why that's funny," she said.

"I know," said Silvio, wiping his eyes. "How about we ask Darren to be in charge of taking the kids to their sports? And then we'll order out food for the workers and he can be in charge of picking it up."

"Perfect," said Sally.

"Stress level down?"

"Just dropped from critical to stable."

"Okay, then, tomorrow we can get to sending out the invitations to the weekend work party. But now…" Silvio stood and stretched. "I gotta go back out."

"What?" said Sally, also standing. "You gotta go back out? At this hour?"

"I'll only be twenty minutes, maybe less. Half-hour at most. Pavio called me just now on my cell. While I was on my way home."

"Pavio called you? The Pavio from Pavio's where we get our pizza?"

"Yeah. One time while I was waiting on our pizza he and I got to talking and I told him I ran a plumbing and heating business. He told me if he ever needed plumbing or heating he'd call. Turns out he wasn't just shooting the breeze. He said he thinks one of his refrigerators is acting fritzy. Which is serious for a pizzeria."

"Well, sure, but, I mean, he calls you at ten-forty-five at night? On your cell?"

Silvio shrugged. "He had my cell number from all our takeout orders. They were cleaning up and about to close when one of his guys noticed the temperature on the refrigerator had dropped. Then it went back up again. Then dropped again. Now it's back up again."

"Maybe the trouble is his thermometer," said Sally.

"Yeah, that's what I'm thinking. But I'll have a quick look. If it's serious, I'll have Kevin come out. He's on call."

"We better get some free pizza out of this," said Sally.

"Nah, I'll bill him good for it. Or maybe if it's nothing I won't. Sometimes you get more bang from the good will than from the buck."

"Whatever you say, Babe." Sally kissed him. "Just hurry back. Thinking about you going back out to work is making me feel exhausted."

"Hey, go to bed. Go now before one of the babies wakes up. I'll meet you there." He kissed her again. "Everything's cool now, right?"

"Right," said Sally. "Everything's..." She pushed back a sweaty lock of hair and chuckled. *"Not* cool. But Good. Hurry back."

After Silvio left Sally went upstairs and checked on the children, took a shower to cool off, then crawled into bed. Tomorrow Silvio would be home. And they'd have their air-conditioning back. Then everything *would* be cool, finally. On Saturday they'd tackle cleaning up and organizing with the help of whichever relatives they could wrangle into coming over and doling out some free labor. Just the thought of having Silvio and a few helping hands for the day made Sally feel calmer. Lighter. It was all good.

She had just dozed off when the jingle of her cell phone jolted her awake, her heart pounding, her brain scrolling through her mental rolodex of who could be calling at this hour, what terrible news was about to come crashing into her life. *Silvio,* she thought.

But the call wasn't from Silvio. Or his mother or his father or his sisters. Or her mother or her brothers. Still, Sally immediately recognized the number on the screen. León, Nicaragua, where it was two hours earlier. *Oh, no,* she thought.

When Silvio arrived home he found Sally sitting on the edge of the bed, looking at the phone still in her hand.

"What's wrong?" he said. He flipped on the light. "Why are you sitting on the...Sally, *what's wrong?"*

Sally looked up. "I'm going to Nicaragua."

Chapter Eleven

Charleston Tilley, Attorney-at-Law, leaned forward in his chair, propped his elbows on his desk and folded his hands. "What you're telling me, then, is that the two of you are planning on traveling with the Guzmans' baby to Nicaragua?"

"Yeah, that's right," said Silvio. "See, I can't let Sally go down there by herself." He played with Sally's fingers as he spoke, a habit of his that Charleston had noticed from the first day they showed up at his office, a pair of nervous working-class white kids, Silvio not much over thirty, Sally a few years younger, with a convoluted story about a couple of undocumented Nicaraguan immigrants with an American-born baby and on whose behalf Sally and Silvio came seeking his help.

Sally chuckled nervously. "I think Silvio was hoping I'd say, 'Hey, don't worry, I can go by myself,' heh, heh."

"No, come on," said Silvio. "I would never let you go by yourself."

"Aw, you know I'm just kidding, Babe, heh, heh." She patted his hand that was entwined in hers.

Silvio pulled in a deep breath. "Not that I'm crazy about going down there."

Sally turned to Silvio. "Me neither, but what else could I do? What else could I say? If you'd have heard Ascensión..."

"Yeah, I know, I know," said Silvio.

Sally turned back to Charleston. "I mean, if you could have heard him on the phone, begging me to bring him and Lupe their baby. He was practically crying. Maybe he was. It sounded like he was. He said Lupe was sad all the time. He was afraid that if Lupe couldn't hold David in her arms again she might..." Sally swallowed. "Die. Of a... broken heart." Sally sniffed.

Charleston pushed the box of Kleenex on his desk towards Sally. Though he had developed a familial fondness for these two good-hearted youngsters, damned if they didn't have a knack for stepping into any garden-variety scenario only to have the garden grow into a jungle of legal, logistical and emotional entanglements. "I'm awfully sorry to hear that," he said.

Sally reached for a Kleenex. "Thanks," she said.

"Okay," said Silvio, "so what do we need to do to go to Nicaragua?"

"What do you need to do?" asked Charleston.

"To get," said Silvio. "What do we need to get? You know, special papers, permission, whatever?"

"You don't need any extraordinary documentation to travel from the U.S. to Nicaragua as tourists. It's the same as if you were traveling anywhere else."

Sally and Silvio looked at each other. "We've never been anywhere else," said Sally.

"You know, with me being married and a father at nineteen, and all, and Sally at twenty-one."

"Of course, it's understandable. In any case, all you need is a passport."

"Huh, okay," said Silvio, "And are we allowed to just take David down there, or what?"

"Yes, you are David's guardians, so you are permitted to travel abroad with him just the same as if he were your own child. You'll need to get him a passport, too. A passport for David and passports for yourselves. With passports you can stay in

Nicaragua for ninety days. If you intended to stay longer than ninety days you would need a visa."

"Oh well, no, we weren't gonna stay that long," said Silvio.

"Just a week or ten days," said Sally.

"Passports, then. And plane tickets."

"Yeah, we knew about plane tickets," said Sally.

"A passport will take six to eight weeks to arrive."

"Six to eight *weeks?*" said Sally.

"Or you could pay extra to have them rushed in about two weeks."

"Yeah, well, we'll have them rushed, then," said Sally.

"Now wait a minute," said Silvio, letting go of Sally's hand and patting the air, "I don't know that we should be rushing this."

"What do you mean?" said Sally. "This is an *emergency.*"

"It's not exactly an *emergency,*" said Silvio.

"It is for Lupe and Ascensión! It would be for us if somebody took our kids away!"

"Aw, c'mon, Sal, I'm not saying I don't…I'm just saying maybe we need to think this through."

"Think *what* through?"

Silvio turned to Charleston, who was now sitting back in his chair, his head resting against one hand. "Okay, Mr. Tilly, how dangerous is it down there?"

Charleston sat up to answer but before he could speak Sally said, "Oh, is that what this is about? You're worried about it being too dangerous?"

"No, I'm not wor…" Silvio sighed. "Yeah, I guess I am." He took Sally's hand again. "Aren't you?"

"Yeah. I guess I kind of am, too."

"For tourists I don't believe that Nicaragua is especially dangerous," said Charleston. "As Central America goes."

"Oh," said Silvio. "So how dangerous it is? Say, North Philly at night?"

Charleston laughed. "Certainly not as dangerous as parts of North Philly at night."

"Maybe Northeast Philly at night?" said Sally.

"Northeast Philly's not *that* dangerous," said Silvio.

"That's what I meant," said Sally. "Not *that* dangerous."

Sally and Silvio looked at Charleston. "Use common sense, of course," he said. "Be aware of your surroundings. Don't give money to the beggars or they'll follow you like an army."

"Beggars?" said Sally and Silvio.

Charleston raised his hands, palms upwards, then folded them. "It's a very poor country."

"Yeah," Silvio muttered.

"People will offer their services left and right and expect to be tipped for it, so be prepared for that. And whatever you do, do *not* get involved in any kind of political activity in that country. Episodes of social unrest break out in the cities from time to time, protests, demonstrations. Steer clear of anything like that."

"Oh, yeah, we will," said Silvio.

"Yeah, we will," said Sally.

"And one more thing. It must be perfectly clear that you are bringing David to León for a visit. Lupe must understand this. She must accept that her son is an American citizen and you are his legal guardians and she cannot keep him there, no matter how hard it is for her to let him go again. Do you think this will be a problem?"

Silvio sighed. "Yeah, it probably will be a problem, but..." He shrugged. "If we bring David down there we're sure as heck not coming back without him. And you know Ascensión is a sensible guy."

"But what if Lupe and Ascensión *did* want their baby back? I mean, to live with them. Is there no way?"

"Oh no, an American child can be returned to their deported parents. But it's quite an involved process that requires collaboration between federal agencies and the consulate of the parents' country. And then there's the question of whether the parents can prove that they can provide materially for their child in a safe environment, considering the conditions that compelled them to leave their country in the first place. All the coordination would take some...Mrs. Jablonski, are you all right?"

Sally was sniffling again. "Yeah, I'm just...Lupe and Ascensión need to see their baby. That's all this is about."

Charleston nodded. "Of course."

"So you think we'll be okay down there?" said Silvio.

Charleston raised his hands again. "If you feel comfortable going, then—"

"I don't," Silvio interrupted. "But, you know..." He shrugged.

"Aw c'mon, Sil, let Mr. Tilley finish."

Sally nodded at Charleston, who smiled. "No problem," he said. "It's understandable that you'd have concerns, never having traveled there before."

"Or much of anywhere," said Silvio.

"This is true," said Sally.

Charleston smiled again. "Look, you speak considerable Spanish, which will definitely be an advantage."

"Yeah, we did have that language exchange going on with Lupe and Ascensión when they were here," said Sally. "We learned a lot from them. And then we took some classes."

"And we have a lot of Spanish-speaking customers," said Silvio. "I practice with them."

"That's a good thing," said Charleston. "And you'll find the Nicaraguans are friendly people, as Lupe and Ascensión are."

"Oh yeah, Lupe and Ascensión are real friendly," said Sally. "And they speak English pretty well, too."

"However I doubt you'll find many people among the general population who speak that much English. But with Lupe and Ascensión accompanying you and watching out for you, you should probably be fine. "

"You ever been?" said Silvio. "To Nicaragua?"

"As a matter of fact, I have. About, oh, fifteen years ago when my daughter was a medical student working there as part of a global health mission. I visited León, where the Guzmans are from. Also Granada, and some of the beaches, and the jungles, the volcanoes. Nicaragua is actually quite a beautiful country with a bounty of natural resources as well."

"No kidding?" said Sally. "I wonder why it's so poor, then."

"Yes, well, there's greed, government corruption and mismanagement, hoarding of wealth and power by the few. But again, even though Nicaragua is the second poorest Caribbean nation after Haiti, it isn't anywhere near as dangerous there as in some other countries. It's not along the South American drug route except for a strip along the east coast called Bluefields, which is nowhere near where you'll be, and even in Bluefields the crime rate is lower than in Philadelphia. So for tourists it is relatively safe there, even in the cities."

"Oh yeah?" said Silvio.

"Emphasize *relatively*," said Charleston. "As long as you're careful."

"Did you like it there? In Nicaragua?" asked Silvio.

"Oh, yes. I liked the country and the people and I had quite a good time. Even though folks on the street and in the marketplaces sometimes called me '*moreno*.'"

"*Moreno*?'" said Sally.

"Black man."

"Oh, you're kidding," said Sally. "Geez, how racist was that?"

"Not at all," said Charleston. "Hard as it would be to believe in this country that a Black person could be referred to by their skin color without offense, in Nicaragua race simply doesn't hold the same cultural weight as in other countries. No offense was intended and so I didn't take any." Charleston chuckled. "That is, once my daughter—whom the locals referred to as '*morenita*,' or 'Little Black Girl'—explained it all to me."

"Huh," said Silvio. "Well, that's different, anyway."

"It is," said Charleston. "And, by the way, you can be prepared to be called 'chele,' which means white man. Mrs. Jablonski, they may likewise refer to you as 'chela.'"

"White woman, I got it. Okay. So, how about the people who aren't Black and aren't white? You know, like the medium brown-skinned people? What are they called?"

Charleston laughed again. "I don't know that there is any word to designate the medium-brown skinned population. That being the skin tone of the majority, I suppose it's considered the baseline."

"So, is that why you went into immigration law?" said Sally. "After you visited Nicaragua?"

"Oh no. I've been in immigration law almost as long as I've been in family law. One time early in my career I took an immigration case, then I took another, and from there the cases cascaded. And so I became an immigration and family lawyer and have found much satisfaction and challenge in the work."

"Yeah, well, you're good at it," said Silvio.

"At both," said Sally.

"Immigration *and* family law, she means," said Silvio.

"Yeah, that's what I mean," said Sally.

"Thank you," said Charleston. "I do appreciate hearing that."

"You're welcome," said Sally. "And you know, we can never thank you enough for all you've done for us. And for Lupe and Ascensión." She reached for another Kleenex.

"This is true," said Silvio. He also reached for a Kleenex.

Charleston smiled. "You are quite welcome as well."

"So I guess we're gonna go get us some passports and plane tickets," said Silvio.

"I trust you'll be in contact with the Guzmans."

"Oh yeah, we always are," said Sally.

"And you also might want to pick up a travel guidebook," said Charleston. "And of course you'll bring along a Spanish dictionary."

"Yeah, we can do that, too," said Sally. "Then I guess we'll be all set."

"Uh, just one more thing," said Charleston. "What about your will?"

"Our...will?" said Sally.

"Yes. Your affairs."

"But..." Silvio swallowed hard. "You just said it's not all that dangerous where we're going."

Charleston folded his hands on his desk. "You've got..." Charleston paused for a mental calculation, "...six children now?"

"Yeah, we've got six now, heh, heh, keeps us hopping. Mostly keeps Sally hopping. With me working such long hours, and all." He cleared his throat nervously. "A will, huh?"

"Yes. Regardless of your trip to Nicaragua, you should be thinking about putting together a will. You do have some considerable assets now, after all."

"Yeah, well, we'll have to do that," said Silvio.

"Yeah, we will," said Sally. "Make a will."

"I can give you the name of an estate lawyer," said Charleston. "But there's one more thing you need to be giving some thought to, and that is naming a guardian for your children who will care for their physical and financial well-being in the unlikely case that anything should happen to you both."

"Oh, boy, yeah, we should take care of that," said Silvio.

"Is there anyone you know, perhaps a trusted relative, who would be willing to take on the role of raising your children for you in the event of...unforeseen circumstances?"

Sally and Silvio looked at each other. Silvio sighed. "I guess we might as well ask..."

"Darren," they said at the same time.

Chapter Twelve

The sun had returned to the sky and was already drying up the surfaces after a particularly light, short rain on this Saturday afternoon. Ascensión had missed most of the shower, which began in earnest after he boarded the bus at the Krukrulitos stop and had greatly abated by the time he stepped off the stop in downtown León not far from *Las Sonrisas*. His shirt was only slightly damp but the brief rain had left his hair in the mass of loose unruly curls that his hair fell into when even the least bit wet.

He stopped across the street from *Las Sonrisas*. He watched the children playing on the patio and the women supervising them. Lupe wasn't among them. He straightened his shirt and ran a hand through his hair. He hoped he looked good enough. He crossed the street and stepped onto the patio. The children stopped their games to look at him. Rafaela, who had been seated on a corner of the patio with a child on her lap, deposited the child on the ground and approached Ascensión.

"*Buenos tardes, señora,*" he said to Rafaela. "I'm Ascensión Guzman. Lupe's husband."

Rafaela's hand flew to her mouth. "Oh!" She gestured for him to wait there and hurried off the patio down the hallway into the kitchen. A moment later she returned followed by Cristela and also Maria, who was still holding a plate and a dish towel.

"*Señor* Guzman?" said Cristela.

"*Sí, señora,*" said Ascensión.

"I'm Lupe's friend Cristela," she said.

"*Mucho gusto,* Cristela," said Ascensión. "May I please talk to Lupe?"

Cristela studied him for a moment. His eyes beseeched her, his face lit with something between hope and fear. "Come," she said, and gestured for him to follow her down the hallway to the room.

Lupe sat on the couch absorbed in the book she was reading to two small children who sat close on either side of her.

"Lupe," said Cristela, "someone is here to see you."

Lupe looked up from her book and gasped when Cristela stepped into the room and revealed Ascensión standing in the doorway.

"It's been three weeks," said Ascensión. "Will you talk to me now?"

Lupe sat speechless, wide-eyed and drop-jawed.

"Will you talk to me, Lupe?"

A small child squeezed by Ascensión, trotted up to Lupe and bounced onto her lap.

"*Oof...*" Lupe caught her breath then squeaked, "Yes."

Cristela flushed the children off the couch and Lupe's lap and shooed them out of the room. "If you two want any privacy you won't find it here. Why don't you go sit on the bench in the yard? It should be dry by now."

"Thank you, Cristela," said Ascensión.

Lupe looked from Ascensión to Cristela, still a little dumbstruck.

"He came here looking for you, *cariño*," said Cristela, cocking her head towards where Ascensión still stood at the door.

"Oh. Yes. Thank you, Cristela," she said distractedly, but then she rose quickly and led Ascensión out of the room through the kitchen to the back yard.

Maria and Rafaela stood in the hallway watching.

"*That's* who Lupe ran away from?" said Maria in wonderment. "He's so handsome, if she doesn't go back to him I'm going to bop her on the head."

Rafaela laughed and put and arm around Maria's shoulder. "So what if he's handsome? Things aren't always as they seem with men." She kissed Maria on the cheek. "You should know that by now, *niña*."

Maria rubbed her pregnant belly and sighed. "Yes, I know."

Lupe and Ascensión sat next to each other on the bench. Lupe looked down at her hands.

"How have you been?" said Ascensión.

"Fine, thank you," she said coolly. "And you?"

"Confused and lonely and missing you," he said.

"Yes," she said. She raised her eyes until they met his. "Me, too."

"Trying to ignore you on the bus every day, that's been the worst."

"Yes, it has been," said Lupe. "And trying to pretend I didn't see you at work."

"I would have gotten down on my knees and begged you to come back to me if I'd thought it would have done any good."

"But I don't understand. Why would you beg me to come back to you after you threw all my things into those two bags and..." Lupe stopped in mid-sentence at the sight of Ascensión shaking his head. "Wait..." At that moment she was hit with a possibility that had eluded her all along. "It wasn't you who threw out my things?"

"Of course it wasn't me," said Ascensión.

"Your mother!" Lupe cried. "It was your mother!" Ascensión nodded and Lupe gasped then laughed glumly and shook her head. "I don't know how she did it, but of course it was your mother who left those bags at my office."

Ascensión nodded again, a tear rolling down his cheek. "The morning of the emergency at Momotombo, remember?"

"Yes, of course," said Lupe.

"Yoolie sent a car to pick me up early. It was my mother who packed those bags with your things and then after I left she ordered Jaime to give them to you."

"How did I never think of that?" said Lupe, reflexively wiping the tear from Ascensión's cheek with her hand and visualizing Violeta coercing poor Jaime into dragging those bags to the bus. "But why did Jaime not tell me? I've seen him at work. Why did he not come up to me and explain to me about the bags?"

"Ah, you know Jaime," said Ascensión. "Always trying to avoid any trouble. He's like a big timid turtle who pulls into his shell at the least noise."

Lupe and Ascensión laughed together at the image of Jaime pulling his bulky self into a massive turtle shell.

"Poor Jaime," Lupe chuckled, wiping her eye. "But you know, *mi amo...*" Lupe cleared her throat and continued in a serious tone. "You know I can't go back to your family's house. I can't especially since I've been officially kicked out by your mother."

"Never mind that nonsense," Ascensión said with a dismissive wave. He grasped his wife's hand. "It's good that you're talking to me now. I didn't know if you would, but it's good that you are, because now we need to talk. You know that I've been promoted to foreman. That means more money for us."

"More money for your family, you mean," said Lupe.

"Things are going to change," said Ascensión. "I promise you."

"How are things going to change?"

"Lupe, my family, my mother...yes, she is my mother and yes they are my family and of course I love them, but you and I...what we've been through together, our time when we were foreigners, illegals, frightened, our time when we had no one but each other, and then our baby David...they could never understand."

Lupe's eyes filled with tears. "I know. How could anyone else understand us?" She looked into his eyes. "We belong to each other."

"And so I've found a place for us, for you and me, I mean. In León."

"Really?"

"I would not lie to you, *amor*, you know I wouldn't."

"No, no, I know you wouldn't."

"You know Alban? One of the mechanics from Momotombo?"

"Yes, I know Alban."

"His uncle died last month and his aunt is moving out of the bottom floor of his family's house to go live with her daughter's family. And so Alban's family wants to rent the bottom floor. He said they'll rent it to me as soon as his cousin returns from Matagalpa. She's there working with her husband's family on the coffee harvest and will be back in two weeks. I've already given Alban half a month's rent in advance to hold it for me. Lupe, will you come back to me?"

"Yes, *amor*."

Ascensión brought Lupe's hand to his lips and gave it several quick kisses before pressing it against his cheek, wet with tears.

Lupe pressed close to Ascensión and placed her other hand on his shoulder. "I know how hard it was for you to do this."

"As long as you come back to me," said Ascensión. "And as long as you still love me."

"How could I stop loving you, *mi amor*?" she said, stroking his head. "I'm not made of stone, and it's because I'm not made of stone that I couldn't stay at Krukrulitos. If I were harder than I am I think I could have. But I'm not. I'm soft."

"I love your softness," said Ascensión, again kissing her hand. "And in a few weeks we'll live together in León."

"But until then..." Lupe sighed.

"Lupe, listen, *mi amor*. I haven't told you the most important thing, the most wonderful thing that I came here to tell you."

"What wonderful thing?" Lupe smiled but then her expression turned serious. "What thing, *amor?*"

Ascensión's eyes again filled with tears. "Sally and Silvio are coming for a visit. They're bringing…"

"*David!*" Lupe cried. "They're bringing David to us!" She threw herself into his arms and began sobbing on his shoulder.

"Yes, *mi vida,*" he said, holding her close. "They're bringing our David to visit us. They'll fly into Managua in one week from today and they'll stay for ten days."

Lupe looked up at him and rubbed the tears from her face. "Ten days?"

"It's not long enough, I know, but…"

"But we'll see our David." She laid her head against his chest. "I'll hold him every minute he's here, I'll never let go of him!"

Ascensión laughed. "You might need to put him down after a while. Or at least let me hold him from time to time."

Lupe laughed though her tears. "I know, I know. I'm just…"

"I know," said Ascensión. "I called Sally. I told her you needed…we needed to see our son."

"You called her? And she and Silvio are coming? Just like that?"

"You know Sally. She always does things just like that."

"She does," Lupe said with a smile. "Ah, Sally and Silvio. They're so good. But do we really have to let David go in ten days? Can't we keep him here with us? He's our son."

"I don't know, *amor.* We didn't talk about that."

Lupe nodded. "David is coming in a week," she said thoughtfully. "*amor,* where will we take him when he arrives?"

Ascensión pulled back from Lupe and took both her hands in his. "Come back to Krukrulitos, Lupe, please. Where else do we have to go? Where else can we take our son?"

Lupe withdrew her hands from Ascensión's and rested them in her lap. She looked down at her hands. "It's true we have nowhere else to take him." She looked up at Ascensión. "But I won't allow your mother or your sister or anyone to be unkind to him. It's one thing for them to mistreat me. But they won't mistreat our son."

"Lupe, they would not mistreat our son."

"I think they would do anything to hurt me. And how better to hurt me than to hurt my baby?"

"No, Lupe, no. No one will hurt our baby. And no one will hurt you ever again, I swear. I won't allow it."

"You won't?"

"I swear it. *Amor*, come back to me, please, come back to me now. I need you. I can't live any longer in Krukrulitos without you. The truth is, my family is driving me crazy. And I'm driving them crazy. I think we all need you there to keep us from driving each other crazy!"

Lupe laughed and shook her head.

"But it's also true that my family is crazy with joy that David is coming. They are so happy and excited that they'll forget all about being mean to you."

Lupe laughed again. "I believe you."

"Lupe, will you come back? Or must I move into *Las Sonrisas* with you? By the way, where do you sleep here?"

"In the room where you found me. I sleep on the couch."

"That small couch? How?"

"With my legs folded."

"Well, I don't think I can fit onto that couch with you," said Ascensión, scratching his head in playful wonderment.

Lupe caressed his face with her hands. "All right, *amor*, I'll come back to Krukrulitos. And I promise not to be…sick…like I was before. When I couldn't get out of bed."

Ascensión's eyes glistened with tears. He removed her hands from his face and kissed her palms. "*Mi vida.*"

"And now I have something to tell you. Perhaps it will make sense why I felt so sick and tired in the morning. And why I've been craving corn flakes."

"Lupe...do you mean...?"

Lupe nodded. Her eyes again filled with tears.

Ascensión playfully hit his forehead with the heel of his hand. "How did I not figure this out?"

Lupe laughed. "How did *I* not figure this out?"

They fell together, their arms wrapped around each other.

Rafaela and Maria stood peeking out the kitchen window.

Maria sighed and rested her head on Rafaela's shoulder. "Ah, just like in the cinema."

"I don't think Lupe will be sleeping on that little couch anymore," said Rafaela.

That evening after the women closed down *Las Sonrisas* Lupe and Ascensión took the bus back to Krukrulitos carrying the shopping bags of Lupe's things, among which were several boxes of cornflakes. Instead of the usual two rows of seats this bus had two long benches, one on either side that ran the length of the bus. And though it being a Saturday evening and the benches not crowded, still Lupe and Ascensión sat close against each other, his arm around her shoulder, her head resting on his chest.

"Soon," Ascensión said, "we'll have—"

"Another child," Lupe finished his sentence. "I know, can you imagine it?"

Ascensión laughed. "I was going to say 'a car.'"

Lupe pulled away from him. "What?" she laughed.

"Something else I had to tell you. I'll need a vehicle for my new job as foreman. You know, in case I'm called in after hours for an emergency. Yoolie has arranged for the *Empresa* to sell me or maybe give me one of the American trucks that they're replacing with Toyotas."

Lupe's face lit up and she clapped her hands with delight. "That's wonderful news, *mi amor*. But do you mean those pickup trucks in the garage behind the machine shop? I can't believe they're getting rid of them. They're hardly old, and still in good shape."

"Ah, well, I suppose the rich Nicaraguans are the same as the Americans, always wanting the newest thing." He pulled Lupe back close to him and kissed her hair. "Me, I want what I have."

"Me too, *amor*," said Lupe.

When Lupe and Ascensión arrived at the house in Krukrulitos Mauricio, Ernesto and Jaime were sitting on the patio while Violeta and Xiomara were in the kitchen cooking dinner. Mauricito and Blanca playing in the yard were the first to catch sight of the couple walking up the path. The children ran to them, opening their arms to Lupe, who bent down to hug them. She picked up little Mauricito and carried him to the house while Ascensión carried Blanca.

Ernesto stuck his head into the kitchen. "They're here,"

Violeta looked up from a pot she'd been stirring and sighed heavily.

"Come on, now," said Ernesto. "You're not being put on the rack. It's not torture."

Violeta shook her head and rubbed her apron across her eyes. "For me it is."

Xiomara put a hand on her mother's shoulder. "It will be all right, *mamita*, we can do this. Think about seeing your grand baby from America soon. You know she has control of him. And of Ascensión, too."

Violeta nodded and rubbed her eyes again. "Yes, I'm coming." Ernesto held the curtain aside for her and she leaned on her daughter as she walked.

After the other family members had welcomed Lupe with smiles and hugs Ernesto gave his wife a light nudge. "Yes, welcome back home, Lupita," said Violeta, smiling, but with a slight strain in her voice. "We're so glad you're back."

"And now the Americans are coming," said Mauricio, laughing heartily. "Who would have thought we'd have a little American in the family."

"*Tia* Lupe," said Blanca, "can we play with the American baby?"

Lupe laughed. "Of course you can, Blancacita. David is your cousin."

"I've made *gallo pinto* with chicken and corn," said Violeta. "But we also have corn flakes and milk if you'd like."

Lupe laughed again. "Thank you, Violeta." She caught Ascensión's eye and raised her eyebrows. He shook his head slightly and led her into the house ahead of the others.

"We can tell them about the baby later," he whispered to her. "First I have something to show you."

He led her into the bedroom. Lupe gasped and covered her mouth with her hands. A long wall of corrugated metal welded to a base running almost the length of the room had transformed the room into two smaller rooms. The opening to each room was hung with a curtain that served as a doorway.

Ascensión pulled back the curtain of the nearer room and motioned for Lupe to enter. Inside the room the metal wall had been painted with whimsical birds and plants in bright colors on a white background.

Lupe stood for a moment speechless.

"It's so small now," Ascensión said apologetically. "We barely have room to move, but…"

"No, no, it's perfect. So beautiful, I can't believe it." She ran a hand along the wall. "Did you paint these birds?"

"I did. I bought the paints in León. But look here." He pointed to a bottom corner of the wall. Lupe saw the word LOVE painted in a replica of the famous sculpture in their snow globe. She threw her arms around Ascensión and kissed him.

"Oh, *mi vida*," she said, wiping the tears from her eyes, "I believe that from now on things are only going to be good for us!"

Chapter Thirteen

Sally knelt on the floor attempting to squash down the contents of her suitcase so as to be able to zip it shut. Silvio, who'd been pacing the floor, stopped to watch her.

"You think maybe you got too much in there?"

"Oh, how the heck do I know?" she said, pulling out a pair of dress shoes.

"Whynch you leave those behind? Where you gonna wear 'em?"

"Fine," said Sally, tossing the shoes aside. "What about these jeans?" She pulled out a pair of jeans and held them up before her.

"Remember, it's like ninety-four degrees there."

Sally tossed the jeans aside. "What else don't I need?"

"I don't know," said Silvio. "I packed a couple pairs of shorts, a couple of tees, a dress shirt. And then there's these pants we're wearing."

"Yeah, okay." Sally fingered the material of the ultra-light multi-pocketed zip-away–bottom hiking pants she and Silvio were wearing. "Good thing we match," she joked. "In case one of us gets lost people will know who to return us to."

"Yeah, ha, ha," he laughed nervously. "Geez, I hope neither of us gets lost."

"Hey, I'll stick by you and you stick by me."

"Will do, Babe. Don't worry about that. How many of those dresses you got in there?"

"I packed three light sun dresses." Sally sighed. "Maybe two will be enough." She pulled out one of the dresses. "Or one." She pulled out another. "There. Now I can get the danged thing shut."

"What about all David's things? You got all David's things?"

"Yep, that's what's taking up a lot of room. But yeah, I got his things."

"Okay, unpack some of David's stuff and give it to me. I got room in my suitcase."

"Nah, never mind. I got it all in."

"Yeah, okay, well…" Silvio pulled in a deep breath. "I guess we're going, huh?"

Sally stood up. "I guess so."

"That place, hotel, whatever, in León where we made our reservations…"

"*Casa de la Recolección,*" said Sally.

"Yeah. You think that place is okay?" said Silvio.

"I don't know. I mean, it looked nice online. And Ascensión picked it out for us."

"Yeah, but, it's only twenty-five dollars a night. What if it's some kind of…I don't know."

Sally sighed. "I don't know, either, but that's where Ascensión said to stay, so I think we ought to trust him. I mean, what else can we do?"

"We're not even gone yet and already I wish we were back home."

Sally stepped over to where Silvio stood and put her arms around his waist. "Don't worry, Babe. We'll be all right."

Silvio put his arms around Sally and held her close. "Okay," he said. "Heck, I guess we should be more worried about poor Darren. I don't know if he knows what he got himself into."

***

In the living room the children were lined up military-style, oldest to youngest, little David busily toddling between his siblings. Darren stood facing the children, barking orders like a drill sergeant with baby Silvia sitting at his feet contentedly sucking on her bottle.

"So Zach, you're in charge of Josh..."

"Yay!" cried Josh, skipping down the line towards his brother.

"Hey, stay in line...eh, never mind. Trina, you're in charge of Sam."

"No she's *not*," whined Sam.

"Yes, I *am*," said Trina.

"*I* want to be in charge!" cried Sam.

"Hey, hey, settle down," said Darren. "Okay, Sam, you're in charge of Silvia."

"*Hmph*," said Sam, nodding and shooting her sister an imperious look then plopping herself down at Darren's feet next to her baby sister.

"Hey, what are you doing?" cried Darren.

"I'm in charge of Silvia," said Sam.

"Fine, fine. Now everybody go play. I gotta go get some work done." He bent down and picked up the baby. "Me and Silvia."

"But, Daddy," said Josh, "we haven't had breakfast yet."

"Oh yeah," said Darren. "Okay, breakfast first."

Sally and Silvio had hauled their suitcases downstairs and set them in the hallway next to David's stroller and car seat and a well-packed diaper bag. Now they stood on the other side of the living room listening to Darren maneuvering the children.

"What do you think?" said Silvio.

"So far so good, I guess," said Sally. "He's only got ten days to go. Anyway, it's time."

"Yeah, I guess," said Silvio.

They entered the living room and were set upon by the children.

"Why can't we come?" whined Trina.

"I want to go to Nicamagua," wailed Sam.

"It's Nicaragua and you're not going, so quit being babies," said Zach.

"Daddy Darren, tell Zach he's not in charge of me!" said Trina.

"Okay, now everybody just...whoa!" Darren realigned his hold on baby Silvia, who threw down her bottle and strained away from him, reaching her arms towards Sally.

Josh sidled up next to Sally and Silvio. He cupped his hand next to his mouth and gestured for them to come close. Sally and Silvio bent down to him and he whispered to them, "I'm going to miss you."

"I know, Babe," she whispered back. "I'll miss you, too."

"But we'll be back before you know it," whispered Silvio. "Okay?"

"Okay," he whispered and hugged them both tightly.

"No, fair," Sam cried, "Josh got to tell a secret and get his own hug."

"Okay, everybody can get their own hug and tell me and Daddy a quick secret if they want," said Sally.

The children lined up and took their turns, told their secrets, and received their hugs. David toddled behind his sisters to be part of whatever was going on, and even Zach lined up behind his siblings to say his good-bye.

"Don't forget about Silvia," said Sam.

"Oh, we're not gonna forget Silvia," said Sally, taking the baby from Darren, kissing and hugging her then passing her to Silvio. "And we're sure not going to forget about you," she said to Darren. She hugged him tightly then said, "We can't thank you enough. You're gonna be all right, right? My mom will be over to give you backup as soon as she drops us at the airport."

"Yeah, I'll be all right," said Darren. David came crashing into the back of Darren's legs. "Oof," he said, looking down at the laughing toddler. "I mean, I think I will."

"All right, then mister, you're coming with us," said Sally, scooping up David.

The younger children then broke into a chorus of entreaties to Sally and Silvio not to go, while Zach began attempting to shove them into being quiet.

"Who wants to go for ice cream?" Darren shouted above the fray.

"But we haven't had breakfast yet, Daddy," said Josh.

"Oh, yeah," said Darren. "Okay, who wants to go get ice cream for breakfast?"

The children broke into cheers.

"Can we go get breakfast *and* ice cream?" said Trina.

Darren sighed. "Yeah, sure."

This brought another round of cheers.

Silvio stepped close to Sally. "Looks like he's got this."

A few minutes later Sally, Silvio and David were waiting in front of the house for Sally's mother to arrive to take them to the airport.

"You really think we oughtta be doing this?" said Silvio.

"I don't know," said Sally. "But we should be okay, don't you think?" She kissed Silvio on the cheek. "I mean, seriously, what's the worst that could happen?"

***

On the other side of customs in the Augusto Cesar Sandino International Airport in Managua Sally and Silvio scanned the crowds for Ascensión and Lupe. Sally nervously pushed David back and forth in his stroller. She said softly into Silvio's ear, "I can't believe all the people here."

"Me neither," he replied softly.

They continued speaking softly into each other's ears, looking around while they spoke.

"I mean, if it's so poor here how come there are so many people traveling?"

"I don't know," said Silvio.

"Maybe they're all tourists, or something?"

"I don't know," said Silvio. "Ascensión said they'd meet us on the other side of customs, right?"

"Maybe they can't find us?"

"How?" said Silvio. "They said the other side of customs, that's where we are, the other side of customs."

"Okay, let's just be calm, they're sure to show up. Maybe they got caught in traffic, or something."

"Yeah, okay." Silvio lifted his shirt collar. "I'm sweating. I don't think this place is air-conditioned."

"I'm sweating too. Maybe they're too poor to afford air-conditioning here."

"Yeah, I wouldn't be surprised about that," said Silvio.

"Or maybe it's not the air conditioning. Maybe we're just, you know, nervous."

"Well, I'm getting pretty nervous," said Silvio.

David began fussing in his stroller.

"Does he need to be changed?" said Silvio.

"I just changed him before we went through customs, remember? I think he just wants out."

"Okay, well, let's take him out before he starts crying, because we don't want anybody to, you know…"

"Yeah, notice us, or anything."

Silvio lifted David from his stroller and passed him to Sally, who began bouncing him in her arms.

"Okay, we been waiting here how long?" said Silvio. He pulled his phone from his pocket. "Almost five minutes. Maybe I better call Ascensión."

"Yeah, we don't want people to think we're just loitering, or something."

At that moment they saw a smiling young man walking towards them and waving. *"Oye, cheles,"* he called.

"Who's that? What does he want?" said Silvio.

"I think he called us '*cheles.*' That's okay, right? Charleston told us about that. Them calling us '*cheles.*' Maybe he's just being friendly, like Charleston said they were."

"Yeah, yeah," said Silvio. He swallowed hard.

"*Hola, cheles,*" said the young man. "*¿A dónde van?*"

"Okay, we know what that means," said Sally to Silvio. "He's asking us where we're going. Should we tell him?"

"Why should we tell him?" said Silvio.

"So he knows we speak Spanish and so he won't try anything?"

"*¿Van a Managua?* To hotel?" asked the man. "I you drive." He mimicked driving.

"*No, vamos a León,*" said Sally. "I wonder if he understood me," she whispered to Silvio.

The man's eyes lit up. "*¡Ah, habla español! ¡Qué bueno!*"

"Oh, wow, I don't believe it, he understood me!"

"Yeah, but why did you tell him where we're going?"

"Well, I mean, if he was just being friendly...Hey, Silvio, why don't you try saying something to him?" said Sally. "Your Spanish is a lot better than mine."

"*Los llevaré a León en mi coche,*" said the man, still miming a driver. "I good drive León. Come."

"Tell him thanks but we're okay," said Sally. "Go ahead, give it a try."

Silvio cleared his throat. "*No, gracias. Estamos...okay.*"

The man looked delighted and clapped his hands. "*¡Muy bien, muy bien español! Ven conmigo,*" he said, motioning them to follow him. "*Los llevaré a León en mi coche,*" he said, again telling them of his intention to drive them to León in his car. "*Es muy barato,*" he added, letting them know that the price would be inexpensive.

"*No, gracias,*" said Silvio. "Oh no," he whispered to Sally. "Look." He pointed to two men approaching them, one of them thin and the other one paunchy. They wore military uniforms with assault rifles slung over their shoulders.

"Oh, no," said Sally. She pressed closer to Silvio and held David tighter.

The young man, unaware of the airport guards standing behind him, continued badgering them to come with him in a mix of Spanish and poor English while Sally's and Silvio's eyes flicked back and forth between the young man and the two smirking soldiers.

Finally the young man threw up his hands in surrender. "Okay, okay." He held out one open palm which he tapped with the index finger of his other hand. *"Propina, cheles, propina,"* he said.

"What, he wants us to *pay* him?" said Sally.

"Propina, that means tip, right?" said Silvio. "What does he want us to tip him for?"

"I don't know, but remember how Charleston warned us that people expect to be tipped for every little thing?" Sally glanced at the guards. "Maybe we should just give him some money so he'll go away, I mean, with those soldiers watching us..."

"Yeah, maybe," said Silvio. He reached into his pocket and pulled out his wallet. "How much? I mean, I don't have any change yet. All I have are these bills. This is a hundred cordobas. That's worth, what, about three dollars?"

"I don't know, maybe that's too much for around here?" said Sally.

"Esta bien, esta bien," said the young man, nodding enthusiastically and pointing to the hundred cordoba bill then to his palm.

"Oh, geez, here come the soldiers," said Sally. "Hurry, give him the money!"

Silvio proffered the hundred cordobas to the young man, but just as the man reached for it one of the guards snatched the bill away.

"You don't get a tip for bothering foreigners," the guard said in Spanish. "Now go on, kid, and leave the tourists alone." He shifted the gun on his shoulder and cocked his head. The young man quickly backed away, hands up, still smiling and excusing himself profusely.

The guard returned the hundred-cordoba bill to Silvio with a polite nod of his head.

"*Gracias, gracias,*" said, Silvio. To Sally he said, "Okay, I guess they are nice here after all."

The guards questioned them in a friendly, curious rather than official tone. Were they from the United States? Where were they going? Was this their child?

Sally and Silvio were able to understand the guards' questions and answered that the child was American and they were taking him to León to visit his parents. The guards appeared to understand immediately.

"Ah," said the thin one, "he is American but his parents are here. What a shame."

"Ummm," agreed the paunchy one. "But how will you get to León?"

"Someone is coming for us," said Silvio. "They're a little late."

"A little late?" said the thin one.

"Ten minutes, more or less," said Sally.

"Maybe they forgot to come," said the paunchy one.

"No, no, they'll be here soon," said Silvio, feeling safer now while chatting with these two friendly officials.

"Yes, that's right," said Sally, also feeling more at ease and happy to be practicing her Spanish.

"My cousin has a car," said the paunchy one. "I'll call him. He'll drive you to León."

"Oh, no thank you," said Sally. To Silvio she said in English. "Boy, they really are friendly here, offering his cousin to drive us all the way to León."

"Yeah, that's really friendly," said Silvio.

"Call your person, tell them you don't need a ride, and my cousin will drive you."

"No, really, that's all right," said Silvio.

"Maybe your person forgot," said the thin one. "You should let his cousin drive you."

"No, no they didn't forget," said Sally. She turned to Silvio. "You don't think they forgot, do you?"

"I hope not," said Silvio. "Do you feel like these guys are getting a little pushy?"

"Yeah," said Sally. "A little."

"My cousin is a good driver. He has a good car. He drives to León all the time. And cheap. Only five hundred cordobas."

"Wait," said Sally to Silvio, "he wants to be paid? He wasn't just being friendly?"

"That's what it sounds like," said Silvio.

"Only five hundred cordobas. Each. The little one is free, of course. And all your luggage, too, that goes for free."

"You should let his cousin take you," said the thin one. "He's a good driver, and honest."

"That's right. If your person doesn't come to get you, someone here might try to cheat you, like that other one." The paunchy guard cocked his thumb back towards the crowd.

"Or even rob you," said the thin one.

Sally and Silvio gasped. The two men stepped closer.

"Oh, my God," said Sally. "Do you think we should let his cousin take us? What if Lupe and Ascensión don't come?"

"I don't know. Five hundred cordobas. That's what, twelve, thirteen dollars apiece?"

"So about twenty-six for all of us?" said Sally. "And he'll bring all our stuff? I mean, that's really not a bad price."

"I don't know," said Silvio. "What if the cousin is, you know, a thief?"

"What if they arrest us, or something, if we don't go with the cousin? Where do you think Lupe and Ascensión are? I gotta be honest, Silvio, I'm getting scared."

The two guards stood patiently watching the exchange between Sally and Silvio, understanding not a word, but smiling and nodding all the same.

"That's it, I'm calling Ascensión," said Silvio.

As he pulled out his phone the two guards stepped closer to Sally and Silvio, hemming them in.

"No, no, put away your phone," said the paunchy guard. He ran a hand along the strap of his gun. "Don't call anyone. They are not coming for you. My cousin will take you. One thousand cordobas. Don't be worried, he's a good man, honest. Come on." He grabbed one of their suitcases while his comrade grabbed the other.

"Oh, my God, they're taking our suitcases. Stop!" Sally cried.

The men had rolled the suitcases only a few steps but stopped and released them. "What's wrong?" said the paunchy one. "We're happy to help you."

"Wait, here," said Silvio, shuffling through his wallet for two five hundred cordoba bills. "Take this, and…"

"Sally! Silvio!"

Sally and Silvio looked over and saw Lupe running towards them, her arms open wide. Behind her ran Ascensión. They pushed in front of the guards, shoving them out of the way. The two enwrapped Sally and their son, then they stepped back and took turns covering David's small face in kisses, sometimes alternating between kissing him and hugging Sally and Silvio. Lupe sobbed breathlessly and tears rolled down Ascensión's face. Sally and Silvio cried as well, though their tears were more from relief than anything else.

"Here, go to your *mamá*," said Sally. She attempted to pass David to his mother but he clung to Sally.

"Didi?" he said.

"That's right, I'm your Didi. This is your *mamá*."

"Mama?" he said. He looked back and forth between Sally and Lupe.

Sally tried again to hand him to Lupe. "Here, go to your *mamá.*"

David looked again at Lupe, studied her for a moment, then reached for her open arms. "Mama," he said.

"Oh *mi amorcito, mi corazoncito,*" she said, kissing him more. "And look, here's your *papito,*" she said, handing him to Ascensión.

"*Oye, mi pequeñito,*" said Ascensión, kissing his face and head.

"Your *papá,*" said Silvio. "Remember?"

"*Papá?*" said David.

"Yes, yes," said Ascensión. "I'm your *papá,* remember?" He wiped his eyes and kissed his son once more.

Lupe hugged and kissed Sally and Silvio again. "My good, good friends," she said. Then she caressed her son's cheek. "Come, my Davicito. We'll show you where you're from."

A crowd of onlookers had gathered nearby, smiling at the happy reunion, some wiping at their eyes. Among them were the guards.

"Your cousin won't be happy to learn that those two Americans got away," said the thin guard.

The paunchy guard scowled and stepped close to his friend so that they were face to face. "Oh, and who's going to tell him, huh?"

His friend stepped back. "Don't worry, Nuncio, I won't say a word. We can always go look for some other tourists for your cousin. Look, there are some backpackers over there looking around. They look like Dominicans or maybe Costa Ricans."

"*Sí,*" sighed the paunchy one. "But backpackers don't want to pay much for a ride. They'll probably just want to know where the bus stop is."

"I know, I know, but we won't find any more easy rich Americans like those two. They are a rare fruit." He put a hand on his friend's shoulder. "Come on, let's at least try those backpackers."

The two guards walked off.

The same man who had tried to give Sally and Silvio a ride returned and now offered to help them carry their luggage. Ascensión nodded and the man grabbed the handles of two of the suitcases and followed behind the group as they made their way across the airport. They came to a stand selling cold drinks and Lupe suggested they stop for a drink before making the trip to León.

Ascensión thanked the man, who let go of the luggage and stood by waiting for his tip. Silvio reached into his wallet and was about to pull out the same hundred-cordoba bill that he'd almost given the man before when Ascensión stopped him. Ascensión reached into his pocket and pulled out a five-cordoba bill. The man thanked Ascensión, accepted the bill then waited, eyeing Silvio's wallet.

"*Gracias, señor,*" Ascensión said in an assertive tone and the man walked off, but not before giving Silvio a disappointed glance.

Ascensión shook his head. "Be careful of over-tipping, my friend," he said. "Five or ten cordobas is enough. Otherwise your wallet will soon be empty."

They bought plastic bags filled with a gold-colored juice pulled from an ice-filled tub. The vendor pierced each bag with a straw. They sat at a table next to the stand, Lupe holding David on her lap. Sally pulled from her bag a sippy cup and squeezed the juice from one of the bags into the cup for David.

"This is the first time I ever drank juice from a bag," said Silvio. "But it sure is good."

"Yes, it's delicious," said Sally. "What kind of juice is it?"

"Oh, probably a mix of guava, papaya, pineapple, coconut, all the juices," said Lupe. "In Nicaragua we like to mix them all."

"And drink them all," added Ascensión. "It's how we keep cool."

Sally held up her plastic bag. "To keeping cool in Nicaragua."

The others held up their bags and joined in the toast.

"To our good friends Silvio and Sally," said Ascensión.

David held out his cup and said "Didi," then laughed along with the others.

After finishing their bags of juice they gathered up the luggage and continued to the airport exit. As soon as they stepped outside the heat hit like a wave.

"Whoa," said Sally.

"Geez, I guess the air conditioning was on inside the airport after all."

Lupe laughed. "Yes, it's hotter than Philadelphia."

"Don't worry, you'll get used to it," said Ascensión.

"Yeah, I don't know about that," said Silvio.

"Now we have to find a car," said Ascensión.

"A car?" said Sally. "You mean *your* car?"

"No, a car or taxi to take us back to León. Or look," Ascensión pointed to the nearby stop, where a bus had just pulled up. "There's the bus."

"No, no, *amor*," said Lupe, "Sally and Silvio and Davicito," here she stopped to plant a kiss on David's head, "they have just traveled for eight hours. We'll get a car to take us."

Silvio pulled a handkerchief from his pocket and mopped his forehead. "So how did you get to the airport?"

"Oh, we took the bus," said Lupe.

"I'm going to have my own car soon, a truck." said Ascensión.

"Ah, look," said Lupe, pointing down the sidewalk. "That blue SUV, where the guards are standing."

Sally and Silvio exchanged a glance then looked in the direction Lupe was pointing. There chatting with driver stood the two guards who had intimidated them inside the airport.

"Yes, that one looks good and big enough," said Ascensión. "I'll go over and get it."

"Whoa, whoa, wait," said Silvio. "Those two soldiers, they were in the airport. They tried to make us go with them. They wanted us to take somebody's cousin's car to Managua."

Ascensión shrugged. "Maybe that's the cousin's car."

"But they were pushy," said Sally.

"Yes," said Ascensión, "you have to watch out for people selling things around here. They can be pushy. You have to tell them no or they will keep pushing."

"So we noticed," said Silvio. "We were afraid they were going to arrest us, or shoot us, or something."

Lupe and Ascensión laughed. "Them?" said Lupe. "They're just airport guards. They're not going to shoot anybody."

"Then why do they have those assault rifles?" said Silvio.

Lupe shrugged. "I don't know. Maybe in case terrorists came, or something?"

"*Terrorists?*" Sally and Silvio cried.

"Don't worry there are no terrorists here," said Ascensión. "Sometimes street riots, but no terrorists."

"*Street riots?*"

Lupe laughed. "Don't worry, there are no street riots in León these days. And if there are just stay away. It's safe. Did the guard say how much the cousin wanted to drive to León?"

"A thousand cordobas for both of us and David," said Silvio.

"*A thousand cordobas?*" said Lupe and Ascensión. The two burst out laughing.

"*Dios mío,*" laughed Lupe. She put a hand on her husband's shoulder. "*mi amor,* go over and talk to that thieving driver. Oh, I'm sorry, my friends," she said when she saw the embarrassment on Sally's and Silvio's faces. "I should not laugh. I was a stranger in your country once, too."

"Oh, it's okay," said Silvio.

"Yeah, we'll learn," said Sally.

"But don't worry," said Lupe. "Ascensión and I will watch out for you."

"We're glad for that," said Sally. "And now I understand how brave you and Ascensión were to come to the U.S. alone the way you did."

Ascensión negotiated with the driver and the guards for a few moments then returned, smiling. "Okay," he said, "the driver will take us to León."

"How much?" asked Silvio, reaching for his wallet.

"You can pay him when we get to León," said Ascensión. "Five hundred cordobas."

"Each?"

"Of course not," said Ascensión. "For all of us."

Sally and Silvio looked at each other.

"How far to León, again?" Silvio asked.

"About eighty kilometers," said Ascensión. "About fifty U.S. miles."

As they walked over to the car Sally whispered into Silvio's ear, "Geez. So we're paying the guy, like, fourteen bucks to drive all of us fifty miles?"

"I know," Silvio whispered back. "Now I feel like the rip-off artist."

"Maybe you could give him a great tip," whispered Sally.

"Yeah, I will," whispered Silvio.

When they arrived at the car the two guards smiled broadly. The paunchy one opened his arms. "Ah, our American friends! You see? I told you my cousin would drive you to León!" He laughed heartily.

The guards helped Silvio and the driver load the luggage while Ascensión and Sally worked on installing the car seat and Lupe waited in the front seat holding David on her lap. After the luggage was packed the two the guards stood around smiling at Silvio.

"*Muchas gracias por su ayuda,*" said Silvio, thanking them for their help.

"*De nada,*" said the guards, still standing there and smiling.

Ascensión came up beside Silvio and chuckled. "They're waiting for a tip, *maje*."

"Wait," said Silvio, "these two guys with assault rifles want a tip?"

"Welcome to Nicaragua," Ascensión laughed. He pulled out two ten-cordoba bills and handed one to each guard. The guards gave Silvio the same disappointed look as had been on the face of the young man who had helped them in the airport, then they shrugged and walked off.

"That was, what, like a quarter a piece you gave them?" said Silvio.

"Don't worry about it, my friend," said Ascensión. "I assure you they are happy right now and are on their way to the juice bar with those ten cordobas."

Silvio sighed. "I have to get used to things around here."

***

Sally and Silvio sat in the back seat behind the driver while Ascensión and Lupe sat in the way back with David buckled into his car seat between them.

"The palm trees," said Sally, craning her head close to the window. "I can't get over the palms and plants everywhere." She turned around to David. "What do you think of all these tropical plants, Baby?"

"Didi," said David, pointing out the window.

"Everything he does makes me smile," said Lupe, planting another kiss on David's cheek.

Along the highway from Managua to León they passed a long stretch of what appeared to be old, rusted corrugated metal structures, shipping containers and dilapidated box cars leaning up against each other.

"What's in all those old containers?" asked Silvio.

"People," said Ascensión. "Those are people's houses."

"Oh, okay," said Silvio, feeling his face redden. "Sorry," he added.

"No need," said Ascensión. "Managua is not Philadelphia."

"That's right," said Lupe. "When Ascensión and I arrived in Philadelphia we found things to be very different and sometimes hard to understand."

"Right, right," said Silvio, staring out the window, still embarrassed by his gaffe yet captivated by the sight of the houses.

Suddenly the sky clouded over, a few drops fell, and seconds later the rain was pouring down in heavy torrents.

"Whoa!" said Sally.

"The heck?" said Silvio. "Where did that come from?"

Lupe, Ascensión, and the driver laughed.

"It's just the rains," said Ascensión. "They come down every afternoon this time of year."

"Seriously?" said Sally.

"Of course," said Lupe. "This part of Nicaragua is in a rain forest. It rains every day during the winter months. But not for long."

"Wait, this is winter?" said Sally.

"Good you didn't come in summer when it's really hot and dry," said Ascensión.

"Yeah, good thing," said Silvio, once again wiping the sweat from his face.

As they drew closer to León the scenery became less urban and more rural, until the margin of the highway was lined with thick tropical foliage, broken by an occasional stretch of field or some houses or a small roadside store.

"I feel like we're in the jungle," said Sally.

"We are," said Lupe. "León is a very old city surrounded by jungle and volcanoes. You'll see."

By the time the driver reached the outskirts of León the rain had stopped and the sun had reappeared. Ascensión leaned forward to talk to the driver.

"You know where *Casa de La Recolección* is? Across from the church?"

The driver laughed. "Which church? You can't spit in León without hitting a church."

"Church of *La Recolección,* of course," said Lupe.

"Of course, of course," said the driver. "I know where *La Recolección* is. But you show me, anyway."

They pulled off the highway into the city where the vista of León, once a Spanish colonial capital, opened before them. Ascensión instructed the driver while Lupe hummed softly to David, who'd been peacefully sleeping in his car seat for most of the trip. Sally and Silvio held each other's hand and took in the sights. They passed through narrow streets lined with low, pastel-colored buildings with red tile roofs and by open-air markets crowded with Saturday afternoon shoppers. On the sidewalks women sat next to small tables with trays of cooked food for sale: egg, rice, red bean and chicken dishes, tamales, custards, squares of corn bread, little cakes and other Nicaraguan fare. They saw public squares lined with palm trees where people strolled or sat on benches and plazas in the center of which were magnificent churches with ornate eighteenth-century Spanish architecture, grimy with age and inattention and worn from centuries of tropical heat and rain. Groups of ragged laughing children and scrawny dogs ran through the streets, running as if with a purpose, as if they had somewhere to be, something to do.

"Wow, this is amazing," said Sally. "I feel like we're in a movie, or something."

Lupe and Ascensión laughed. "Yes, we know the feeling," said Lupe. "We felt the same when we arrived in the United States."

"Especially Philadelphia," said Ascensión.

"Oh, yes, especially Philadelphia," said Lupe.

"They're from Philadelphia?" asked the driver, recognizing the word from the English being spoken by his passengers.

Sally and Silvio looked at each other.

"Go ahead, you can speak to him," said Lupe. "You need to use your Spanish."

"Okay," said Silvio. He cleared his throat and said, "*Sí, somos de Philadelphia.*"

"And you speak Spanish, *que bueno*," said the driver. "My cousin has a friend whose uncle moved to Philadelphia. In two thousand seven. Back when…you know."

"*Sí, sí,*" said Ascensión. "Now you need to turn at the next street and we're almost there."

They rode for a few moments in silence then Sally turned around to Lupe and Ascensión. "Back when what?" she asked in English.

"Change of presidents," Lupe replied softly. "Politics. Best not to talk about it. Best to change the subject."

"Okay," said Silvio. "What's with those packs of dogs in the street?"

"Oh, you don't have to worry about those dogs," said Lupe. "If you don't bother them they won't bother you."

They passed a street corner where two young, slovenly-looking soldiers with assault rifles slung over their shoulders slouched against a wall.

"Oh, geez, what about those soldiers with the rifles?" said Silvio.

"Them?" Ascensión laughed. "Same as the dogs."

Chapter Fourteen

"Silvio." Sally put her hand on Silvio's arm. "Would you look at that."

The driver had just left his passengers and their belongings on the sidewalk in front of the *Casa de la Recolección* across the street from a sweeping plaza in the center of which rose up the *Iglesia de la Recolección*. The majestic church was built of bright yellow stone, with an asymmetrical façade in which were set a dozen and a half swirling columns joined to a three-tiered structure topped by a balcony and a bell tower.

"Wow," said Silvio. "Is that a famous church?"

"Yes," said Lupe. "Perhaps not the most famous church in León, but some say the most beautiful."

"Well, it's beautiful all right," said Silvio. "I mean, different, but beautiful. Must be the biggest one, too."

"Oh, no," said Lupe. "*La Recolección* is not the biggest church in León. The *Basílica de la Asunción* is the biggest cathedral in Central America. You must visit the *Basílica* while you're here, and all the churches!"

Ascensión laughed. "There are a hundred churches in León, *mi amor*."

"No, not a hundred, *mi amor*. But there are at least a dozen beautiful churches here built in the 1700s by the Spanish colonizers. You must see at least some of them."

"Yes, School Teacher Lupe," Ascensión said with a wink. "But we can give these Americans a Nicaraguan history lesson later. Right now they would like to check into their hotel."

"You take them inside," said Lupe. "I'll be right back." She gave her son one more kiss then she dashed off.

"Where did she go?" said Sally.

"Oh, don't worry," said Ascensión. "She'll be right back."

"And this is our hotel, huh?" said Silvio.

"Yes, this is *Casa de la Recolección*."

Sally and Sally stood for a moment hesitant, looking over the *Casa de la Recolección*, a long, low, red tile-roofed building with a stone wall exterior in the same shade of bright yellow as the church across the way minus the age marks that stained the church. The only break in the solid yellow stone wall was the entrance, an old-looking wooden double door with an arched top above which was painted the name of the hotel.

"So, what, there's a hotel on the other side of that door?" said Sally.

"That's right," said Ascensión.

"You been here before?" said Silvio.

"No," said Ascensión. "But I've heard it's very nice."

"Looks kind of like a, you know, a…fortress, or something," said Sally, though the word both she and Silvio were thinking was *prison*. "But, I mean, it's a nice color, and all," she added hopefully.

"Yeah, the color is nice," said Silvio. Once again he pulled out his handkerchief and wiped his face. He was now sweating more profusely than before.

"Yes, don't worry, you'll be very safe inside," said Ascensión, though this remark somehow failed to make them less anxious. "Here, you hold David," he said, handing the baby to Silvio, "and I'll ring the bell for them to come and let us inside."

"Wait, what?" said Sally, "You have to ring a bell to get in and out of here?"

Ascensión pressed a button next to an intercom alongside the door. "Probably only to get in."

A voice spoke through the intercom and after an exchange between Ascensión and the voice one of the double doors clicked open. They gathered the luggage and Ascensión pulled open the door. He turned back to Sally and Silvio, who still lingered a step behind him. "Come," he said.

Sally and Silvio exchanged a glance. "See you on the other side of the door," said Sally.

Silvio responded with a short nervous laugh then he pulled in a deep breath. "Okay, let's go."

On the other side of the door was a short stone passageway that opened into a lobby with bright white walls and deep brown parquet floors. The walls were hung with colorful folk-art paintings and shelves that held intriguing indigenous objects and curios. The room was otherwise decorated with large painted pots of tropical plants and a few rustic-looking side tables on which were smaller plants. Placed around the room were comfortable-looking pieces of cushioned rattan furniture, love seats, rocking chairs, and glass-topped coffee tables. Against one of the walls was a water cooler. There were a few guests in the lobby, reading or looking at their phones, a couple of them perusing the board games, books and magazines stacked on a wooden table against the wall. The room was cool from ceiling fans and several floor fans but at the same time bathed in light as the lobby opened to a beautiful outdoor courtyard in the center of which was a large, lush garden where there grew a variety of palm trees, colorful flowers, and other tropical flora, all strung with tiny white lights.

Next to the entrance was a reception desk manned by a tall, dark man who appeared to be in his mid-thirties wearing a light, loose ochre-colored peasant shirt, baggy tan pajama pants and sandals. He had hazel-green eyes and curly black hair pulled back into a ponytail and a neatly trimmed beard. He was speaking on the phone in quick Spanish but when he spotted Sally, Silvio,

Ascensión and David he smiled and nodded to signal that he'd be right with them.

The group stood in the middle of the lobby taking in their surroundings.

"Okay, this is *really* nice," said Sally.

"Yeah, it is," said Silvio. "Like we're in a whole different..."

"...country," said Sally. They looked at each other and laughed.

"See, I told you it would be nice," said Ascensión.

"Yeah." said Silvio. He lowered his voice, "But do you think this place is really only twenty-five bucks a night like it said online?"

Sally pulled in a deep breath. "I guess we're about to find out."

The man at the reception desk hung up the phone and called to them in perfect English, "Hey, sorry about that. Just leave all your stuff there, Dante or I can help you with it. Are you our Philadelphia guests?"

Sally and Silvio stood for a moment in drop-jawed silence, then they followed behind Ascensión to the desk.

"You...you're...*American?*" said Sally.

"Canadian," he said. "But I went to grad school in the States."

"You did?" said Silvio.

"Yep," he said.

"And you're Canadian?" said Sally.

"As Canadian as a guy can be who has an Indian mother, a wife from Kentucky, an MBA from Cornell, and two kids and a hotel in Nicaragua."

"This is your hotel?" said Sally. "I mean, you own the place?"

"Yep," he said. He extended a hand across the desk. "Nikhil Trudeau."

They shook hands and made introductions around.

"So," said Silvio, "your name is Trudeau? Like, you know, the President of Canada...?"

Nikhil Trudeau laughed. "Everybody asks that. Yes, I'm a Trudeau but no relation to the Prime Minister."

"And you have two kids?" said Sally.

"And a wife."

"Well, that's...I mean, that's...great," said Silvio.

"You see?" said Ascensión. "Don't you like this place?"

"Oh, yes, we do," said Sally. "Don't we?" she said to Silvio.

"Oh, yeah, we do," said Silvio. "And it's what, nine hundred cordobas a night? Is that right?"

"That's right," said Nikhil. "Now let's get you checked in before your little guy here runs out of patience."

"Oh, he's a good boy," said Ascensión. He reached out and took David from Silvio's arms.

Nikhil looked from Ascensión to Silvio and back again. "You need a baby bed for the room?"

"No, no," said Ascensión. "This is my *majito*." He kissed David's chubby cheek. "He comes home with me today."

While Nikhil was checking in his guests a female voice came over the desk intercom. "Niki, would you kindly send Dante to fetch these groceries and carry 'em in for me?"

Nikhil spoke into the intercom. "I thought Jazmín went with you to the market."

"Oh, she was going to, but she had to..." There was a sound of whimpering and the voice responding, "All right now, let me just tell Daddy...Niki, could you please just...Nikhil junior here is havin' a hissy and Georgie beshat himself..."

"Okay, come on in, Cassie, leave the groceries," said Nikhil.

"Well, Honey, I'm not about to leave these groceries," said the voice.

"Okay, hang on," said Nikhil. He looked up at his guests and smiled apologetically. "Sorry, give me a minute."

He picked up his phone just as a young man appeared in the lobby from the courtyard. "*Oye*, Dante," he called to the man. He spoke a few words in Spanish and the man nodded and hurried towards the door.

A few moments later Cassie Trudeau entered pushing a baby in a stroller while a whimpering little boy who looked to be about four years old attached to her by a wrist cord followed close behind. She appeared to be in her early thirties, small but sturdily built, with wide brown eyes and a smattering of freckles across her nose. She was dressed in a peasant skirt and loose blouse with a kerchief tied around her long, light-chestnut hair.

Nikhil hurried from behind the desk to the little boy, whom he detached from his wrist cord and scooped up into his arms. "Hey, hey, what's the matter, Buddy?"

"Oh," said Cassie, "we were at the market and he wanted a coconut slice from Marco's."

"Why didn't you buy him one, *mamita?*" Nikhil began bouncing the boy in his arms.

"Seriously, Honey? From Marco's? You know everything from Marco's, why, it's nothin' but hepatitis on a stick."

"You hear that, Buddy?" said Nikhil, blowing a raspberry on his son's cheek and making him laugh.

Sally and Silvio alternated between watching the hotel owner converse with his family and exchanging questioning glances with each other. Ascensión, however, seemed perfectly at ease, babbling with David and making him laugh.

"Do you think he forgot about us?" Sally whispered to Ascensión.

"Huh?" said Ascensión, looking over from his son. "Oh, no, don't worry. He'll be back."

"Look, let me tend to Georgie and Niki Junior," Cassie was saying, "and you go on and take care of..." Cassie looked to the desk where Sally, Silvio and Ascensión with David stood waiting. She broke into a friendly smile. "Are y'all the folks from Philly?"

"We are," said Sally.

"Why, welcome. Nikhil and me were to Philadelphia once. Loved y'all's cheese steaks. Nikhil'll be right on over. *Hola, guapito,*" she said in a baby voice, waving to David.

"*Hola, señora,*" Ascensión replied also in a baby voice, holding his son's hand and making him wave back.

"Okay," Cassie said to her husband, "now you put that boy down and get these folks from Philly squared away." Before shepherding her children through the lobby into the courtyard she turned and pointed a finger at Sally and Silvio. "Y'all are gonna love Nicaragua. But drink bottled water. The water here in our coolers is safe, too. And *always* wear your sunscreen, hear?"

After Nikhil finished checking in his guests he helped them with their luggage and led them into the courtyard. The hotel was one story built around the courtyard, to which all twelve of the guestrooms opened. The garden in the center was surrounded by a smooth stone tile patio protected from the sun and rain by an overhang. On the patio were hammocks, more rattan rocking chairs, loveseats set around coffee tables, some picnic tables, and another water cooler. Nikhil greeted the guests on the patio as he passed by.

"And here you are, room number five," said Nikhil, opening the door to the room for his guests.

The room was small and plain but clean, with two queen beds, a wooden armoire, two chairs, a small table on which were set two glasses, and a floor fan. At the far end of the room was a rustic-looking wooden door on which was printed the word *baño*. Inside the room the heat was sweltering.

"Don't worry, it'll cool off when you open the window and turn on the fan," said Nikhil.

Silvio pointed to a tall, vented metal box on wheels in one corner. "What's that?"

"Oh, yes, I forgot about that," said Nikhil. "That's the air conditioner."

"*Air conditioner?*" cried Sally and Silvio.

"It's a hundred and fifty cordobas a day to use it," said Nikhil. "That's about, oh, five American dollars if you're interested."

"Yes!" Sally and Silvio cried.

Nikhil wheeled the portable unit away from the corner and plugged it into a wall socket. "I'll go get you the remote."

After he left Sally plopped down onto the edge of one of the beds. Silvio plopped down next to her. Sally bent her head over and lifted her blouse slightly to wipe her dripping face on the blouse's edge. "Phew, sorry, guys, but I had to do that. Geez, how the heck could anybody forget about air conditioning here?"

Ascensión laughed. "Nobody thinks about air conditioning here. Don't worry, you'll get used to it."

"Never," said Sally.

Silvio grunted his agreement.

Lupe whisked in through the open door, looking happy and breathless. She held a paper bag in one hand and the air conditioner remote in the other. "Here," she said, handing Sally the remote, "the *hotelero* asked me to give this to you."

"Oh, thank God," said Sally as she and Silvio both lunged for the remote.

"Sally, shut that window, shut the door," said Silvio as he hit the remote buttons.

"High," said Sally, "put it on high, max."

"High, yeah, max," said Silvio.

Lupe and Ascensión laughed as Sally and Silvio parked themselves on the floor, their faces in front of the cold air blowing from the air conditioner vent.

"Who can stand all that air conditioning in the middle of winter?" asked Lupe, still laughing as she set the bag on the table then took David from Ascensión's arms.

"Yeah," said Silvio. "Right. Winter."

"So when is the hot time of year?" Sally asked without turning her head away from the air vent.

Lupe sat on the bed and held David on her lap. "Oh, February, March, April, May. Then it starts to cool off in June into the lower thirties."

"Nineties in American Fahrenheit," Ascensión added. "*Amor*," he said to Lupe, "why were you out of breath just now when you came in? You weren't running?"

"Well, I was hurrying back with some food." She set David on the floor then rose from the bed and stepped over to the table and pulled from the bag a box filled with plantains, corn bread, several bottles of water and two paper plates. She set two pieces of corn bread on each plate then shook the plantains onto the plates, piling more on one plate than the other. "Come over here, sit and eat," she said to Sally and Silvio. "We'll go out for dinner later but this will hold you over." She took one bottle of water and the plate with the lesser amount of plantains and sat on the bed and motioned for Ascensión to sit next to her.

Sally and Silvio pulled themselves up from the floor and sat at the table. They dug hungrily into the plantains, still warm and crispy, and the fresh cornbread.

"Oh, my God, what did they do with these bananas?" said Sally. "They're delicious."

"They're plantains," said Ascensión. "We eat them all the time."

"They're great," said Silvio. "And this cornbread? Man, I'm gonna be eating this all day while I'm here."

Lupe and Ascensión laughed again. "You'll have no problem finding cornbread," said Ascensión. "Someone is selling cornbread on every street corner."

"Cornbread, plantains, beans and rice, cakes, custard, you can buy anything to eat on the street," said Lupe.

"But where did you find these plantains?" said Ascensión. "They're nice and brown and crisp."

"Over by the market," said Lupe.

Sally put down the plantain she was holding and Silvio held his piece of cornbread suspended in mid-air.

"Uh...from Marco's?" said Silvio.

"*Marco's?*" said Lupe looking horrified. "Of course not Marco's! Nobody buys food from Marco's."

Sally and Silvio looked relieved and continued eating.

"But how did you know about Marco's?" said Lupe.

"The *hotelero's* wife warned them," said Ascensión.

"Ah, good," said Lupe. "No, I bought this food from a little old *abuelita* who probably just brought it from her kitchen."

"Well, somebody's grandma sure can cook," said Silvio.

"All the grandmas in Nicaragua can cook," said Ascensión.

David now sat on Ascensión's lap while Lupe fed him pieces of plantain and cornbread and gave him sips of water from the bottle.

"Look at our son," she said. "He knows how to eat the food of his people."

"Oh yeah," said Silvio, "that little guy's a great eater. Eats like a little football player."

"But, *amor*," said Ascensión to his wife, "no more running to and from the market. From now on you walk."

Lupe laughed. "Running won't hurt me. Remember all the pregnant American women we used to see running? And look how healthy their babies are."

"*Pregnant?*" said Sally and Silvio together.

Lupe nodded and smiled. Ascensión kissed her cheek.

"Oh, my God, congratulations, you guys," said Sally. She and Silvio hurried over to the bed and Lupe and Ascensión stood to hug them. "So happy for you," said Sally, hugging each of them hard.

Sally switched places with Ascensión and sat next to Lupe on the bed so that the women could discuss pregnancies, babies, and other maternal subjects while the men sat next to each other at the desk.

"Look," said Silvio, "I just want to let you know that it's great that you and Lupe are expecting and this doesn't change anything as far as me wanting you to come to work for me."

"Thank you, my friend," said Ascensión. "This baby also doesn't change our desire to come to the U.S."

"Okay, good," said Silvio. "So we're still on the same page, and all. And look, I know the visa is taking a while, but I want you to know that Charleston is still on it and I'm still on it. It's just...this kind of thing...immigration, you know...it's taking a while these days."

"Yes, we know the feeling about immigrants in your country."

"No, no, not all of us are like that," said Silvio. "You know that, right?"

"Yes, we know," said Ascensión.

"Yes, of course we know," said Lupe, joining the men's conversation. "And we know that you are doing all you can for the visa. But don't worry about that today. Today we're all happy. You rest for an hour or two and we'll take David out for a walk in his stroller to meet our friends at *Casa de las Sonrisas*."

"*Casa de las Sonrisas?*" said Sally.

"House of Smiles," said Lupe. "It's a shelter for street children where I work on the weekends."

"Street children?" said Silvio. "You think that's, uh..." He and Sally exchanged a look.

"But first, Ascensión," said Lupe, "would you get me a glass of water?"

Ascensión took the glasses from the table, entered the *baño*, then returned and handed one of the filled the glasses to Lupe.

"Wait a minute," said Silvio. "Aren't you not supposed to drink the water?"

Lupe and Ascensión laughed again. "*You* are not supposed to drink the water, or our Davicito, either, at least until you have been here long enough to get used to it. We have been drinking it all our lives." They toasted each other with their water glasses then drank.

After Ascensión and Lupe left with David Sally and Silvio flopped down next to each other on the bed.

"So, here we are in a hotel room, no kids," said Sally.

"When's the last time we had this kind of privacy?" said Silvio.

"When's the next time we'll have it?" said Sally.

"So…what should we do?"

"Take a shower, maybe? See what happens next?"

"You think it's safe?" said Silvio.

"What, taking a shower?" said Sally.

"Taking a shower, seeing what happens next," said Silvio. "I mean, seeing as we're in this foreign country, and all."

"I think people take showers—and all the rest—in foreign countries. I mean, otherwise why would they have a shower stall? And a bed?"

"Yeah, I guess," said Silvio.

"So what do you say?" said Sally. "Shall we get in the shower then see what happens next?"

Silvio turned to Sally and smiled. "Yeah, okay."

Silvio and Sally opened the door to the *baño* and stepped inside.

"Oooh," said Sally.

"Well, would you look at this," said Silvio.

The bathroom had walls and floors of bright blue tile. There was no shower stall as such, but attached to the far wall was a shower head and faucet positioned over a drain in the floor. Against one of the side walls was a mirrored sink above an open cabinet on the shelves of which were towels, soap and shampoo, while against the opposite wall was the toilet. The roof was thatched palms that covered only as far as the sink and toilet. The shower was open to the sky and over the unroofed sections of the walls were visible the tops of palm trees and other tall exotic plants.

"Oh, how, cute is this?" said Sally.

"Uh, this bathroom's outside," said Silvio.

"Just the shower is," said Sally.

"Yeah, and the shower is, like, right in the room. I mean, no shower curtain, or anything."

"I know," said Sally. "Kinda sexy, isn't it?"

Silvio smiled. "Yeah, it kinda is. Okay, let's give it a try."

***

"Whoa, wait, what, there's no hot water?" Sally hopped out from under the shower.

"Huh, doesn't look like it," said Silvio. "The water's not that cold, though."

"The heck it isn't," said Sally, wrapping her arms around herself.

"Aw, come on back in," said Silvio, reaching for Sally and pulling her back under the shower next to him. "We'll shower fast and warm up afterwards."

After they toweled dry they returned to the bedroom and climbed under the sheets.

"Damn," said Sally, "now I'm cold and all we've got is this sheet. You think there's any blankets in that armoire?"

Silvio got out of bed and walked over to the armoire. "Huh, I don't see any. Maybe I oughtta turn off the air conditioning?"

"Yeah, that's a good idea. It's kinda freezing in here. And maybe open the window, let a little heat in?"

"Eh, I don't know about opening the window. Here, I'll open the bathroom door. That leads to the outside."

"Yeah," Sally said with a yawn. "That should work." She yawned again, turned on her side and pulled the sheets up over her shoulders.

Silvio looked around for the air conditioner remote, which he finally found lying on top of one of the pieces of luggage. After he turned off the air conditioning he opened the bathroom door and stepped inside for a moment to warm up from coldness of the room. Then he crawled into bed next to Sally to find her softly snoring. Silvio yawned then sighed, "Yeah, me, too, Baby." He turned on his side, pulled up the sheets and closed his eyes.

An hour later, refreshed from their nap, Sally and Silvio sat out on the patio. Nikhil appeared from the lobby pushing a cart filled with bags of fruit juice which he offered to the guests, stopping to chat for a moment with each guest.

"How's it going?" he asked Sally and Silvio as he handed them each a bag of juice with a straw.

"Hey, thanks," said Silvio as he reached for his juice bag. "Going good, going good. This juice in a bag is something different."

"But we're loving it," said Sally, poking a hole into her bag of juice. "Oh, by the way, the hot water doesn't work in our shower."

"Oh yeah," said Silvio, "and could we get a couple of blankets?"

Nikhil scratched his head. "Well, I could scratch up some blankets. If you really want them. But I can't do anything about the hot water. There's no hot water anywhere in this part of Nicaragua."

"*What?*" said Sally and Silvio. Then Sally said, "You're telling us there's no place to take a hot shower *anywhere* around here?"

"Oh, I think maybe you could find a hot shower at, say, the Imperial Hilton in Managua. But anywhere else? Not likely. But look, you're in the hottest part of Central America. There's no need for hot showers."

"Uh, that's debatable," said Sally.

"Unless you keep your air conditioning cranked up. Otherwise why would you need blankets and hot water when it's ninety-four degrees outside?"

"This place is gonna take some getting used to," said Silvio.

Nikhil chuckled. "It always does. Why don't you try turning off the AC and turning on the fans instead? Might help you get acclimated quicker."

"Yeah, okay, I guess we could try that," said Silvio. "Seeing as we're gonna need all the help we can get."

"Hey," said Sally, "have you heard of a place called, what was it Silvio, 'Casa de las Sonrisas?'"

"Yeah, I think that's what they called it," said Silvio. "A place for street kids? Our friend works there."

"Las Sonrisas? Sure, I know them. One of the ladies, Rafaela, she comes over here and gives us a hand once in a while when we need some extra help. Sometimes we send food over there if we have a lot of leftovers."

"Oh," said Sally. "So it's, you know, safe? I mean, it's just that our friends were going over there with their baby."

"Oh sure. They're good people, Rafaela and Cristela and the other ladies who help with the kids. And there's even an American who helps out there sometimes…shoot, I can't think of her name. Hey, Cassie," Nikhil called to his wife, who appeared on the patio carrying two rolls of toilet paper. She walked over to where he stood with Sally and Silvio. "Cass, what's the name of that American chick, the redhead, who sometimes hangs with Cristela over at Las Sonrisas?"

"Yonny, Yellie, I don't know, and I'll thank you kindly not to refer to any female who hasn't just hatched from an egg as a 'chick.'" Cassie sounded irritable and she looked tired.

"Where you going with that TP?" asked Nikhil.

"Oh, those Belgian backpackers in room ten."

"They want more? What are they doing with it? Eating it?"

"Huh, they'd best not be flushing it, and if I don't see it in their trash can then I'm guessing they're either eating it or stuffing it into their backpacks for down the way." Cassie turned to Sally and Silvio. "By the way, you know not to flush the paper down the commode, right?"

"Well, yes, we saw the note in the bathroom," said Sally. "But why? Plumbing problems?"

Nikhil chuckled. "All over Central America. It would take an army of plumbers to replace all the old pipes in this neck of the world."

Sally and Silvio glanced at each other. "Is that so?" asked Silvio.

"It's so," said Nikhil. "So what do you say? The U.S. has sent armies down here for a lot less beneficial reasons than to fix the plumbing. How about you send some troops to help us with that?"

"Oh you come on, now," said Cassie, playfully bopping her husband with a roll of toilet paper. "These folks don't want to hear your politics and neither do I." She winked at Sally and Silvio. "Don't pay him any mind, he's just joking with y'all."

"I was," said Nikhil. "No offense."

· "No, it's okay," said Silvio. "I think that's kind of a good idea."

"Silvio's a plumber," said Sally, and immediately wished she hadn't when she saw Cassie and Nikhil's eyes light up.

"That so?" said Cassie.

"You're a plumber?" said Nikhil.

"That's right," said Silvio. He gave Sally a look.

"Oops," said Sally. She looked apologetically at Silvio.

"Well, if you happen to have some time during your stay..." said Nikhil.

"It's just a problem with one of our toilets," said Cassie.

"Dante usually fixes these things for us," said Nikhil, "but he says we need a plumber for this one."

"But the plumber he always gets for us is his wife's cousin's husband, and his wife and her cousin aren't talking now so he can't ask the cousin's husband," said Cassie.

"Can't you just get another plumber?" said Sally.

"Dante said that if we did his wife's cousin's husband—that's the plumber—wouldn't appreciate it," said Nikhil.

"Which means we can't fix the toilet, which means we can't fill the room..." said Cassie, twisting her hands.

"...until the plumber's wife makes up with her cousin," said Nikhil, also twisting his hands. "But we don't want to impose on you."

"No, we sure don't," said Cassie.

"But if you did happen to have a little time..." said Nikhil.

"We'd have to pay you the local rate," said Cassie. "We couldn't near afford what you make in the States."

The two looked at him with such anxiousness and hope that Silvio sighed, "Well...I mean, I guess could have a look. But I don't have my tools, or anything."

Cassie and Nikhil looked overjoyed. "Oh that's no problem," said Nikhil. "Dante can lend you his."

It turned out that the broken toilet was in the room next to Sally and Silvio's. Dante knelt next to Silvio as he investigated the problem and Nikhil stood over both of them. Sally sat in the bathroom on a chair she brought in from the bedroom, fanning herself with a magazine that had been left on the bedroom table.

"Corroded inner valve," Silvio said, showing the rusted piece to Dante and Nikhil. To Nikhil he said, "Tell Dante if he can get me one of these I can fix it pretty easy."

Nikhil explained in Spanish to Dante, who took the piece, nodded, and left.

A short time later Sally and Silvio were back out on the patio, this time lying next to each other in a wide hammock.

"Funny," said Silvio.

"What is?" said Sally.

"You know what was wrong with that toilet?"

"I don't know," said Sally. "I think you said a corroded...something or other?"

"Inner valve. A corroded inner valve. You remember who else's toilet had a corroded inner valve?"

Sally laughed. "How the heck would I remember who else's…oh, no, wait a minute…you don't mean…not…"

Silvio nodded then they both burst out laughing.

"*My* toilet," said Sally. "*My* toilet the day I called for a plumber and *you* showed up…the day we met…and damn near slugged each other."

Silvio laughed again and pulled Sally closer. "Boy, what a pair we were, huh? A couple of strangers. Both of us mad at the world."

"Well, we were mostly heart-broken strangers," said Sally. "Our divorces, our kids…and now look at us. Hey, what if we could have seen into a crystal ball that day you came to fix my toilet? What if we could have seen that you and I would end up together?"

"Married."

"With six kids between us."

"In Nicaragua swinging in a hammock."

"I sure would have felt better seeing all that," said Sally.

"Me, too," said Silvio. "A *lot* better. But then, you and me, we felt better soon enough after that day, didn't we?" He kissed her forehead.

"Mmmm." Sally closed her eyes. Silvio closed his as well.

"*Señor, señor.*"

Sally and Silvio opened their eyes to see Dante standing over them smiling. In his hand was a new valve. He spoke to them slowly enough, with profuse gesturing, so that they understood something about calling his wife's cousin's husband, who brought him the valve, but don't tell his wife…or something like that.

Silvio showed Dante how to replace the valve, after which Dante called Nikhil to show him the functioning toilet, impressing upon him that his wife's cousin mustn't find out about her husband's surreptitious delivery of the new valve.

"Man, you don't know how grateful we are," Nikhil said to Silvio. "What do we owe you for this?"

"Aw, don't worry about it," said Silvio. "Last time I fixed one of these it brought me really good luck."

"Hope it does again," said Nikhil. "Oh, and I put a couple of blankets on your beds. And the air conditioning is on us."

***

Sally, Silvio, Lupe and Ascensión sat around a table in a three-walled restaurant which opened out into a square lined by palm trees. David sat in a highchair between his parents, who took turns spooning into his mouth a mixture of mashed plantains, red beans and rice.

"Gallo pinto con plátanos y crema," said Lupe, passing around one of several platters of food that had been set by the server on their table.

"That's beans and rice with plantains, vegetables, meat, and cream sauce," said Ascensión. "And these are *nacatamales,*" he said, passing around another platter. "Rice, vegetables and meat wrapped in corn dough and cooked in a plantain leaf. But don't eat the plantain leaf. Lupe, give them some corn bread."

"Try the *baho,*" said Lupe, serving Sally and Silvio helpings of the dish made of beef, green plantains, cassava, onions and peppers and topped with coleslaw. "You'll like it."

"I'm liking all of it," said Silvio, digging into the pile of food on his plate. "And the beer, too." He raised his bottle of *Victoria.* "Here's to great food, great friends," he raised his bottle a little higher, "and great beer."

"And here's to our wonderful friends Sally and Silvio," said Lupe, raising her bottle of water. "You have made us so happy and brought our David back to us."

Sally and Silvio glanced at each other. "For a while," said Sally.

"Yes, don't worry," said Lupe. "We know it's only for a while. But we won't think about that tonight. Tonight we'll pretend it's forever."

"Aw, sure, why not?" said Sally, again raising her bottle of *Victoria*. She took a sip and almost choked on it. She pointed towards the square. "Oh my God. What the heck just happened?"

"What?" said Lupe and Ascensión.

"That," said Silvio. "Out there, outside. It was just day, now all of a sudden it's night."

Lupe and Ascensión laughed. "That's how it is here. It's day, then boom, it's night."

"At a quarter after six," said Lupe. Her smile disappeared and she gasped. "It's a quarter after six! Oh, no, Ascensión, the last bus to Krukrulitos will leave soon! We stayed too long at *Las Sonrisas*, it's my fault." She turned to Sally and Silvio. "But I was so happy to bring David to see our friends there, and they had a party for us, and Yoolie—our good friend, you'll meet her—she was there and she brought cake, and David played with the children, and it was so nice, and that's why we were so late getting back for dinner."

"*Calma, calma,*" said Ascensión, resting a hand on his wife's shoulder.

Sally turned to Silvio. "Couldn't we set them up at our hotel? Then they could spend the night and wouldn't have to worry about rushing for the bus."

"Sure," said Silvio. "You can just spend the night at our hotel."

"Oh, no, we couldn't bother you that way," said Ascensión. "We'll find a taxi to take us home."

"No, please," said Sally. "Spend the night at the hotel."

"Can we, *amor*?" said Lupe. "It would be so much easier. And so nice to spend more time with Sally and Silvio. We were going to come back and get them tomorrow morning to bring them to Krukrulitos. This way we won't have to."

"You're bringing us to Krukrulitos?" said Sally.

"Yes, we're bringing you to our house to meet our family and have a big Nicaraguan breakfast," said Ascensión.

"But can't we stay the night in León with Sally and Silvio?" said Lupe. "It would be easier for David, see how tired he is." She reached and pulled the yawning baby, his hands and mouth sticky with his dinner, from the highchair and cradled him in her lap. "And we could give him a nice *bañito* in the shower there."

"Well…" said Ascensión. "Maybe we could. I'll have to ask my mother."

"Ask your mother?" said Sally.

"I mean, uh, *call* my mother," said Ascensión.

"Yes, call your mother and tell her we're staying here. Tell her, uh… that we missed the bus. Or no, tell her that our American friends are nervous to spend their first night in Nicaragua alone. Tell her David is so tired. Tell her we'll bring David and our friends *pronto* tomorrow morning."

Sally and Silvio exchanged another look. Ascensión stood, reaching into his back pocket for his phone. He pulled in a deep breath. "I'll be right back."

He returned from making his call looking rattled.

"Ascensión?" said Lupe.

"You okay, Man?" said Silvio.

Ascensión quickly smiled. "Yes, yes, of course, everything is fine."

Lupe took her husband's hand. "Thank you, *amor*," she said.

"Of course, of course," he said. "It's fine. We'll stay with Sally and Silvio tonight, no problem."

At that moment the lights blinked out in the restaurant and all the buildings around the square went dark.

"Uh-oh," said Silvio.

"Don't worry," said Ascensión. A moment later the lights blinked back on. "You see? Every night the electricity goes out for a few hours. But all the businesses in town have generators. Some of the houses do, too."

"But why do the lights go off every night?" Sally asked.

"Because so many people do not pay their electric bills," said Ascension.

"And so instead of making some go with no electricity and others having electricity all the time, everybody gets electricity some of the time and goes without some of the time," said Lupe.

"Hmmm. Well, I guess that's one way of dealing with the problem," said Silvio.

"But of course the rich people all have generators so it isn't a problem for them," said Ascensión.

"It isn't a problem for us, either, because Ascensión built a generator for our house," said Lupe.

"Wow," said Sally.

"I remember that time when you were living in Philly that you showed me how to fix a generator," said Silvio. He lifted his beer bottle in salute to Ascensión. "You're good at your stuff."

"You are," added Sally.

Lupe jumped in. "And he will be so good when he comes to work for you in the U..." She stopped, suddenly worried about tempting fate with too much hope.

"No, no, it's still gonna happen," said Silvio. "Like I told Ascensión, Charleston is still on it."

"We've just gotta have patience," said Sally. "And faith."

"We still have patience, and faith, too," said Lupe.

"It'll all be good," said Sally. "You'll see."

"When we finish dinner we'll go for a walk and get ice cream if you're not too tired," said Lupe.

"Too tired for ice cream?" said Silvio. "Not me."

"Not me neither," said Sally. "But let me call the hotel now and make sure they have a room for you."

"A room for us?" said Lupe. "Why would we need a room for us?"

"Yes, don't spend the money for another room," said Ascensión. "There are two beds in your room."

Sally and Silvio looked at each other. Sally said, "But, um, wouldn't you like some, you know, privacy?"

"*Privacy?*" Lupe and Ascensión said at the same time. They looked at each other and burst out laughing.

Later that night Sally and Silvio lay in each other's arms under the sheets, comfortable after another cool shower and the breeze of the room fan.

"Now, this feels okay," said Silvio.

"We must be acclimating, like Nikhil said. But I feel kind of guilty, persuading Lupe and Ascención to take their own room by lying to them that I was going to set the air conditioning on 'high' all night."

Silvio chuckled. "Nah, it was worth it. Probably for them, too. I mean, to have a night to themselves."

"Speaking of which, what do think was going on with Ascensión? I mean, the phone call, his mother…"

"Yeah, I noticed that, too. He was acting kind of funny."

"I wonder if he has mother issues."

Silvio shrugged. "I wouldn't think Ascensión would be the kind of guy to have mother issues. But then, I guess you never know, huh?"

Sally yawned. "I guess not."

***

Jaime entered the patio from the kitchen holding a bottle of beer in each hand. He sat down next to Ernesto in front of the television and handed Ernesto one of the bottles. "She's crying again," he said.

"These women," said Ernesto, taking his beer. "Do they never run out of tears?"

Jaime opened his mouth to reply, but he no more knew what to say or do about his mother-in-law sobbing her heart out in the kitchen than did her husband, so both men drank their beers and watched the soccer game being played on the screen before them.

In the kitchen Violeta sat at the table surrounded by her daughter and several women who stayed even after all the other relatives had left upon hearing that Lupe and Ascensión would not be returning to the village that night with their child.

"It's those Americans," said *tia* Pilar. "They think they own everything. Even our children."

One of Violeta's relatives spoke up gently. "Violeta, *querida*, maybe it really was just that the baby was tired. Maybe they were all tired."

"Of course they're too tired to come home to their family when they could spend a night in a fancy hotel," Xiomara said bitterly.

"All I know," said Violeta through her tears, "is that woman has taken my son away from me and now she has my grandson, too."

"But *tia* Violeta," said Lidia, "aren't they coming back tomorrow morning? For the big breakfast?"

"Of course, of course," said *tia* Pilar, waving her hand in disgust. "They'll always come back when there's food to be had."

"But not to help make it," said Xiomara.

"Don't worry, Xiomara," said one of the women, affectionately rubbing Xiomara's back, "we'll help you and your mother get the breakfast ready."

"That's not the point," said Xiomara. "*Lupe* should be here to help us instead of spending the night in a fancy hotel with the Americans and keeping that baby to herself instead of bringing him to his family who loves him." Xiomara began sniffling. "And who would *never* give him up, *never*."

Violeta wiped her eyes. "She abandons her baby, abandons her husband, and what does she get for it? She gets rich Americans to travel all the way down here to bring her baby to her and put her up in a hotel. She gets her husband, my son, who should have left her on the street, to chase after her and bring her back into this house, pregnant again with another baby that she'll probably abandon, too. And am I allowed to say a word to her, to even open my mouth in my own house?"

"Nobody is allowed to say a word to her," said Xiomara. "Or else Ascención will bite off their head."

Violeta began tearing up again. "My son, my *own son* won't even stand up for me."

"It's a sad situation when a son won't even stand up for his own mother," said *tia* Pilar.

"Oh, I don't blame Ascención," said Violeta. "He's always been the perfect son. Until now. *She's* the one who made him change, I know it." She began sobbing into her hands while the women tried to comfort her, one stroking her hair, another rubbing her back.

"She's spoiled, spoiled, spoiled!" cried *tia* Pilar. "But what do expect when you let a princess from Managua into your house? Abandoning her own child! Someone should teach her a lesson!"

Violeta lowered her hands and looked up. "Yes," she said. "Yes, someone should."

Chapter Fifteen

"Where do you think they are?" said Sally. She knocked again on Lupe and Ascensión's hotel room door.

"They're sure not here," said Silvio, looking around.

"Oh, they're yonder in the electrical shed," said Cassie, who appeared on the patio pushing a cart holding covered plates of food.

"You give room service?" asked Sally.

"Why, we'll give you whatever service you want," said Cassie. "Long as you pay us for it." She rolled her cart up next to Sally and Silvio. She planted one hand on her hip and waved her other hand for emphasis, hamming it up as she spoke. "Breakfast is seventy cordobas—about two American dollars, right?—but those toilet paper-eating backpackers in room ten? They want to be *served* their breakfast, lazy old things. Fine, I'll serve 'em. Cost 'em a hundred and fifty cordobas extra for the service, but I'll serve 'em, oh, I *will* serve 'em." Cassie sighed dramatically. "I expect I'd best be about my serving. 'Bye." After she'd rolled her cart a few feet she stopped and turned back to Sally and Silvio, who by now were laughing helplessly. She pointed a finger at them. "By the way, y'all's breakfast is free. 'Less you want to be served, too."

"No, no," Silvio laughed, wiping his eyes. "But hey, can you tell us again where our friends are? In the electrical shed, you said?"

"Over there, though that door," she said, pointing to a wooden door in a corner on the other side of the courtyard. "It'll be unlocked." She then continued on with her cart to room ten.

"What the heck are they doing in the electrical shed?" said Sally.

"Huh, maybe the toilet's not the only thing that was on the fritz around here."

"You think maybe they can sniff out repair people?"

"Probably for a mile," said Silvio.

They found Ascensión on the other side of the door in a small room on the wall of which were fuse boxes, switches, and assorted wires. He knelt on the floor hunched over a large generator, a needle-nose pliers in one hand and a small thin wire in the other. Nikhil was hunched next to him, closely watching him work.

"You see this?" said Ascensión, showing Nikhil a small section of wire. He caught sight of Silvio standing in the doorway and waved him over. "*Oye*, Silvio, come, see this."

"What have you got?" said Silvio, entering then kneeling over the generator between Ascensión and Nikhil.

"A short in this wire," said Ascensión. "That's why the electricity was going on and off during the night. Can't have that, eh, *hombre?*"

"It's been a problem," said Nikhil.

"But is okay now, I've spliced together a new piece."

"Hey," said Silvio, "if Ascensión says it's okay, it's okay. He knows his generators."

Sally still stood in the doorway. "Uh, yeah, good morning, guys."

The men turned towards Sally. "Aw, sorry, Babe," said Silvio. "You know us guys and our generators."

"*Oh*, yeah," said Sally. "I know all about guys and their...generators. Ascensión, where's Lupe and David?"

"Here we are," said Lupe, coming up behind Sally, pushing David in his stroller. "I was getting David some milk. But you're not finished yet, *amor?*" She continued in Spanish, "If we're late for breakfast you know they'll blame me."

"*No te preocupes,*" said Ascensión. He stood and brushed off his jeans then said to Sally and Silvio, "All ready to go now?"

"Wait, what do I owe you?" said Nikhil.

Ascensión waved his hand. "Don't worry about it, *maje.*"

"Are you kidding?" said Nikhil.

"It was not a big thing."

"Hey, well, thanks. I owe you."

Ascensión chuckled. "I'll remember that, *maje.*"

The group traveled in two taxis to Krukrulitos and their arrival at the Somarriba's was greeted with cheering and excitement by the family members who'd been waiting at Mauricio's house on the patio and in the yard, on which were set an assortment of chairs and a few tables which relatives had brought from their houses. The relatives gathered around and alternated between fussing over Lupe, Ascensión and David and Sally and Silvio, who came laden with treats they'd picked up that morning at the market, bags of *rosquillas*, the traditional doughnut-shaped Nicaraguan cookies.

Ernesto reached for David, who was munching on a *rosquilla*. "*Oye*, give me my grandson. His great-grandfather Mauricio wants to meet him."

"Where's *mamá?*" asked Ascensión, handing his son to his father.

"She and Xiomara are in the kitchen with some of the women making the breakfast. Ah, look at this big boy," said Ernesto, bouncing David in his arms and kissing his cheek.

"All that American food," said one of the men.

"He's very healthy," said one of the women.

"The Americans must be feeding him well," said another.

"Bah, he needs some good Nicaraguan food," said Ernesto. "Come, *nene*, your grandma Violeta wants to feed you."

"Wait, let me wipe off his hands and mouth first, he's covered in *rosquilla*," said Lupe, reaching into her purse for a baby wipe.

"No, no," laughed Ernesto. "His grandma will be happy to see him enjoying his *rosquilla* like a little *Nica*."

As the group walked from the lawn towards the house Cousin Lidia, who was carrying her own baby, sidled up next to Lupe.

"*Lupita*, you know, some of us…"

Lupe stopped. "Yes, Lidia?"

"I mean…*all* of us…everybody is very happy today for you and Ascensión."

Lupe put her arms around Lidia and her child. "Oh, thank you, *Lidiacita*."

After Lupe had entered the house Lidia stood in the yard with several other women.

"Should I have warned her that Violeta is upset?" said Lidia.

"What for?" said one of the other women. "If Lupe doesn't know by now that she's a thorn in Violeta's side she never will. Let's go see these Americans."

Sally and Silvio found themselves standing in the middle of the yard handing out *rosquillas* to the children and practicing their Spanish.

Sally turned to Silvio. "You remember that day I called for a plumber to fix my broken toilet and you showed up at my door?"

"What? Well…yeah, of course I do, but…what, you're still thinking about that crystal ball?"

"Yeah. This time I was thinking that what if at that moment, I mean the moment I answered the door and we laid eyes on each other for the very first time, what if the crystal ball appeared right then and we saw ourselves a year later standing together in a jungle clearing handing out cookies? What do you think we would have thought about that?"

Silvio laughed. "I would have thought the future had gone crazy. Heck, maybe it has."

"Yeah," Sally chuckled. "That's about the only explanation I can think of. Hey, you think it's okay to be giving these kids cookies before breakfast?"

"Eh, nobody's telling us not to," said Silvio. "And it's making us some friends."

"Oh, speaking of friends, did it sound to you like Lupe said that if we were late getting here everybody would blame her?"

"Yeah, I thought she said that, too. But then Ascensión told her don't worry about it."

Sally tsked. "I wonder what that was about?"

"I don't know, but I guess it's all good. I mean, nobody seems mad at anybody."

"All these relatives gathered together in one place? Believe me, somebody's mad at somebody."

A fat, friendly looking young man came up to Sally and Silvio. "I'm Jaime, I'm married to Ascensión's sister. Welcome to Krukrulitos."

"Thank you, Jaime," said Silvio. "I'm Silvio. This is my wife, Sally."

"*Mucho gusto,*" said Jaime. "Ah, are those *rosquillas?*"

"Yes," said Sally, offering Jaime a cookie.

"Mmmm, fresh," said Jaime, biting into his cookie.

One of the women standing nearby laughed. "Jaime, those are for the children!"

"No, no," said Silvio. "We have plenty. Please, here." He handed a bag of cookies to one of the adults and gestured that it should be passed around.

Lupe came hurrying out from the house to the yard. "Sally! Silvio! I'm so sorry! How did we leave you all alone out here!"

Sally laughed and gestured to the children and adults around them. "Well, we're not exactly all alone."

"That's right, they're with me," said Jaime, throwing one arm around Silvio's shoulder while still eating his cookie.

Lupe laughed. "Yes, thank you, Jaime, you're all doing wonderfully. But come, Sally and Silvio, meet the others, and it's almost time to eat."

Lupe led Sally and Silvio to the house, stopping to introduce them to Mauricio, who was enjoying the festivities from his chair on the porch. He reached out to Sally and Silvio and took one of their hands in each of his hands. "Welcome, welcome to my home," he said.

"Yes, this is *abuelito* Mauricio's home," said Lupe. She opened her arm and gestured around her. "And all this land is his."

"And yours too, of course, *chiquita*." Mauricio removed his hands from Sally's and Silvio's and wrapped them around Lupe's. "No matter what all those old hens in the kitchen say."

Lupe bent forward and wrapped her arms around Mauricio in his chair. "Thank you *abuelito*, thank you."

Sally and Silvio exchanged a glance.

On the other side of the curtain the kitchen was crowded and bustling with women scooping food from pots on the stove onto plates that were set out on the kitchen table. In a corner of the kitchen sat an old woman who looked to be keeping an eye on the kitchen activity. At the table Ascensión sat next to an attractive older woman who shared his handsome features and who held David on her lap.

"Violeta, here, you eat first," one of the women said, setting a plate of food in front of her. "You've been working since dawn and this is your special day." The woman caressed David's face and planted a kiss on his chubby cheek. "Who can believe how beautiful he is? He looks so much like his grandmother."

The women agreed in chorus that it was quite unbelievable how beautiful this child was and several stopped to fuss over him and his grandmother, whom everyone agreed should immediately eat something.

"No, no, don't worry about me, feed the others first," replied Violeta. "Ascensión, where are your...? Ah, look, here they are! Our American friends!"

Attention turned from the food and the baby to the Americans standing in the doorway.

"Everyone," said Lupe, "these are our good friends Sally and Silvio. Sally and Silvio, this is Ascensión's mother, Violeta. And over there," she gestured towards the greatly pregnant woman who was transferring slices of corn bread from a pan to the plates on the table, "is Ascensión's sister, Xiomara."

"*Mucho gusto*," Xiomara said coolly, without stopping her work.

"I think we met your husband," said Sally. "Jaime?"

"Yes, they met me," said Jaime, standing in the doorway munching on another cookie.

"What are you eating?" said Xiomara in a stern tone, as if she were speaking to a child. "Is that a *rosquilla?*"

"We brought them," said Silvio to distract Xiomara's attention away from her beleaguered husband. He held up a bag of the cookies. "Here, do you want one?"

"Before breakfast?" Xiomara sounded horrified. "Jaime, why are *you* eating that cookie before breakfast? I've been on my feet since dawn fixing this good food and you're eating *rosquillas?*"

One of the women put an arm around Xiomara's shoulder and led her over to the table. "*Xiomarcita,*" she said, "your poor husband is hungry, and you need to eat, too, for the little one." She patted Xiomara's stomach. "Get yourself some food, sit down, someone else can cut the cornbread."

"I can help," said Sally. "I can cut the cornbread."

"No, of course you won't work," said Violeta with a warm smile. "You are our guests."

"That's right, Sally," said Lupe. "I can finish the bread." She strode to the counter and began cutting and serving squares of cornbread. "Sally, Silvio, get yourselves a plate. Ascensión, you, too, and fix a plate for *abuelito* Mauricio. Go sit by him on the patio. Tell him all about America, he'll love to talk to you."

"Oh, ho, ho," Xiomara said from where she now sat at the table rubbing her back. "Look at little Lupita coming into the kitchen after all the work is done and taking over." She said it with a smile, as if she were joking. "But really, Lupe," she added, "you know we don't expect *you* to work. Yoselin," she called to one of the women, "will you finish the cornbread?" To Lupe she said, "You just go feed yourself and don't worry about *abuelito* or anyone else."

Lupe stopped and stood for a moment open-mouthed. Her eyes darted around the room to see if all the women were looking at her, wondering what she would do or say. She saw Yoselin take a step towards her then stop. Lupe was too embarrassed to look at Sally or Silvio, but her eyes finally landed on Ascensión, who stood and picked up a plate of food from the table then said to her, "*Querida*, just put a piece of cornbread on this plate for *abuelito*. Sally and Silvio, take a plate from Lupe and come, we'll sit out on the patio. Lupe, come out and join us when you've finished working in the kitchen." Ascensión looked defiantly at his sister and nodded to Lupe, who mouthed the word *gracias* to him then continued with the cornbread.

Violeta chuckled. "Such a fuss over the cornbread! Of course you can work in the kitchen if you want to, Lupe, dear. Nobody in this house will stop you from working when you feel like it. We just don't want you to wear yourself out."

"I'm fine, Violeta," said Lupe.

"Of course she is," said Sally. All eyes in the kitchen were now on the Americans who stood holding their plates of food. Ascensión stopped in the doorway and turned back to the kitchen. Sally looked around the room and smiled but moved a step closer to Silvio. Very softly in English she said, "Back me up, Sil."

"Yes, Lupe is a very strong woman," said Silvio, also offering the friendliest smile he could manage. "She's the strongest woman we know."

"Oh, she is?" said Violeta, still smiling.

"Yes, she is," said Sally with a nod for emphasis. "And a hard worker."

"And smart," said Silvio, also nodding.

"And brave," said Sally.

"And strong," Silvio added once more for good measure.

"*Gracias,*" Lupe said softly.

The other women in the room looked at each other, some covering a smile. Violeta and Xiomara looked taken aback.

Tia Pilar spoke up from her corner. "Maybe for an American she's strong, but we Nicaraguans, we're much stronger. We have to be."

"At least those of us who didn't grow up rich with lots of servants," added Xiomara with a smile and looking directly at Lupe.

Several of the other women also looked at Lupe, including *tia* Pilar, who nodded and mumbled, "*Sí, sí.*" However some of the women purposely looked away from Lupe so as not to embarrass her more. Ascensión stood in the doorway as if frozen, holding the two plates of food. Lupe continued to put cornbread on plates, showing no reaction.

Violeta broke the excruciating silence. "*Oye,* enough joking," she chuckled. "Is no one hungry? Sally, Silvio, don't you want to eat?"

"Yes, I'm very hungry," said Silvio, sniffing the plate of food appreciatively. "Ummm."

"Me, too," said Sally. "This looks delicious. Thank you, Violeta and everyone, for making all this beautiful food."

"Our pleasure," Violeta said sweetly. "Ascensión, why are you still standing in the doorway? Bring *abuelito* his breakfast. Sally and Silvio, go and eat. Someone go tell everybody to come to the kitchen, the food is ready."

All the women hurried outside to fetch the relatives, each one wanting to escape the tense scene in the kitchen, leaving Lupe, Violeta, Xiomara and tia Pilar.

"I'm finished with the bread," said Lupe. "Violeta, I can take David for a while."

"Fine, take your son," said Violeta. Her warm smile was replaced by a look of cold hostility.

"I just want to give you a break so you can eat," said Lupe, lifting David from Violeta's lap.

"Fine, fine," said Violeta. "Take him. Go to your American friends. Do what you want."

"Lupita always does what she wants, doesn't she?" said tia Pilar sweetly.

"Always," said Xiomara, equally sweetly.

"But I only…" Lupe looked at the three women, tears welling up in Violeta's eyes, animosity radiating from the eyes of the other two.

Lupe whisked her son from the kitchen onto the patio. From the other side of the curtain she heard Xiomara say, "Just watch her run tattling to Ascensión!" followed by Violeta sobbing, "My son *and* my grandson…she takes *everything* from me," followed by *tia* Pilar scolding, "Oh, you stop that crying now, Violeta. Look here comes everyone. That's right, wipe your eyes, stand up, look happy, don't give her the satisfaction. You'll have your due, and she'll have hers."

Lupe hurried across the patio to where Ascensión sat with Mauricio and also Sally, Silvio, and several other relatives who had gathered around the American guests. Lupe stopped and closed her eyes and felt her heart pounding as she was hit with a terrible thought: *Might they hurt her David to hurt her?*

"Hey," Silvio said in English, "what are you trying to do, squeeze the stuffing out of him?"

"What?" Lupe opened her eyes and saw the group on the patio smiling at her. She realized how tightly she was holding David. "Oh, no," she answered him in English, "I just…I'm just so happy to have him." She kissed her son on his forehead.

"Here, let me hold him now," said one of the women, opening her arms to take David.

"Yes, don't keep this beautiful little treasure all to yourself," said another, stroking David's cheek. "Let all of us have a turn."

"That child's feet haven't touched the ground since he arrived in Nicaragua," Sally attempted to say in Spanish, and succeeded well enough that the others in the group laughed.

Ascensión rose from his seat and stepped over to where Lupe stood and said softly into her ear, "Let them hold him, *mi amor*, he'll be all right."

Lupe looked into her husband's eyes then gingerly handed her son over to the woman who stood waiting to take him. She then took a seat and Ascensión brought her a plate of food that she didn't want and she could neither focus on the conversation going on around her nor keep her eyes off her son as he was passed around from relative to relative.

But after a while she relaxed. Ascensión's family members fussed over David and kissed him and bounced him, and when Violeta finally exited the kitchen looking benevolently matriarchal she opened her arms to David and held him lovingly and basked in grandmotherly pride. Even Xiomara playfully whisked him away from Violeta and set him at her feet and played with him then watched him carefully while her children played with him. *They all love him*, she thought with relief and joyful gratitude. *They may hate me, but they love him.*

***

The meal was over and most of the relatives had gathered up their children and gone back to their houses before the arrival of the afternoon rains. Lupe was in the house napping with David in her and Ascensión's bed. Xiomara dozed on one of the patio hammocks while her children played in a corner. The rest of the family sat with Sally and Silvio on the porch watching the rain, chatting and asking about life in the United States. Violeta and Ascensión brought out mugs of coffee and plates of homemade *picos,* cookies filled with sugar and cheese. After she finished handing out the coffee and cookies Violeta returned to the kitchen.

"Is your mom in there by herself cleaning up the dishes?" Sally asked.

"Oh," said Ascensión, looking around for his mother. "She probably is."

"My wife is a real work horse," said Ernesto proudly. "Always working."

"My daughter has always been a hard worker," added Mauricio, sounding just as proud.

"I see where Ascensión gets it from," said Silvio.

"Yes, my grandson is a hard worker, too," said Mauricio. "And my granddaughter. Both are just like their mother."

Sally turned to Silvio and said in English, "Yeah, well, the woman may be a regular Clydesdale, but she shouldn't be in that kitchen in this heat washing all those dishes by herself."

"She's probably used to the heat," said Silvio. "Unlike me." He pulled his handkerchief from his pocket and mopped his brow, which made his hosts laugh and state what Silvio had just observed, that Americans weren't used to the Nicaraguan heat.

"Even so, I don't feel right. C'mon, let's go help her."

"You think that might be rude here?" said Silvio. "To offer to help with the dishes?"

"It's not rude," Ascensión cut in. "But I doubt my mother will let you, her guests, or any of us except for Xiomara or Lupe help her with the dishes. She often washes them by herself."

"Well, she's not washing them by herself today," said Sally. "C'mon, Silvio."

As Ascensión had warned them, Violeta refused to let Sally or Silvio help with the dish washing or any part of the kitchen clean-up. But she invited them to stay in the kitchen to talk to her while she worked. Sally and Silvio complimented her on her wonderful cooking and her hospitality.

"Not at all," said Violeta with a smile. "It's an honor to have Americans in my home. And my son says you are such good people."

"Thank you," said Sally.

"Your son is a good person, too," said Silvio.

"And so is Lupe," added Sally.

"Ah, yes, thank you, they are," said Violeta affectionately. "But I must tell you the truth. Although Lupe has been part of my family for years there's something about her I don't understand. I shouldn't ask you, but since you knew her so well in the United States, perhaps you can explain it to me?"

Sally and Silvio caught each other's eye briefly. "Well, uh," Silvio said, "I don't know if we know her *that* well."

"You didn't know her that well? That makes it all the harder to understand."

"Harder to understand what?" said Sally.

"Why she gave away my son's baby to you. Oh, *Dios mío,* forgive me," she quickly added, reading the taken aback expressions on their faces. "I can see I shouldn't have asked."

"No, it's okay," said Sally as soon as she'd found her tongue. "Lupe didn't give us their baby."

Violeta chuckled tersely. "Did you *take* their baby?"

"No," said Silvio. "We didn't take their baby."

"Hmmm," said Violeta. "She didn't give you their baby and you didn't take their baby. How did you get their baby? Forgive me again, I just want to know. "

Sally and Silvio sat speechless, neither feeling equipped to explain the American foster care or immigration systems in Spanish.

Silvio finally took a stab at a rough explanation. "Uh, well, see, Ascensión and Lupe had to return to Nicaragua because they don't have a visa yet and David is American, so…"

"Oh, so America won't allow children to go home with their parents? To be with their family, their grandparents and aunts and uncles and cousins?"

"No, no, it's not like that," said Sally. "Not exactly."

"It's complicated," said Silvio.

"Ah, complicated," said Violeta. "Or maybe Lupe wanted to leave her child in the United States so he could have a better life than his poor family could offer him here in the jungle?"

"Lupe didn't want to leave their son and neither did Ascensión," said Sally. "They were very sad. It almost killed Lupe."

"Oh," said Violeta. "I know of women who would die before they would give away their children. You see how little we have here in Krukrulitos. Women have nothing else to live for but their children. Maybe in a rich country like the United States it's different. And Lupe is from a very rich family from Managua. So perhaps it wasn't as hard for her."

"No, no, it was hard for her," said Sally. "It was really hard."

"She and Ascensión are coming back to America for David as soon as they can," said Silvio.

"Oh, they are?" said Violeta. "But I don't understand why they need to return to the United States for David. He's here now. Why won't you just leave him here?"

"We can't," said Silvio. "We have to bring him back."

"Why?" said Violeta. "His parents are here. His family is here. Do you think we wouldn't love him and feed him and care for him well enough?"

"No, it's not that at all," said Sally. "He's an American. He doesn't have a visa right now."

"Oh, that's right, he's an *American*. I keep forgetting an American child cannot live in Nicaragua."

"No it's not..." Sally stopped when Silvio put a hand on her arm and shook his head slightly.

"You have a really nice family," said Silvio.

"Yes, everyone is so nice," said Sally, taking Silvio's cue.

"And Ascensión is the smartest man I ever met," said Silvio.

"Thank you, I'm very proud of Ascensión and all my family. And I love my grandchildren, they are the most important thing in the world to me. But my heart longs for the one who can't be with me." Her eyes began to tear up.

"We understand," said Sally. "And we're sorry that David has to be so far from you."

Violeta wiped her eyes on her apron and smiled. "Ah, never mind me. I'm just a foolish old woman. Tell me, Sally and Silvio. Do you have children?"

Silvio chuckled. "We have five."

"*Five* children? *Qué bueno!*"

"Well, they keep us busy for sure."

"Of course," said Violeta. "But...again, I don't understand."

"You don't understand?" said Sally. "What, why we have five children?"

"No," said Violeta. "I don't understand why with five children of your own you needed to have my grandchild, too."

Sally and Silvio again sat speechless. "Uh, we just wanted to help," said Silvio.

"Ah, yes, of course," sighed Violeta. "Americans are so helpful."

***

The sun had returned and now Silvio and Sally strolled around the Somarriba property encompassed by the surrounding jungle. They stopped to look at the line of volcanoes off in the distance.

"This is like a scene from a movie," said Silvio.

"It is," said Sally. She cocked her head back towards the house. "Complete with the drama."

"Oh, yeah, that," said Silvio. "Boy, you sure called it right when you said in a group of relatives there's always somebody who's mad at somebody."

"Yeah, well, it looked to me like some of those somebodies were mad at Lupe."

"I wonder why?" said Silvio.

"And *I* wonder how you say 'passive-aggressive bitches' in Spanish," said Sally.

"*Putas pasivas-agresivas.*"

They turned around and saw Lupe, up from her nap, standing behind them.

"Oh, uh…hi, Lupe," said Sally, reddening. "Were you, uh…? Hey, we didn't mean anything, really, we were just, uh, you know…"

Lupe hurried over to Sally and hugged her hard. "Please don't worry," she said. "It's okay that you were talking about me." She pulled back from Sally and wiped a tear from her eye. "I have so few friends in this village. But while you and Silvio are here I know I have at least two."

This time Sally hugged Lupe then kissed her cheek and Silvio put his hand on her shoulder. "You know you do, Babe," said Sally.

"Then I won't worry about the *putas pasivas-agresivas* today. Look," she said, opening her arm to the vista before them of jungle and volcanoes. "Do you like it?"

"It's amazing," said Sally.

"Is that smoke coming out of some of the volcanoes?" said Silvio.

"Yes," said Lupe. "These are all active volcanoes so there's often a little smoke."

"And look at those two palm trees," said Silvio. He craned his head back and gave an appreciative whistle.

"Those are *señor* and *señora* Frondosa," said Lupe. "They're *abuelito* Mauricio's favorite trees. Me, I feel a little sorry for them."

"What, you feel sorry for the trees?" said Silvio.

"Because they don't fit in with the rest of the trees."

Sally thought a minute, then she said, "Well, no. But at least they have each other."

Lupe smiled. "Ah, that is true. So perhaps I should be happy for them instead. As long as one doesn't die before the other."

"Anyway," said Silvio, "we sure don't have anything like that in Philly."

"No," Lupe laughed, "but you have buildings even higher than *señor* and *señora* Frondosa. Come, look at this." She led them about five hundred feet deeper into the property to a spot where Momotombo rose up above the horizon.

"Wow," said Sally and Silvio at the same time.

"This is Momotombo, one of the biggest volcanoes in Nicaragua."

"Momotombo?" said Sally. "Isn't that the same name as the power plant where you and Ascensión work?"

"Yes, we work on Momotombo."

"Wait," said Silvio, "you work *on* the volcano?"

"Yes. The power plant is *on* the volcano. The energy for the power plant comes from the volcano."

"Wow," said Sally and Silvio again.

"Looks like that bad boy is really smoking up a storm," said Silvio. "Does it always smoke that much?"

"No, not always that much," said Lupe.

"Oh," said Sally. "Is it, you know, dangerous?"

"Oh, no, it's not at all dangerous. Engineers from all over the world work there and we have visitors and give tours all the time. It's a very big geothermal plant." Lupe's eyes lit up. "But you must come up and visit the Momotombo plant! You can meet our boss, Yoolie. She's an American, too, and wonderful like you."

Sally and Silvio chuckled. "I don't know how wonderful we are," said Sally.

"But sure," said Silvio, "I'd love to see the geothermal plant on the volcano. Whata you say, Sal?"

"Sure," said Sally.

"Wonderful," said Lupe. "Come tomorrow."

"Tomorrow?" said Sally. "What about David? Didn't you want us to take him back to the hotel with us and watch him tomorrow while you were at work?"

"I think he could stay here, don't you? He is doing so well with the family."

"Yes, he does seem to be doing fine," said Sally.

"Probably because he's used to getting passed around like a little football with our kids," Silvio chuckled.

"You can leave him here tonight, then. In this family we have all the things we need to take care of a baby. And Ascensión's mother and sister and cousins will take good care of him. The *putas pasivas-agresivas* may not like me, but they love Ascensión and they love children. I trust them completely."

They strolled around the property for a while with Lupe showing them the gardens and the animals in their pens then stopping in to say hello to the relatives who sat outside or called to Lupe from the doorways of their houses. As they were heading back to the house they saw Ascensión approaching them carrying David. Upon catching sight of them Ascensión broke into a broad smile. *"Ahí estan,"* he said.

"Yes, here we are," said Lupe. She hurried towards them then kissed her son on his cheek and her husband on his forehead. "What have you and our *pequeñito* been doing?"

"Listen to this," said Ascensión. *"Oye, maje,"* he said to David, who responded with something that sounded rather like *"Oye, papá."*

Lupe squealed with delight and everyone laughed and clapped, including Baby David.

Chapter Sixteen

Ascensión and Lupe had advised Sally and Silvio to take an early bus from their hotel to Momotombo.

"How early?" they'd asked.

Lupe and Ascensión had looked at each and shrugged. "About eight am," Ascensión had finally said. It was agreed that Ascensión and Lupe would meet them at the Krukrulitos stop.

"How will you know which bus we're on?" they'd asked. Ascensión and Lupe appeared to think on it for a moment then Lupe said, "Why don't you call us when you get on the bus?"

Now Sally and Silvio bounced along with the other riders seated on the bench that ran the length of the canvas-covered military-style deuce-and-a-half truck that had stopped to pick up the workers and other Monday morning passengers at the bus stop to which Nikhil and Cassie had directed them a block from the *Casa de la Recolección*.

"Wait there and keep your ears peeled," Nikhil had advised them. "The driver of every vehicle that stops will get out and announce where the vehicle is going. Eventually a vehicle headed for Momotombo will arrive."

Silvio scratched his head. "By vehicle you mean…what? A bus?"

"A bus, an old school bus, a truck, a van. Anything that can take on passengers is a bus around here," said Nikhil. "Anyway, if other folks are climbing on board it should be safe." Cassie nodded in agreement.

"Should be?" said Sally.

"Oh, yeah," said Nikhil.

"Totally should be," Cassie agreed.

Sally and Silvio looked at each other.

"Maybe we should, like, take a taxi?" said Sally.

"Nah," said Nikhil. "A couple of American tourists who don't yet know how to negotiate a taxi ride? The driver will take the long way and charge you double and you won't even know you're being charged double."

Sally and Silvio both smiled. "Yeah, we've kinda already been there," Silvio chuckled.

"We almost got hooked into taking a taxi on our own from the airport for a thousand cordobas," said Sally.

"A thousand cordobas?" Nikhil laughed.

Cassie laughed, too, but then turned to her husband, "Now, come on, Honey, you know that you and me got ourselves a little bit rooked a time or two in the beginning."

"True," said Nikhil. "Anyway, you can depend on the bus to get you there."

"Eventually," Cassie added.

"And for pennies," said Nikhil. "You're in León, do as the locals do."

"Okay," said Sally. "I guess we've done crazier things than take a bus in a strange city."

"Yeah, I guess we have," said Silvio. "So do you know if there's a bus around eight o'clock?"

This time Nikhil and Cassie looked at each other and laughed. "Just go out and stand at the stop," said Nikhil. "The bus'll come when it comes."

"And don't y'all worry," said Cassie. "You'll be fine."

Nikhil and Cassie had been right: The bus came when it came and they were fine. That is to say, as fine as two nervous white

Americans could be who were sitting—bouncing—and sweating on a crowded bench facing another bench crowded with people whose eyes were fixated on them as if they were some sort of curiosities. Which, on this army truck bus, they in fact were.

A very elderly woman with her white hair pulled back in a bun stared at Sally and Silvio until she succeeded in catching Silvio's eye. Then she said, "¿A dónde van, chele?"—Where are you going, White Man?

When it became clear from his answer that he understood Spanish the passengers broke into smiles and peppered Silvio and Sally with questions on who they were, where they were from, what they were doing in León, how they liked Nicaragua.

While the truck lumbered through town people got off and on at the stops, the benches alternately losing and regaining occupants along the way. However after the truck crossed the highway that separated the city from the road that led to the jungle villages and up to Momotombo, all the riders except for Silvio and Sally wore ENEL badges around their necks or clipped to their shirts.

After they had been traveling along the jungle road for some time chatting with their fellow passengers, Silvio patted Sally's knee. "Hey," he said to her, "is it just because it's so hot in this truck or does it seem like we've gone a long time without stopping?"

"Huh?" said Sally, who'd been conversing with a pleasant young woman sitting next to her. "Oh, yeah. Yes, it does." Sally and Silvio looked around them, though there were no windows in the truck to reveal exactly where they might be.

"Como?" asked the girl Sally had been talking to. The other passengers looked expectantly at Sally and Silvio, waiting to hear what they had been conversing about in English.

When they asked how soon until Krukrulitos, some of the passengers chuckled, others shook their heads sympathetically.

One of the passengers said that they had surely passed Krukrulitos by now.

"What?" gasped Sally and Silvio.

The passenger explained that the driver wouldn't have stopped because the truck was full. Once the benches were full the truck would not stop unless someone pulled the cord to get off. Otherwise anyone waiting at a stop would have to catch the next bus.

"Oh, no, now what do we do?" said Sally.

"I'll call Ascensión," said Silvio, reaching into his pocket for his phone.

The passengers advised Sally and Silvio to stay calm. There would be no phone reception on this truck in the jungle, they said. Buses and cars, no problem, but no one could get service on the trucks in the jungle. Nobody knew why. But their friends would surely be on the next bus and would meet them at Momotombo. The passengers then got into a discussion of what should be done with the two Americans while they waited for their friends to arrive from Krukrulitos. They should come inside the plant, the gate guards would surely let them inside. After all, they were Americans and friends of...who were they the friends of?

"Lupe and Ascensión," Sally told them.

"Guzman," Silvio added.

Yes, of course, a few of them knew Ascensión, a few others knew Lupe. They could wait for the Guzmans inside the gate...maybe they could wait at the Visitors' Center, yes, that would be nicer...even better, someone could call Yoolie and tell her there were two Americans at the Visitors' Center, wouldn't she want to meet them?

At the mention of "Yoolie" Silvio and Sally sat up in their seats.

"Yes!" said Sally. "We know about Yoolie! From Lupe and Ascensión!"

The passengers smiled and nodded. "Then we must go and find her for you," said one.

"She'll want to meet you," said another.

"That's okay," said Silvio. "We'll just wait somewhere for the Guzmans. We don't want to bother Yoolie."

"*Por supuesto que no!*" said a passenger. "Yoolie won't mind. She's an American, too." The passenger smiled widely, as did most of the rest of the passengers on the truck.

When the truck arrived at the gate of the Momotombo geothermal plant the passengers hurried to the gate, many of them explaining at once that there were two Americans here to see Yoolie, which message confused the guards, who were accustomed to being notified prior to the arrival of important visitors, nor were they used to said visitors arriving via public transport. As Silvio and Sally, the last passengers to exit the truck, approached the gate, one of the guards upon spotting them pulled out his phone to call Yoolie.

"Yoolie's not picking up," said the guard.

"I passed her just now heading up to generator five," said a guard in a jeep who had pulled over to see what the excitement was about.

"Is it okay if we wait here?" Silvio said to the gate guard who had just tried calling Yoolie.

"What is your business here at Momotombo?" the guard asked.

"They are tourists and friends of Ascensión," said one of the workers.

"Ah, friends of Ascensión," said the guard with a smile. "But where is Ascensión?"

"The truck was too full to pick him and Lupe up," said another worker. "But Yoolie is expecting them."

"Oh," said Sally, "See, I don't know if, uh..." She turned to Silvio and said softly in English, "Wait, do you think maybe she's actually expecting us?"

Silvio shrugged. "Beats me what's going on." In Spanish he said, "Please don't trouble yourselves. We can wait here."

"Why don't I take them to generator five?" said the guard in the jeep. "She's probably still there."

The two gate guards looked at each other and shrugged. "If Yoolie is expecting them…"

The guard in the jeep motioned for Sally and Silvio to get into the jeep. Afraid not to, they got into the jeep. As they drove off the other workers waved.

The jeep wound up the road along the slope of Momotombo until it arrived at generator number five. For the length of about ninety feet ran a complex of massive cylinders, pipes, wires, gauges, and several small towers emitting a flow of steam. There were a few workers milling around, including a helmeted welder in protective overalls who was working with an acetylene torch on a spot at the far end of the generator.

"Would you look at that," said Silvio.

"Wow," said Sally.

The guard, who, though he spoke no English, understood that these Americans were expressing their admiration, sat tall and stopped his jeep in front of the generator.

"There are four other generators besides this one," he said, "but number five is the most important one. Momotombo gives power to them all."

"That's one big volcano," said Silvio.

"Yes," the guard said proudly, "it's a big volcano." He pointed towards a jeep parked a few feet away. "There's *señora* Yoolie's jeep, you see? She's here somewhere." He pulled out his phone and dialed a number but hung up a few moments later. "She's still not answering. But you can ask one of the men where she is." He gestured to Sally and Silvio that they should exit his jeep.

"What the heck are we supposed to be doing here?" said Silvio as he and Sally stood at the worksite, looking around for they knew not whom or what.

"Damned if I know," said Sally. "I feel flipping ridiculous."

"Maybe if we hang around long enough Lupe and Ascención'll get here and find us," said Silvio.

"But how will they know where to find us?" said Sally. "Hey, why don't you try calling Ascensión again. See if they're off the jungle bus yet."

Silvio made the call then hung up. "No reception. They must be on an army truck, too. Hell, we should've just waited at that gate."

"Ha, it's not like we didn't try."

They stood for a few moments longer then Sally said, "Okay, I'm starting to feel like an idiot just standing here and all these guys looking at us."

"Okay, so let's ask those two guys who are coming towards us," said Silvio.

"Uh, ask them what?" said Sally.

"I don't know," said Silvio. "I guess ask them where this Yoolie is."

"Except that we're not actually looking for Yoolie. *Señora* Yoolie Whoever-She-Is doesn't have a clue in hell who we are."

"Can we help you?" asked one of the workers.

"Um, we're looking for Yoolie," said Sally. "*Señora* Yoolie."

Both men smiled. "Ah, *señora* Yoolie," said one. He looked around then said to the other man, "Have you seen Yoolie?"

The other man looked around. "There's her jeep," he said.

"Yes," said the first man. "You can wait by her jeep."

"Okay, *gracias*," said Silvio. To Sally he said, "Like we're not already waiting by her jeep."

"We're at least ten steps away from her jeep," said Sally. "Oh, for crying out loud, let's just keep calling Ascensión and in the meantime let's at least walk around, or something, so we look like we belong here."

"We don't look like we belong here," said Silvio, pulling out his phone, dialing, then hanging up. "But okay, we could look at this generator, I guess. Better than being on that crazy hot truck."

"For sure," said Sally. "Okay, so let's look at the generator."

They began walking along, looking at the generator. As they approached the far end the welder, who had been working hunched over on one bended knee, straightened up then appeared to catch sight of them.

"Oh great," said Sally. "Now that welder guy is looking at us."

"He probably wonders what we're doing here."

"Maybe we better go say something to him."

"Like what?"

"Like what else?" said Sally. "Tell him we're looking for Yoolie."

"Yeah, okay," said Silvio. "What harm can it do?"

They hurried over to the welder, who continued watching them as they approached.

"Uh, *con permiso*," said Silvio, using the polite form of interrupting.

"Buscamos a señora Yoolie," Sally finished for him.

The welder put down the torch, stood, and removed the helmet. Sally and Silvio found themselves looking into the freckled face of a tall, blue-eyed, red-haired woman.

"Yo soy Yoolie," said the woman.

Sally and Silvio looked at each other then at Yoolie, who looked back at them, and for a moment all three stood looking at each other.

"Uh, you're American, right?" Silvio finally said.

"Yes?" said Yoolie. "Are *you* Americans?"

"Yeah," said Sally, "We're Sally and Silvio—"

"Jablonski," Silvio finished for her. "And we're here because, uh, well, see..." He looked at Sally for help explaining why they were there.

"Wait..." said Yoolie. "You're *Sally* and *Silvio*? The Guzmans' friends from Philadelphia?"

"What, you've heard of us?" said Sally.

Yoolie's perplexed expression changed to a smile. "Why, yes, I have. The Guzmans told me about you. How you helped them. And it's you who brought Baby David here to see them."

Silvio and Sally breathed audible sighs of relief. They were in friendly territory. "Yeah," said Sally. "That's us."

"It's a pleasure to meet you," said Yoolie. She slipped off her protective gloves, switched the helmet she carried from her right arm to left arm and extended her right hand to shake with the Jablonskis. "I'm Julie Pursglove. 'señora Yoolie' since I moved down here. But please go ahead and drop the 'señora.'"

"Happy to meet you, Jul…Yoolie," said Sally.

"You don't *know* how happy," said Silvio, wiping his arm across his sweating forehead.

Yoolie chuckled. "I can guess. But of course I *am* wondering what you're doing up here on the volcano looking for me?"

Sally and Silvio began speaking at once.

"Well, we were going to meet Lupe and Ascensión to go see the volcano where they work-"

"See, we're staying in León, at a hotel—"

"They said we should take the bus and meet them, but—"

"And we took the bus, from the hotel, right? Well, near the hotel—"

"The bus, actually it was a truck, and it didn't stop at Krukrulitos, so—"

"We were supposed to meet them, Lupe and Ascensión, I mean, but—"

"Everybody on the bus said—"

"So when we got here, I mean, to the gate, everybody on the bus, er, the truck—"

"Whoa, whoa, *stop*," laughed Yoolie, patting the air with her free hand. "I'm getting the gist, but could you slow down some?"

"Ah, could you explain, Sil?" said Sally, sounding slightly breathless. "I'm feeling a little, uh…"

"Follow me to that storage shack, over there," said Yoolie, pointing to a small nearby cinderblock structure. "It takes a while to get used to this heat. Even at this hour."

"You're telling me," said Silvio, again wiping his forehead.

"Especially when your day starts with a ride in an army truck," said Sally.

Sally and Silvio sat on two of the half a dozen molded plastic chairs scattered around the storage room with a fan blowing in their direction. Yoolie had given them each a bottle of cold water she retrieved from a small refrigerator. She stepped out of her overalls, under which she wore khaki pants and an ultra-lightweight long-sleeved shirt, and returned her gear and equipment to one of the supply closets. Meanwhile Sally and Silvio explained, this time more coherently, how they ended up on Momotombo looking for her.

When they had finished their story Yoolie chuckled, "Welcome to Nicaragua. And to Momotombo."

"Aw, thanks," said Silvio. "Hey, could I trouble you for another bottle of that cold water?"

"Certainly," said Yoolie. She fetched them each another bottle from the refrigerator. It occurred to her that Lupe and Ascensión's benefactors were not at all as she had pictured them. She had imagined an older couple, middle-aged at least, exhibiting the self-assurance and self-regard of age and affluence, people with a long-established social conscience and the means to take under their wing two young undocumented immigrants and their child.

But these two were just a couple of bewildered youngsters themselves—Sally didn't look thirty, and Silvio, this supposed successful business-owner, looked just barely that. Along with her curiosity about them Yoolie felt an immediate affection for them and concern for their well-being, these babes in the wood. Or rather, the jungle. Still, they obviously weren't completely helpless. They apparently spoke some Spanish and had succeeded in sorting themselves out so far. Which was good because, whatever her personal interest in them might have been, right now she had other concerns that she needed to tend to sooner rather than later.

"So, you, uh, do a lot of welding around here?" Silvio asked.

"Not as a rule," said Yoolie. "But I was up here early this morning and I noticed a couple of spots on the tubing." To herself she added, *Why were there were scorch spots on the tubing?*

"Oh, yeah, I know how that goes," said Silvio. "Sometimes it's easier to do it yourself."

"Um-hmm," said Yoolie, adding to herself, *It would be a helluva lot easier than to have to deal with that snotty nitwit Alejandro, but I better try and get him up here anyway to have another look at the volcano.*

"That's probably why you didn't hear your phone when the gate guards were trying to get ahold of you," said Sally. "I mean, because of the welding noise."

"No doubt," said Yoolie. "Which reminds me, I need to return their calls." She pulled out her phone. "Tell you what, I'll also see if someone is available to come fetch you. It's air conditioned in the Visitors' Center so you can wait there until Ascensión and Lupe—"

"*Ay, ay, ay, Dios mío,*" cried Lupe as she burst through the door of the shack. She rushed to Sally and Silvio still sitting in their chairs and bent to hug each of them awkwardly. "The guards told us you were up here, and then we got a ride from the one in the jeep…"

Ascensión hurried in behind her. "*Perdónenos, muchachos,*" he said breathlessly. "The bus…"

"Don't worry about it," said Silvio. "We're fine, aren't we, Sal?"

"Oh, yeah," said Sally. "We're good." She raised her water bottle in a mock toast.

"I'm sorry, Yoolie," said Lupe. "When I got to work I was going to ask you if Nico could give our friends a tour of the plant."

She chuckled then added, "But they found their way up to the generator on their own."

"They did," said Yoolie. She turned to Silvio and Sally. "Look, I'm sorry. Ordinarily I'd be more than happy to have Nico from the Visitors' Center give you a tour of the plant. But the generator might be needing just a little maintenance today, so…"

"Uh-oh," said Silvio. "Is that why you were out there welding just now?"

Ascensión looked dismayed. "You were welding, Yoolie? What, on number five?"

"Yep," said Yoolie. She gave the smallest shake of her head then cocked her head ever so slightly towards Sally and Silvio. Ascensión gave her a barely perceptible nod, but sufficient to let her know that he understood that she did not wish to further discuss the generator in front of their guests.

But Silvio picked up on their communication. "Say no more," he said. He stood and motioned for Sally to do the same. "We'll get going. I know how generators can be."

"That so?" said Yoolie.

"Por supuesto," said Ascensión. "He is a plumber. And he also knows about generators."

"I mean, not a lot about this kind of generator, but…anyway, at least we got to see it. So I guess Sally and me'll take you up on that ride back to the gate. Then what? Wait for another bus to town?"

Yoolie sighed. "Tell you what. Ascensión, I'm going to stay up here for a while. You take my jeep. Drop Lupe off at my office so she can get to work and then go ahead and drive these guys back to León. When you get back you need to go on down to the motor pool first thing and pick up your truck. The paperwork's all ready to sign it over to you."

Ascensión smiled broadly and Lupe clapped her hands in delight. "Our truck is ready? Oh thank you," she said, giving Yoolie a hug.

"Thanks, Boss," Ascensión said. "And Lupe," he teased, "you shouldn't be hugging *la jefa*."

"It's okay," Yoolie sighed.

***

Ascensión and the others piled into Yoolie's jeep and as soon as they were out of sight Yoolie pulled out her phone and dialed the number of *Los Caminadores*.

"Yoolie! What's up, my girl?"

Yoolie recognized the voice of the young Dutch volunteer. "Hey, Jan. Any Momotombo tours scheduled today?"

"Today? Hmmm...Let...me...No, none today. None tomorrow."

"Okay. Do me a favor, Jan?"

"Anything in the world for you, *señora* Yoolie."

"Can you call me—or leave a message for anybody who's on duty to call me—before the next Momotombo tour is scheduled?"

"I can if you want, Yoolie. Something going on?"

"Oh, no. Just a scheduling thing with the geothermal plant."

But that was what her Grandma Pursglove would call a whopper fit to choke Satan's mule. The truth was that Yoolie had a bad feeling about the volcano.

***

Lupe stepped out of the jeep in front of Yoolie's office but then turned back. "Sally," she said, "would you and Silvio please stop at Krukrulitos and visit David?"

"Oh...sure," said Sally. "We could do that, huh, Sil?"

"Yeah, we could," said Silvio.

Ascensión looked uneasy. "I'm sure David is fine," he said.

"Of course he is," said Lupe. "But it will make him happy to see Sally and Silvio, too." She clasped her hands together. "And we want our David to have so much love and be as happy as can be!"

"*Sí, sí, por supuesto, amor*. But how will they get back to León from Krukrulitos?"

"The bus, of course," said Lupe. "Or taxi."

"Yeah, I think we're gonna want to take a taxi this time," said Silvio.

"Okay," said Ascensión. "But...Maybe you could tell my mother you just stopped in to say 'hi?'"

"Isn't that what we're doing?" said Silvio. "Stopping in to say 'hi?'"

"Yes, that's all they're doing," said Lupe. "Saying 'hi' to David. And your family, too, of course." She stepped back into the jeep for a moment to kiss Ascension's cheek. "Don't worry, *amor*, all will be well."

Ascensión sighed. *I hope so,* he thought.

***

Ascensión pulled up to the gravel road that led to the dirt path to his family's house. "When you're ready to leave you can call *El Rayo* taxi service in León to come and pick you up. Only call *El Rayo*. I know Santos, the owner. His drivers are all honest. I'll text you the number."

"Great," said Sally. "Thanks."

"Can I leave you off here? It's just a short walk to the house."

"Wait, aren't you coming in with us?" said Sally.

"No, no," said Ascensión. "I'll see David tonight. Now I have to get back to Momotombo with Yoolie's jeep."

"But is it okay to just show up at the house like this?" said Silvio. "You wanna at least call your mom and let her know we're coming?"

"No, it's not necessary. My mother will be happy to see you. Please give David kisses from Lupe and me."

As they walked towards the house Sally said, "Yeah, I bet his mom'll be happy to see us."

Silvio laughed. "Real happy."

"You see how fast Ascensión hauled ass back to work? He was probably worried about his *mamá* breaking his nougats for bringing the Americans back."

Silvio laughed again. "I sure hope she doesn't start breaking mine."

"Ha," said Sally. "Yours and mine both."

They found David on the patio happily playing with his cousins Mauricito and Blanca while Xiomara and their great-grandfather Mauricio watched them. But as soon as he caught sight of his foster parents he began crying and toddling towards them with outstretched arms.

"Didi, Didi," he cried.

"Oh, oh, oh," Sally cooed as she scooped him up in her arms and kissed his cheek. "Hey, fella, what's the matter, huh?"

Xiomara looked momentarily confused. "No one told us you were coming back to take David."

"We didn't come back to take him," said Sally.

"We just stopped by to say, 'hi,'" said Silvio.

Mauricio stretched out his arms. "Welcome, welcome," he said.

"You didn't need to come by to check on him," snapped Xiomara. "He was doing fine. Now you see he's crying."

"What's wrong?" said Violeta, hurrying from behind the house where she had been tending to the animals. "Oh, what? You're here? Are you taking David?"

"No, no," said Silvio.

"They just came by to say 'hello,'" said Xiomara, her voice dripping sarcasm.

"To say 'hello?'" said Violeta.

"They were worried about David," said Xiomara.

"We weren't—"

"What?" Violeta cut Sally off. "You didn't trust me to take care of my own grandchild for one day?"

"No," said Sally, "we just…" she turned to Silvio and said softly in English, "Should we throw Lupe under the bus, or what?"

"Nah," said Silvio. "Lupe has to live with her. Better let her think we're the villains."

"What are you saying?" Violeta snapped. "You were talking about Lupe! She put you up to this!"

"Well, uh, no, uh, see," said Sally, "Lupe and Ascensión, they just thought—"

"*Lupe* thought," Violeta cut her off. "*Lupe* told you to come here, didn't she? David was happy here with his family, playing with his cousins, but she sent you here to make him unhappy so that you would have to take him with you. Well, fine! Take him with you! Take my grandchild away from me! Take him away from his aunt and his cousins and his great-grandfather!" Violeta stormed into the kitchen in tears.

"What's going on?" said Ernesto, who appeared from behind the house carrying a basket full of eggs. "Why did Violeta run off and leave me with these eggs?"

"The Americans came to take your grandchild," said Xiomara.

"What?" said Ernesto.

"No, really, we don't want to take him," said Sally. "We just stopped in for a visit. Here, I'll put him down and he'll be fine, then we'll…"

But when Sally sat David back down on the ground he stood and grabbed her leg. "Didi, Didi," he cried.

"Maybe if we stay for a little while he'll get busy playing again," said Silvio.

"Yes, stay for a cup of coffee," said Mauricio.

"No thanks, we're good," said Silvio, pulling out his handkerchief and wiping his forehead.

"You want a beer?" said Ernesto.

"No," said Violeta, appearing in the kitchen doorway and wiping her eyes. "You came to take my grandson. So take him and go." She turned and disappeared again into the kitchen. Xiomara followed behind her.

Ernesto waved a hand dismissively. "Sit," he said. "I'll get you a beer."

Sally and Silvio declined his offer and he, too, disappeared into the kitchen with his basket of eggs. A moment later there was the sound of arguing and crying coming from the kitchen.

"Sit, sit," said Mauricio, then he, too, rose and went into the kitchen. Sally and Silvio looked at each other, shrugged, and sat. David, seeing that his Didi and Didi weren't leaving him, returned to playing with his cousins.

"Okay," Sally sighed. "I guess we've been in more awkward social situations."

"Yeah, right," said Silvio. "So what are we supposed to do now? Leave and take David with us?"

"Or sit here and listen to the fighting?" said Sally.

"We shouldn't have stopped," said Silvio.

"I know, but what were we supposed to do?"

"Beats me," said Silvio. "Tell you what. I'm gonna go in there and ask them what we should do."

"You're a braver man than me," said Sally.

"I don't know about that." Silvio got up from his chair and headed towards the kitchen when Violeta stepped onto the patio the carrying David's diaper bag which she set on the ground.

"How did you get here?" Violeta asked.

Silvio and Sally exchanged a glance then Silvio spoke up. "Well, see, we were visiting Momotombo—"

"To see the electrical plant," Sally finished.

"Right, we wanted to see the plant," said Silvio. "And then afterwards Yoolie lent Ascensión her jeep—"

"So we could stop in," said Sally. "To say 'hello.'"

"Of course," said Violeta with a wave of her hand. "The Americans help the Americans."

"It wasn't exactly like—"

"My son drove you here?" Violeta cut Sally off. "Why didn't he come in to *'say hello,'* too?"

"Well, see, he had to get back to work," said Silvio.

"Really?" said Violeta. "He didn't have five minutes to come in and say 'hello' to his mother and father after he drove all that way?"

"It wasn't that far," said Silvio. "It's just a mile or so up the road."

"*Uhhh!* Fine! Tell him he can back come and get you now!"

"Um, we were going to call a taxi," said Sally.

"*El Rayo,*" said Silvio.

"*Uhhh!*" Violeta scooped up David and held him tight, planting kisses all over his face and head while the tears rolled down her cheeks. "Good-bye, *mi amor, mi corazón.* Remember that your *abuelita* loves you so much and will miss you."

"We can bring him back a little later," said Silvio.

"Maybe after his nap?" said Sally.

"*Uhhh!*" said Violeta. She set David down then she rushed into the kitchen, brushing past her husband, who stood in the doorway.

"Bring him back a little later," said Ernesto. "Just call *El Rayo.* Santos will take you whenever you need to go somewhere."

"Yeah, Ascensión told us about *El Rayo* and Santos, and all," said Silvio.

Ernesto stepped onto the patio and picked up his grandson. "See you later, *majito.* I better go in and let your *abuelita* yell at me for a while. She'll be fine by the time you come back." To Sally and Silvio he said, "You sure you don't want a beer?"

***

260

They stood at the end of the gravel drive by the side of the main road waiting for their taxi. Sally and Silvio took turns holding David, sometimes setting him on the ground where he amused himself playing with the small stones.

"Maybe we should have stayed on the patio until the taxi came," said Silvio.

"I couldn't take it anymore," said Sally. "Geez, and I thought my mother-in-law was a trip."

"What?"

"Oh, I don't mean your mom. I meant my first mother-in-law. Darren's mom. Donna." Sally rolled her eyes. "Your mom I love. You know that, right?"

"Oh, yeah. Violeta, she kinda reminds me of my Aunt Rosalia."

"On your Italian side or your Polish side?"

"She's on my Polish side." Silvio chuckled. "Boy, can Aunt Rosalia rock the drama. And she can hold a grudge from here to South Jersey and back. But she's a great cook and she'll do anything for you. When she's not breaking your—"

"Nougats," Sally and Silvio said at the same time. They both laughed. "Yep," said Sally, "your aunt sounds like Violeta, all right. Oh, crap. I guess now we have to call Lupe and tell her we have David."

"Maybe we shouldn't call her just yet," said Silvio. "I mean, she's at work, and all."

Sally tsked. "Yeah, it might be better to wait a while. Or wait 'til she calls us. She'll probably call us, don't you think?"

"I guess. I don't know. Unless she gets busy at work, or something."

"Okay, so let's don't call her if we don't have to," said Sally. "I mean, if we make sure to get David back to the house before she and Ascensión get home from work we should be okay. Then Violeta can just spin the story however she wants."

"Right. Hey, here comes our ride." Silvio pointed to the brightly painted taxi slowing down as it approached them. "With all the back and forth we'll be doing old Santos is gonna turn out to be our best friend."

***

"Ah, *señora* Yoolie. So you're having trouble with your equipment? Again?"

"Yes." There was a slight distortion in the line. Yoolie supposed Alejandro must have his phone on speaker.

"And you need my help again?" he said.

Yoolie wanted to say, *Isn't that what you're getting paid for?* But she said, "Yes, Alejandro."

"Of course I would like to help you any way I can. But if you're having trouble getting your men to maintain the equipment…"

Be cool, she warned herself. *Don't let him bait you.* "I don't think it's the equipment," she said. "I think it's the volcano."

"You think it's the volcano?" said Alejandro. "What, you're a geologist now?"

"No, Alejandro," she said in as calm a voice as she could muster, "I'm not a geologist. *You're* the geologist. But I have a bad feeling about the volcano."

"A bad feeling about the volcano?" said Alejandro. "What do you mean by a bad feeling about the volcano? That you don't want to date the volcano?"

Now Yoolie could hear male voices snickering in the background. Of course. Alejandro had an audience, likely some fellow engineers standing around wasting time with him, and so he was ragging her, showing off for the guys. The prick. "No," she said. "I mean I'm concerned."

"Thank you for making it clear what you mean. After all, we are from different cultures. I suppose in the United States women can have feelings for whoever they want. Even for a volcano. But

262

in Argentina where I'm from and here in Central America women have feelings only for men." Laughter in the background and she heard someone say, "Ask her if she wants to see *your* volcano" and she heard Alejandro laughingly answer, "No, no, *hombre, por favor,* not *my* volcano!"

"FOR GOD'S SAKE, ALEJANDRO, WOULD YOU QUIT FUCKING AROUND AND..." Now Yoolie heard louder laughter and whistles. Shit. She pulled the phone away from her ear for a moment. She rubbed her forehead and pulled in a deep breath. "I'm asking you to please have your people take another look at the monitors and also get someone up here *pronto* to take a tiltmeter and a hydrology reading."

"And *I'm* asking *you, señora* Yoolie, to please do your job instead of always telling me how to do mine!"

"Look, at least just check on the..." The phone went dead in her hand. "Sweet Jesus," she muttered and wondered what she should do now. Was Alejandro right? Did he in fact know what he was doing? Was she being paranoid?

She walked the length of the generator, stopping to look at parts. Was that another scorch mark? Or just dirt? She put on a glove and knelt down to examine the length of tubing that she had welded earlier. She touched a spot where she'd soldered. Why was the solder still soft?

"Yoolie, I'm back."

Yoolie looked up and saw Ascensión standing over her, smiling. "I picked up my new truck from the motor pool. I drove it up here. It's beautiful. Drives like...how do you say in English? A charm. Ah, here comes Nico with your jeep." Ascensión waved the jeep over.

"Okay, thanks, Ascensión."

"No, I must thank *you,* Yoolie. For the truck. And for all you've done for Lupe and me. And for helping our friends Sally and Silvio today."

"No problem," said Yoolie.

"Now what's going on here? With the welding?"

Yoolie took off her glove and handed it to Ascensión. "Feel that spot where I soldered this morning."

Ascensión felt the solder. "Why is this still soft?"

Yoolie sighed. "I don't know."

"Yoolie," said Ascensión. "What if the problem isn't with the tubing or the wires or the turbine or any part of the generator? What if the problem is..."

"The volcano," said Yoolie.

"*Madre de Dios,*" said Ascensión. He stood and handed Yoolie back her glove.

"I'm going to take a look at generator number four," said Yoolie. "Would you go look at number three? Check the wires, the couplings, the tubing..."

"Everything, yes," said Ascensión.

"But don't make a big thing of it. No need to spread alarm or rumors. It's probably something with this generator."

"Yes, of course," Ascensión agreed. "The problem is probably with this generator."

But their words belied the worry in their eyes.

***

The first call came from Ascensión.

"It's generator three," he said. "It's making The Squeak. And there are two wires that look...not good."

"Oh, no," said Yoolie. "Generator four has shorted out, too. I think the governor is broken, but generator two is taking up the slack, so it's hard to...wait, I have another call..."

The second call was from one of Alejandro's subordinates, a young Indian geological engineer.

"Yoolie...Yoolie..." He sounded breathless. As if he were running. Or hyperventilating.

"What is it, Ravi?"

264

"Yoolie...I'm sorry about the phone call...Alejandro...it was rude...to you. Some of us felt badly afterwards. You and I, we've always been friends."

"Forget it," said Yoolie. "Look, I need to talk to somebody, fast. The volcano...there's something wrong, there has to be."

"You're right, Yoolie. After Alejandro hung up...Yes, he behaved like a pig to you, but after he hung up he did have us check the monitors. A few of us went up to the south slope and ran a tiltmeter and a hydrology."

"And?" Yoolie could feel her heart pounding as a drop of sweat fell from her forehead into her eye.

"A buildup of...of...magmastatic pressure."

"For God's sake, calm down, Ravi, please, and explain to me what this means."

"We think the pressure of the magma against the rock layer is causing vents in the layer, sending up too much heat."

"Too much heat?"

"Too much heat for the volume of water in the reservoir. The excessive heat was causing too much steam to be directed to the governors. That's what was causing your equipment to malfunction. More water should have been dumped into the reservoir, don't you see?"

"Dammit, Ravi, of course I don't see! Why the hell didn't you people report this to me?"

Ravi was sobbing now. "We didn't...Alejandro never...I don't know...and now the volcano..."

"Jesus. Where's Alejandro? Get him on the line. Now!"

"He's gone," Ravi sobbed.

"*What?*"

"He said he has a wife and children."

"*A wife and*...Jesus, Ravi! Are you telling me the volcano...?"

"We think...we're not sure, but...maybe a phreatomagmatic eruption...a result of the hydrothermal system... it could be very explosive, or...it's hard to tell."

"Wha...? When? How much time do we...?"

"Hard to tell. Soon, we think. Maybe tomorrow, or...maybe today."

"*Today?*"

"Maybe. It's hard to tell. But soon. Probably. "

"Jesus, Ravi, we've got to shut this place down and get everybody out of here!"

"Yes, yes, shut down all the generators, you don't want the power running."

"Damn right I don't want the power running!"

"Of course, of course," said Ravi. "An electrical explosion could destroy the power grid."

"And set the whole damn jungle on fire!"

"Call ENEL," said Ravi. "Tell them—"

"Forget ENEL! I don't have time to argue with those suits! I need every one of your engineers to get their asses on the line! I'll need a crew to shut down the turbines and another to open the safety valves to divert the steam. And somebody's got to evacuate the workers."

"The engineers have all gone." Ravi was crying again. "I'm sorry, Yoolie. I'm on my way to León. I have a wife and children, too. In Bhopal. Good-bye, Yoolie."

The third call was Ascensión again.

"Yoolie, what's going on up on number four?" he asked. "I think number three is down, but number one is still backing it up."

"Shut them down!" said Yoolie.

"Shut them...?"

"Just shut them down! You can do that, right? And open the safety valves?"

"Yes, I think I...but...what...?"

"The volcano. We've got to shut the whole plant down! Now!"

"I'll get a crew, together," said Ascensión. "It'll be faster."

"No, wait...forget about the generators. Send all your workers home. Shit! Call the *estación de autobuses* in León, tell them to send every bus and truck they have to Momotombo. In the meantime get everyone off the geothermal plant, call the motor pool, have them send every vehicle and every driver to pick up every person they can find and get them to the gate. Tell everyone when they get to the gate to start walking—running if they can—away from the plant."

"But what about the turbines? And the safety valves?"

"I'll turn off the goddamn generators myself!"

"By yourself? Yoolie, you can't—"

"Just...just...*go!*" She shouted.

Ascensión followed Yoolie's orders but the first person he called was Lupe.

Lupe was waiting for him outside Yoolie's office and she quickly slid into the driver's seat of the truck.

"You haven't driven since we lived in Philadelphia," said Ascensión.

"It's fine. I haven't forgotten. Are we in danger in Krukrulitos?"

"I don't think so. The village is at least a mile from the volcano. And you know how our volcanoes go off."

"Yes," said Lupe. "I know how our volcanoes go off when they're not hooked up to a power plant."

"On your way out of the plant pick up as many people as you can fit into the truck and the cab. Don't explain, just tell them to get in. Drive them as far as Krukrulitos and they can walk the rest of the way to León or wherever they need to go. I'll get the *chicos* at the motor pool to help me get everyone to the gate. They can start walking. Buses should be coming soon but in the meantime they can walk."

When Lupe pulled in front of the motor pool she turned to Ascensión. "*Amor,* I don't want to leave you here," she said.

"I know," he said. "But you need to go and be with—"

267

"David," they said together. "I know," she said.

"And I have to stay. But as soon as the plant is evacuated and the generators shut down I'll leave. I'll borrow a jeep. Don't worry. The volcano may not even erupt today. And if it does, you should be safe. But just in case..."

"I have the truck," she said. "But we'll be safe. I'll keep David safe."

"I know, *mi vida*. I'll be home soon." He kissed her forehead then climbed out of the truck.

As he walked away she called to him. "Jaime," she called. "What about Jaime? Make sure he gets out."

"Yes, yes, I'll be sure and find him."

Ascensión quickly gathered a crew to help him, and within minutes the evacuation of the Momotombo geothermal plant was underway. The gate guards waved through workers, most of them on foot, a few in cars, out the front gates in an orderly fashion onto the macadam road that led to León and the jungle villages along the way. There was no rush or panic; in fact as they walked to the gate the workers joked about this supposed eruption, for the volcano gave no outward appearance of unusual activity, only the serene wisps of smoke that always drifted gently from the basin of the volcano to the sky.

Ascensión found Jaime among a group of workers walking towards the gate. Jaime climbed into the jeep that Ascensión had accessed from the motor pool.

"Are they trying to clear us out for an American photo shoot like everybody is saying?" Jaime joked nervously. "Or is the volcano really about to explode?"

"It's not a photo shoot," said Ascensión. "But you know what's been going on with the generator wires and now..."

Jaime's eyes widened in fear. "The volcano is about to explode?"

"We don't know what the volcano is or isn't about to do. But Yoolie is shutting down the generators and I'm evacuating the plant. And you need to leave now. I'll drive you to the gate. You can start walking. Maybe fast."

When they arrived behind the crowd at the gate Jaime climbed out of the jeep, walked towards the others, then turned around and began running after the jeep, waving his arms and calling to Ascensión. Catching sight in his rear-view mirror of Jaime trotting behind him, Ascensión stopped and backed up. Jaime climbed back into the jeep.

"No," said Jaime, breathless from his brief sprint, "I want to…stay…I can…help Yoolie's crew…with the generators."

"Yoolie doesn't have a crew," said Ascensión. "She's shutting down the plant by herself."

"What? Why doesn't she have a crew?" Jaime looked around. "And where are all the other engineers?"

"I don't know," said Ascensión. "But she's shutting down by herself and I'm in charge of the evacuation."

"*Válgame Dios*," Jaime muttered. He hesitated a moment, looked behind him towards the gate, then said, "I'm staying with you. I'm going to help Yoolie with the generators."

"What?"

"I know as much about generators as anyone. You know I do."

"I know you know about generators," said Ascension, "but…"

"Somebody needs to help Yoolie. Take me to where she is."

Ascensión stared for a moment at his brother-in-law. Then he headed towards the slope of the volcano where he knew Yoolie was in a mad dash to shut down the generators.

When they reached the generator where Yoolie's jeep was in view Ascensión said, "You sure you want to do this, *maje?*"

Jaime pulled in a deep breath. "You and Lupe are my friends. You two are the most kind-hearted people in your family. Everyone else thinks I'm a clown."

"No, no, *hombre*, nobody thinks—"

"Even Xiomara," Jaime cut him off. "But today I'm going to be a man." Tears welled up in his eyes. "If something happens to me…"

"Nothing's going to happen," said Ascensión. "You and Yoolie will have all the generators shut off in forty-five minutes, maybe less. Then I'll come and get you and we'll leave together." He patted the wheel of the jeep and chuckled, "In this jeep that I'm going to borrow."

"If something happens to me," Jaime continued, "you'll take care of your sister and our children."

Ascensión grasped Jaime's shoulder and squeezed it lightly, his own eyes tearing up. *"Por supuesto, hermano."*

"Thank you, my good friend," said Jaime. He exited the jeep and began walking towards Yoolie, who'd caught sight of him and was now eagerly, imploringly, beckoning him.

***

Lupe dutifully drove about the plant urging people to hop into her and Ascensión's new truck. When the cab and bed were filled she headed to the gate, which was crowding with exiting workers, Ascensión having already recruited a crew to spread the word of the evacuation.

Some of her passengers who lived in the villages along the road between Momotombo and León implored her to take them home, and though she was beyond anxious to get back to David in Krukrulitos she could not bring herself to leave them off along the way and make them walk. Nor could she bring herself to ignore the pleas of the rest who lived in León and pressed her to take them into the city. And so Lupe passed by her own village and drove into León. *David is fine,* she kept telling herself. *If he weren't someone would have called me. Maybe Sally and Silvio are still there with him. David is fine. Our baby is fine.*

***

"Dang, there goes the fan," said Sally.

"Isn't it a little early for the electricity to be fritzing?" said Silvio.

"Don't ask me," said Sally.

They sat in their room resting from the morning's adventures. While David napped Sally and Silvio munched on plates of fried chicken, rice, and crispy brown plantains they'd bought on the street from the same elderly *abuelita* from whom Lupe had bought food a few days earlier.

"I wonder if it's safe for us to be eating all this street food," said Sally. "I mean, I wonder if it'll make us sick, or something."

"Nah. Anything that tastes this good can't make you sick." Silvio licked his fingers then wiped his hands on a paper napkin. "Hey, look who's up."

Sally lifted David from the bed and kissed his cheek, still warm and rosy from his nap. "What do you say, Bud?" she said. "You want to go back to your *abuelita* Violeta and wait for your *mamita and papito?*"

"Didi," said David.

***

"So, where is everybody?" Sally asked as they pushed David in his stroller into the empty lobby of the *Casa de la Recolección*. Even the reception desk was unmanned. "Hello?" she called to the empty room.

"They're probably across the courtyard turning on the generator," said Silvio. "And, you know, maybe checking on things."

"Yeah, I guess," said Sally. "Oh well, let's just go outside and wait for Santos."

They found Nikhil and Cassie, each with one of their children in their arms, among the crowd of people standing around looking off into the distance, some of them holding up their cell phones. Santos was there standing next to his cab, which was parked in front of the *Casa de la Recolección*.

Nikhil caught sight of Sally and Silvio and waved them over. "Look at that smoke," he said.

"The heck is that?" said Silvio.

"Momotombo, we're guessing," said Cassie.

"Momotombo?" said Sally. "Wha…what do you mean?"

"The electricity's off," said Nikhil. "The internet's down, too. The electric company doesn't turn off the power in the middle of the day."

"Could something have happened at the plant?" Sally asked.

Nikhil shrugged. "There is a volcano up there…"

Santos walked over to where his American customers were standing and, straining to understand what these *cheles* were discussing but understanding the words *Momotombo* and *volcano*, he began explaining that a little while ago he'd seen what looked like a convoy leaving the *estación de autobuses*. He'd called to one of the bus drivers, his friend Rafe, who told him that the Americans were doing a photo shoot at Momotombo and so the plant was being evacuated. "But Rafe never knows what he's talking about," said Santos. He gestured towards the smoke. "I think it's the volcano." To Sally and Silvio he said, "You don't want to go to Krukrulitos now."

"We've got to call them," said Sally. She began frantically rummaging through her purse but Silvio pulled his phone from his pocket. He was tapping in Lupe's number when a moan rippled through the crowd.

"Cell service is down," someone from the crowd called.

"Oh my God," said Sally. "Lupe…Ascensión…" She gripped Silvio's arm and he covered her hand with his. "What should we do?"

"*Quédense aquí*, y'all," said Cassie. "Just in case."

"Yes, stay here," Santos agreed, and though he hadn't understood that Cassie had also said it, he, too, added, "Just in case."

***

Minutes before the black cloud was visible from León, Yoolie and Jaime were hastily flipping the last switch, pulling the last lever, then scuttling down the slope of Momotombo. They made it to Yoolie's jeep, and had they made it a few minutes sooner the jeep would have outraced the earthquake that turned the road beneath it into a rolling wave so that the jeep could not escape the cascade of massive rocks that shot from deep inside the crater into the sky, then seconds later rocketed to earth, crushing Yoolie's jeep and its two passengers too quickly for them to feel even a final moment of terror or pain.

***

When Ascensión was satisfied that the plant was cleared he joined the members of his evacuation crew who were busy herding to one side of the road those who were leaving in vehicles so that those leaving on foot could stay safely on the other side.

When the buses from León arrived, Ascensión and his crew saw to it that everyone boarded in an orderly fashion. He then sent his crew home and he turned around and sped back to the geothermal plant, his destination the slope of Momotombo where he intended to pick up Jaime or help him and Yoolie finish the shutdown. Had he arrived minutes earlier he, too, would have been caught in the sudden deadly rain of volcanic rock that crushed Yoolie's jeep. Instead he felt the roll of the earth just before the jeep spun and was flipped onto its side so that it served as a partial barricade against the still-steaming rocks that tumbled down the road towards him. Ascensión scrambled from the jeep and outran the rocks until he reached more level ground and was able to veer from their path as the rocks gradually lost velocity and bounced to a piled-up stop.

Ascensión ran down the road towards Krukrulitos, breathless and bruised from the overturning of the jeep, sobbing, the tears rolling down his face as he prayed. *Please God, save them! Jaime, Yoolie, please, Santa Maria, please save them! Santos Angeles, save them! Santo Domingo, save them, please, save them!*

But even as he commended the deliverance of his friends into the hands of God and the angels and saints, it was to himself that he commended the task of saving his wife and child.

***

Minutes after Momotombo's phreatomagmatic eruption of black smoke and deadly rock Lupe stood in Violeta's kitchen crying.

"*Where is he? Where is he?*" she sobbed.

Violeta stood with her back to Lupe as she stirred a pot of chicken and rice for dinner. "I don't know why you keep asking me," she said coolly. "I told you, if you don't trust me to care for your child, then fine, don't ask me where he is."

"Is he with Sally? Tell me!"

"I told you. Ask your friend Sally yourself."

"And I told *you*, I can't! My phone is dead! *Where is he?*"

Violeta turned around to face Lupe. "Look, first you send the Americans to check on me. *Me*, David's grandmother! Then you leave your work in the middle of the day driving this fancy American truck to come here and check on me yourself! As if I'm not good enough to take care of my own grandchild!" Now Violeta was crying.

"What? No! I told you, the volcano—"

"Yes, yes, your story about the volcano." Violeta waved her hand dismissively and turned back to her pot on the stove, weeping softly and wiping her eyes on her apron.

"It's true," Lupe cried, "everyone is evacuating!"

"Where's Ascensión?" sniffed Violeta. "Why didn't *he* evacuate?"

"He'll be here soon, he…Violeta, *where is David?*"

Ernesto stepped into the kitchen. "Oh, *por el amor de Dios*, Violeta, stop tormenting the girl." To Lupe he said, "The Americans took him back to León. Now stop all the shouting."

Lupe collapsed into a chair, put a hand on her chest, and pulled in a deep breath. "Oh, thank God."

"*I'm* tormenting *her?*" cried Violeta. "First she sends the Americans, then she drives herself here in that fancy American truck, then she tells me some story about the volcano…"

"Enough, enough," said Ernesto. "It's not a story. Lupe, where are Ascensión and Jaime?"

"Ascensión is helping to evacuate Momotombo. Jaime is probably on his way home. Or maybe he stayed with Ascensión."

Ernesto nodded gravely. "Come outside."

Violeta and Lupe hurried out the door and followed Ernesto to the back yard where the rest of the family members had gathered and were staring at the eruption of Momotombo.

"You drove yourself home in that big truck," Xiomara snapped, "and you left Jaime and Ascensión behind!"

"Oh, *Dios mío*," Lupe gasped, covering her mouth with her hands. Then she pulled herself together and said calmly, "No. Ascensión knows what he's doing. He has a jeep. He'll get everyone out safely and he'll be back home soon. And he'll bring Jaime with him."

"How do you know he'll do that?" Xiomara shrieked, now waving her arms at Lupe. "You took the truck for yourself and you left them!"

"No, no, I didn't, I—"

"You left them!" Xiomara was screaming now, the tears rolling down her reddened face. "You left my husband, you left *your* husband, you…you…you left your *own baby! Your own baby!*"

275

Lupe closed her eyes and pulled in a deep breath. Then she said gently, "No, Xiomara, I didn't leave my baby. And for the sake of your own baby you must calm down."

"Leave her alone," said Violeta. "How could anyone be calm knowing her husband is up there?"

"She's right, Violeta," said Ernesto. "Xiomara must calm down."

The relatives nodded and murmured agreement.

"*Ohhh!*" Xiomara grabbed her stomach and doubled over its bulk as much as she was able.

The others encircled her, the women putting their hands on her shoulders, back, and stomach.

"What's wrong, *mija*," her mother said, nudging aside the other women. "Are you in pain? Is it the baby?"

"*Oh…oh,*" Xiomara gasped.

"She needs to calm down," her father said. "She's over-excited herself. Bring her inside."

"Yes, calm down, *mija*," said her mother. "Come inside, this is too much for you."

Violeta, assisted by several other women, led Xiomara towards the house. Lupe joined the women helping Xiomara but Violeta swatted her away. "You've caused enough trouble. You can just stay here and…" Violeta waved her hand dismissively. "…do whatever you please."

A cry went up among the onlookers as what looked like a flight of small orange stars soared through the sky off in the distance then disappeared into the jungle below. A dozen small nova-hot lava bombs the size of dinner plates had been jettisoned from deep inside the volcano with such force that they landed a mile away in the jungle area surrounding Krukrulitos.

A few minutes later there was the smell of smoke and the sight of flames flickering a hundred yards away through the foliage. There were cries of *"Fire!"* and people scrambled in confusion this way and that, but it was Lupe who took action.

"We need to leave, now! Everybody gather the children and put them into the back of the truck. I can drive." To the daughters of old *tia* Pilar she said, "Run and get your mother, she can go into the truck, too."

"It will take several men to hoist Pilar into the truck bed," said Ernesto.

"Fine, do it," said Lupe. "Where's Mauricio? The men will need to lift him into the truck, too. And somebody go and get Xiomara. She needs to ride in the truck. We may need to take her to the hospital. Call everyone else who's not here, tell them to leave, now, tell them to start walking or running if they can."

"Where should we run to?" One of the women asked as she gathered her children around her.

"Go to León," said Lupe. "Everybody go to León…to *Casa de la Recolección*. The Americans Sally and Silvio are there. With my David. Tell the hotel owners that Lupe says they owe her husband a favor. They'll know what that means." She looked around. "Where's *abuelito* Mauricio? Someone go and find him and put him into the truck as well. And gather all the children, put them on the truck!"

Little Blanca ran up to Lupe and wrapped her arms around Lupe's waist. "I want *mamá*," she cried.

Lupe scooped up Blanca and carried her towards the truck. "Look, there's your *mamita*, she's in the truck." She pointed to Xiomara, who had been helped into the truck bed and sat against the side, her knees drawn up against her stomach, her head down and her eyes closed. Her mother Violeta sat next to her with an arm around her daughter's shoulder.

As Lupe put Blanca onto the truck she looked over the others sitting on the truck bed. "Violeta, where's Mauricito? Is he there?"

At the mention of her child Xiomara's head sprang up. She looked around then cried, "Where's Mauricito? Where's my baby?"

"Shhh," said Violeta. "He must be with one of the relatives. Someone will bring him here in a moment."

But after *tia* Pilar had been hoisted into the truck bed and all the other children were accounted for three-year-old Mauricito was not among them, nor was old *abuelito* Mauricio.

"*My baby!*" Xiomara cried, "*where is my baby?*" She tried to stand but the pain brought her back down. "*Find my baby,*" she moaned. "*Somebody find my baby!*"

"I'll go find him," said Lupe. "Ernesto, you stay here until I get back. Violeta you stay with Xiomara and the children."

"My father," Violeta called after her, sobbing, "Find my father!"

Ernesto followed after Lupe as she hurried away. "Lupe," he called. When she turned around he said, "Don't worry about *abuelito!* Find Mauricito! If you don't make it back in time..." He gestured towards the approaching wall of flame.

"I'll make it back in time."

"But if you don't..."

"Then you know how to drive the truck," she snapped, and she ran off. She ran from yard to yard and house to house, calling for Mauricio and Mauricito. The smoke began clouding the air, stinging her eyes and making her cough but she lifted her shirt and covered her mouth and nose with its edge and kept running and calling. Outside of Cousin Lidia's house she heard crying and found Mauricito inside where he'd run to hide from the fire, huddled in a corner, sobbing for his mother. When he saw his *tia* Lupe he scampered over to her, arms outstretched. She whisked him up into her arms and he wrapped his arms around her neck and burrowed his head against her shoulder.

"Shhh, shhh, don't cry now, *mi bebé, mi chiquitín,*" she cooed, holding him close against her and kissing his head while she ran back to the truck.

When she was in view of the truck she caught sight of Ernesto waving at her. "Mauricio," he called and pointed. She turned and looked behind her. There was Mauricio, who had been back tending his cornfield when the fire broke out, now stumbling and disoriented in the smoke.

Lupe quickly kissed Mauricito one more time then set him down. "Run now," she said, pointing towards Ernesto. "There's your *abuelito* Ernesto, run to him as fast as a monkey!"

Lupe then ran back to grab Mauricio but by the time she reached him he, too, had wandered into Lidia's house, thinking it to be his own. Lupe ran into the house after him, unable to see what Ernesto, still watching from the distance, watched in helpless horror.

When Lupe was a teacher she had, among the lessons she taught, covered lessons on palm trees, whose shallow, fibrous root systems grow above the ground and spread laterally like a mat on the soil floor around the trees. She'd taught her young students that a palm tree's root system not only drinks in moisture for the tree but serves as a strong support system that allows palms to withstand even hurricane-strength winds. And she knew from her lessons that if a palm tree's root system were to be destroyed the tree, sitting upon the soil without brace or buttress to hold it up, would fall over. Still all those lessons were nowhere in her mind as she ran into Lidia's house and the palm trees *señor* and *señora* Frondosa, their surface supporting root system burned up by the fire rolling across the jungle floor, came crashing down onto the house's flimsy corrugated metal roof.

Ernesto stood for a moment paralyzed by disbelief and shock before he turned and jogged back to the truck, the words beating like a tattoo in his brain, *they're dead, they're dead, they're dead*.

"Where are they?" Violeta cried when Ernesto arrived, breathless, back at the truck.

"Dead," he said.

"What? My father? *No!*"

"Both dead. We have to leave. Watch the children."

Ernesto then pulled the truck from the path in front of the family's house out to the gravel road that led to León. The truck had rolled only a few yards forward when Ernesto heard Violeta cry out for him to stop. Ascensión ran up alongside the truck and hooked his hands over the windowsill. He was out of breath, his face bruised and tear stained.

"David," he gasped.

"He's safe in León with the Americans. Get into the truck."

"Lupe...where is Lupe?"

Ernesto cocked his head back towards the family's property. "Mauricio wandered into Lidia's house. Lupe ran in to save him. The palm trees fell. On the house. Lupe and Mauricio..." Ernesto could say no more. He broke down into breathless sobs.

Ascensión backed away from the window. "No. No." He began running back towards the house.

Ernesto climbed from the truck and called after his son. "Come back! She's gone, *mijo!*"

"No!" Ascensión called back. "You wait here!"

"The fire..."

"*You wait here!*" Ascensión screamed.

Violeta stood up in the back of the truck and cried out, "No, *mijo, no!*"

But Ascensión did not even turn back to look at her and kept running. Violeta continued to call to her son until he disappeared into the smoky haze. Then she slumped back down onto the truck bed, her face in her hands. "Why," she sobbed, "why is my son throwing away his life? For that...*useless* girl!"

Ernesto didn't answer his wife, he knew she was distraught. But he thought, *that useless girl saved our grandchild.*

By the time the remains of Lidia's broken house came into Ascensión's view the fire had reached the edge of the yard, blocking his way. The bits of flame that had clung to the roots of the fallen palm trees were now creeping up their trunks. He cried out Lupe's name then fell to his knees and coughed and sobbed into his hands.

"*Please God, please God, please God,*" he prayed, over and over, begging God for a miracle as the flames surrounded him.

And at that moment God gave him a miracle. It was the same miracle that occurred every day at this time when the skies opened and the afternoon rains poured down.

Ascensión looked up and where a wall of fire had been there was now a wall of water and steam. He scrambled to his feet then ran through the mud towards the house, ignoring the steam and the heat from the ground that penetrated through his shoes.

The giant palms had hit Lidia's house on the right side and in the middle, causing the left side of the roof to flip up a few feet from the ground. Ascensión crawled far back into the space between the roof and the ground and amidst the rubble came upon the body of his wife. He pulled her out from beneath the roof then sat in the mud and the rain, holding her to his chest.

"Please, *mi amor,*" he sobbed, "please don't leave me, *mi corazón, mi vida,* please don't be dead." He pulled her face close to his and whispered hoarsely to her, "How can you be dead, *amor?* How can you be dead?"

Then the sensation of breath against his cheek told him that she wasn't.

Chapter Seventeen

"Boy," said Cassie, "when our friend Lupe collects on a favor, she *really* collects."

"Ha, tell me about it," said Sally. The two women stood in the kitchen of the *Casa de la Recolección* dishing up plates of food for the crowd of villagers waiting in the dining room. Several dozen residents of Krukrulitos of all ages had straggled into Cassie and Nikhil's hotel three days ago and had been taking refuge there since.

Cassie sighed. "Well, what were we supposed to do?"

"Just what you're doing, I guess," said Sally.

"So much for our hotel business," said Cassie.

"If my mother were here she'd say, 'God will provide.'"

"In these parts you'd best believe that," said Cassie. "Anyway, foreign volunteers will be pouring on down here any day to help repair the village. A few of 'em already are."

"Thank goodness the phone and electricity are back on," said Sally.

"For sure. Supposedly they got the generators turned off in time up on Momotombo so the eruption didn't destroy the whole power grid. I expect they got 'em up and running again already."

"Yeah, Ascención told us that all the engineers who flew the coop before the volcano blew are back now. Bastards." Sally rubbed the back of her hand across her eyes.

Cassie put down her ladle and put an arm around Sally's shoulder. "I'm so sorry about your friend Yoolie. And Ascensión's brother-in-law and grandfather."

"It's just so crazy," Sally sniffed. "I met Yoolie just that day. I was talking to her only a few hours before. And Jaime the day before."

Cassie handed Sally a dry cloth to wipe her eyes. "I know, Hon," she said. "They're the heroes."

"And that poor old man, Mauricio. And Lupe...I just don't know what to do." Sally began sobbing into her cloth.

"You're doing the best things you could do for Lupe. Visiting her in the hospital every day like you've been doing, bringing David with you, talking to her. They say people in a coma are responsive to that sort of thing. Helps 'em come 'round."

"I hope so," said Sally, wiping her eyes. "Ascensión's hardly been away from Lupe's side for the last three days. Even Ascensión's parents stop in—well, it's probably just their son they want to see–but they stop into Lupe's room every day while they're in the hospital visiting Xiomara."

"She doing okay now, Xiomara?" asked Cassie.

"Looks like she will be," said Sally. "But her baby..." Sally sighed and shook her head.

"Why, I'm sorry to hear that," said Cassie.

"Yeah, me too," said Sally. "Lose your husband, your baby and your grandfather at the same time...just so sad."

"And Xiomara's mother, when she's here and not at the hospital she doesn't come out of her room. I expect we'll have to keep bringing her food to her."

"I'll bring her a plate," said Sally.

"That's okay, I'll have Dante...*Oye*, Dante," she said to her assistant who came into the kitchen for more plates of food. "When everybody's fed have one of the folks bring a plate to...uh, what's her name again?"

"Violeta," said Sally.

"Right," said Cassie. "She's in her room still."

Dante shook his head. "Poor lady."

Cassie sighed. "I know. Say Dante, you know where my kids are?"

"And David?" said Sally.

"Por supuesto," Dante assured her. "Jazmín took your boys out to play in the courtyard. But David's relatives took him again. He's out here sitting on someone's lap eating plantains and rice." Dante chuckled. "You have a little *nicaragüense* there."

"He eats like one," said Sally. "Loves his plantains."

"Who loves his plantains?" said Nikhil, entering the kitchen carrying a five-kilo sack of plantains. Behind him came Silvio with a ten-kilo bag of rice slung over one shoulder and a ten-kilo bag of red beans slung over the other.

"Oh, thank goodness y'all are back," said Cassie. "Here, gimme those plantains, I need to fry up another batch. I had to ration 'em, gave everybody just a mouthful. Now I can give 'em a decent portion."

"Hey, hey, don't go too crazy on the portions," said Nikhil. "Who knows how long we'll have to be feeding these folks."

Cassie took the sack from her husband and dumped the plantains onto the kitchen counter. "God'll provide," she said.

***

The kind nurses and doctors at the Oscar Danilo Rosales Hospital gave Ascensión what assurance they could, explaining that it wasn't uncommon for someone with a traumatic brain injury such as Lupe had received to drift in and out of consciousness and to seem confused and disoriented for a while. But her breathing was good and her heartbeat steady and strong. And so, miraculously, was the heartbeat of their unborn child.

"Your little one is a fighter, I can tell," said one of the nurses while roving with a stethoscope around Lupe's slightly swelling middle. She then listened for Lupe's heart. "Sounds like her mother is, too."

"She is," said Ascensión, blinking back a tear.

The nurse put a hand on Ascensión's shoulder. "We'll give her some time, then."

It was on the third day as Ascensión sat by Lupe's bed, holding her hand and recalling to her some happy times they'd had back when they lived in Philadelphia, that Lupe wrapped her fingers around his and her eyes fluttered open. "*Amor,*" she said weakly.

Ascensión gasped. He leaned in close to her and kissed her face. "Are you back, *mi amor?* Have you come back to me?"

"Your face," she said, reaching up towards him then wincing and dropping her arm.

"It's nothing," said Ascensión. "Just a few scratches."

"David," she said.

"He's safe, he's fine. He's with Sally and Silvio at *Casa de la Recolección.*"

"Oh," she said, closing her eyes, "that's good." A few moments later she opened her eyes again. "I dreamed David was here."

"Yes, he's been here to see you. Sally and Silvio bring him every morning. They'll bring him again tomorrow. You'll be better then."

"Our baby...Is it...?"

Ascensión rested a hand on Lupe's belly. "She's here, *amor.* Safe and fine. She's strong. She's a fighter."

"Are we having a little girl?"

"I think so. But we'll see, won't we?"

Lupe smiled and nodded.

"Sleep more if you want to," said Ascensión.

"I'm very thirsty," said Lupe.

Ascensión filled a glass from the pitcher on the table next to Lupe's bed. He elevated her gently but when she made the effort to sit up on her own she yelped in pain.

"Let me lift you, don't try yourself," said Ascensión.

"What happened to me?" She said.

"A few broken ribs and a concussion. You've been out of it for a few days. Here, drink."

Lupe took a drink of the water then she said, "The fire...*abuelito* Mauricio."

"Here, drink some more," said Ascensión.

"I remember now. I went into Lidia's house to find *abuelito*."

"Yes, yes. Here, let me lay you back down."

"No, I want to sit up now."

At that moment a nurse entered the room. "Oh, *que bueno*," she said, clapping her hands. "Our *niña* has come back." The nurse took Lupe's pulse then looked into her eyes with a pen light. "Yes, you look better now," she said. "Are you hungry?"

"Oh, yes," said Lupe.

"Wait," said Ascensión. In a corner of the room sat a bag from *La Unión*. Ascensión reached into the bag and pulled out a box of cornflakes. Lupe laughed. "Can she eat this?" Ascensión asked the nurse.

"What is it?" she asked. Ascensión opened the box then handed it to the nurse. She looked over the box and its contents. "Is this some American food?"

"Corn flakes," said Ascensión. "It's cereal. You eat it in a bowl with milk."

The nurse poured herself a small handful. "Hmmm. Tastes good. Yes, I think our little patient can eat this with some milk. Unless she'd rather a bowl of *gallo pinto*."

"No, no," said Lupe. "Cornflakes, please."

The nurse left and returned a few minutes later with a bowl and spoon and a small plastic bag of milk. After Lupe finished her cornflakes and drank another glass of water she appeared much better, as if she'd finally come back to life. Then she asked, "What about *abuelito*?"

"*Abuelito*? He..." But there was no need for Ascensión to say anything more. Lupe could read the answer to her question in her husband's face. She reached for his hand. "I'm so sorry, *mi amor*," she said. "I tried…"

"Oh, don't cry, now," he said, though his own eyes were brimming. "I know you tried to save him. They told me you found Blanca and you saved Mauricito." He rested his hand on her middle. "And you saved our baby."

"Did anyone else from the village…?"

"*Tia* Pilar. She had a heart attack while they were trying to get her off the back of the truck in León."

"Ah," said Lupe. She found herself unable to dredge up much sorrow for *tia* Pilar. "But everyone else is all right?"

"You're getting tired, now," said Ascensión. "You should rest. We can talk later." He moved to lower her back down to a lying position on the bed but she resisted.

"Please tell me. Tell me now. Who else…?"

"Really, you need to rest."

"Ascensión. Tell me."

"Xiomara's baby," he said.

Lupe gasped and covered her mouth with her hands. Then she lowered her hands and said, "Now I remember. Xiomara wasn't well in the truck, but I didn't think…What about Xiomara? Is she all right?"

"Yes. She'll be all right."

"Oh, thank God."

"I know that Xiomara hasn't been kind to you."

"It doesn't matter. I'm thankful for the sake of her children. And for your sake, *amor*. And for Jaime's sake. Poor Jaime. How is he doing?"

Ascension hesitated, tried to speak, then burst into tears. He shook his head.

"What?" said Lupe. "Did Jaime…did he…? Wait, didn't he come back from Momotombo? Yoolie…What about Yoolie?"

Ascensión shook his head again. When he could speak he told her about Jaime, how Jaime had bravely insisted upon staying with Yoolie to shut down the generators. Ascensión told her what he'd learned from the news, of the rocks beneath which the bodies of Jaime and Yoolie were found. Lupe's sobs hurt her chest but she couldn't stop herself.

The nurse whisked into the room. "*Señor, señora,* what's going on? *Calma, señora* Guzman, we can't have you upset like this. Think of your baby."

To Ascensión the nurse said, "She needs to rest now. Help me lay her down, gently now, watch her ribs." When they had lain Lupe back down the nurse said, "You're too upset, *señora* Guzman. I'm going to give you a little something to help you sleep. Perhaps you should go home and get some sleep, too, *señor.*"

But Ascensión stayed next to his wife until she drifted off to sleep. Then he settled into the chair next to her bed and closed his eyes and dozed. This hospital room that he shared with his wife and their child was as close to a home as he had at the moment, anyway.

***

Lupe could hear familiar voices: Ascensión, Ernesto, Violeta. The voices were soft and muted and she couldn't tell if they were nearby or far way. She opened her eyes and saw her father looking over her. He was sitting next to the bed. Holding her hand. She must be dreaming.

"*Papá?*" she said groggily.

"Yes, Lupita. It's me, your *papá.*"

Lupe closed her eyes again. Yes, of course she was dreaming.

"Lupe," she heard him say. "Lupe, it's me. Your *papá.*"

"*Papá?*" She opened her eyes. "*Papá?* You're here?"

"Yes, *mi corazoncito.*"

"But…" She closed her eyes again for a moment, still trying to determine whether what she'd just seen was real. But when she

288

opened her eyes her father was still there. And there were Ascensión and his parents sitting in chairs across the room. "*Papá?*" she said. "You're not angry?"

"*Angry?* I've been searching for you for over two years, *mija.*"

"What?" Lupe struggled to sit up.

"Wait, wait," Daniel Paloma said, putting a hand gently on his daughter's shoulder. "Ascensión, come help me, she wants to sit up. And would someone please pour her a glass of water?"

Violeta jumped up to pour the water. She handed Lupe the glass and said sweetly, "Here, drink now, *querida.* Thank God you've come back to us. I've been praying to the Blessed Virgin. I've visited you every day." To Daniel Paloma she said, "Lupe is like a daughter to me."

Lupe sputtered on her water.

When Lupe had finished drinking her father took the glass from her. "Why did you never call me?" he said. "I've been trying, I've been..." He put a hand over his eyes and broke down into sobs.

"*Papá...Papá...*I don't understand." She spoke haltingly, her own eyes filling with tears. "You disowned me. When I married Ascensión. You told me never...never to come back again. "

Daniel shook his head. He pulled a handkerchief from his pocket and wiped his eyes. "I was angry, I...Maybe I was angry that I was losing you, too. Just like I lost my Clara...your *mamá.* But I was wrong. I was wrong."

"You were looking for me?"

"For two years. You didn't know? How did you not know?" He looked around the room. "How did she not know? Ernesto? Violeta? How did she not know?"

Ernesto and Violeta glanced at each other then lowered their eyes.

"What's going on here?" said Ascensión. "*Mamá? Papá?*" When neither responded he walked over to the bed and sat on the edge next to Lupe so that he was facing her father. "Dr. Paloma. What in the world are you talking about?"

"Yes, *papá*," said Lupe. "What in the world *are* you talking about?"

Daniel Paloma told them of how he tried to call Lupe but her cell number was out of service. He went to León to find her and Ascensión, to ask their forgiveness and to make sure they were all right. He went to *Reparaciónes León* but the store was shuttered and the Guzman family was gone. He asked around and learned that the family had moved to Krukrulitos to live with the Somarriba family. And he thought, *my daughter. Living in poverty in the jungle.*

But when he got to Krukrulitos Lupe and Ascensión weren't there. Violeta told him that they had fled to the North months ago and that no one had heard from them since nor knew how to contact them.

"She told me this in the presence of her husband and her daughter," said Daniel. "I don't know where the other family members were when she told me this, but of these three, nobody told me otherwise."

"What?" said Ascensión. He looked at his parents. "You told him you didn't know where we were?"

"So you did know," said Daniel. "You did know. You knew but you didn't tell me."

"Well…" said Violeta. "Well…you were a bad father…as you said…and so…"

"…And so you lied, *mamá*," said Ascensión. "And you, *papá*, and Xiomara, too."

"Yes, I was a bad father," said Daniel. "And a bad father-in-law. As bad as I had been to my own daughter, I had been just as bad to Violeta and Ernesto's son. So maybe I deserved it. Maybe I even suspected that they were lying. And if they were, I hoped that over time their hearts would soften, just as mine had. And so I begged their forgiveness and I begged them to ask your forgiveness and Ascensión's forgiveness if ever they heard from you, and to please, please contact me if they did, just to ease my mind that you both were safe, that you were all right. Because they could just as easily have been telling me the truth and I was so worried. But even though I was suffering in my mind, on that day I saw how this family was suffering in their need. And so I gave them some money."

"A lot of money," said Ernesto. "It kept us from starving."

"I came by one more time, months later, to give them more money and to beg them again to tell me if they heard any news of my daughter or their son. By then the family appeared to be doing better. I wondered if perhaps you had made it to the United States and were now supporting them. Violeta took the money I offered and then told me I had only myself to blame if I never heard from my daughter again."

Here Daniel again broke down into tears and Ascensión put a hand on his shoulder. "*Mamá*, how could you?"

Violeta was crying softly. "I've just lost my father and my grandchild. My poor widowed daughter has lost her baby and her husband. How can you talk to me like that now, *mijo*?"

Ascensión shook his head. "I'm sorry, Dr. Paloma."

Violeta stood. "You apologize? To *him*? I'm your *mother*! Your *mother*!" She rushed from the room, now sobbing loudly.

Ernesto stood and followed his wife but stopped in the doorway and turned back to the room. "Dr. Paloma, I'm sorry that I didn't call you before today. But a man has to keep peace with his wife. She's the heart of the family." He turned and left the room.

"It's true that my mother is the heart of the family," said Ascensión. "But sometimes that heart can be hard."

"I understand well how hard a heart, even a good heart, can sometimes be," said Dr. Paloma. "Tell me, where were you? When you went up North? Did you make it to the United States?"

"We did, *papá*," said Lupe.

"Lupe was very brave and strong," said Ascensión.

"We both were, *mi amor*," said Lupe.

Dr. Paloma sighed. "If only I had known. I could have helped you out. I have contacts there, you know."

"You do?" said Lupe. "No, *papá*, I didn't know."

"Of course I never told you, but yes, I do. What happened? Were you deported?"

"Yes, *papá*, we were. But now we have American friends. They helped us." Lupe, feeling tired from the effort, closed her eyes.

Ascensión told Daniel the story of their life in Philadelphia and their friendship with Sally and Silvio and about the lawyer Charleston Tilley and the visas he and Lupe were waiting on so that they could return to the United States and eventually apply for green cards. And he told Daniel about their son David.

"I have a grandson? A grandson?" Daniel began sobbing again. "Oh, thank God. It's more than I deserve. Where is he, my little *nieto*? In Philadelphia?"

Lupe opened her eyes and smiled. "He's here, *papá*. In León. You can see him today."

Ascensión told him of how Sally and Silvio brought David to Nicaragua.

"But where is David? Is he safe?"

"Yes, yes," said Ascensión. "He's at *Casa de la Recolección*, it's a hotel across from the church, it's—"

"I'll find it," said Daniel. He still held Lupe's hand and now he reached for Ascensión's hand as well. "Lupe, my daughter. And Ascensión, my son. I came to ask your forgiveness and now I realize I've forgotten to do it. Can you both forgive me?"

"Yes, *papá*, I forgive you," said Lupe.

"I do, too, Dr. Paloma," said Ascensión.

"Please, call me Daniel from now on." Daniel released Ascensión's hand and turned back to his daughter. "Listen, Lupe, you'll be all right, *mija*, I promise you will. I know the doctors at this hospital and they know me. Many of them teach at the University. They're the best in Nicaragua."

"I know I'll be all right, *papá*," said Lupe. "I have to be. I have to survive and be strong again. For David. And for the child I'm carrying now."

"The child you're...?"

Lupe nodded.

Daniel took his daughter's face in his hands and kissed her forehead then on both cheeks. "Lupe, after your mother died for so many years I felt dead inside. But now I feel as if my life is starting over. I'm so happy. So thankful to God..." Again he was too overcome to speak.

"*Papá*, go and see David now. *Casa de la Recolección.*"

Daniel pulled a handkerchief from his pocket and wiped his eyes. "Yes, yes." He kissed his daughter and son-in-law then he left.

Ascensión stroked his wife's hair for a moment. "Can you forgive my family?"

Lupe reached for his hand. "Today you forgave my father and so did I. Of course I forgive your family. Today we must all forgive each other."

A tear rolled down Ascensión's face and he kissed her hand. "*Mi luna, mis estrellas,*" he said.

Lupe's eyes suddenly opened wide. "*Amor,* you must go to Cristela for me."

"Cristela?"

"Yes, go to *Casa de las Sonrisas* for me. Find Cristela and tell her I sent you to share with her my sorrow for Yoolie. Try to comfort her if you can. For me."

"Yes, all right," said Ascensión. "If you want me to."

"Yoolie and Cristela were...*amantes.*"

"What?" said Ascensión. "Yoolie? And Cristela?"

"I'm sure of it," said Lupe. "Everyone at *Las Sonrisas* knew."

"*¡Vaya!*" said Ascensión. "I didn't."

"Will you go now to her, *mi amor*?"

"Yes, but first…" Ascensión pulled something else from the *La Unión* bag that held the cornflakes.

"My phone?" said Lupe. "You found it?"

"You left your purse in the truck before you went to rescue Mauricito. My father gave it to me, and so I brought your phone here. For when you woke up and might want it." He placed the phone on the table next to her bed. "Now you can call me if you need me." He kissed her cheek one more time and said, "I don't want to leave you alone."

"I'm all right, I promise."

After her husband left Lupe rubbed the small mound just below the center of her body. "I'm not alone," she said softly. Then she reached for her phone. Her father's contact information she'd deleted long ago, what use had there been to keep it? But it didn't matter, she still remembered her father's number.

***

The *Casa de las Sonrisas* was crowded with children and adults, many of them villagers displaced from the fire who stood or sat around on the patio, some of them eating plates of rice. Ascensión didn't see Cristela or any of the other usual workers among the group on the patio, which led him to assume that they must be bustling around in the kitchen or perhaps tending to children in the room. He decided not to bother Cristela right now, to return another time when she might not be so busy, but then Rafaela appeared on the patio followed by pregnant Maria, each woman carrying two plates of rice. They handed out the plates of rice then collected four empty plates to take back to the kitchen to wash then refill for those who still waited to eat.

"*Madre de dios*," Rafaela cried upon spotting Ascensión. "Maria, look who it is!" The two women hurried over to

Ascensión and attempted to hug him as well as they could with the plates in their hands.

"How are you, *mijo?*" said Rafaela. "How is our little Lupe?"

"She's come around," said Ascensión. "She's going to be fine. Our baby is fine."

"Oh, thank God! Here, Maria, *cariño,* take these dishes back to the kitchen." To Ascensión she said, "What a terrible thing. Poor Yoolie." She wiped her eyes with her apron.

"How is Cristela?" said Ascensión.

"Of course her heart is broken," said Rafaela. "But how does she have time to grieve?" Rafaela swept her hand across the scene on the patio. "All these people, looking for food. Luckily some of the volunteers from *Los Caminadores* came by with a twenty-kilo bag of rice. But the volunteers, their hearts are broken, too. Everyone loved *señora* Yoolie." She shook her head. "But poor Cristela."

Ascensión looked around. "Where is Cristela? I came to see her."

"She had a phone call. She went back to the yard for some quiet. While you're waiting can you help us?"

Ascensión was in the kitchen washing and drying dishes when Cristela came in from the yard. Her face looked drawn and there were dark circles under her eyes. Ascensión hurried over to her but before he could speak she said, "We don't have enough dishes for all these people, we have to keep washing them...and we've run out of beans, but I think we have enough rice...it would be better if we had more beans, and some tortillas...and all these people, we can't make the rice fast enough, we should have another pot or two..."

"Cristela," said Ascensión, "would you like me to go to the market for you? Buy some beans? Some pots?"

Cristela laughed a little. "Can you believe it? I was just thinking I'd ask Yoolie to go, and then..." She covered her eyes with her hands and Ascensión wrapped his arms around her and held her close while she sobbed breathlessly. Then she pulled away from him and rubbed the back of her arm across her eyes. "We have enough rice for now. We'd better just wash the dishes."

Cristela washed dishes while Ascensión dried and set the dishes next to the stovetop from where Rafaela and Maria filled them with rice and then brought them out to the patio.

"You were among the last to see her," said Cristela.

"Yes, I was," said Ascensión. "She gave me one of the old trucks from the motor pool. I was so happy to have that truck. Now I'm even more happy because that truck saved Lupe's life. I took her to the hospital in the truck that Yoolie gave me."

Cristela didn't answer, but nodded, swallowing hard and blinking while she continued to wash the dishes.

"And then Yoolie told me to evacuate Momotombo, to get everyone to safety while she went to shut down the generators by herself because those *pendejos* engineers abandoned the plant. My brother-in-law Jaime was the only one who stayed to help her. And he, also...you know."

"I'm sorry," said Cristela. Then she put down her dishrag, closed her eyes and leaned against the sink as if she needed support to keep standing. "I can't bear it," she said.

Ascensión took her elbow. "Cristela, here, lean on me."

But she waved him away. "No, I'm all right. I'll be all right."

"I'm so sorry," said Ascensión. "Yoolie, she was such a good person."

"She was," said Cristela. "She was the best person I ever knew. And I loved her more than I ever loved anyone. And I miss her more than I can say."

"I know," said Ascensión. "I miss her, too. And Lupe is heartbroken. She sent me here to tell you that we share your sorrow. If there's anything we can do..."

"You have already done something for me by coming here today. And Lupe also has already done something for me. I was on the phone just now. It was Lupe's father who called me. Lupe had called him and asked him to help *Las Sonrisas*. He called to ask me what I needed. He promised me that my *Casa de las Sonrisas* would be provided for." Cristela wiped her eyes on her apron. "So now I know that my purpose will go on. And this will help me to go on."

Rafaela hurried into the kitchen followed by Santos, owner of *El Rayo* taxi service. Santos carried two five-kilo bags of beans.

"Look what God has sent us," said Rafaela.

Santos plopped the bags of beans onto the floor and wiped his brow. "God and a rich doctor from Managua. He called me and I hurried to the market like that..." He mimed a lightning bolt, "...and zip, zip, zip, here's everything he asked me for. *Oye, maje*," he said to Ascensión, cocking his head towards the door. "There are two big bags of tortillas, a box of plates and silverware, and four pots. You want to give me a hand?"

"*Dios mío*," said Cristela, her eyes filling again with tears. "He did provide."

"Hurry and get the pots so we can start soaking the beans," said Rafaela. "Cristela, now there are even more people on the patio, some of them not villagers, some of them from this neighborhood. They saw all the people eating and now they want to eat, too. There's even that foolish girl and her mother who left little Pablito here! Shall I send them away?"

Cristela took Ascensión's hand. "No," she said. "We'll feed as many as we can."

Chapter Eighteen

Lupe and Ascensión stood on the other side of customs at the Philadelphia airport waiting for Sally and Silvio to come and fetch them. Their friends were late, but the Guzmans waited calmly. This time around the United States was not a strange, fearful country for them. And this time around they had visas.

Someone came over to them and in typically friendly American fashion led them to some empty chairs so that Lupe could sit. Ascensión sat down next to Lupe and took her hand. Lupe looked around in wonder.

"*Amor,*" she said, "are we really here? Are we really back in the United States?"

"We are," said Ascensión. "Thanks to your father."

Lupe shushed her husband then glanced left and right. Then she leaned in close to him and said softly, "We don't even know for sure that it was my father's influence that caused our visas to be approved so quickly."

Ascensión laughed. "*Calma, mi amor.* Nobody's listening. And besides, as you say, we don't know that your father had anything to do with our visas. And if he did, what difference would it make?"

"I don't know," said Lupe. "I just think it might be better if no one thinks that my father might have helped us get our visas. And if even we don't talk about it."

"Talk about what?" said Ascensión, miming a zipper across his lips. "I only meant thanks to your father for giving us money for our new apartment."

"Ah, yes, we can thank my father for that," said Lupe.

"And we must also thank...What's his name, again? The guy who found our apartment for us?"

"'Darren.' I think Sally said he was her ex-hus... *¡Oye, querido!* Look!"

Sally and Silvio came hurrying towards them, Silvio pushing David in his stroller. Ascensión helped Lupe up from her chair and soon she was hurrying in their direction. After a quick but tearful reunion among the friends Ascensión scooped up David from his stroller.

"Oh, *amor*, I can't believe how much he's grown in four months," Lupe cooed, playing with their son's hands, legs and feet.

"Hey, he's not the only one who's grown," said Sally. "Look at you, Girlfriend. Seven-and-a-half months along and you look like you're about to pop."

Lupe laughed and rubbed a hand over her belly.

"Speaking of which," said Silvio, "ask Sally why we were late picking you up."

"Oh, don't worry about it, *maje*," said Ascensión. "It was no problem."

"No, ask her," said Silvio.

"All right," Ascensión laughed. "Sally, why were you late picking us up?"

Sally and Silvio exchanged a mischievous glance. "I was in the bathroom. Being sick."

Their friends' eyes widened with concern. "You were sick?" said Lupe. "Oh, no. Are you better now?"

Sally and Silvio exchanged another glance. "I will be," said Sally. "Probably in about another month or so."

It took Ascensión a few moments to grasp what Sally was saying, but Lupe understood immediately, and the friends fell into another round of hugging and loud, happy cries.

"My God, we're putting on a show right here in the airport," said Sally, wiping her eyes with her sleeve. "They're gonna kick us out, for sure."

"Oh, not at all, Hon," said an elderly lady who was among the small crowd of people who had stopped to see what the commotion was about. "It's nice to see young people so happy."

"Yes, we are so happy," said Lupe, also wiping her eyes while bravely trying her English on this group of Americans. "My friend, she is having a baby, too. But, you see, we are more than friends. Their family is my family. And my family is theirs."

There was a collective *Ahhh* among the now smiling crowd and a smattering of applause.

"Well, that's very happy news, Hon," said the lady. "The world can always use a good dose of happiness. You just keep spreading it."

"Oh, we'll be spreading it, all right," Sally said. "We're gonna have eight kids among us."

Her remark was followed by more applause, laughter and good wishes.

Then Sally and Silvio helped Lupe and Ascensión gather their belongings and the two families that had become one made their way across the terminal. Through the glass walls a bright, sunlit blue sky shone over the cityscape. It was a beautiful day in Philadelphia.

ABOUT THE AUTHOR

Novelist, playwright, and blogger Patti Liszkay lives in Columbus, Ohio. Her comedy *The Cosmic Oy* was produced by Curtain Players and she co-wrote with composer Elmer Cabotage the comic operetta *The Town of Hard Times*. You can follow Patti's blog *Ailantha* at www.ailantha.com.

NOTE FROM THE AUTHOR

Word-of-mouth is crucial for any author to succeed. If you enjoyed *Tropical Depression*, please leave a review online—anywhere you are able. Even if it's just a sentence or two. It would make all the difference and would be very much appreciated.

Thanks!
Patti

We hope you enjoyed reading this title from:

BLACK ROSE
writing™

www.blackrosewriting.com

Subscribe to our mailing list – *The Rosevine* – and receive **FREE** books, daily deals, and stay current with news about upcoming releases and our hottest authors.
Scan the QR code below to sign up.

Already a subscriber? Please accept a sincere thank you for being a fan of Black Rose Writing authors.

View other Black Rose Writing titles at www.blackrosewriting.com/books and use promo code **PRINT** to receive a **20% discount** when purchasing.

www.ingramcontent.com/pod-product-compliance
Lightning Source LLC
Chambersburg PA
CBHW010514100726
47903CB00009B/2744